Olivia Ryan lives in Essex with her husband and three daughters. Before becoming a full-time mum, and now a novelist, she worked as a secretary, spending her lunch breaks writing stories and poetry.

Visit her website at www.oliviaryan.com

Also by Olivia Ryan

Tales from a Hen Weekend
Tales from a Wedding Day

Olivia Ryan

TALES
FROM A
HONEYMOON
HOTEL

piatkus

PIATKUS

First published in Great Britain as a paperback original in 2009 by Piatkus

Copyright © 2009 by Olivia Ryan

The moral right of the author has been asserted.

A CIP catalogue record for this book
is available from the British Library.

ISBN 978-0-7499-4176-5

Typeset by Action Publishing Technology Ltd, Gloucester
Printed and bound in Great Britain by Clays Ltd, St Ives plc

Papers used by Piatkus are natural, renewable and recyclable
products sourced from well-managed forests and certified in
accordance with the rules of the Forest Stewardship Council.

Piatkus
An imprint of
Little, Brown Book Group
100 Victoria Embankment
London EC4Y 0DY

An Hachette UK Company
www.hachette.co.uk

www.piatkus.co.uk

For Cheryl and Jon, with love, on your marriage

Acknowledgments

With thanks to Donna Condon at Piatkus for so
much help and guidance with this novel

S	M	T	W	T	F	S
				1	2	3
4	5	6	7	8	9	10
11	12	13	14	15	16	17
18	19	20	21	22	23	24
25	26	27	28	29	30	

June

Korčula, Croatia

Gemma

It's evening when our little boat approaches the island from the mainland, the sun sinking behind the dark huddle of land that gradually takes shape, as we chug nearer, into folded mountains, gently rippling into slopes of vivid green, and, finally, rising out of the twilight as if they'd been hiding from the night, clusters of houses perched precariously on cliff-tops and hillsides and down on the shore. We hold our breath, watching the dusky landscape gradually drawing nearer, the flickering lights of windows and street lamps casting their shimmering reflections on the inky sea.

The boatman steers steadily closer and suddenly a promontory looms proud of the coast, cluttered with a confusion of red-roofed, stone-walled buildings, sheltered by ancient fortified walls and topped by a

1

high-spired church. There's a cheerful tangle of white masts on the boats bobbing in the harbour beneath the walls.

'Korcula Town,' says the boatman. 'It's the main town of Korcula island. Your hotel is just outside of it.'

'Do we have to walk?' says Andy, looking doubtfully at our two heavy suitcases wedged under the seats of the boat.

'No. I take you to your hotel.'

'Do we swim ashore?' I whisper to Andy as we chug a little further down the coast.

But almost as soon as I've spoken, we're pulling into a little wooden jetty where the boatman jumps out, ties up the boat and heaves our cases out.

'This way,' he says, heading off into the gloom with a suitcase under each arm as if they were no heavier than shopping bags.

'Quick, Gem,' says Andy, laughing as he helps me out of the boat. 'I think he's doing a runner with our luggage!'

'As long as he leaves *my* case behind . . .' I begin, gasping suddenly and holding on to Andy's arm as I nearly slip over on the slimy surface of the jetty.

This is a new joke between us. We thought we'd lost one of our cases at Dubrovnik Airport – the one with all my clothes in. After all the things I've had to think about for the wedding, during the last few weeks, I completely forgot my usual rule about packing half of our clothes into each case, so that if we lose one, neither of us has to go naked or wear dirty clothes for the entire holiday.

'You're *supposed* to be naked for your honeymoon,' Andy teased me when I said this to him after we finally found the missing case on the wrong luggage carousel.

2

'That's a male myth,' I retorted, laughing, 'like the one about not getting out of bed for the whole two weeks.'

'You mean that's not going to happen?' he said, pretending surprise and disappointment.

'Well, I suppose it depends on how nice you are to me ...' I amended with a flirty smile. But we both knew quite well that, after all the stresses and strains of the wedding preparations, the journey (including the three-hour coach trip from the airport, plus this short boat ride over to the island) was going to leave us both so shattered that if there was going to be any lying in bed naked tonight, it was more likely to involve a long, long sleep than anything more energetic!

We catch up with the boatman on the shore. In front of us, a flight of shallow steps leads up to a white, balconied building with a steeply sloping roof and large open windows overlooking the sea.

'This – your hotel,' he tells us proudly, as if he'd built it himself. 'You go this way, up steps. Reception is through door at top.'

Andy thanks him and passes him a couple of notes. He takes my arm and we watch the little boat turning and beginning the journey back to Orebic on the other side of the channel, then he squares his shoulders, picks up the cases and I follow him up the steps.

The insignificant-looking door at the side of the small hotel opens into a surprisingly spacious foyer with an artistic display of greenery and a couple of comfy-looking sofas – although, to be honest, anything would look comfy after a couple of hours on a plane and three on a coach. We head over to the reception desk where a solemn-looking man with wavy dark hair combed over a balding pate, and wearing a bright red bow-tie, welcomes us to Hotel Angelo and introduces himself as Tomislav, the hotel manager.

'I do not mind,' he says rather grandly, 'if you like to call me Tomi.' And with a little bow he proceeds to give us quite a lengthy speech, in rather formal English, about how much he hopes we will enjoy our stay. He then relieves us of our passports in return for our room key and calls a porter to take our luggage up to the second floor.

Once inside our room, Andy immediately collapses on the bed with a groan of exhaustion. I head straight for the windows where a French door opens on to the balcony.

'Look at *this*,' I breathe, half to myself – but a minute later Andy's beside me, leaning on the balcony rail, and together we stare at the view. Back along the coast, the lights of Korčula Town and the little harbour are blinking up at us. In the other direction the mountains of the mainland undulate against the grey horizon. Little boats, tied up in the harbour, bob gently on the shallow waves. Below us a middle-aged couple sit hand-in-hand at the edge of the sun terrace, watching the light fading across the sea.

'It's beautiful,' I say, sighing and hugging Andy happily.

'Perfect,' he agrees. 'Absolutely perfect. Well done, Gem.'

Croatia wasn't Andy's first choice for the honeymoon. He'd originally wanted us to go back to Egypt. We went there a couple of years ago, to one of the Red Sea resorts, and although we both enjoyed it – the weather, of course, was the main attraction, as well as the superb snorkelling off the coral reefs – I was actually a bit disappointed by Sharm-el-Sheikh. As a teenager, I'd fallen in love with the whole idea of Egypt. I'd seen an advert once – a huge golden sun rising over the desert, with a procession of camels being led by a smiling and very good-looking boy in a white djellabah and sandals. I'd cut it out and put it under my pillow. I'd like to say that to me it represented the Promised Land, but in all honesty I probably just had the hots for the camel boy. Of course, I didn't think I was going to find him in Sharm-el-Sheikh, any more than I expected to find camels. But long after the page with the advert on had been crumpled up and thrown away, long after I'd finished studying the Nile Delta in geography lessons, my fascination with Egypt had continued, bolstered by library books and TV documentaries about Tutankhamun. But, of course, Sharm-el-Sheikh is a modern resort and it had about as much to do with the history and romance of Ancient Egypt as Milton Keynes does. I didn't want to go back there for our honeymoon.

'We could go to a different Red Sea resort this time,' Andy had suggested when we'd started looking at brochures this year. 'And a five-star hotel, as it's our honeymoon. All-inclusive.'

'I don't particularly want five-star,' I protested. 'Or all-inclusive. I just want to go somewhere . . . a bit more special.'

'Florida, then? Or the Caribbean? Australia even?' He was flicking through the pile of brochures we'd brought home.

'No. It doesn't have to be *far*. It just has to be . . . special.'

He laughed at me gently, teasing me as usual about being a hopeless romantic.

5

'You choose then,' he said with a shrug. 'It'll be special enough for me, Gem, just being with you. Being married to you.'

He's good at saying the right thing, I'll give him that. But he does tend to leave the major decisions to me. It was great when it came to furnishing our house.

What colour do you think we should have in the lounge?

I don't mind. It's up to you.

Do you like this leather sofa? This cream rug? These brown curtains?

Yes. If you do.

Sometimes I could hope for a bit more enthusiasm. It's not that I ever wanted to take charge, or be the dominant one in our relationship; just that Andy's so easy-going, and someone has to get things done! But at least I got to choose the honeymoon. The pile of brochures was doing my head in, but a couple of days later I was thumbing through a copy of *Weddings Today*, and there in the honeymoon section, under the heading 'Croatian Island Dreams', was a feature specifically about the island of Korčula. The picture showed the view of the little town that we just saw from the boat – but in sunshine, with the roofs shining bright red and orange, a pink morning light warming the church spire and the old stone walls, the sea such a bright turquoise it hurt your eyes to look at it. As I read the article, becoming more and more excited by the description of the little harbour, romantic views and steep cobbled streets packed with restaurants, bars and quaint little shops, a reference to the Hotel Angelo – 'perfect for honeymooners' – caught my eye. 'Charming, friendly small hotel in wonderful location on the edge of the bay, all rooms with balconies and lovely sea views.'

'This is the place,' I told Andy, with such conviction that he got straight on the internet and found the hotel before he'd even finished reading about it. We booked the same day. And here we are, Mr and Mrs Andrew Collins, married since yesterday, together since we were fourteen and in the same class at school. Happy in love and together forever.

Ruby

'There's another new couple arriving,' I tell Harold, who's dozing in his chair next to me. It's getting dark now; we've sat here on the sun terrace outside the hotel since dinner, watching the sun go down over the sea, and it's still so warm I've got no desire to go back inside. 'I wonder if they're honeymooners too.'

'Why should they be?' he says, opening his eyes and following the direction of my gaze.

The young couple are at the bottom of the steps, by the jetty. They turn and watch their boat heading back to the mainland. The girl gives the boatman a friendly wave as her partner picks up the cases and starts to climb the steps.

'Because the hotel's been recommended, apparently – in a wedding magazine. The manager – Tomislav – said so. They've been flooded out with bookings from British honeymooners. Quite funny, really. He says almost every couple he's checked in this week has got the free Champagne and flowers in their room.'

'Good for their business, then. Nice touch, wasn't it?'

'Yes. I'm not sure it was a good idea to drink *all* the Champagne before we had dinner, though! I still feel tipsy, and look at you – you're half asleep!'

He smiles ruefully and squeezes my hand.

'Sorry. I'm not very good company, am I?'

'Don't be daft. It was such a long journey, wasn't it? No wonder we're both tired. We'll be all right tomorrow,' I try to reassure him, wondering even as I'm saying it whether in fact he will be all right at all.

He's made the biggest, most amazing effort to get here in the first place – to please me, to come for our honeymoon to the romantic island I've dreamed about visiting ever since I read a novel set here, in the former Yugoslavia before their war. Harold booked the honeymoon to please me. He arranged the flights and the hotel and gave me the confirmation print-outs as a surprise, a couple of weeks before our wedding. I wasn't expecting a honeymoon, you see: not because we couldn't afford it, but because Harold had said it wouldn't seem right in the circumstances. I didn't argue because I understood. Of course I did. But he must have thought it over, and decided to put his own feelings aside to please me.

'Isn't that what it's all about, Rube?' he said when I almost cried with surprise and pleasure at his thoughtfulness. Korčula, of all places! How had he even remembered that I wanted to come here? 'Doing whatever it takes to please each other?'

'But . . . will you be OK?' I asked him doubtfully. 'Is it *really* what you want?'

'I want to marry you, Ruby Atkins. More than anything . . . it's what I've wanted all these years!' he said fiercely, holding me in a bear-hug as if he was afraid I was going to run away. As if!

'I know. But – a honeymoon too? You're sure you feel up to it?'

'I'm sure,' he said, nodding as determinedly as though he'd agreed to take part in the London Marathon.

I think that's how it feels, actually, to him. I almost feel guilty now for agreeing to this. But when we arrived this afternoon, when we saw this sweet little hotel and the view from our window, when we'd showered and changed and sat on the balcony drinking our Champagne, I thought: You've done it, Ruby girl. You've not only married the love of your life, you've mended his broken heart and made him whole again.

Daft old cow. Been reading too many of those romantic novels again, I suppose. Looking at him now, seeing the tired, sad look back in his eyes again, I'm not so sure. The trouble with those novels and romantic films is that there are places they don't go, things behind the scenes they don't show you. You never see the beautiful heroine shaving under her arms or coping with nasty periods. You don't see the tall dark handsome hero caught out with a bad attack of diarrhoea. Or not being able to get an erection.

'They *look* like they might be on their honeymoon,' I say, watching the young couple again as they disappear round the side of the hotel with their suitcases.

'How can you tell?' says Harold with a smile.

'I don't know. Body language. She reminded me a bit of my Karen,' I add wistfully. Same long dark hair, same melodic laugh ringing out in the distance. Same sort of age as Karen when she married Stuart. Except that Karen's been divorced now for nearly a year. Like mother, like daughter.

'They looked a bit more cheerful than that last pair anyway,' says Harold, closing his eyes again. 'I doubt whether *they're* on their honeymoon. She looked totally bloody miserable.'

'I think she was pregnant.'

Harold's eyes fly open again.

'Good God, woman! You don't miss much, do you? We didn't get much more than a glimpse of them!'

They arrived earlier, while it was still light. While we were drinking the Champagne on the balcony. We watched the boat tying up at the jetty and the boatman, who seems to be a familiar figure here, helping them out with their luggage. Even from our balcony we could hear the guy calling after the girl as she struggled with a suitcase: 'Put it down, Jo! For God's sake! You'll hurt yourself!'

'I'm not an invalid!' she called back irritably. 'I'm all right, it's not heavy.'

He took the case from her, nevertheless, as they climbed the steps. She was frowning slightly as they came closer and I saw her pass her hand over her stomach, just once, with the expression of mild surprise I remember so well from when my babies were growing inside me. Swimming around energetically like wriggling little tadpoles, before they got so big that the movements were more restricted, more like being dug on the inside of my belly by sharp little elbows and knees.

'Are you sure you're OK, babe?' I heard him ask her anxiously before they disappeared out of sight round the corner.

'I reckon she's about four months. Maybe four and a half. Not big enough to be any further on.'

'Amazing,' says Harold, still smiling at me. 'It must be some sort of female instinct. Something you're all born with – this innate understanding of pregnancy and childbirth. Jeannie used to talk about it and understand it all, too, even though we never had any ...' He pauses and sighs heavily. 'Sorry, Rube. Sorry.'

'It's OK.' I reach out and take his hand, holding it loosely in mine. Loosely the way I've always tried to hold him – as if I always knew that if I gripped too tightly, I'd squeeze all the hope out of him. 'We can still talk about her, can't we, Harold? Let's never think we have to stop talking about Jeannie.'

He swallows a couple of times, not looking at me, staring out over the darkened bay.

'Shall we go inside now?' he says flatly. 'I don't know about you, but I'm feeling dead beat.'

'Yes,' I agree, trying to sound cheerful. 'It's been a long old day, hasn't it?'

'We'll be all right in the morning,' he says again, helping me to my feet.

Well, let's wait and see. That's what I'm used to anyway. Waiting and seeing.

Jo

I wish he wouldn't do this. Fuss, fuss, fuss. I keep telling him: I'm pregnant. Not sick, not dying, for God's sake. I'm sorry, it's all just a bit over the top. It's getting on my nerves.

'You must be tired, babe,' he says, almost as soon as we set foot in the room. Our room. Our *honeymoon* room. Jesus, it does feel weird.

'I'm OK,' I say, for the twentieth time since we got off the boat.

'Have a lie down. Close your eyes. I'll get you a drink of water . . .'

'No, Mark! I *said* – I'm OK!' I don't like the tone of my voice – snappy, irritated. I feel like a bitch. I make an effort, try to smile at him.

'Look, they've left us Champagne. Pour some of that out instead.'

'*You* mustn't drink it,' he reminds me sternly.

'I know that.' I drank orange juice all through my own wedding reception yesterday. Am I likely to have forgotten already? 'I just want a sip. A tiny, tiny sip – before I forget what it tastes like. I'm not going to hurt the baby with one sip. Trust me. I've read all the books, too.'

He's been getting them out of the library. *Healthy Pregnancy*; *The Expectant Father's Guide to Life before Birth*, and *Nine Happy Months*. That one reminds me of a title of a film I saw once – I think it was just *Nine Months* – where a surrogate mother runs away to Australia because she changes her mind about giving the baby up. It was supposed to be a romantic comedy but it made me cry buckets, and that was *before* I got pregnant. God knows what I'd be like if I watched it now; I cry at the least little thing. Hormones, I suppose.

He opens the Champagne and pours it – a full, fizzing glassful for him; a trickle in the bottom of the glass for me. He looks at me doubtfully as he hands it to me, then changes his expression swiftly as he sees me grit my teeth with exasperation.

'Sorry, Jo. I'm just trying to be . . .'

Careful. Protective. Concerned. He doesn't say any of these – he doesn't have to. He's said it all enough times already. I know he means well. He cares about me, cares about the baby – which, really, is more than I could have asked for.

Again, I make the effort to smile. To raise my glass to him. To see the answering smile he gives me as he clinks his glass against mine.

'Here's to us,' he says softly. 'To our honeymoon.'

'To our honeymoon,' I echo, the words feeling strange and foreign on my tongue – as strange and foreign as the taste of the Champagne after months without drinking any alcohol.

I haven't missed it. Even without Mark's constant nannying, I would have been determined to keep myself fit and healthy for this baby's sake. My little boy – the reason I'm living. The only reason I haven't fallen apart. I've only known about his existence for twenty weeks but already he's changed my life. When I think about it too much, it makes my head spin and my heart race with panic, so that I have to sit down and take deep breaths and Mark goes into an overdrive of concern. I'm only twenty-one. Up till a week or so ago I was a student, taking my final exams, and now I'm a married woman and I'm going to be a mother. It's ridiculous, impossible. I can't get my head around it. I've promised, in church, to love and cherish this man, in sickness and health, till death do us part, forsaking all others, etc, etc, etc. If I get ideas about walking out on him now, I'll have the vicar, God and all the angels to reckon with, to say nothing of solicitors. I'd have to give him half my worldly goods, always supposing I had any. What the hell have I *done*?

I put down my empty glass and go out on to the balcony. The older couple we noticed sitting on the terrace when we arrived are still there. She's gazing out to sea; he looks like he's dropped off. Is that what we'll be like in thirty or forty years' time – me and Mark? Sitting out our days together, dozing and staring into space? If we're still together. I put my hands up to my head as I catch myself thinking this, wanting to push the thought back into my brain – push it back and keep it back. I *can't* think like this on the day after my wedding, for God's sake! I've done it now. Made the promises. Made up my mind. This is *it*. Get on with it, girl. Mark's a lovely guy. He loves me. He'll look after me. No negative thoughts allowed, not now.

He's joined me on the balcony, sipping his Champagne, his arm slung loosely across my shoulders as we watch another little boat, like the one that brought us across to the island, chugging up to the jetty. A girl and a guy climb out and follow the boatman, holding hands and laughing together. He's tall and slightly built, sandy-haired, pale-skinned. She's dark and pretty – *vivacious*-looking. Their voices carry clearly in the still twilight air – happy voices, teasing and joking, full of cheerfulness and confidence. Here on their holiday, expecting to have fun, have a great time together. I find myself smiling as I watch them climbing the steps. Mark, watching me, gives me a gentle hug as he sees the smile.

'Happy?' he asks quietly.

'Yes.'

It's a lie, but I owe him this. I owe it to *myself* to keep up this effort, keep pretending, keep trying to be happy. To myself, to my baby, to my parents who, despite the shock of my pregnancy and the double shock of the sudden engagement, put aside their worries to give me a beautiful wedding yesterday. But, most of all, I owe it to this man who loves me enough to take me on for life – and not just me, but someone else's baby too.

I've made a choice, and I have to make it work. *I'm* not the baby around here any more.

S	**M**	T	W	T	F	S
				1	2	3
4	5	6	7	8	9	10
11	12	13	14	15	16	17
18	(19)	20	21	22	23	24
25	26	27	28	29	30	

June

Gemma

Breakfast is being served at tables out on the terrace, overlooking the sea. It's hot already at only nine o'clock. I'd planned to have a long lie-in this morning, but to my surprise I woke up just after seven, feeling refreshed, as if I hadn't just had a long journey – to say nothing of the most exhausting day of my life on Saturday!

'Hello, *wifey*,' teased Andy as soon as I opened my eyes. He was propped up on his elbow beside me, looking like he'd been watching me sleep.

I hit him with my pillow.

'Don't call me that! Unless, of course, you're happy to be addressed as *hubby*!'

'I'd consider it an honour,' he said, laughing and ducking as I clobbered him with the pillow again, just for the hell of it.

Within minutes we were rolling around on the bed,

play-fighting like we were still a couple of teenagers. I really do wonder sometimes if we're actually mature enough to be married. I suppose it comes from knowing each other when we were still at school, young and silly. It's so easy to slip back into that again. So comfortable, knowing everything about each other, having no pasts, no secrets. Like two halves that fit faultlessly, perfectly, together.

The view over the bay this morning is even more stunning than when we arrived last night. The sea is an even deeper shade of blue than it was pictured in the magazine. Lots of little boats are out on the water; people are putting out chairs and sunbeds on the paved area in front of the hotel, and there are already a couple of brave souls swimming off the rocks.

'Shall we explore the town today?' suggests Andy, nodding towards the cluster of buildings rising up above the harbour in the distance. We've both been to the buffet table and loaded our plates with all kinds of fruit, bread, jam, cheeses and cold meats – enough to feed an army – and we're gazing at the view while we're eating.

'Yes, I'd like that. I wonder how long it takes to walk in?'

'Ten minutes, love, that's all,' says a voice from the next table before Andy has a chance to reply.

'Sorry?' I'm a bit put out by the interruption. It's the middle-aged, rather plump lady who was sitting outside the hotel last night, holding hands with her husband. She's on her own this morning, at the next table to ours.

'Don't go by the road. If you walk along the path here, by the coast, it takes about ten minutes, but the road at the back goes inland and it's a much longer walk. I went that way yesterday afternoon, soon after we arrived. To stretch my legs a bit – after the journey, you know? Is this your first time here? Is it your honeymoon?'

I don't know which question to answer first so I just nod mutely at her, hoping this'll be enough to deter her from talking any more. But, of course, I didn't reckon with Andy. Here we go, I think to myself with resignation as he turns in his seat, smiles at the lady and introduces himself. Don't get me wrong – Andy's the friendliest bloke in the world and I love that about him. It never takes more than five minutes for him to strike up a companionship with someone, and more often than not buy them a beer. That's fine – in fact, it's great, normally. We've made some good friends in pubs and on plane journeys and even in supermarkets because of his ability to chat to anyone; to charm the birds out of the trees. But right now, this week, just for once – I really wanted it to be just me and him.

'I'm Ruby,' the lady at the next table's saying. 'Lovely to meet you both. Anything you want to know about Korčula, fire away.'

She sits back, arms folded across her considerable chest, apparently expecting a barrage of questions.

'I take it you've been here before, then?' I say, to be polite and because it's obvious now that we're not going to get a quiet breakfast on our own.

'No, love. Our first time too. Beautiful, isn't it?'

'Yes . . . but . . .' I frown at her, puzzled. 'Are you an expert on the island or something?'

She laughs loudly at this, tossing back her head of close-cropped strawberry-blonde hair.

'Not exactly an expert but I've read a lot about it. Always fancied coming here, you see, ever since I read about it in a novel, years ago, when it was still Yugoslavia, you know? It was about Marco Polo. He was born in Kočula, did you know that? Very romantic story, all about the history of the place – got me interested so I borrowed all the books I could out of the library and read up on it. I wanted to come then but of course there was the war here – ninety-one to ninety-five that was. You probably know that already. But Harold . . . bless him. That's my husband Harold, you'll meet him later, he was too tired to come down for breakfast this morning . . . he's such a dear that without even telling me he arranged this trip for our honeymoon . . .'

'It's your honeymoon?' I say in surprise, having had trouble keeping up with her rapid-fire speech up till now. 'Oh! It's ours, too.'

'Congratulations, love. I thought you might be honeymooners. The hotel's full of 'em – featured in a magazine apparently. Anyway, it's easy to tell: you look so happy together. Get married on Saturday, did you?'

'Yes.' Andy smiles. 'You too?'

'Yep.' She runs her fingers through her hair and sighs contentedly. 'A quiet do, it was. Just the basics, in the register office – not a full-blown church do like my previous ones.'

'Previous ones?' I blink at her. 'How many times have you been married, Ruby?'

'It's the third time for me, love. Second for Harold.'

'Blimey!' says Andy, giving her a look of amused respect. 'Glutton for punishment, aren't you?'

'No, it's third time lucky for me. The other two were both a disaster, mind you, so I'm due a good one.' She pauses, nodding to herself thoughtfully. 'We both are. How about you two? Big wedding with all the trimmings, was it?'

'A bit too big,' I tell her, laughing. 'Started off planning a nice quiet little affair with just the family and a few friends, and suddenly – bang! It kind of *grew*. It was like a monster . . . out of our control! Every time I turned around, another half dozen people were added to the guest list . . .'

'And another couple of hundred quid on the bill!' says Andy.

'Ah, it's worth it, though. Special day. Once in a lifetime, isn't it – if you're lucky in love, and you look like you are. Not like me. Shouldn't have even bothered the first time – too young. We didn't want a fuss this time. We're both past the age for having a lot of fuss made. My kids all came, of course – apart from Trevor, but it's a long way from Australia, I couldn't really expect it – and their families, my grandsons and granddaughters. It was lovely to have them all together. I had a wonderful day.'

I smile at her.

'Good for you. Why not!'

'That's what Harold said. He was all for me dressing up and enjoying myself. Even though he didn't feel much like it himself.'

She pauses, looking down at her breakfast plate, and I feel obliged to ask.

'Is he not well, then – Harold?'

'He's . . . not ill,' she replies a bit guardedly. And then, shrugging as if deciding she might as well explain, adds: 'He's . . . been bereaved, you see. Taking quite a while to get over it.'

'Sorry to hear that,' says Andy kindly. 'Was it someone very close to him?'

'Yes, love. Very close. His wife.' Andy nearly chokes on his coffee, and Ruby goes on quickly, giving him a fleeting smile: 'His first wife, you understand.'

'Of course. I see.' Andy raises his eyebrows at me and we both have to look away.

I have no idea what to say next, but Ruby continues calmly: 'Harold is the love of my life, you see. But we couldn't get married. Not until his wife died.'

I can feel my chin drop. Andy's eyebrows are up in his hair. He's sipping his coffee to stop himself from having to look at her.

'It's not quite like it sounds,' Ruby amends quickly. 'We didn't push her under a train or anything like that.'

'Glad to hear it,' I mutter faintly.

'She was very ill. Very ill for a very long time.' Ruby suddenly sits up straight and takes a deep breath as if something's hurting her. 'She was in hospital for years. You can't imagine it. You don't want to.'

'Poor thing,' I say, softly.

'And poor Harold!' says Ruby firmly. 'She – Jeannie – she was out of it in the end. Didn't know anything about it. Harold looked after her himself for as long as he could. He did his best, but it was too much for him finally. He used to visit her every day, though. Right up to the end.'

'Even though you two were . . . *together*?'

'Of course. How could he not? She was still his wife. But she'd have wanted him to be happy. She was a lovely girl, was Jeannie. She'd only have wanted the best for Harold.'

'You knew her too, then? Before she was ill?' Andy asks.

'I knew her all her life, dear,' says Ruby calmly. 'Of course I did. She was my sister.'

'She probably had cancer or something horrible. Or one of those what-do-you-call-its . . . regressive

20

diseases,' says Andy as we stroll along the path into town a little later.

'Degenerative?'

'Yeah. Probably wasted away in hospital while her old man and good old Ruby were *consoling* each other.' He pretends to leer disgustingly.

'That's sick!' I protest. 'I don't know *how* she could have . . . got together with Harold at all. He was her sister's husband!'

'I'm surprised she told us,' says Andy with a shrug. 'We'd only just met her! What were we supposed to say?'

'I know — I was horrified. She seems like one of those people who can't help telling you their life history straight off. And she didn't seem the least bit embarrassed about it, did she? It sounds gross! I suppose. . . I suppose it must be *legal* to marry your brother-in-law, if your sister dies?'

'It might be legal, but it's just a bit weird, isn't it? I can't help wondering if they did really bump the poor cow off. Poison her or something.'

'You watch too many rubbish films,' I tell him, laughing. 'Oh — don't! Andy, no — it's too hot!' He's tickling me, trying to make me run away so that he can chase me. 'Come on. Walk nicely. Look at the pretty little boats.'

'*Walk nicely, look at the pretty boats,*' he mimics teasingly. He stands up straight and walks along in front of me with perfect posture like a mannequin. 'I suppose, Mrs Collins, now that we're an old married couple we're expected to behave with dignity and refinement. Yeah?'

I grab him from behind and we wrestle for a few minutes before I end up out of breath.

'Nah,' I tell him cheerfully. 'Refinement? Dignity?

21

Sod that for a game of cowboys. Plenty of time for dignity when we're dead.'

'Try telling *that* to Harold Whatsisname's last wife!'

'Not funny. And can we leave off talking about them now, do you think? I don't really want to spend the whole of my honeymoon debating other people's marriages, Andy. I'd rather concentrate on our own, since it's only two days old.'

'Me too.'

He slips his arm through mine and we stroll in a companionable silence. Past another, larger hotel; past a couple of little cafés with tables and chairs outside; past a stretch of shingly beach where a handful of people are stretched out on towels facing the sun. It's not particularly crowded and certainly not over-commercialised. I think I'm going to like it here. I feel a bubble of excitement starting in the pit of my stomach and rising up through my chest. *Our honeymoon.* The most romantic two weeks of my entire life, stretching out in front of me like a promise. I deserve this, don't I, after the stress of the wedding? I just know it's going to be perfect.

Our wedding day wasn't quite so perfect. Don't get me wrong, it was lovely: marrying Andy, standing together at the front of the church, smiling at each other as we made our promises – and then dancing together at the reception, celebrating with all our friends, lots of them friends from school who'd known us both for half our lives – *that* was all perfect.

It's just . . . my family.

I feel bad even saying this. I know I should be grateful to my mum. She helped out so much with the wedding preparations and she was in a state of high excitement for the whole year we were planning it. But

I had the feeling that the excitement was all about the dresses, and the flowers, and the menu, and her own outfit, of course, and which aunties were coming, and who was sitting on which table ... rather than about seeing her eldest daughter getting married. At times, what with my long-lost father taking over the financial side of things by sending his huge guilt-money cheque in the post, and my mother trying to take over practically everything else, I began to wonder whose wedding this actually was. Andy's response, typically, was to shrug and tell me to let them get on with it. But I had this strange feeling, once or twice during the reception, that I was actually at someone else's wedding, watching this family celebrating ... this family of strangers who had nothing to do with me.

I was an only child until I was sixteen. My earliest memories were of Mum and Dad fighting, so I always assumed that they hated each other too much to have sex any more after I was born. As I got older, Mum used to confide in me about Dad and his affairs. Although it ensured that I fell out of love with my father for ever, in some ways it made me feel grown-up and a bit special – like I was her best friend instead of a kid still at school who shouldn't really have been concerning herself with her parents' marital problems.

'I'm going to leave him,' she used to tell me, 'as soon as I've got enough money together. We'll pack up and move to Devon. Just you and me – it'll be lovely.'

She had an old school friend who lived in a little village in Devon. We'd been down there to stay with her once for a holiday – it was a kind of dummy-run for the Leaving Dad plan. I'd been about eleven and had just started making friends at my new senior school. The idea of the holiday was exciting – especially as Dad wasn't coming with us – two whole weeks with no arguments. But the reality was totally different. Mum's friend Sarah was a single mum with two little boys who fought even more than Mum and Dad did. When they weren't fighting, they were throwing things, breaking things or burying things in the garden. I wanted to murder them both. And, to make matters worse, my mum thought they were 'sweet' and lavished loads of time and affection on them, leaving me feeling left out and bored.

There was nothing to do in the village. I wandered around the streets on my own, but after five minutes the streets ran out and there was nothing but fields in every direction. There was one shop, that hardly sold anything, and no park. The local children and teenagers hung around on the village green and whispered about me. After two days I wanted to go home – and *this* was the wonderful new life my mum had in mind for us both.

'I don't want to move to Devon,' I said the next time the subject came up back home. 'I don't like it there. I'd miss my friends.'

'You'll make new ones,' she told me curtly. 'And try thinking about *me*, Gemma. Don't *I* deserve to start a new life, after all I've been through?'

In the event, we didn't move anyway because my little sister came along – and that was the most astounding and horrifying thing of all.

'How *can* you be pregnant?' I demanded.

Did Mum have boyfriends, like my dad had girlfriends? Was she just as bad as him all along?

'I'm not too old, Gemma!' she protested, misunderstanding me.

But why was she having another baby at all?

24

Wasn't I good enough for her any more? Did she need a new daughter? Or, even worse, was she hoping for a little boy like the horrible ones in Devon she'd seemed so keen on?

'But you don't love Dad. You hate him. You wanted to leave him.'

She looked at me serious-faced for a minute, before shaking her head and sighing.

'You don't understand,' she said quietly, and changed the subject.

She was dead right there – I didn't understand. Not at all. I was quite an immature fifteen-year-old but I believed I knew pretty well all there was to know about sex. I was already *going out* with Andy. He was my second boyfriend; the first one had been all about experimenting with snogging and, to be honest, I hadn't even enjoyed it much. But with Andy it was different. I was with him because I *liked* him so much. Because he got picked on by the bigger, tougher boys and didn't fight back. Because I saw something in him that they didn't seem to see. He was *nice*. He was kind, and gentle, and interested in what I had to say. When he kissed me, I knew it wasn't about seeing how far I'd let him go. It was about him liking me as much as I liked him.

I asked myself how I'd feel if Andy were as mean to me as my dad was to my mum. Would I still fancy him? Or if he went out with another girl while we were still supposed to be going out – would I still have this tingling, desperate urge to have sex with him? You had to be *joking*.

I stopped listening to Mum's problems after that. I didn't have much sympathy for her any more. If things were really that bad between them, she wouldn't have got pregnant. And if she really wanted to start a new life – just me and her, the way she'd always said, the way that had always made me feel like we were really close, best friends as much as mother and daughter, sharing a secret together – then she wouldn't have wanted another child.

My dad left, anyway, before my sister Claire was even born, as if to rub salt in the wound. He'd finally fallen in love with one of his girlfriends, apparently. I looked at my mum with distaste as she dripped tears over the new baby's head and wondered how she could have been so pathetic, demeaning herself by continuing to want someone who treated her so badly. Looking back now, of course, with the benefit of maturity and hindsight, I can understand the hurt, resentful child that I was back then, but I wish I hadn't been so contemptuous of my mum. I wanted, so much, to hug her and make things right between us, but couldn't bring myself to do it. Instead I spent more and more time with Andy and my friends, started my nursing training when I was eighteen and left home as soon as I was qualified. And however much I'd like to have a closer relationship with Mum, I know it's not going to happen. It's my own fault for being such a spoilt bitch back then. Claire's sixteen now, the same age that I was when she was born – and she's Mum's golden girl. I can't compete. I don't even really belong.

'What're you day-dreaming about?' Andy asks me affectionately, pulling me closer to his side. 'One of those hunky doctors at work?'

It's an ongoing joke, and I play along with it. He knows I'm not interested in anyone else – never have been, never will be. I look, sure, and have a giggle with the other girls at work. But I tell you what, even if

George Clooney asked me out on a date I'd tell him I needed to get home to Andy.

'Yeah – the good-looking new paediatric registrar. I wanted to ask him to the wedding but I thought you'd be jealous,' I tease.

'No problem. I was too busy looking at the girls on the beach there, in their tiny little bikinis.'

I smack him playfully and we fall together again, laughing. Secure in our love for each other – no handsome doctor or teenager in a bikini is ever going to touch it. We're indestructible. We're eternal. And we're married!

Ruby

These young people. They do make me smile. Everything's so black and white, isn't it, when you're young? They're either head over heels in love, everything perfect, wonderful, all-singing and dancing – or it's terrible, the end of the world, you're miserable and probably going to die.

I know. I've been there. More times than they've had hot dinners.

I've been watching these two young couples. Come on, give me a break: it's the most fun I get, at my age – watching the world go by, and all the crazy people in it! The ones I was chatting to earlier – Andy and Gemma – are obviously besotted with each other, running along together like a pair of kids: laughing, teasing, playing tag. They look about thirty but they act a lot younger – charming in a way. She's tall, dark, pretty and happy-looking; he's very slender, pale and freckly with an open, honest-looking face. I like them.

Now I'm watching the other two – the young pregnant girl and her husband – having their breakfast. They're in their early-twenties, I'd guess. Round about the same age as my Jodie – my youngest. Think they're grown up, of course – well, they should be, shouldn't they? I'd had my first two kids before I was their age. That's when you *really* know what being grown-up's all about, isn't it? When you're crying from the sheer bloody exhaustion of getting up in the middle of the night, half a dozen times or more, every single night, because your old man's too damned lazy to take a turn, but you've still got to get up in the morning and make the bottles and change the nappies ... no lying in bed all morning getting over hangovers from binge drinking like some of today's so-called adults, eh? Still, I suppose you can't blame them. They work hard and earn the money, don't they? Might as well spend it before the Government takes it off them.

These two look like a miserable pair of buggers, if you ask me. If I hadn't heard him say something to her about it being their honeymoon, I'd never have believed they were newlyweds. What's the point? That's what I ask myself: what's the point in getting married these days anyway – now they don't have their parents or the Church breathing down their necks, threatening them with hellfire and damnation for immoral behaviour – unless they're so happy together they can't bear *not* to be married? Baby or no baby, it doesn't seem to be a necessity any more. My Karen, that's my elder daughter, she's a single mum and doing all right, best she can do in the circumstances – not that I'd recommend it as a lifestyle choice, you understand, but it sure as hell beats the alternative of being married to someone you can't stand.

Looking at this pair, it's hard to tell whether they're happy together or not. She looks sad and tired, leaning on the table as if she's having trouble staying upright. She's very pale, with long fair hair and delicate features, and she's nibbling half-heartedly at slices of fruit – juicy mango, knobs of yellow banana, sticks of bright pink papaya – but not in the normal whole-hearted way most people would. She's taking it from his hand as he offers it to her across the table, feeding her like a sick child as he strokes her arm with his free hand. He's big and dark and muscly – next to her he looks massive.

'Come on, babe,' I hear him say eventually. 'Just eat a little bit of yoghurt. A couple of spoonfuls. For me.'

She sighs loudly.

'Mark – give it a rest, OK? I'm not feeling hungry. I'll eat later. Don't worry, the baby won't starve.'

To be honest, I can understand why he seems so concerned. She doesn't look healthy. Girls these days seem to pay too much attention to so-called healthy eating while they're pregnant, if you ask me – messing around with lettuce and carrots and wasting away till they look like refugees with baby bumps. She could do with some good solid steak and kidney pie and some apple crumble and custard. Not that she knows how to cook it probably. My daughters are just as bad – ask them about pudding and they get a low-fat yoghurt out of the fridge.

'All right, then,' says the husband, finishing his coffee, still stroking her arm with his fingers. 'As long as you're going to eat something later.'

'I will,' she says, looking irritated. 'When I'm hungry. I still feel a bit sick from the journey.'

'Do you?' Now he looks even more worried. 'Do

you want to go back to the room for a lie down?'

'No!' She's struggling now, I can see it, not to snap his head off. Poor guy – he's trying his best but he's getting it so wrong. She closes her eyes for a moment, probably counting to ten, and when she looks back at him she's managing a forced kind of smile. 'Please, Mark, don't keep fussing and worrying about me. If I need you to worry, I'll tell you, OK?'

'OK.' He smiles back at her. He's got a nice smile. He looks a nice guy – the gentle giant type, probably. I don't suppose she realises how lucky she is, that he cares about the baby at all. I had two husbands who couldn't give a damn. 'Sorry, sweetheart.'

Sweetheart. It's an old-fashioned word for such a young man to use. It's what Harold used to call Jeannie. For a minute, the memories come rushing back at me like the wind, almost making me dizzy. Jeannie at eighteen, my petite and pretty younger sister, her glossy dark hair tied up in a pony-tail, her eyes flashing with excitement as she talked about Harold Dimmock, her boss at the publishing company where she'd just started work. It was one of the many that had sprung up in London in those heady days of the early-70s. Unlike the exhilarating years of the 60s when I was a teenager, with the exciting new culture of youth and pop and cheap fashion, life in 1973 felt somehow more grown-up and serious. We'd had decimal currency for a couple of years and had just joined the European Community and got VAT. In London, the centre of business, there was an air of optimism and new possibilities everywhere. It sounded like my little sister's head had been turned by it all.

'I'm in love, Ruby!' she sang, twirling round on the spot, too full of joy and exhilaration and *life* to keep still. 'I'm in love with Harold, and he's in love with me!'

I couldn't get much sense out of her, so I talked to my mother about it instead.

'How *much* of a boss is he? A manager? Her department head?'

'His father owns the company, dear. Apparently.'

'Shit,' I said. 'What's he doing messing around with our Jeannie?'

He was twenty-six, the younger Dimmock of Dimmock & Dimmock Ltd, and his father owned several companies, so despite his relative youth, Harold was Managing Director of the publishing enterprise. Jeannie was a secretary, fresh from school. Livid at the thought of her being taken advantage of by an older, worldlier man, I made a phone call straight away and demanded to meet him. I'd planned to give him a piece of my mind: 'Stay away from my sister if you know what's good for you, buster.' But when I stormed into the restaurant where he'd booked us a table, I took one look at him and melted. He didn't look like the Managing Director of a company. He looked young, and nice, and normal. His tie was crooked, his shirt looked crumpled, his hair was fashionably long and tousled, and when he smiled at me with those soft brown eyes, I felt like we were sharing a secret.

Harold and I were the same age. Apart from his privileged background and my impoverished one as a mature student with two young children, we had a lot in common. Over dinner, instead of discussing his relationship with Jeannie, we talked about books, and poetry, and films, and music. We liked the same things. We laughed at the same things. We liked each other.

'I came here today,' I remembered eventually over coffee, ' to tell you to leave my sister alone.'

'I know,' he said quietly. 'Go on, then.'

'Leave my sister alone,' I repeated. 'Why are you going out with her anyway? She's just a *baby*.'

'She's not. She's a beautiful young woman with a mind of her own. You just think of her as a baby because she's your little sister and you feel protective . . .'

'Of course I do! And how do you think my mum feels about this? She's worried sick. You're *much* too old for Jeannie.'

He sighed.

'I kept trying to tell myself that, at first. I tried to stay away from her. I tried to resist it, Ruby, but it's no good. . .'

'Please don't try to tell me you're in *love* with her?'

'Yes. I am.'

For a full minute we sat and stared at each other through the steam from our coffee.

'Prove it,' I demanded, childishly.

'OK, I will. I'll love her, look after her, protect her, give her everything she wants. And I won't sleep with her. Whatever you think – I won't. Even if she begs me!' His eyes sparkled at me and I looked away, blushing. 'Not until we're married.'

'*Married*!' I shouted, almost dropping my cup.

The couple at the next table looked at me and smiled. They probably thought I was being proposed to.

'Yes. We're going to get married. I've asked Jeannie. She's accepted.'

'But...' How the hell was I going to report *this* back to Mum? 'Look, you *can't*. She's only eighteen. She'll change her mind. She'll want someone younger!'

'She won't,' he said calmly.

I took a deep breath.

'Look, Harold – I know what I'm talking about. I got married at seventeen ...'

'You're married?' he queried, glancing at my naked ring finger.

'No. Divorced. My point exactly.'

'I'm sorry.'

'No. No – don't be sorry! Look, that's what I'm trying to say – it was a rubbish marriage. We were too young. We didn't love each other...'

'But we do. And *I'm* the same age as you, Ruby. I know what I'm doing.'

'Maybe – but does Jeannie?'

He sighed and smiled at me sadly.

'If you love your sister, please give us your blessing.'

'What if I don't?'

'We're still going to get married. And you'll risk losing us both.'

He looked at me very pointedly as he said 'both'. I had to look away. I felt awkward and uncomfortable with him staring at me like that. I knew what he meant. It was only our first meeting but we'd got on so well – I really liked him. I had to admit, I'd be hard placed to find a better man for my sister. If only she was a bit older ...

'OK,' I said reluctantly. 'I suppose I'll have to trust you.'

'I won't let you down.' He was still staring at me. 'I promise.'

33

'I'll hold you to that,' I muttered. 'And you've got to meet my mum. And my dad.'

'Is that a threat?'

He was smiling now.

'Yes. Be warned! Jeannie's under twenty-one so you'll have to ask their permission to marry her. They'll give you a much harder time...'

I stopped. It was supposed to have been me that gave him the hard time about this. That was why I'd demanded to meet him. What was the matter with me? How had I caved in so spectacularly? Just because someone with beautiful brown eyes sat staring into mine, making me promises I had no idea if he was going to keep?

'I've enjoyed tonight, Ruby,' said Harold, planting a kiss on my cheek as we left the restaurant. 'I'm so glad we're going to be friends.'

'Family,' I amended, flustered by the kiss. 'If this wedding really goes ahead.'

'Family,' he agreed, giving me an appraising look. 'That's even better, isn't it?'

I didn't argue. I already knew I was going to speak in his favour to my parents, and that he was going to be my brother-in-law. And also that I was half in love with him myself.

The young couple have got up from their breakfast table. I ought to go, too. I've been sitting here for ages, drinking coffee after coffee, wondering if Harold is going to come down and join me, but now the waiting staff look as though they're wanting to clear up and go home. As I get to my feet, the young husband nudges me with his elbow, he's trying so hard to hang on to his pregnant wife as they pass me.

'Sorry!' he says, touching my arm briefly and looking genuinely contrite.

'No problem.' I give them both a smile. 'Enjoy your breakfast? It's your first day, isn't it? I saw you arrive a couple of hours after us. Is it your first time in Croatia? When's the baby due?'

Harold's always telling me I do this – fire too many questions at people at the same time. I always forget, until I see this look of confusion on their faces.

'My turn to apologise,' I add quickly. 'I should have introduced myself first. I'm Ruby.'

'Pleased to meet you, Ruby,' he says politely. 'I'm Mark, and this is my wife Jo.' It's the way he says it – *wife* – the proud smile, the look in his eyes. I was wrong: they *are* happy together. Well, at least – *he's* certainly happy. 'Yes, we just got here yesterday. We're on our honeymoon.'

'I've never been to Croatia before but Mark has,' says Jo quietly. She gives me a quick smile. 'How could you tell – about the baby? I thought I was hardly showing.'

'A mother's intuition,' I tell her. 'You've definitely got that look about you, but let me try and guess . . . you're about four months?'

'Four and a half. The baby's due at the end of October – I had my twenty-week scan two days before the wedding! But I haven't put on much weight because I was really sick for the first three months.'

'Jo wasn't too keen on coming away at all at first, were you, babe?'

She shakes her head.

'I couldn't imagine flying anywhere. Couldn't even manage a car journey!'

'Poor you,' I sympathise. 'I was like that with my

first one. Never actually sick – just nauseous, morning, noon and night. It wore off, though, after the first three months.'

'Yes. Luckily mine's a lot better now, too. And when we saw the article about this hotel in the wedding magazine, well – Mark thought I'd like Croatia. And I decided maybe I did need a break.'

'That's right, you must need it. I'm sure it'll do you good. Build you up,' I say. I don't go so far as to say she looks a bit peaky. None of my business, after all.

'Yes. Well – I think we're going to sit and relax in the sun for a bit,' she says. 'Have a nice day.'

'You too. Take care.'

I watch them heading out of the dining area, Mark holding her gently beneath the elbow as if she was old and infirm. I smile to myself. It must be frustrating for her, all his fussing and over-the-top concern, but I find it quite endearing, really. Probably because the fathers of my own children weren't like that at all. But there you go – things were different in those days.

'I was just thinking about coming to find you,' says Harold, looking up from his book as I go back into our room. 'Nice breakfast?'

'It would have been nicer if you'd been with me,' I say, putting my arms round him.

'Sorry, Rube. I just couldn't face it. I'm not really hungry anyway.'

'Never mind. Perhaps we'll have a nice lunch somewhere in the town, later on.'

'Yes. Perhaps.' He puts down his book and stares out at the sea.

'Or just a couple of sandwiches, then. On our own somewhere.'

I'm trying not to sound impatient. I know he can't help it. He's got this far – arranged the surprise honeymoon, made the effort to get here, done his bit to please me – and now he looks like slipping back to how he was before the wedding. Silent, brooding, not wanting to do anything or go anywhere. It's so sad to see him like this, when he was always such an energetic, vibrant man – so happy, so full of enthusiasm for life. Before life knocked him for six.

'Come on,' I urge him gently. 'Let's have a little walk along the seafront . . .'

'I don't really feel like it, Rube. You go.'

'No. I'll wait for you to feel more like it.' I pick up my sunglasses, book and sun hat. 'Won't you at least come and sit down on the terrace with me? Where we sat last night?'

'All right.' He heaves himself to his feet as if it's an almighty effort. 'Anything to stop you nagging, woman,' he adds with a smile.

That's better. If it takes a little nag to make him look more cheerful, then nagging's what I'll have to do.

We sit on the sun terrace outside the hotel. No one else is out here now – apparently it's mostly used for breakfast, and again in the evenings when people sit here to relax with their drinks – it looks like most people prefer to sit down on the rocks by the sea during the day, or round the little pool at the side. This is only a small hotel and the evening meal is served inside, but the restaurant, although it's clean and fresh, seems a bit basic. It appears that most of the guests prefer to go out and eat in one of the restaurants in town.

Below us, down on the rocks, Jo and Mark are propped up on a couple of towels. His voice drifts up to me, saying something to her about keeping in the shade and being careful.

'Look at that sea,' I tell Harold. 'What a beautiful colour. It's almost too blue to be real.'

'Why don't you go down to the beach and have a swim, Ruby? I'll watch you. There are lots of people in the sea.'

'It's not really a beach. Those people are swimming off the rocks, but they look a bit slippery to me. I'd be nervous of slipping and breaking my ankle.'

'Yes. We're not as young as we used to be, are we, girl?'

He's teasing, but I don't really like the way he says this. It makes me feel sad – like he thinks we're all washed up, had our day and ought to be shunted off to an old folks' home.

'We're only fifty-eight, Harold,' I tell him. 'Not ready for the knacker's yard yet.'

'Maybe that's just how I'm feeling. Maybe I'm just tired.'

'Yes. Maybe.'

I don't know what else to say to him. I was so happy when we arrived here yesterday, imagining all the days out we were going to have together – walking around the town, taking the bus to the little villages on the other side of Korčula that I've been reading about in the guide-book, or even hiring a car and exploring on our own. Harold always used to love driving in foreign places – he found it challenging and exciting. Now I'm wondering if I was just kidding myself. He's not even ready for the challenge of *being* here.

'We have to try,' I say, taking hold of his hand and looking at him earnestly, before he buries himself

38

back in his book again. 'Harold – we should be trying to get the most out of this holiday. Out of this *life*. Jeannie would have wanted that. She would!'

He looks at me for a moment, sighs and shakes his head.

'It's not that I don't understand,' I go on, desperately. 'I loved her too!'

'I know you did,' he says, quietly. 'I'm sorry, Rube. Sorry about . . . *everything*.'

'Nothing to be sorry about,' I retort, turning away quickly before he can see the tears that have sprung up in my eyes.

Silly nonsense, crying over nothing. Crying isn't going to change anything. I don't know what is, though.

'I just feel *so tired*,' he says, closing his eyes and lifting his face to the sun. 'Like I've been running, and running, and running, for half my life, and now – now I've suddenly stopped – I could just lie down and sleep for ever.'

This is a long speech for Harold. He normally leaves most of the talking to me – or, as he would say, perhaps he just can't get a word in edgeways.

'Of course – it's a reaction. To all the stress.' Years and years of bloody stress. Tell me about it. 'These two weeks will do us both good. Let's just relax today and see how we both feel tomorrow. Yes? Maybe then we'll feel like swimming right round the headland there, going for a ten-mile hike, and . . .'

'Paragliding off the harbour walls?' he says sarcastically.

'I don't see why not.' I laugh and pick up my book, pulling my sun hat down over my face so that he can't see that I may be laughing but the tears aren't very far behind.

But I'm not giving in to sadness. We can't *both* give in to it. It's lovely sitting here, after all, with the sun beating on my bare legs and the turquoise sea sparkling with a thousand diamonds below us. If you're in heaven, Jeannie, then I reckon I could feel closer to you in a place like this. I don't think it can be so very different.

	S	M	**T**	W	T	F	S
					1	2	3
	4	5	6	7	8	9	10
June	11	12	13	14	15	16	17
	18	19	(20)	21	22	23	24
	25	26	27	28	29	30	

Gemma

Yesterday was lovely. A perfect first day for a honeymoon. We walked all round the walls of the old town in the morning, and then found a nice little place, next to the harbour, with tables outside overlooking the sea, where we had lunch and a bottle of wine. Andy went swimming off the rocks in the afternoon, but to be honest I was feeling too full up with lunch, too dozy from the wine, so I just sat on the rocks and watched him.

I've been in the sea this morning, though, and it was beautiful – clear, right to the bottom. It's a bit of a job getting out: the rocks are pretty slimy and I had to get Andy to give me a hand. He laughed at me and said I looked like an old woman, stumbling about and hanging on to him, but sorry, I don't want an accident. Not on my honeymoon, thank you very much.

I pick up my towel and head for the flat rocks at the

41

top, near the hotel steps. There are a couple of people sitting up there already and as I get closer I realise they've been watching me struggling out of the water. How embarrassing.

'That didn't look easy,' says the man.

'No. It'd be OK if the rocks weren't so slimy. Now I know why so many people around here are wearing those plastic shoes for swimming!'

'We heard someone saying they're on sale on the stalls in the town. Very cheap,' he says.

'Oh – thanks. I'll get myself a pair, then. Better than breaking my neck.'

He seems a pleasant enough guy, but somehow I really can't imagine *him* in a pair of cute little coloured plastic shoes. He's big, broad-shouldered, with bulging muscles and thick dark hair on his arms. His wife hasn't spoken yet. I glance at her and notice she's pregnant – although I don't suppose it would be showing if she weren't in a swimsuit. She's very young – not much more than a teenager – and in contrast to her partner she's slender and pale with long blonde hair.

'When's the baby due?' I ask her. Not just to be polite. I'm really interested, not to say a little bit envious. Andy and I are planning to start a family soon; since we've been together so long already, we decided that once we were married it would be the logical next step. I'm really excited about it.

I smile at this girl as she puts her hand tenderly over her bump as if to protect it from the world, and says: 'October. Long time yet.'

'Lovely. How lovely. I bet you're looking forward to it.'

'Yes.' She glances at the guy and hesitates. 'Yes, but . . .' And then she drops her eyes, shakes her head and doesn't say any more.

'Jo was quite sick for the first few months,' he tells me, taking her hand gently in his and holding it. 'So she's still feeling a bit . . . tired. Washed out.'

'Poor thing. Well, I'm sure a week or two of this lovely sunshine will do you good . . .' I begin, but I'm interrupted by Andy, bounding towards us over the rocks as if it was no more difficult than skipping across a well-manicured lawn. He's been taking photographs of the view across the bay – but as soon as he's seen me talking to someone, he wants to join in. I can't help smiling. He's like a big friendly playful Labrador sometimes.

'Hello there! I'm Andy. How're you doing? I'm just about to get us a couple of beers. Can I get you anything?'

To be honest, his enthusiasm for making friends can sometimes be just a tad embarrassing. Like now. I kind of feel that this couple, Jo and Mark, might have preferred a quiet rest in the sun, but Andy's getting them drinks and babbling on about the restaurants and bars in the town and, before you know it, he's invited them to join us for lunch.

'I thought we'd be having lunch on our own together,' I say when we're back in our room, changing out of our wet swimming things.

'Oh! Sorry, Gem,' he says, looking surprised. 'Don't you think it'll be fun? They seem like a nice couple.'

'Yes. But we're on our honeymoon,' I say a bit sulkily. 'And so are they! They might really prefer to be on their own, too.'

'I didn't think of that. I should have done. I'm a prat, aren't I?' He looks at me, puppy-dog eyes round with regret. 'But look, Gem – we've got the whole of the rest of our lives together! We'll *always* be together! It'll be nice to make a couple of friends while we're here, too.'

'OK. I guess.'

They do seem nice, too, although I think Jo's still feeling a bit rough, whatever she says about being over the morning sickness. We're eating at a cute little café just along the coast from the hotel. We've all ordered huge plates of seafood with salad. The fresh air and the swimming have given me an appetite, but Jo's picking at her food and Mark keeps trying to encourage her. 'Come on, sweetheart. Think of the baby.'

'Of course I'm thinking of the baby!' she says eventually, flashing him a look of annoyance. 'I think of *nothing else* but the baby!'

Andy and I look at each other uncomfortably.

'Do you know whether it's a boy or a girl?' I ask her, to break the awkward silence that follows.

'A boy. Jacob.'

'Ah, that's lovely,' I say. 'It's one of the names I like for a boy, too.'

'Are you ... expecting ... as well?' asks Mark, looking at my stomach.

I laugh. I know I could do with losing a bit of weight. 'Not yet. But we're going to start trying soon. That's why we got married. We've been together since we were fourteen ...'

'Really!' exclaims Jo. 'Childhood sweethearts? How romantic.'

'Yes.' I have to try not to sound smug whenever I tell anyone this. People are always surprised and impressed. After all, not many couples can say they've been together almost twenty years before they married, can they? 'And now we're ready to start a family, so we got married.'

44

'I wanted to marry you anyway, Gem,' points out Andy. 'You know that.'

'Yes, yes, I know ... of course, we would have got married anyway,' I laugh. 'But we're so looking forward to having a baby together.'

'Want another drink, Mark?' says Andy.

I glance at him, suddenly aware that he's changing the subject because it's not particularly tactful to talk about our plans for a baby when, for all we know, Jo's pregnancy might have been an accident. They might not really have been ready for a baby yet. In fact, that wouldn't surprise me at all. She's far too young, and they can't have been together very long, can they? They might actually be *sorry* that she's pregnant. I mean, not everyone's relationship is as stable as ours. Maybe they only got married because she was pregnant. That can be a terrible mistake, can't it?

'How long have you and Mark been together?' I ask her when we've finished eating.

'Not long,' she says.

'We've *known* each other for quite a while, though, haven't we, Jo?' he puts in. 'As friends.'

'Yes.' She smiles at him. 'Friends.'

'Andy and I are best friends, too,' I tell them happily. 'Best friends, lovers, and ...'

'And now an old married couple,' Andy finishes for me, laughing.

We've lingered a long while over the after-lunch drinks and coffees, and now Jo and Mark are heading back to the hotel while Andy and I are going on into the town. I want to buy a pair of those swimming shoes.

'Very glamorous,' jokes Andy as I pick up a bright blue pair. 'Going to try them on?'

I do, and of course this makes him laugh as they

45

don't exactly tone well with my dark green shorts and yellow vest top.

'They'll look fine with my blue bikini,' I explain, getting the money out of my purse. 'I'm not risking a fall on those rocks. They're bloody dangerous.'

'You could always sit down on the jetty and slide into the water from there. That's what Jo says she's going to do.'

'Yes, I don't blame her. If I were pregnant, I'd do the same. She needs to take care of herself.'

We wander the cobbled streets for a while, and Andy takes photos of the church, the harbour and the little huddled houses. Being a professional photographer, he's always there with the camera; it's his hobby as well as his job – and the little town is certainly photogenic. We climb the church tower and look out over the chessboard of red and orange tiled roofs spread out below us.

'Shall we stop for a drink?' he suggests when we climb back down. We head for a café with bright yellow tablecloths and umbrellas, where waiters in white shirts are swaying between the tables with trays of cold drinks and ice creams.

It's nice sitting in the shade, sipping a tall glass of fresh orange juice.I look up at Andy, smiling, on the point of making a remark about how lovely it is here, how happy I am. But he's not looking at me. He's staring at someone a couple of tables away from us. He's actually got his glass of Coke halfway to his mouth and his jaw's dropped. He looks like he's seen a ghost. I follow his gaze. There's a group of girls, about our own age, sitting together and chatting over their drinks. One of them is stunningly beautiful. She's blonde, with a figure to die for, wearing a cropped top that shows off her tiny waist, and tight white shorts displaying long tanned legs. As I'm looking at her, she raises her sunglasses and I realise that she's staring back. At Andy.

'Who's that?' I ask him.

She's smiling at him now, actually raising a hand as if to say hello, but still he's just staring like a zombie. He puts down his glass, suddenly and without drinking. His hand's shaking.

'Come on, Gem,' he says brusquely. 'You finished? Let's go.' He fishes in his pocket for some money and leaves it on the table with the bill. 'Ready?'

I'm still looking at the girl. She's watching us, but she's stopped smiling. She's realised she's being ignored. I suppose she might have made a mistake, thought he was someone else.

'You haven't even drunk your Coke,' I tell him, frowning. 'What's the matter?'

'I . . . don't want it. Got a stomach ache,' he says, feebly rubbing his stomach but darting surreptitious glances at the table where the girls are sitting. I know a fictitious stomach ache when I see one.

'Who is she?' I'm still sitting down, watching him. He looks over again, anxiously, fiddling with his sunglasses, running his hand through his hair.

'Come on, Gem. Let's go,' he repeats.

'Andy: who is she?' I ask him again as we start to walk away.

'Who?' He's staring straight ahead as we pass closer to her table.

'That girl,' I whisper, nodding with my head. 'She's still looking at you, Andy. Do you know her?'

'Of course not!' He laughs. 'Probably just fancies me, Gem.'

He's relaxing now that we're walking away from the café. We're turning a corner, out of her sight. I can almost hear him breathing more easily as we head back into the maze of little streets criss-crossing the main road through the town.

'Don't change the subject. Why should I mind if she's someone you know? Or if you fancy her!' I'm joking, but obviously I'm *hoping* he doesn't really fancy her. She's so bloody obvious, so tarty and cheap-looking.

'I don't know her. She looked a bit like one of the models I used to photograph, years ago, that's all. 'Course I didn't fancy her!' He laughs and hugs me. 'I don't fancy anyone except my little wifey!'

'Well, that's just as well.' I'm slightly mollified, but I still feel uneasy. I don't know why he'd get so flustered about someone who just looked like someone else. 'I need you concentrating on me, Mr Collins, while we're on our honeymoon!'

'I am!' he laughs, giving me a hug.

I try to relax and put his strange behaviour out of my mind while we're looking around the town. Instead, I find myself thinking about Jo, and how young she seems to be having a baby. Most of the couples Andy and I know are leaving it till their thirties to start families. We've always agreed that we'd get married first, and then hopefully start our family during the next year or so.

'It must be so exciting for Jo and Mark,' I muse.

'Having a baby already? I don't know. I expect they've come to terms with it, but I bet they hadn't planned it so young. It wasn't what *we* wanted, was it?'

'No – but it's different now, isn't it? We're both ready.' I pause. 'You *are* ready to start trying for a baby, aren't you, Andy?' I add as he hasn't responded.

He shrugs.

I give him a look of surprise. 'What? We've talked about this often enough. We've always said we'll start trying for a baby after we get married.'

'Yes. After. Not *straight* after. Not immediately, before the bloody wedding cake's even been eaten. I didn't think we'd be talking about it on our *honeymoon*.'

I'm so staggered, I have to stand still to recover. I can't believe I'm hearing this. Andy never talks to me in this sort of tone.

'No need to snap my head off. I didn't mean that. I didn't mean we were going to jump straight off the plane home and buy a pregnancy testing kit.'

He turns and grins at me a bit sheepishly.

'I know. Sorry. Of course we'll have a family, Gem. But there's no rush, is there?'

'*Rush*!' I laugh. 'We've been together over eighteen years! We've been living together for nearly eleven! I'm thirty-two, I'm not getting any younger ...'

'All right, all right!' We've stopped at a shop window. It's an art shop – paintings of Korčula harbour jostling for position alongside still-life images of fruit and black-and-white photographs of old folk dressed in traditional costume, carrying baskets of fish. 'You're thirty-two, Gemma, not fifty-two. We've still got plenty of time. We've only just got married. Let's enjoy being on our own, can't we, before we start thinking about babies?'

'But ...' I'm trying to stay calm, but this is bothering me slightly. It seems at odds with everything we've ever said before on the subject. 'But that was the whole *point* of getting married, wasn't it? We said ... because we've already been together so long, we planned it this way ...'

He turns to face me. He's definitely not teasing.

He's looking at me like he's going to impart a funda-mental truth, and it's going to hurt me.

'*You* said, Gemma. *You* planned it. As always, you just assumed I'd go along with it.'

I stare at him, tears spurting into my eyes. No! No, we're *not* going to have an argument! We never have arguments! I'm not *letting* us have an argument, not on our honeymoon! Why is he being like this? I can't believe it.

'Don't cry,' Andy says at once, softening, putting his arm round me. 'I'm not saying it isn't going to happen – just that the timing's got to be a joint decision.'

'I know! I know, but I thought . . .'

'You just assumed.'

'All right, I bloody *assumed*! Why wouldn't I? You never have any opinions, Andy! You let me choose the furniture, the carpets, the holidays . . .'

Shit. We're arguing.

'On this, I have an opinion. I don't want to rush into it.' His face is set, immovable. He doesn't seem to care that I'm crying now. Crying, on our honey-moon! This is *awful*. It's all going wrong.

'Let's talk about it again when we get home,' he says. 'Come on. Let's not argue, Gem. It's not worth it.'

Not worth it. Not *worth* it? I keep playing this over and over in my mind as we stroll back to the hotel. Despite what Andy says now, we've *both* always agreed on this before – and suddenly he doesn't even want to discuss it? It's *not worth it*? First the girl he stares at but claims he doesn't know, and now this? What's going on with him?

OK: I'm not having my romantic honeymoon ruined. I'm going to have to try to imagine that none of this has happened; that we haven't had the conversation about babies at all; that Andy hasn't spoken to me in that harsh, stern tone and accused me of leaving him out of the decisions. I'll just stay off the subject, at least for today, and by tomorrow whatever's upsetting him will have blown over and we'll be back to normal again. He'll probably apologise and say of course, of course we're going to start a family – isn't that what we've always agreed?

I look at him sideways as we walk along. He's frowning to himself and staring out at the sea. He seems really unsettled and odd since he saw that girl.

'*Did* you know her?' I ask him again, quietly. 'I don't care who she is – I'd rather you tell me the truth, Andy.'

'I am,' he says, turning to face me. Andy's not the type to tell lies, so he's no good at it. He's normally straightforward and honest, and his colouring doesn't help him either: he's pale-skinned, with light red hair, and when he's hot, or anxious, or embarrassed, he colours up in a way he can't hide. His response comes out awkwardly, quivering on his voice like a leaf hanging on a branch. Waiting to fall. Waiting for the one tiny puff of wind that's going to bring it tumbling down.

'I have no idea who she is, OK?'

It's no good. We both know he's lying.

And I feel like my whole world's caving in around me.

Jo

I've had my enforced rest, which Mark seems to insist is necessary even though I'm perfectly fine

51

and not tired any more, and we've come down to sit out on the sun terrace overlooking the sea.

'Here you are, babe,' he says, pulling out a chair for me. 'Sit here. This one's in the shade.'

I grit my teeth and try to smile my thanks. This is awful. I've got another four and a half months yet of being treated like an invalid. The trouble is, I know he means well, he's being so sweet, but … oh, I know what the problem is really. The problem is me! I'm not ready for this. I feel like I've been turned from a fun-loving student into a shaky old woman without a mind of her own, and I can't even rebel because I've signed up for it.

'Hello again, love,' calls a cheery voice. 'Having a nice day? How are you feeling now? Managed to eat something yet, have you?'

'One question at a time, Ruby!' protests the guy sitting with her, who I presume is her husband. 'Give the poor girl a chance to answer.' He smiles at me. He's got a nice smile, brightening up his face and making him look younger. He's probably about sixty – sprightly-looking for his age, with smooth silver-grey hair and chiselled features. Probably a very handsome man until he developed the lines of sadness now showing around his eyes. 'Hello, I'm Harold. You must be Jo and Mark? Ruby's told me all about you. I'll apologise now, on her behalf. She doesn't mean to be nosy. It comes from years of being a French teacher and constantly asking all the pupils their names, where they live, and whether they've got any brothers or sisters.'

'Oh, God!' I smile back, despite myself. 'I remember those French lessons! I used to cower at the back of the class and hope Madame Dupont didn't pick on me. Did you used to shout at your pupils in French and scare them out of their wits because they didn't know what you were saying?'

'Of course not!' she laughs. 'I was a *nice* teacher. I still am, actually, although I've retired from mainstream education. I just do home tutoring now – so much more civilised. The classroom was becoming a jungle. Trust me, if I'd shouted too hard at any of those little savages, their parents would have been suing me for their hurt feelings.'

'I don't know how you stood it,' comments Mark, shaking his head. 'You have my admiration.' He glances at me, grins and adds: 'Students these days, eh? Nightmare!'

'I'm not even a student any more,' I say, quietly, the familiar feeling of panic washing over me.

'What were you studying, love?' asks Ruby.

'Sports science. I took my final exams two weeks ago. Just got to wait and see whether I've passed, now. And whether there are any career prospects available for a sports science graduate with a baby.'

'Don't start thinking about that just yet,' Mark tries to soothe me, as always. 'We can manage . . .'

I swallow hard. I'm not going to go over all this again – not now, not in front of this other couple. How he's going to earn enough for both of us, how I won't need to work, but how we'll be able to afford child care when I decide I'm ready to start. It's not what I want. I don't want him to think that's why I married him – so that I could sit at home with my baby while he works extra hours, looking for private patients as well working long days at the hospital. But what else can I do? The baby's got to come first, now, I know that – and I haven't got a job. I haven't even graduated yet.

'Don't look so worried,' he whispers to me now. 'Everything's going to be fine.'

'You wait,' says Ruby, smiling at me kindly. 'Once the baby's born, you won't be thinking about going out to work for a while, trust me. You won't even have time to consider it!'

'I suppose you were OK, though, when you had your children. I mean – teaching is really compatible with parenthood, isn't it? I've been thinking about it as a possibility myself. If I get my degree, of course,' I add quickly.

'I wasn't a teacher back then. Oh, no – I qualified much later. Went back to college when my boys – my first two children – started school. After I'd left my first husband.'

I look at Ruby with new interest.

'Life must have been very difficult for you. How did you manage?'

'I had a good mum,' she says with a faint smile. 'She took me back, me and my two babies. I was only seventeen when I got married – pregnant, of course. It still wasn't really the done thing, in those days, being an unmarried mother, so it was assumed by everyone that Eddie and I would have to get married. Total disaster, but what else could you expect? We were just two kids, playing house, having kids ourselves without really understanding what we were doing.'

'That's so sad,' I say. Seventeen. It doesn't seem very long ago since I was seventeen myself, still in the sixth form, working for my A levels, going out with my friends, looking forward to the future. Before I met Ben.

'Yes. It's a wonder my Trevor survived!' Ruby goes on with a throaty chuckle. 'I didn't even like babies, I'd had enough of them at home with being the eldest girl,

54

expected to do all the work and look after the little ones. I thought it'd be great to get away from home, live with Eddie in our own little place and be looked after in return for some housework and the occasional bit of nooky. Had no idea what I was letting myself in for. Especially as I didn't even love him.' She sighs. 'Never mind. We all make mistakes, don't we? That's life. My mum helped me bring up my boys, along with my brothers and sisters, and they didn't suffer. I hope not, anyway.'

'Of course they didn't, Rube,' says Harold stoutly. 'They've turned out great, and so have your girls. You know how proud you are of the lot of them.'

'How many children have you got, Ruby?' asks Mark.

'Only the four. Two sons and two daughters. My youngest, Jodie – she's probably about your age, love – was twenty-three last Christmas. She's talking about getting married to her boyfriend, but I've said to her: "Jodie love, you're too young. Don't make the same mistake as me ..."' Ruby stops speaking, shaking her head, and adds quickly: 'Sorry – me and my big mouth. I'm sure you two have done the right thing. You seem very happy together. It works for some, of course, marrying young. Especially when there's a baby ...'

'Yes. That's it, exactly. That's the only reason we got married,' I agree, without thinking. Then I see the look on Mark's face and amend quickly: 'I mean, the only reason we got married so young. Of course.'

There's a silence. Ruby and Harold go back to looking out at the sea. They remind me a little bit of my own parents – always staring at the sea when we were away on family holidays together. 'What are you looking at?' I used to ask them, irritated, as a young teenager by their apparent lack of desire to *do* anything. 'We're just relaxing,' Mum used to say with a patient sigh. 'For once in our lives.' I understood when I was older, of course. They both had demanding jobs, and my younger brothers and I were hard work. It was fine for us to run around on holiday, in and out of the sea, playing sport, getting sweaty and dirty and using up all the energy that had been thwarted during our days in the classroom. We weren't the ones who'd be going back after two weeks to wash and iron all those grubby clothes, tidy up the house and garden and go straight back to work. Harold and Ruby have had hard enough lives, too, I suspect. No wonder they just want to sit back, now, and gaze at the sea for a while.

I look at Mark. He's doing the same – but there's a sadness, a tension, about his mouth as he gazes at the ocean, and that's because of me. I hadn't meant to say it – about only getting married because I'm pregnant. He's knows it's true, of course, but I don't mean to rub his nose in it.

'Sorry,' I whisper, although I don't know how it can help.

He nods and squeezes my hand, still looking hurt, and I feel a momentary flash of resentment that overrides my sympathy. It's not my fault he wanted to marry me. I didn't make him. I didn't ask him to love me. He should have left me alone. I'd have managed, I'd have been all right. Me and my baby. He didn't have to get involved!

'I think I'll go for a swim,' I say abruptly, getting up and looking around for my towel. 'The sea should be really warm by now.'

'I'll come with you,' he says instantly.

'You don't have to. I'll be perfectly OK.'

'I don't want you to take any chances ...'

'Mark, swimming's the best exercise for me!'

'I know. But the pool would be safer. Those rocks are so slippery...'

I sigh. 'I'll get in and out off the jetty. I'll sit down and slide in, like the old lady, like the invalid you seem to think I am. I'll swim in a nice gentle breast-stroke and I won't tire myself out. All right?'

I don't wait for his answer but walk off, down the steps to the beach, carrying my towel and feeling hot and sick, and wishing I wasn't such a bitch. But I can't help it. He's going to drive me mad before this baby's born. It's bad enough him nannying me about what I eat, what I drink, how much I sleep and every other bloody thing − but *swimming*, of all things − that's what I *do*! I know exactly what I'm doing − I bloody well should do. It's what I'm best at.

It's how I met Ben.

It was my first term at uni. I was only just eighteen. When I look back now, I can't believe that fresh-faced, innocent, enthusiastic girl was really me. I feel a hundred years older than I was then. A thousand years wiser. I wanted to join every club available, take part in every sport, play for every team. Swimming was always my first love, and I was good: I knew I was good. So did everyone at the university swimming club − I was signed up to the squad as soon as I tried out. Ben was the squad's trainer. He was in his late-twenties, fit, good-looking, oozing testosterone. He took a particular interest in me, which I assumed was because of my potential. He told me if I trained hard enough, I could compete nationally. Maybe even internation-ally.

It turned my head in the way only a young, naive, inexperienced head can be turned. I'd had a couple of boyfriends before I went away to uni – nothing serious. Now, they seemed like sad and pathetic schoolboys compared to this amazing spec-imen of a man who was suddenly filling my dreams and turning into a mega-crush.

That's what it should have stayed – a crush. Nothing wrong with a crush, is there? It's a fairly normal thing for an eighteen-year-old girl to have on an older, attractive man. The worst you can end up with from a crush is a heap of unfulfilled dreams. Better than a broken heart and a ruined life any day. Better than being pregnant and married to the wrong man.

I'm walking towards the jetty when I see Gemma and Andy heading back towards the hotel. I can tell instantly that there's something wrong. They seemed so deliriously happy when we had lunch together, it made me ache. Every time she looked at him, her eyes lit up. They've been together so long, they've got their own jokes and funny little catch-phrases. It's the sort of relationship I'd have liked ... the sort of relationship *anyone* would like. But they're the lucky ones who actually got it. Now something's happened. They're not holding hands. They're walking about a yard apart, and as they come closer I can see she's been crying while he looks like he's just lost something. Or seen some-thing terrible. They're not talking.

'Hello,' I venture. They both look at me and try to smile. I don't know what else to say. 'Just going for a swim,' I try.

'Good idea,' says Gemma, her voice coming out slightly strangled. 'I think I'll join you.'

She takes out a pair of blue plastic swimming shoes, shoves her bag at Andy and then walks with me to the jetty, ignoring him. He watches for a moment and then sighs heavily and heads for the steps. Gemma strips down to her bikini, shrugging herself out of her shorts and top without saying a word, and puts on the shoes.

'Oh, you bought a pair!' I sit down on the edge of the jetty, preparing to slide off into the water in my new safety-conscious manner. 'They're cool. I might get a pair, too. It might stop Mark from nagging me.'

She doesn't say anything. We both get into the water and I swim a little way before looking back at her. She's still standing on a rock, holding on to the edge of the jetty.

'Are you OK?' I call to her. She nods and begins to swim towards me, stopping when she gets within her depth and breathing hard.

'I was just watching you. You're a good swimmer.'

'Thanks. It's my thing. I swam for the university, and for the county . . . before I got pregnant, of course.'

'You'll carry on, though, won't you? No need for you to give up after the baby's born . . .'

'I only swim for fitness now,' I say, more sharply than I'd intended. 'I've finished with competitive swimming.'

'Pity. I wish I had something I was really good at,' says Gemma wistfully. She splashes past me, head up, arms doing a furious kind of crawl, legs splashing water in all directions.

'Mark worries about me swimming,' I say, half to

myself. I turn on to my back and belt out to sea in a fast backstroke. The water here is calm, almost like a pond. No rough waves to dive through. No sneaky currents to power against. Easy and warm and relaxing. When I turn and tread water, I see Gemma watching me again, back in the shallows. I swim over to her, slowly, steadily, enjoying the strength of my arms and the heat of the sun.

'Why?' she says as if there hadn't been a break in our conversation. 'Why does he worry? Swimming's good for you when you're pregnant.'

'I know. It's not that. It's just . . . oh, look, it's a male pride thing. My . . . ex . . . was my swimming coach.'

'Oh. Right. So he's jealous of your swimming, is that it?'

'Kind of.' Worried that I'll swim for Ben's squad again one day. Worried that I'll get hurt again. Or that he will. 'Men are strange,' I say with a shrug, shaking the water from my hair. I'm purposely being flippant. I don't really want to discuss this with someone I've only just met. But she sighs at once and agrees vehemently.

'You can say that again. I thought I knew my husband inside out, but suddenly I feel like I don't know him at all.'

I don't want to hear this either. I don't really want to exchange intimacies with this girl who's on her perfect honeymoon with her perfect husband, who's one of the lucky ones, finding her true love at only fourteen and marrying him and *still* wanting to complain. I hold my nose and duck-dive under the water, swimming away from her, pushing against the tide with the strong muscles in my chest and arms that Ben once purported to love so much, kicking away from Gemma with her soulful eyes and her

60

sighs of misery over some imagined silly slight, some exaggerated lovers' tiff. She must be ten years older than me, but I feel like I've lived forever in comparison. She doesn't know she's born.

By the time I swim back, she's out of the water again and is sitting on the jetty, kicking her feet, drying off in the sun. I shake my hair out of its pony-tail and raise my hand in farewell to her.

'I'd better go back to Mark, before he comes looking for me.'

'OK.' She doesn't move. When I get to the top of the steps, I turn back and see her still sitting there, looking at her feet kicking the surface of the water. She should just get her arse over here and make it up with Andy, whatever it is. It can't be that bad, can it?

As it happens, Andy's with Mark. When I look for him on the sun terrace, Ruby glances up from her book and tells me: 'He's in the bar, love. That other young chap – Andy – came up an hour or so ago and asked if any of us fancied a drink. Your Mark's gone with him.'

This surprises me, to be honest. Mark's not a drinker, really. He likes a couple of beers, or a glass of wine, but he's not the type to go boozing with the boys and it's definitely not like him to go off to the bar with someone he hardly knows.

'Thanks, Ruby. I'll go and shower. Probably see him back in our room.'

I've showered, dressed and am drying my hair by the time he returns. And he's trying hard not to slur his speech.

'You're surely not pissed!' I grin with surprise and something like satisfaction. He's very health-conscious and always nagging me about the dangers of drink. I never expected to see *this* – especially when he couldn't have been in the bar for much more than an hour.

'Only a little bit. I'm not used it these days, Jo.' He throws himself down on the bed and watches me in the mirror as I brush my hair. 'I couldn't say no. Poor guy's in a bit of a state.'

'Oh, God, don't tell me. I was just swimming with Gemma. They've had some sort of a row, haven't they? I didn't want to hear about it.'

'Not a row, as such. He's just got himself into . . . a bit of a dilemma.'

'Huh.' I put my brush down and turn to face him. 'I thought they were the perfect couple? She was quite irritating at lunch, sounding so smug about how long they've been together and how wonderful everything is. So everything's not as rosy as she thought it was? Well, sorry, but that's life, isn't it? That's the reality of it. Nobody's life is bloody perfect, at the end of the day.'

God, I sound so bitter. I want to take it back. I want to take that injured look out of Mark's eyes, stop him turning away from me with the long-suffering sigh I'm beginning to get so used to.

'What happened, then?' I ask him, trying to sound interested. 'What's up with them?'

'Never mind,' he says, picking up his book. Shutting me out. 'Nothing you want to hear about. As you say – just life, not being bloody perfect.'

Well, I'm not like Gemma. I don't believe in a perfect life. Not any more, anyway.

	S	M	T	**W**	T	F	S
					1	2	3
June	4	5	6	7	8	9	10
	11	12	13	14	15	16	17
	18	19	20	(21)	22	23	24
	25	26	27	28	29	30	

Gemma

By the time we went to bed last night, after an uncomfortable meal in the hotel's own restaurant because neither of us felt like walking into town with the atmosphere between us souring the evening air, I'd tried to convince myself I must be making something out of nothing. I told myself I must have imagined seeing the panic in Andy's eyes when he caught that girl looking at him, and then hearing the dishonesty rolling off his tongue when he told me he didn't know her. It just couldn't have happened – could it? Andy's not like that; he doesn't have secrets from me. And anyway, how ridiculous to think that he'd recognise someone he saw in such an out-of-the-way place as a small island in Croatia. I must have been over-tired.

And as for the baby conversation – I just blew that up out of nothing. I don't know why I was making such an issue of it. I suppose talking to Jo got me thinking about starting our own family, but Andy's quite right really – we never said we'd try for a baby *immediately* after the wedding! We have plenty of time to make our plans once we get home.

I feel stupid now, and cross with myself for spoiling a day of our honeymoon. I don't want to look back on these special two weeks and only remember how I sulked and cried and showed off like a spoilt brat.

Andy had a few drinks with Mark while I was swimming yesterday afternoon.

'Nice guy,' he tells me now that we're talking again. After we've made it up in the best way possible – making love under the crisp white hotel sheets, with the morning sunshine filtering through the curtains. We're just leaving the breakfast table now, and Jo and Mark have passed us on their way in. 'Bit of an unusual situation he's in, though.'

'How do you mean?'

'He told me . . . once he'd had a couple of beers, you know . . . that he's not the father of Jo's baby.'

'Oh my God! What – did she have an affair with someone else while they were engaged?'

'No. He only asked her to marry him when she found out she was pregnant. The father's a friend of his. *Was.* Treated her really badly, apparently. Mark didn't go into details, but it sounds like the guy dumped her when she got pregnant.'

'The bastard! Poor Jo.' I think about this as we go back up to our room. 'Actually, it kind of fits. She doesn't seem as crazy about Mark as he obviously is about her. And she told me yesterday that her ex was her swimming coach. That'd be the pig who dumped her, I suppose. Sounds like she's married Mark on the rebound. I hope she's done the right thing.'

'Mark seems to be worried about that too. He

thinks she might be having second thoughts already. Thinks she still hankers after the other guy.'

'Poor Jo,' I say again. 'We're so lucky, Andy, aren't we – you and I? Having each other, being together all these years. Some people have such an awful time, like Ruby with her failed marriages ...'

'And her carry-on with her sister's bloke!' he reminds me, laughing. 'Maybe it wasn't all bad!'

'I think we should just appreciate how lucky we are. That's all I'm saying.'

'So do I.' He kisses me gently and we hold on to each other for a minute. I like to think we're both contemplating our good fortune, having found a soul mate at such an early age, with no problems and no worries about each other. Regretting our argument of yesterday and putting it all behind us.

'What are you thinking about?' I ask him dreamily.

'How long before I can get the first beer of the day,' he says, ducking quickly before I hit him.

Andy wants to go somewhere different today. I'd have been quite happy to carry on chilling out around here, but he's keen to explore more places and take more photos. He's got the guide-book and he's reading bits out to me.

'No point hiring a car, really, Gem. There's a good bus service from the town, apparently. We can get a bus to this place here – look.' He shows me the map. 'Lumbarda.'

'Sounds like a dance.'

'Or a backache,' he laughs. 'It's a little village with nice sandy beaches. Not very far away. Shall we give it a try?'

'OK! Why not?' I don't want any disagreements today. I throw some towels, sun cream and books into our back-pack, and we set off to the bus station in the town.

Turns out the bus only runs once an hour and we've got half an hour to wait. We buy bottles of water and sweets to pass the time, and ten minutes before the bus is due, Andy calls out: 'There's Mark and Jo! Hey – Mark! Hi! Where're you off to?'

They cross the road and join us at the bus queue.

'Just walking into town, going to mooch around the shops and maybe buy Jo a pair of those swimming shoes you got yesterday, Gemma. I don't want her slipping on those rocks and even the jetty's quite slippery . . .'

I see Jo raise her eyebrows. Looks like she's really fed up with his fussing.

'We're getting the bus to Lumbarda – supposed to be the best beaches on the island,' says Andy enthusiastically. 'Come with us! Go on, it'll be great!'

I try not to sigh. I so wanted a nice romantic day on our own. But I don't think Mark's up for it anyway.

'We . . . ell,' he says, considering. 'I don't think so. Jo gets so tired . . .'

'Mark!' she snaps. 'I'm not tired, and I hardly think a bus ride and a sandy beach will overstretch me. Don't be such an old woman!'

I turn away. It was bad enough arguing ourselves yesterday, I don't want to get involved with other people's scrapping. But while they're still prevaricating, the Lumbarda bus pulls up and we're getting elbowed out of the way by local women with huge shopping baskets climbing aboard.

'We're going then,' I tell the others quickly. 'See you later.'

'We're joining you,' says Jo firmly. 'Come on, Mark.' She's stepped on to the bus before he can disagree.

It's already crowded and we don't manage to get seats near Jo and Mark.

'I'm not sure that was such a good idea,' I say as the bus pulls away.

'Why?' Andy looks at me in surprise. To him, it can never be a bad idea to make friends. New friends everywhere we go, but still it's never enough to make up for the past. The days when he didn't fit in, didn't measure up to some stupid teenage idea of cool; when he wasn't smart enough, sporty enough, big enough, cocky enough – when the only ones who talked to him were the ones who subjected him to their endless petty tortures. The *accidental* trips on the stairs. The drinks spilt in the school canteen, pens and books and money stolen from his bag, cruel jokes, nudges, whispers, insults, stupid laughter at nothing, just to make the idiots feel bigger and better about themselves. I was his only friend in those days, and it didn't matter that we both got teased about that too. I could stick up for myself, and I stuck up for Andy. I always will, of course – not that he needs it any more. He's a better man than all his tormentors put together. They didn't grind him down. But they did leave him with a need to surround himself with people who like him. Everybody does like him, these days – that's the thing. But he goes on drawing them around him like a comfort blanket. Even now, on our honeymoon, when I should be enough for him. Shouldn't I?

'I just thought we'd have a quiet day together, on our own, you and me,' I protest with a shrug. 'But never mind.'

'Sorry.' He frowns. 'I didn't think. I'll make it up to you tonight, Gem. We'll have a really nice meal at a posh restaurant. On our own. Yeah?'

'OK.' I smile. 'That'll be nice.'

I look round for the others, and finally see them towards the back of the bus. Jo's staring out of the window, looking as if she's miles away or at least would prefer to be – and Mark's watching her, the anxiety never far from his eyes. I sigh and lean closer to Andy. I wish we hadn't had that argument. I wish I could rid myself of the doubts that are still niggling away at the back of my mind, despite everything I'm telling myself. But at least we haven't got *their* problems.

The village of Lumbarda is really small, with just a cluster of houses, restaurants and a small hotel surrounding the little harbour. The famous sandy beaches are actually a bit of a walk from the village, and predictably Mark begins to fret about Jo feeling tired, hot, thirsty, sick, in need of shade, water, a bigger hat, different shoes, medical attention or a bloody ambulance. God, he's beginning to drive *me* mad, just listening to him. What the hell's he going to be like when she goes into labour? He'll probably insist on taking over and having the contractions himself.

'I think Jo's fine,' I tell him quietly when I can get a word in edgeways. 'She's looking really fit and healthy.'

This is actually a bit of a lie. I'm sure she's fit – having seen her swimming yesterday – but she's pale and too thin. I don't think that's anything to do with the pregnancy, though. From what Mark's told Andy, I suspect it's because she's bloody miserable.

'I'm a nurse,' I add, hoping this will convince him I know what I'm talking about. I work on a paediatric medical ward, and haven't had anything to do with obstetrics since I did my training, but people always assume that nurses are experts in every human condition under the sun and ready to leap into action with our first-aid kits at the suggestion of anything from toothache to gout.

'Really?' He looks at me with interest, falling into step with me out of earshot of the other two. 'Well, we've got something in common then. I'm a physiotherapist. I specialise in musculoskeletal cases – so my patients mostly have broken limbs, torn muscles or tendons, or they're post-surgery – and my real interest is sports injuries. I'm doing a bit of private work for a sports injury clinic in the evenings. I don't have anything much to do with the medical cases, so this is all a bit outside my sphere of reference.'

'Jo's not *ill*, Mark!' I laugh at him. 'Pregnancy isn't a sickness!'

'But don't you think she looks . . . a bit peaky?'

'Well, if she had severe early-pregnancy sickness she's probably lost a bit of weight, but the baby won't have suffered. She'll start blooming now she's midway, you'll see!'

'Thanks, Gemma. That's really reassuring. I worry about her . . . not looking after herself properly. The pregnancy wasn't planned, you see,' he confides. 'It's been a shock for her. She's had to adjust to the idea of being a mum before she was ready.'

'Of course. That must have been difficult. But there are lots of compensations for having children at a young age. She'll be fitter for coping with the birth than an older mum. And for coping with the lack of sleep – all the demands of a little kid. Older mothers can have a really tough time.' I sigh without even realising I'm doing it. 'I sometimes wish *I'd* had children while I was still in my twenties.'

Shit. I didn't mean to say that. I had *no* intention of bringing up this subject again today, and certainly not to this guy I hardly know from Adam.

'Do you?' He looks at me in surprise. 'But you've got your career.'

'Oh, yes. I'm a staff nurse on a children's ward – I love it.'

'I suppose that makes you hanker after kids of your own?'

'Perhaps,' I agree, trying to sound nonchalant about it. 'But like Andy said yesterday – there's no rush, of course.'

I watch Andy as he walks ahead of us, chatting companionably to Jo, and have to give myself a little shake and change the subject.

The beach is long and wide, open and windswept. If it hadn't been such a breezy day, it would have been lovely. As it is, there aren't too many people here and – hot from the walk – we all go in for a swim straight away. There are bigger waves here than in the sheltered waters outside our hotel. I'm not a good swimmer and soon I'm struggling against them, spluttering and scrambling to my feet if one goes over my head. Jo and Mark are striking out into the deeper water where there aren't any breakers to contend with and they're racing each other: Jo, obviously, because she can, because she enjoys it, because she's winning every time; Mark, I suspect, because he doesn't want to let her out of his sight.

After swimming we sit on our towels in the sun to dry off and within five minutes both the guys have stretched out and fallen asleep.

'Typical!' I remark jokingly to Jo. 'They're good company, aren't they?'

'I should think Mark's glad to close his eyes and blot out my moaning,' she says. She leans back on her elbows and sighs. 'I wish I could help it. He's

70

being so considerate and caring, but it just gets on my bloody nerves.'

'I can imagine. There's nothing worse than being treated like an invalid, is there? But, as you say, at least it shows he cares about you and the baby.'

'I know. That's why I feel like such a bitch.' She closes her eyes and for a minute I think she's dozed off too. Then, suddenly, she blurts out: 'You don't know how lucky you are, Gemma.'

'How do you mean?'

'All the stuff you were saying yesterday lunchtime, about being each other's soul mate, and Andy being the love of your life . . . I know you seemed a bit upset with him later on, but that's life, isn't it? Everyone has their ups and downs, but you seem so happy together.'

'I *do* know that. But, Jo, it's exciting and wonderful, too, to be having a baby. Even if it wasn't what you expected just yet.'

'I know. I know I should feel like that. But – just between you and me – it's the *circumstances*. Mark isn't the father. He only married me out of pity.'

'Pity? Oh, I can't believe that. He seems crazy about you!'

'Maybe. He says he is, of course. I don't know . . . I find it hard to believe anything, any more. Ben said he was crazy about me, too, but when the chips were down he dumped me like a . . . like an unwanted bit of *rubbish*.'

I feel I should put my arm round her, but I hardly even know her. I wish she wasn't telling me this, really: it's difficult to know how to respond.

'I'd say you're too good for him, then, in that case. You're better off with Mark, I'm sure. Were you friends with him for a long time?'

71

'Only since I was seeing Ben. He was a friend of Ben's, really, at the university. Mark was a post-grad student; he and Ben are both fitness fanatics and they used to work out together. Of course, Ben didn't tell too many of his friends about me . . .'

'Why not?' I'm beginning not to like the sound of this Ben at all.

'Oh!' She turns to look at me, her face deceptively impassive. 'Didn't I tell you? He's married. Married with two children. I was only ever his bit on the side, Gemma. What an idiot, eh? The oldest story in the book.'

'Oh, God, I see. Did you know that, though? When you met him, I mean?'

'Of course not. I was over the moon when he asked me out. I thought this was *it* – the man of my dreams. He was full of shit – all the stuff I wanted to hear, about how I'd come along and changed his life, blah, blah, blah. He seemed conveniently to forget that he had a wife and twin daughters at home. By the time I found *that* out, it was too late; I was completely in love with him. I should have walked away but I didn't . . . and, in the end, I couldn't.' She closes her eyes and lies back on the beach, sighing. 'I wish I had.'

I'm clamping my teeth together with anger. The bastard! How could he do that – to Jo, to his wife and his children!

'Poor you,' I tell her gently. 'You've had a rotten time.'

Why are men so crap at being faithful? My dad was just the same. Why didn't he ever think about all the pain he was causing Mum and me? And why did I never think before about the girls he had his affairs with? Or, if I did at all, just presume they were the kind of girls who slept around with married men and deserved all they got. But what if, like Jo, they fell in love with him, without even knowing he was married or that he had a daughter at home who was holding her mum's hand while she cried? I hated my dad for doing that: for putting us through that, and not even caring.

'Are *you* OK?' asks Jo, sitting up and frowning at me. 'What is it?'

'Nothing. Sorry. I'm just cross – for you. How dare he? How dare he treat you like that? Why are some men such bastards?'

'It was my fault for falling in love with him.'

'No! No, of course it wasn't! He shouldn't have let that happen!' I take a deep breath and try to calm down. This isn't helping Jo at all. 'I suppose, when you found out, he told you he didn't love his wife any more?' I ask her quietly.

'Yes. He was going to leave her ... but it was the children. I couldn't compete with his children. He'd always put them first, of course. So, in the end, I reasoned ...'

'That if you got pregnant, he'd leave his family for you and the baby?'

She nods miserably.

'But he didn't,' I add, crossly. 'He didn't want to know.'

'Told me I'd better get rid of it,' she whispered.

Neither of us can speak for a few minutes. I reach out and take hold of Jo's hand. It's all I can do. If I try to say anything right now, I'm going to explode. I want to kill this fucking Ben. I hate him almost as much as I hate my dad. I'm glad Jo's with Mark instead of him. There's no comparison. Mark could fuss and irritate her for the rest of her life and he'd still be a knight in shining armour compared to Bastard Ben.

73

'I think I went slightly crazy,' she says tonelessly. She grips my hand but doesn't look at me. 'I was feeling so ill — sick, tired and scared. Sorry for starting a baby so carelessly and selfishly, and then finding out that its father didn't even want it. But when he said that — about getting rid of it — I finally snapped. I wasn't going to do it. I wanted this baby.' She lays her free hand protectively over her stomach and a ghost of a smile flickers across her face. 'I wanted it, and I was going to keep it, and love it, no matter what. Even without him. In *spite* of him.'

'Good for you,' I tell her softly.

'That's not what Ben said. He told me I was a fool; that I'd tie myself down and ruin my life. Of course, he was more concerned about the baby ruining *his* life. It hadn't occurred to me until then, Gemma, that he didn't actually love me at all.' She says this almost wonderingly, as if it's still a strange notion to her. 'He never did. Not at all.'

'So how did Mark come into it?' I ask, to try to move her along.

'He phoned me the very next evening. Apparently he was the only person Ben had confided in. He'd known about our affair, didn't like it but kept quiet because he was Ben's friend. Ben had told him about my pregnancy and said he wasn't going to see me any more. "Too heavy" was the expression he'd used. Nice, eh? He didn't even tell *me* that, but he told Mark. Apparently, Mark felt sorry for me. And when I started crying on the phone, he asked if he could come round. I don't know why I said yes: I was so low at that point, I think if Jack the Ripper had been nice to me I'd have asked him to come round.'

'I can understand that.'

'Mark was . . . just what I needed at that time. He

brought me flowers. Let me cry. Let me talk about Ben. Tried to persuade me to eat when I felt so sick and so pissed off with life, I could easily have starved. He started to look after me, and I so needed looking after. I desperately wanted to keep the baby, but I felt too weak and too ill to take care of myself. Does that make sense?'

'Yes. Yes, it does – absolutely. But I still don't see why . . .'

'We got married?' She sighs and shakes her head. 'It was Mark's idea. Within a couple of weeks, he was telling me he'd always liked me. I found that a bit strange because, of course, I'd never taken much notice of him. I didn't look at anyone else when Ben was around. And it was slightly spooky to think that all this time, this guy had apparently fancied me . . .'

'Wishing Ben would leave you alone so that he could make a move?'

'Exactly. But when he offered to stay around so that he could look after me and the baby . . . do you know what? . . . it sounded so good. After all the years of sneaking around, being a mistress, a dirty little secret to be hidden away, it actually felt good to imagine myself as part of a proper partnership, with someone who obviously really cared about me, who seemed to care about the baby almost as much as I did. It was actually such a relief to *let* go. To lean on him. Let him take me over. I was too ill to worry about whether it was the right thing for me to do or not. It was easy and convenient so I went along with it. Of course, he told me I should stay away from Ben. Stay away from him and give up the swimming, he said. Don't ever be tempted to go back to it. In Mark's mind, you see, if I go back to competitive swimming, I go back to Ben. He can't let that happen because he knows I'd go back to Ben permanently if I could. If he'd have me.'

'Even now?' I can't believe this. Is she mad? 'After what he's done? The way he's treated you?'

She doesn't even answer. She doesn't have to.

'In a way, I feel sorry for Mark,' she admits. 'It's Ben's baby, whatever he does or says. Mark suggested getting married because he thought that would make the baby *his* in some way. "I'll be a father to it," he told me, and I know he means it. He means well . . . that's the trouble. I just laughed at him at first. Get married? The idea was absolutely ridiculous. But then I spoke to Ben.'

'You phoned him?'

'No. He called me. He'd found out I was seeing Mark and he was absolutely furious. "He's not having you!" he yelled at me – even though he didn't want me any more himself. I finally lost it; yes, I know it was long overdue. I called him a heartless bastard, and told him that if Mark could love me, and look after me and the baby, it was more than *he* could do. Not only was I going to stay with Mark, I was going to marry him too, and there was nothing Ben could do about it.'

Yes, I can understand it now. I can almost feel it myself – the wretchedness, the hopeless, helpless misery, the bitterness and fury and desire to hurt him back. To feel that she'd somehow got even. And, in doing so, hurting herself even more.

'If Mark hadn't been so determined to take care of me, take on the baby, take over our lives – it just wouldn't have happened. Anybody else would have said no, you're doing it for all the wrong reasons – which I was, of course. But he was thrilled. He wanted to do it instantly – the sooner the better. It should have rung alarm bells: he wanted us to get married before

76

I could change my mind. Come to my senses. But all I could think about was, I'll show him. I'll show Ben Newton I don't need him. We fixed the wedding for the first available date after I finished my exams – last Thursday – there were no weekend dates left but we didn't care, it didn't matter. Then I had to tell my parents. They were shocked and upset . . .'

'Yes, I bet they were. Do they know . . . about the baby not being Mark's?'

'I didn't tell them at first. Then, when I was talking to Mum one day, it all came out in a rush – a bit like I'm telling you now, Gemma. Mum and Dad have been brilliant. They must be so disappointed in me, but they haven't shown it. They helped out with the wedding, arranged the reception, and even paid for this honeymoon.' She sniffs and smiles. 'Mark saw it advertised in that wedding magazine. He loved Croatia when he came here before so he got in and booked it quick. If nothing else good comes out of all this madness, at least I've had a holiday. To recover . . .'

'From Ben?'

'From all of it. Because I'm so worried I've done the wrong thing! Am I crazy? I've married someone I don't even love . . . It isn't fair on him, apart from anything else.'

'But you still went through with it. Jo, *why*? Why didn't you back out, tell him you'd changed your mind – even at the last minute?'

'Because then Ben would think he'd won. And I would've had to live the rest of my life knowing he was smugly thinking I still loved him.'

Whereas now she has to live the rest of her life knowing she made a terrible decision, for all the wrong reasons.

'But I do still love him anyway,' she adds in a tiny

voice. 'I think about him every day – all the time I'm with Mark. It's tearing me apart. Making me ill. Doing my fucking head in.'

Love? For God's sake! That's not love, is it? I think it's masochism.

Ruby

They gave us a wave as they went off for the day.

'Going to Lumbarda!' Andy called cheerfully. 'We think it might be a dance!'

'Have fun,' I said, smiling at them as they strolled off, holding hands, their arms swinging in the sunshine.

Twenty minutes later the others went off in the same direction. Not holding hands.

'I don't really *do* breakfast, Mark,' I heard Jo saying impatiently. 'I'm never hungry till later on in the day.'

'But now, you really should be trying ...'

'Please, Mark – I'm sorry, but you're giving me a headache. I'm perfectly fine. Let's talk about something else.'

I sighed to myself sadly as I watched them disappear out of sight down the coast path, and I'm still thinking about them now, on and off, while I'm sitting here with Harold in silence, reading my book. I wonder what's wrong between them: something obviously is. Maybe just the girl's pregnancy, making her feel snappy and moody. She probably hasn't really come to terms yet with being a mum at such a young age. I remember that feeling only too well. But these things happen in life, don't they? They happen, and you just have to get on with them.

'I'm going for a walk,' I tell Harold, standing up

suddenly, letting my book drop off my lap with a smack on the tiled floor. I feel inexplicably restless, fed up with sitting still, fed up with being patient and understanding and gentle. 'Want to come?'

He looks up, surprised by my tone.

'No. I'm OK, Rube. It's nice sitting here . . .'

Suit yourself, I almost say. But, of course, I don't – and I wouldn't, ever. I love him, I'll support him, and wait for him, as I've waited for him all my life. But it's my life, too, and my holiday. My *honeymoon*. I need more than a seat in the sun.

I meet them as I'm walking into town. All four of them, coming back from the bus station, chatting together like old friends. It makes me smile, but at the same time it gives me a pang in my heart, as sharp as indigestion.

'Hello, Ruby,' says Andy, the friendly, freckly one with the sandy hair. 'How are you doing? Where's Harold?'

'Oh, he's back at the hotel, enjoying his book.'

'We're just going to get an ice cream,' he says. 'Want to join us?'

He gestures to the little café next to the marina, where the others are already exclaiming over the colours and flavours of ice creams on the menu.

'Hey, look at this!' calls Gemma. 'Swinging sofas!'

She jumps on to one and starts to swing it, giggling and patting the seat next to her for Jo to join her.

'Careful,' Mark warns her predictably, but Jo ignores him and throws herself on to the seat next to Gemma, joining in with the laughter. It's nice to see her looking a bit more cheerful. Gemma's probably good for her – she seems a straightforward, no-nonsense sort of girl.

'Come on, Ruby,' says Andy insistently, taking my arm and leading me like a bride to the other end of the swinging seat, holding it still for me while I sit myself down. 'There! Now, what ice cream would you like?'

This sure as hell makes a change from sitting on the sun terrace, I think to myself as I swing gently back and forth, listening to the two girls chattering, and savouring my mint choc sundae. Then I instantly feel guilty for even thinking this, sit up straight and look at my watch, wondering how long I've been gone.

'It's only half-past four,' says Gemma, noticing. 'We got the bus back from Lumbarda a bit earlier than we'd planned. It was too windy on the beach, but we had a nice lunch there.'

'And now we're filling up with dessert!' puts in Jo, happily digging her spoon into an ice cream that looks impossibly pink with sprinkles of candied fruit.

I glance at Mark and see him smile with satisfaction. He must be relieved that she's eating, whether it's healthy food or not. To be honest, I'm relieved too, and I hardly even know her. After seeing Jeannie literally fade away, I get twitchy at the thought of anyone not eating.

'Was the bus trip fun?' I ask them all, between mouthfuls.

'Yeah – it didn't take long. But the bus was packed with local people – they come into town for their shopping, of course, from all the villages,' says Gemma. 'Quite an experience. No nice polite English queuing to get on the bus. You have to join the throng and shove, or you don't get on!'

'You and Harold would enjoy it,' says Mark. 'But take an early bus, before it gets too busy.'

'Maybe,' I say, doubtfully, thinking again of the ridiculous notion I had, before we came away, of hiring a car. Harold's just not showing any interest in that. Any interest in anything, really. 'We'll see.'

There's an awkward silence. They all probably wonder what the hell I'm doing, wandering about on my own on my honeymoon. Probably think Harold and I have fallen out.

'Tell me about your weddings,' I say brightly to the girls, to change the subject. 'Did you both have church weddings? What were your dresses like?'

It's cosy, sitting alongside Gemma and Jo, swinging slowly in the sunshine while the two boys, sitting on another sofa opposite us, are talking about football and cars, the way young men do. I listen as Gemma describes the church, the flowers, her sister and her best friend dressed in pale green, her mother in her green and cream dress and big hat, taking charge of everything and making Gemma wonder whose wedding it really was.

'But it was lovely,' she adds quickly. 'We *are* grateful to Mum. It was a really special day. We'll remember it all our lives.'

'Of course you will. Your wedding day is always special,' I agree, smiling at her as she strokes the brand new ring on her finger. 'Your ring's beautiful.'

'I'd have loved a white-gold ring like that,' says Jo, sounding wistful as she admires it. She drops her voice. 'Mark wanted me to wear his grandmother's ring. It's a family heirloom, and I suppose it was kind of expected.'

She holds up her hand for Gemma and me to inspect it.

'But it's gorgeous!' exclaims Gemma. 'So unusual. That's *so* romantic, Jo – having a family heirloom. I'd have loved something like that, but our families aren't really into heirlooms and stuff.'

'It *is* gorgeous,' I agree. 'Very special.'

'I suppose.' Jo shrugs and checks that Mark's not listening. 'Wouldn't have been my choice, though. To be honest, I think it's a bit ugly.'

I nearly ask her why she didn't tell Mark it wasn't to her taste, but I bite my tongue. It might be a sore point.

'I think it's lovely, dear,' I insist. 'What was your wedding dress like?'

She describes the simple cream dress as if it was nothing more special than an outfit from Marks & Spencer – not that there's anything wrong with that if money's tight, of course.

'I didn't have any bridesmaids. We planned the wedding fairly quickly, you know – because of the baby. We had a quiet ceremony in the church near my parents' home and the reception in a marquee in their garden. It was good.' She nods curtly as if this is the best she can say about it. 'All went well.'

I think back to our own wedding on Saturday. Four days ago – is that all? The memories already seem to be fading. That's the trouble with getting older; even the important things, things you think you're never, ever going to forget, become wispy, cloudy, like out-of-focus photographs, in no time at all. I can picture Harold, though – standing at the front of the room, turning round to smile at me as I walked in with my son Richard. No father to give me away this time. No mother to cry in the front row. Too late for them both to see me finally marrying the right man – they're both gone now. Gone believing Harold would be married to their darling Jeannie till the end. Thank God they never had to know how awful that end would be.

*

'Where have you been?' asks Harold when we get back to the hotel. He's still sitting in the same position on the sun terrace. The only time he's moved all day was to go inside with me for some lunch. 'I thought you were only going for a walk ...'

'I was. But I met up with those two young couples, and they persuaded me to stop and have an ice cream with them. It was lovely – the café had those big swinging sofas outside. We sat and chatted, watched the boats in the marina. You'd have loved it. I'll take you there tomorrow.'

'Perhaps.' He sighs. 'I'll see how I feel.'

I sit down next to him and take hold of his hand. 'How *do* you feel, Harold? Tell me. We're not even talking about it and it's not right. We can't carry on like this, pretending nothing's wrong.'

'You know what's wrong,' he says, looking down at his feet with a pained expression. 'You *know* how I feel, Rube.'

'Yes. Of course I do. But we talked this all through, didn't we, when we agreed to get married? We both agreed she would want us to be happy! You were happy on Saturday, weren't you, when you married me?'

'Of course I was happy. It was what I'd dreamed of for so long, Ruby! But I can't feel happy about us being together, without feeling this pain – this terrible pain inside! It's like I'm betraying her every time I smile at you. Every time I kiss you. Every time I hold you ... in bed. Betraying her again.'

'But we never did, Harold. We never did betray Jeannie. And we're not betraying her now. You *know* that.'

'Knowing it is one thing, Ruby. Stopping the

83

feeling is something else. I can't just turn it off. I can't stop feeling that this, you and me together – being happy together – isn't right. It's still not right.'

'You *will* stop feeling like it. You have to make an effort, though, darling. *Try* to believe me. *Try* to be happy, and you will!'

'I thought so too. I thought I would otherwise I'd never have married you, Ruby. Now ... I don't know.' He rubs his fingers across his forehead as if he's soothing a violent headache. 'I don't know whether I should have married you at all. I can't be a good husband to you.'

'Of *course* you can! You will! You *are*!'

'No! I'm not. We both know it. I can't even make love to you – what sort of husband does that make me?'

'It doesn't matter! For God's sake, Harold. Sex isn't the only thing – it's not important. I don't care about that.'

'But *I* care. I care that I want to, but I can't. I can't because of Jeannie. It's *never* going to be right, Rube. I love you; I've always loved you. But I shouldn't have married you. It isn't fair. I'm not going to make you happy.'

'That's a *stupid* way to talk, Harold Dimmock!' I retort crossly. Crossly, to hide the shaking of my voice, the quaking of my heart. 'Four days after our wedding, and you're talking like this! Come on, stop sitting around out here on your own being morbid and miserable. Take me out to dinner. Drink some wine and have some fun! It's our *honeymoon*, Harold. We're *through* with guilt and sadness. We've had enough of them!'

'I know.' He gets to his feet, slowly, heavily, like an old man, leaning on his chair. 'But I think the guilt and sadness have got so deep into my bones now, Ruby, that I can't let go of them.'

No such thing as can't, I think to myself, as I follow him back up to our room. It's what I tell my pupils when they say they can't do something. Can't conjugate the verb *avoir*. Can't translate a page of their set book. Can't write an essay in French about their holidays. No such thing as can't. Just start doing it, and you'll see that you can. Maybe if Harold just starts being happy he'll see that he can be. I just need to persuade him to *try*.

Unfortunately, my powers of persuasion aren't enough to make him take me into town for dinner. We eat in the hotel restaurant again. Don't get me wrong, it's nice enough: three choices of main course after the ubiquitous cold fruit soup – which is actually a lot better than it sounds – as well as a good selection at the salad bar, which you can have for an alternative main course or a starter. The desserts are a bit unimaginative, though. Every night so far it's been the same choice, delivered in a monotone by our sturdy, grim-faced waitress: apple, pear, ice cream, cake. The cake is a sponge, sometimes iced, sometimes with a kind of jam, not something I wanted to try again having experienced it once. We normally opt for the ice cream, which is a different flavour every night. Harold might be feeling sad inside but at least he's making an effort for other people, and he's trying to make the waitress smile.

'What's for dessert tonight, love?'
'Apple, pear, ice cream, cake.'
'I'll have the treacle pudding then, please.'
She looks at him in bewilderment.

'We have apple, pear, ice cream, cake,' she repeats slowly.

'Oh. I'll have a banana, then.'

'No bananas. Only apple, pear ...'

'Take no notice of him,' I tell her, laughing. 'He's being funny.'

'Funny?' She frowns, considering this. Maybe not a word she learnt at school. Or not a concept she's used to.

'Don't worry. We'll both have ice cream,' I tell her gently. 'Don't tease her, Harold,' I say as she walks away. 'I don't think she's got a sense of humour.'

The ice cream tonight is vanilla. It doesn't quite compare to the mint-choc sundae I had earlier, but it's OK. At this rate, I'll put on another stone by the time we go home.

We go out on to the terrace to have coffee, and before too long we're joined by Jo and Mark.

'Did you eat here tonight too?' I wonder.

'No. We went to the little Italian place next-door. We had a table overlooking the sea. The food was very good.'

'That sounds lovely,' I say, wistfully.

'Mark thinks the food here is a bit unimaginative,' says Jo with a shrug.

'That's quite true. Especially the desserts,' I add, nudging Harold, who smiles and repeats in our waitress's stony voice: 'Apple, pear, ice cream, cake!'

'You should try the place next-door tomorrow night,' suggests Mark. 'I'd definitely recommend it.'

'Thanks.' I nudge Harold again. 'That'd be nice. Perhaps we will.'

I mean to say, what difference does it make? Why is it OK to eat in the hotel restaurant, but too much effort to walk to the little restaurant next-door where the food is so much better? Or maybe that's the problem: it's not just too much effort; more like too much *enjoyment*.

'We'll see,' says Harold, giving me a wary smile.

'Well,' I say, cheerfully, 'to be quite honest I'm actually thoroughly pissed off with eating breakfast, lunch and dinner here in the hotel every day. So tomorrow, Harold, *I'm* choosing where we go. We'll have lunch down by the harbour, and dinner at this place next-door. OK?'

There's a momentary silence, a raising of eyebrows between Mark and Jo, a look of pain in Harold's eyes, and I know I've probably gone too far. I should have waited till we were on our own to throw down this particular gauntlet. I've embarrassed him in public. I shouldn't have done that.

'Absolutely,' he says, without meeting my eyes. 'Good idea.'

'Does he always agree with everything you say, Ruby?' asks Jo with a little giggle. 'You'll have to tell me your secret!'

'Oh, I just nag him into submission,' I tell her with a grin. 'Don't I, darling?'

'She does,' he agrees. 'I wanted to wear my old green cords and brown shoes for the wedding, but she just wasn't having it! Made me buy a new suit – can you believe that?'

The other two are laughing now. It's OK. The awkward moment has passed. We chat comfortably for a while about weddings, clothes, and families. Jo seems to have come out of her shell a bit. She's a nice enough girl. She'll probably be fine once the baby's born and she settles down again, gets used to the new life she's going to have.

'I expect you're both getting really excited about

the baby now,' I say, smiling at them encouragingly.

'Yes.' Mark's nodding enthusiastically. 'Now that Jo's beginning to feel better. I've been too worried about her, up till now, to get excited.'

'Understandable.' I smile.

'He fusses too much.' Jo shakes her head. '"Eat this, Jo; eat that, Jo." Always nagging me about eating.'

'You have to *eat*, Jo,' says Mark, looking to me for support.

I feel my smile slipping slightly. 'Well, it is important . . .' I glance at Harold. He's looking down at the floor. Not smiling at all. 'Important to eat properly when you're pregnant,' I finish quickly.

'You see?' Mark looks at Jo triumphantly. 'That's what I keep telling you . . .'

'Christ!' she exclaims. 'Not again! Will you ever let up about the whole *eating* thing, Mark? For God's sake!' She laughs. 'Anyone would think I was *fucking anorexic*!'

'Don't say that,' says Harold. He gets to his feet, almost knocking over his chair. 'Don't ever say that! It's not funny. Don't joke about it.'

Jo stares at him in surprise.

'I only meant . . .'

'I know what you meant,' I tell her quietly. 'It's OK. It's just . . . a sensitive subject.'

'God! Sorry.'

She looks at Mark, who shakes his head and adds: 'We didn't know, mate . . .'

'Of course you didn't, love. It's all right, forget it. Come on, Harold, I think it's probably time we were going.'

He sighs, closes his eyes, takes a deep breath and nods.

'Yes. OK. Sorry I sounded off like that. It's just . . .

not something to be flippant about. Believe me.'

I look back at them as we go inside and head for the stairs. They're sitting in silence, looking at each other, eyes still wide with shock. Well, if nothing else, perhaps that'll stop them arguing.

I take Harold's arm and give it a squeeze to show I understand. But, sadly, the light-hearted atmosphere of earlier has gone – and I don't think it's going to be easy to recapture it.

	S	M	T	W	**T**	F	S
June					1	2	3
	4	5	6	7	8	9	10
	11	12	13	14	15	16	17
	18	19	20	21	22	23	24
	25	26	27	28	29	30	

Gemma

Well, this time, there's no getting away from it.

We saw her again last night – the blonde girl with the face of an angel and legs the length of Southend Pier. We were having the romantic dinner Andy had promised me, just the two of us, under the stars, at a restaurant on the edge of the sea. It was wonderful – the scent of the pines, the warm night air, the wine, the music. Everything I'd dreamed of. At last, I was thinking, this is just how I imagined a honeymoon should be. And then I looked up, and there she was. Standing there, beside our table, in her shimmery strapless mini-dress, her skin glowing, her perfectly made-up face beaming.

'Andrew,' she said – and it was a purr of a greeting, a caress of a greeting. 'It *is* you, isn't it? I *thought* I saw you the other day, but you didn't recognise me. How *are* you?'

I stared at her, feeling coldness and fear wash over me, making me shiver.

'Aren't you going to introduce us?' I heard myself say, as if from a distance, '*Andrew*?'

He didn't answer, and when I looked at him, he'd dropped his eyes and was playing with his fork. I waited. The girl glanced from one of us to the other, frowning slightly. Or was it a sneer?

'This is Caroline, Gem,' Andy said at length, finally looking up. His eyes were beseeching me. 'I worked with her once, on a photo shoot for *Elle*. Caroline – this is Gemma. My wife.'

'Well, hello, Gemma,' Caroline said brightly, without missing a beat. I didn't respond. I couldn't. I looked from her, grinning happily as if she'd just bumped into a film star at the very least, to Andy, looking wretched and awkward, scratching his head and shifting uncomfortably in his chair, and I said, frostily, to my wine glass: 'We were just leaving, actually.' We weren't. We hadn't even finished, but Andy wasn't arguing. 'I'll get the bill.'

I called the waiter and paid the bill, left a tip and got to my feet. All the while Caroline continued to smile at Andy, and to prattle on about how wonderful Korčula was, and how wonderful the scenery was, and how wonderful the food in this restaurant was, until she finally cottoned on that Andy was still staring at the table and fiddling with his fork – and then she looked at me with some sort of gleam in her eyes, and said, well, she'd better be going, but it was *wonderful* to catch up with him once more, and *wonderful* to meet me, too, and perhaps we'd bump into each other again while we were over here.

'Wonderful,' I muttered to myself as I stood up to

leave, scraping my chair loudly on the concrete. 'Fucking wonderful.'

'Gemma,' Andy tried as I walked off. 'Gem – wait. I'll explain. Let me explain!'

'I *asked* you to explain the other day!' I threw back at him, loudly, making people stop and stare at us. 'But you wouldn't. You said you didn't know her. You'd never met her. You *lied* to me, Andy! You *lied*!'

It's the worst thing, the very worst thing. The thing we promised we'd never do, no matter what. Nothing could be so bad, we said, when we first became an item – recognised our love for each other, formalised it with the engagement ring I've been wearing for so long – nothing could ever be so bad that we couldn't confide in each other. It's what I've always believed in: our honesty, our lack of deception, our refusal to have secrets that hurt each other. It's what defines us, what sets us apart from people who cheat and mess around, wrecking relationships, wrecking lives. People like my dad.

'It was just . . . easier,' said Andy, trying to take hold of my arm. 'Listen! I just thought it would be easier than trying to explain. I didn't think I'd see her again.'

'Oh, I see.' The ground felt like it was rocking beneath my feet. My voice dropped from a shout to a moan, from a moan to a whimper. 'So that makes it all right, does it? All right to lie to me and cheat on me, as long as I'm not going to find out?'

'Did I say I'd cheated on you, Gemma?' he retorted loudly. How dared he raise his voice at me? How dared he expect me to believe a word he said?

'Then why did you need to lie?' I asked flatly, walking on again.

'I don't know. It was stupid. I should have just told you,

I know I should — but I was frightened you wouldn't believe me.'

'Well, you're right. I don't.'

'I haven't even *told* you yet . . .'

'You don't need to. Don't forget, Andy, I'm the fucking *expert* in cheating and lies. I grew up with them going on all around me.'

'I know! I *know* that, Gem, and that's why I was worried about telling you . . .' He was standing still in the middle of the path, calling after me, pleading with me. For a moment, I wanted nothing more than to run back and wrap myself in his arms. To say it didn't matter, wasn't important, nothing mattered so long as he never left me.

But I couldn't do that. That's what my mum kept doing.

I ran ahead of him back to the hotel, let myself into our room and was in bed before he even came in. I turned my back and pushed away the arm he tried to put across my waist when he lay down beside me.

'I'm sorry I lied, Gemma,' he whispered in the darkness. 'I know you're angry with me. We'll talk all this over in the morning. OK?'

I closed my eyes and let the tears scald my eyelids.

'She's a model,' he says now, sitting on the bed, watching me brush my hair in the mirror. Angry, despairing strokes of the brush that hurt my scalp but make me feel like I'm in control. 'Her name's Caroline Starr. I worked with her about six years ago when I was doing the shoot for *Elle*. You remember? It was a great contract — the first one I'd got with one of the big magazines, just after I lost the work on the travel brochures.'

I don't reply. Of course I remember the job with *Elle*.

Of course I remember the desperate worry of him losing the contract with the travel company. To reply would be as fatuous as it was for him to ask me that.

'She was modelling underwear,' he says on a long sigh. He stops, looks at me warily. 'I have to photograph girls modelling underwear, Gemma. There's nothing sleazy or sinister about it . . .'

'Of course you do!' I snap, throwing down my brush. 'Don't talk to me as if I'm stupid! Of *course* you have to take those photos – it's never worried me in the least! Did you ever worry, when I worked on the adult wards, about me giving male patients bed baths? Dressing them or helping them in the toilet? For God's sake – are we *children* now?'

'No. I'm sorry. I'm just trying to explain. She modelled underwear, and she was good at her job. Not stroppy and awkward and demanding like a lot of them are. We got along well. That's all. We just got along well.'

There's a silence. I stare back at him in the mirror.

'And that's *it*? You lie to me, tell me you don't know her, because you just *got along well* with her?'

'No.' He looks uncomfortable. 'As far as *I* was concerned we just got along well.'

'I see. And?'

'You know me, Gemma. I don't do subtlety, or hints, or reading-between-the-lines. I'd never been *flirted with* before, not so far as I know anyway. I never expected it. Didn't recognise it. I just thought she was nice. Fun. It was great working with someone I could chat to, have a laugh with, feel comfortable with . . .'

'And?'

'Don't keep saying "And" like that! That was all there was to it, from my point of view. We had lunches together, she introduced me to other people – I

94

thought that was great, too. More contacts. More work. That was all I was thinking about.'

Listening to this, I can almost believe it. I do know Andy. I do know how unlikely he would find it that any girl, never mind one as beautiful as Caroline, would fancy him. After all those years of cruel taunts and teasing at school, he was left with no confidence at all in his power to attract the opposite sex, and it just wouldn't have occurred to him that he was encouraging this girl's attentions by going out to lunch with her, indulging in friendly banter and getting to know her friends. I could almost believe it, sure – except that he'd kept it from me.

'If that was all there was to it, you'd have told me. We *always* told each other stuff like this. I told you about that Egyptian doctor who came on to me in the sluice room, and the patient who said he wanted to marry me . . .and that time one of the consultants got drunk and tried to kiss me at the hospital party . . .'

'Yes! Yes, *exactly*, Gem – you told me about all those things because there was something to tell! Something you wouldn't have wanted me to hear from anyone else, in case I got the wrong impression. Something innocent but open to misinterpretation. Yes? But with Caroline it was just – a friendly working thing. Or so I thought.'

'So why the big deal now? Why the pretence yesterday, the lies, the big stupid secret?'

'Because of the way it ended. I never told you about her because we stopped being friendly the day she asked me to sleep with her.'

'And you refused?' I study him suspiciously.

'What do you think? I was just totally gob-smacked. I hadn't seen it coming at all, or I wouldn't have been encouraging it.'

'So that was all right, then. You refused, she presumably felt rejected, you weren't friends any more. Still no reason to lie, was there?'

He looks down at the floor. 'It wasn't quite as straightforward as that, unfortunately. I don't think Caroline was used to rejection. She wasn't just upset – she was livid. She didn't just stop being friendly, she turned downright nasty.'

'Oh, look, I don't think I want to hear any more,' I say. 'This is crap, Andy. I don't care how nasty she was, how livid she was – you could have told me about it. If you didn't have a guilty conscience, for whatever reason, you'd have told me.'

I grab my bag and start to head for the door. I don't know where I'm going or what I'm going to do. I can't even think straight. I just know I need to get away from him.

'Don't go!' he calls after me. 'Gemma, don't just walk out. We have to talk about this. You're right – I did have a guilty conscience.'

I stop, my hand on the door handle. I feel like sinking to the floor.

'Go on,' I tell him, dully.

'Because I was such an idiot. Because of what she *said*, and because I was stupid enough to let her get away with it.'

'I don't understand. Get away with what?'

'She told people – people in the business, people who mattered, people who might have given me work – that we'd had a fling, and she'd dumped me. And that after it was over I'd kept on pestering her for sex. I was bloody annoyed when I found out these rumours were going around, but I reckoned it was her way of saving face – and that having it out with her would probably just make things worse. You *know* what I'm like, Gem, I hate

96

confrontation. I didn't have any more work to do with her so I just stayed away from her, ignored all the whispers and waited for it to die down and be forgotten. I couldn't tell you then. I just knew how it would sound. No smoke without fire – all that crap.' He looks at me miserably. 'You don't trust me any more now, do you?'

'If you'd told me all this at the time, it would have been different,' I say stonily. 'But now, Andy – now I just don't know what to think, to be honest.'

'I wish I could change things, go back and deal with it differently, but I can't. What can I do?'

'You could have confronted her when you saw her last night. Asked her why she'd been such a mega bitch. If it was true.'

'It's in the past, Gemma,' he says, wearily. 'Not the sort of stuff you want to rake over six years later. She's probably completely forgotten.'

'Oh, right! She tells all these vicious lies about you and then *forgets*? I don't think so!'

He sighs. 'This is getting us nowhere. Look, I know you're angry, and suspicious, and I deserve it. I'm so, so sorry, but – she's just a bitch who caused me a lot of trouble.'

I think I believe him, actually. I *want* to believe him. This is Andy – my good, decent, caring Andy. Surely he's not even capable of doing anything to hurt me? He must be telling the truth.

There's just a tiny, insistent whisper in the back of my mind about the possibility of someone's head being turned. Someone who's never been the focus of female attention – who's been with the same girlfriend since puberty. Who has no idea what it'd be like to have a quick shag with someone else – and who's being offered it on a plate. Who might, just might, think, Why not? She'll never know.

It takes me all of two minutes to decide that I'm going to ignore the whisper in my mind and tell Andy I believe him. But I've got a horrible feeling it's going to take me a lot longer than that to be sure I really mean it.

'Once you lose your trust in someone,' my mum told me years ago, back when I was about thirteen or fourteen and she used to talk to me about my dad's affairs, 'you never get it back. It can't be rebuilt. That's it – gone.'

It was different for Mum, of course. Dad hadn't tried to deny anything when he was caught out the first time. There wasn't any point. My uncle – Mum's elder brother – had seen him out in public with this woman, kissing her in a way that had nothing to do with polite friendship. Of course, Dad promised it was a one-off, that it'd never happen again – but two weeks later my uncle saw them again. From then on, the promises became a farce. He didn't believe them himself, even while he was making them. 'You should have left him the first time,' I told Mum several times over the years, with the harsh intransigence of youth. But, of course, I don't really believe she actually wanted to leave him. Not then, and not later, despite all the talk about the village in Devon. It was just a pretence – a game she played in her own mind to stop herself from feeling powerless. The truth was, I reckon she'd made a conscious decision to tolerate his unfaithfulness from the very beginning. That was what I couldn't understand as a teenager. And I'm still not sure I can.

I think about it while we're breakfasting, in semi-silent politeness like mere acquaintances, passing knives and cups, nods and single words between us.

Could I tolerate it if I found out Andy was lying about this? If I found out *now*, on our honeymoon? If I had to go home to friends and family welcoming us back from the most romantic two weeks of our lives, knowing that our marriage had begun with the cancer of deceit already gnawing at its guts?

'I'm going to have to trust you, Andy,' I tell him now, quietly, reaching for his hand across the table. He grabs it gratefully, like a drowning man holding on for his life. 'If I don't, then everything's pointless, isn't it? The wedding vows . . . our whole lives, really.'

'I wish I hadn't lied to you. I just didn't know how else to handle it.'

'I can understand that,' I say with a sigh. 'But, equally, I wouldn't know how to handle it if you cheated on me. I'm not my mum.'

'I know. And the point is, Gem – I'm not your dad either.'

Jo

When I woke up this morning I couldn't remember where I was. I'd been dreaming I was back at my student house, in my hard little narrow bed under the eaves in the back bedroom, where the paper was peeling off the walls and the thin blue carpet had unrecognisable stains distorting its ugly floral design. In my dream, my housemates Sara and Colleen were trying to wake me: shaking me and calling me, laughing because I wanted to stay asleep. 'But your baby's crying,' they were shrieking. 'We're not going to feed him for you. He's your baby – you've got to do it.'

'Jo!' Mark's voice intruded into the babble of

their laughter. 'Jo, are you all right? You're dreaming!'

'Ben!' I said. Thank God. It was just a dream. There was no baby. Just Ben, here with me, holding me in his arms, waking me gently from this nightmare about babies and feeding ... And then I opened my eyes, just in time to see Mark closing his, in pain.

'I'm sorry!' I blurted, wide awake now, sitting up and taking hold of his arm. 'Mark, I'm sorry – I was dreaming. I didn't know where I was.'

'You remember now?' he asked, quietly, looking at me with an attempt at a smile.

'Of course. We're on our honeymoon. How could I forget!'

'Would you prefer to go back to sleep?'

'No. No – look at the time! I'll get up now, and have a shower, and ...'

'I meant, Jo, would you prefer to go back ... to your dream? Instead of the reality.'

'Mark, it was only a dream,' I said, rattled. 'I can't help what I dream. I don't have any control over it.'

'No, I realise that. We all have dreams.'

'Yes.' I looked at him carefully. 'What do you dream about?'

'Oh, just silly things,' he said dismissively, turning away. 'About us staying together, being happy. All that.'

'That's not silly,' I told him gently. 'It's what I'd like, too.'

This is the problem, you see, with someone loving you too much. It makes you feel ungrateful, even though you didn't ask for it. My parents gave me my own TV one year for my birthday. It might

100

have been my fifteenth. I'd asked for something else – I can't even remember what, now. Probably some sportswear or something for my bike. I can still remember the tight feeling of the smile I fixed on my face all day, pretending to be thrilled because I couldn't rebuff their generosity, and the disgust I felt with myself for *not* being thrilled. I told one of my brothers, years later.

'That's the price we pay for growing up,' he said philosophically. 'As a child, you could've been forgiven for being straight and saying you didn't even want it. As an adult, you have to pretend.'

I'm not exactly pretending with Mark. I promised to love him and I will. I do, in a way. I love him for loving me, for rescuing me, for *not* being someone who only wants me in a limited way, as a sideline to his life, an optional extra. But it's hard being adored. It's a lot to live up to, being someone's dream. Especially when your own dreams are still about someone else entirely.

I've done a lot of swimming today. I'm beginning to feel better: I'm eating a bit more, even if it's not as regularly or as ravenously as Mark might like, and I'm feeling stronger. I can feel the fresh air and exercise, the sunshine and the relaxation, working on me, helping to heal the damage caused by all the stress of the last few months. Studying for my final exams and finishing my course work would have been stressful enough, without everything else. But, of course, it's the *everything else* that's ground my system into meltdown. Am I ever going to recover? If I stayed out here in Croatia for ever, resting in the sun, swimming in the calm, warm sea, concentrating on my health and looking after my baby, would I discover one day that I wasn't even suffering any more?

I turn over to float on my back, staring up at the perfect blue sky and remembering what someone once told me about love being an illness. It strikes you down unexpectedly, makes you feel delirious for a while and ghastly afterwards, there's no medicine, no antidote, but you *do* recover. Eventually. Everybody does. Apparently.

'Are you getting tired?' Mark calls, swimming up alongside me. 'Don't overdo it.'

'No, I won't, don't worry.' I close my eyes and take deep, healing breaths of the tangy warm air.

'And don't get chilled – you ought to get out now if you've finished swimming – dry yourself off and . . .'

'I haven't! I *haven't* finished swimming!' For God's sake. Give me a break! I flip over and dive beneath the surface, kicking smoothly away and surfacing in a strong crawl, powering out to sea, away from the warm shallows, away from the people milling around the edges with snorkels, with children, with ball games and Frisbees. Away from Mark and his constant worrying and nagging and caring. Away, in my head, from my exhausting memories and regrets. After a few minutes I slow down into a steady easy rhythm. Stroke, stroke, breath. Stroke, stroke, breath. It's as natural to me as walking. Out here, with the murky unknown depths beneath me and the open sky above, I feel free. I've escaped from it all, left it behind. Maybe I'll just keep on swimming, all the way across the channel to Orebić, carry on down the coast to Dubrovnik, or maybe pop across to Italy. Just keep on swimming like this for ever.

When I do stop and turn, treading water, to look back at the coastline behind me, our hotel looks like a miniature house perched on the rocks. People are unrecognisable moving specks. They all look the same from this distance, which for some reason I find oddly comforting. I smile to myself, catch myself doing it, and think: That's a start. Then I realise how far I've swum, and acknowledge that maybe Italy would be just a tad ambitious. Maybe next time!

I swim back at a steady pace and am still smiling when I climb out on to the jetty, happy to feel the heat in my muscles and the tingling of my skin.

'What the *hell* were you doing?' says Mark, appearing suddenly at my elbow with a towel, which he tucks round my shoulders as if I was a geriatric patient in need of a blanket. 'I've been worried *sick*. I lost sight of you *ages* ago! I tried to come after you but I couldn't even *see* you. I was on the point of finding a life guard ...'

'Mark.' I feel the smile dropping from my face. 'I *am* a life guard.'

'For all I know, you could have got cramp, got into trouble and drowned!'

'I've got a gold medal for survival. Jesus! I was swimming in a calm, warm bloody bay, not shark-infested storm waters!'

'You've been ill, Jo, and you're pregnant. Your fitness is *not* what it was. You need to understand ...'

'No!' I've had enough. 'No – listen! *You* need to understand. Getting pregnant didn't rob me of the ability to think for myself. Nor did getting married to you!' I pause, stare at him for a moment and nearly don't go on. But I do. 'I didn't expect all this stuff when I agreed to marry you.'

'What's that supposed to mean?' he asks very quietly. 'You're having regrets, I suppose. You think it was a bad idea.'

'I didn't say that.'

'But you do, don't you? You'd still have preferred Ben, I suppose – despite everything! You still hanker after him, still dream about him. What am I supposed to do? How am I supposed to compete? If *I* treated you like shit, dumped you and the baby and ran away so fast I left scorchmarks, maybe you'd want *me*?'

'Don't be *stupid*. I can't be doing with all this, Mark. I married you – what more do you want?'

'Something you don't seem to be able to give me,' he says quietly.

'Then I'm sorry!' I get to my feet, slipping slightly on the wet wood, and shake off his hand crossly when he tries automatically to steady me. 'You knew the score. I'm trying. That's all I can do. Don't *hassle* me! Oh!' I've slipped again, almost overbalancing. This time, I don't shake him off when he reaches out a hand to save me. We stand for a moment, holding on to each other, not meeting each other's eyes.

'I'm sorry too,' he says. 'I shouldn't have said all that. It's just . . . I was worried about you. I can't help it.'

I'm about to answer him, tell him wearily to forget it, let's not argue, let's not make things even harder for both of us than they already are. But I'm looking at my hand, holding on to his arm where he stopped me from falling. There's something wrong. Something missing. For a moment I can't even think what it is.

'Shit,' I say, realisation making me feel sick. 'My ring.'

'What?'

'My wedding ring. Your grandma's ring, Mark. It's gone. I've lost it. Oh, *no*. I'll go back out and find it!' I'm actually trying to wriggle out of his grasp. 'I'll swim out again in the same direction. Check the seabed. Look over the rocks ...'

'Don't be ridiculous.'

'I'll find it, Mark! I promise, I'll find it! Let me go – I'll start looking now. Go and get my snorkel ...'

'There's no point, Jo. You won't find it now. It doesn't matter.'

'It does!' I'm trying not to cry. 'I'll swim underwater till I see it. It'll shine, won't it – in the sun?'

'No. Not if it's out there – in the deep water. In the seaweed, or fallen into a crevice between the rocks. You'd never be able to see it, much less get it out.'

'Yes, I will! I've got to! Come on, Mark – get the snorkels. We can both look. If we look now, before the tide turns, we've got more chance ...'

'*I'll* have a look. In a minute, if it makes you happier. But I *don't* want you going back in the water right now.' He turns to face me, and for a minute I think he's angry with me about the ring. But then I see he's smiling – just a little smile, at the corners of his eyes. 'I don't care if you think I'm nagging, or being an old woman, or if I'm not as much fun as Ben – no, I mean it! You might be a gold medallist, you might be the best swimmer in the whole bloody world, but all I care about is – you're my wife now, and I love you. And you're tired, you're upset, you need a drink and a rest, so unless you want to push me off this bloody jetty, I'm *not* letting you get back in the water!'

I'm almost as shocked by the length and vehemence

105

of this speech as I am by my own reaction, which is to bow my head meekly and murmur, 'OK, then.' The obvious sincerity of what he's just said has hit home, robbing me of all my previous annoyance and making my chest heave and my eyes swim with tears.

He leads me, with the towel still wrapped round me, back to the hotel, where he takes me up to our room, gets me a cup of tea while I shower and dress, and waits until I'm lying, half asleep now, on the bed before picking up his own snorkel and heading for the door.

'Please find it!' I whisper, child-like, as he goes. 'I'm *so* sorry, Mark.'

'You didn't even like that ring,' he says gently, turning back to stroke the hair out of my eyes.

'I did! Of course I . . .'

'Liar,' he says affectionately. 'I know you didn't. I shouldn't have asked you to wear it.'

'But it was your grandma's.'

'She'd have understood. She was a good sport. She'd see the funny side of this. If we don't find it, Jo – or even if we do! – I'll buy you a new one. I should have done that in the first place. It's my own fault.'

'Oh, Mark.' My eyes fill up with tears again. Why am I being so pathetic and over-emotional? 'You shouldn't be so nice to me.'

'Why not?' He laughs. 'It makes me happy.'

But after he's left and I think about this, it doesn't make *me* happy at all. All it does is make me cry even harder.

	S	M	T	W	T	**F**	S
					1	2	3
	4	5	6	7	8	9	10
June	11	12	13	14	15	16	17
	18	19	20	21	22	(23)	24
	25	26	27	28	29	30	

Gemma

I think Andy and I are fine again now. Perhaps, in a way, the whole stupid thing with Caroline has given us both a shake-up: tested us, if you like, and ended up making us even stronger. I'm going to try to stop going over his story in my mind, wondering about it, doubting bits of it. Of course, I really wish he'd been able to confide in me at the time, but, well – it's water under the bridge now, and one day we'll probably laugh about it. I hope we don't bump into her any more, though. I think I'd find it quite difficult not to slap the silly bitch round her silly lipsticked mouth.

We had a good day yesterday: we got the ferry over to the mainland to have a look around Orebić in the daylight. We picked up the boat there on Sunday, of course, when we arrived, but apart from looking at it in the distance across the sea from our balcony, we didn't know anything about it. It turned out to be a nice little resort, with sandy beaches and some really good restaurants along the seafront. We had such a wonderful lunch in one of them, we were still too full up in the evening to eat again and were just sitting outside our favourite little bar near the hotel, having a drink, when Jo and Mark turned up. They were on their way into town to see the Moreška – Korčula's famous sword dance and drama. It's advertised all over the town and described in the guide-books but Andy and I had forgotten that it's only staged on Thursday evenings. So the four of us went together to watch it, and ended up having a great evening – although I'm somewhat surprised at myself. I'd always imagined wanting Andy totally to myself on our honeymoon, but with the couple of minor discrepancies of opinion we've encountered – I prefer not to think of them as arguments – and the underlying tension about bloody bitch Caroline, it's possibly been better to surround ourselves with some new friends for at least part of the time, to lighten the atmosphere and keep us off the scary topics.

The open-air stage where the Moreška takes place is just at the edge of the old town. It was absolutely packed; Andy commented that every tourist in Korčula must have turned out to watch it. I immediately wondered whether Cow-face Caroline was somewhere in the crowd, but I tried not to dwell on it.

Basically, the Moreška originated with the conflict between Moors and Christians, and it's been performed in Korčula for over four hundred years. They have loads of local guys dressed up as the Red Army and the Black Army. They act out the story of the conflict between the two armies, with the Red King's girlfriend being captured by the Black King, who wants to have his wicked way with her but, of course, she refuses because she loves good old Red. The two armies perform this ritual sword dance and obviously, in the end, the Black King gets beaten and it all works out happily ever after. Well, till next Thursday anyway. The performers have to be pretty fit and do loads of practice and apparently it's a real honour for their families if they get picked for one of the leading parts. I was quite taken by all of this. I used to be in the drama group at school, you see, so I can kind of appreciate the work that goes into a performance like this. Having said that, I only ever got picked for parts in The Chorus, apart from this one time when I was Maria, A Cleaning Lady, in a modern version of some pantomime or other. My part was described as: *Enter Maria, angrily, from L., brandishing a broom.* I'd like to say it was an honour for my family, but none of them even bothered to come and watch it.

We walked back to the bar with Jo and Mark afterwards for another drink. She seemed a bit quiet, but it was only when she started rubbing her ring finger and looking at Mark unhappily that I noticed. She'd lost her ring in the sea, apparently. I know she'd told me she didn't like it, but still, it must be terribly upsetting to lose your wedding ring, especially as it was Mark's grandmother's. He was going out of his way to be understanding and nice about it. Apparently he'd been out with his snorkel and searched the area where Jo had been swimming, but hadn't found it. He'd reported it to the hotel reception, though, so you never know: someone might find it and hand it in.

'But I'm going to buy Jo a new ring anyway,' he said, smiling at her. 'I should have done that in the first place.'

'He seems such a nice guy,' I say to Andy this

morning. We're going for a walk today, round the other side of the headland where our hotel's situated and then along the next bay, where we've heard there's a climb to a church on top of a hill. We've eaten so much since we've been here, with not much exercise apart from a bit of swimming, that we both think the climb will do us good. It's easy walking so far, following the road along the coast, and we're chatting about Mark and Jo as we go.

'Maybe a bit too nice for his own good,' says Andy with a shrug.

'How do you mean?'

'I just wonder if he's going to end up getting hurt. If Jo still hankers after this other bloke, and he's the father of the baby . . .'

'But he's married! And he didn't want anything to do with her or the baby.'

'That's what he says now. But what's the betting, after it's born, that he starts demanding his *right* to see the kid?'

'Tough shit!' I say, with feeling. 'If Jo's got any sense, she'll tell him to get stuffed. He wanted her to get rid of it!'

'But whether she likes it or not, if he *does* decide he wants to get involved with the kid, she can't refuse, can she? Bottom line is, it's his child. Not Mark's.'

'I don't think that awful Ben is going to risk his wife finding out about the affair. I can't see him suddenly announcing that he's the father of Jo's baby and demanding to have a say in its life.'

'Can't you?' He frowns. 'If it were me, I'd want to. I'd want a say in its life.'

'What – if you'd had an affair, and it meant I was going to find out?' I retort. 'I don't think so, Andy!'

'That would be my mistake, and I'd have to live with

it. I couldn't go through life, knowing there was a child out there who was a part of *me*, being brought up by some other guy.'

I raise my eyebrows at him. 'So: let me get this right. Say you'd had an affair, and the woman told you she was pregnant, what would you do?'

'No, this is just *theoretical*, Gemma. It's not actually going to happen, is it, so it's easy for me to say . . .'

'But *theoretically*, then. You've had an affair – let's say, with that Caroline person . . .'

He stops dead in his tracks and stares at me. 'Oh, great, Gemma. Thank you *so* much for bringing that up again! You said you believed me . . .'

'I'm just saying . . . *theoretically*, Andy. You've had an affair and she tells you she's pregnant – what do you do?'

We're standing at the side of the road now, both of us, with our hands on our hips, staring at each other. I can't believe I'm being like this. What's wrong with me? Why can't I just let it go?

'I'd have to take responsibility,' he replies, sounding a bit uneasy now. Then he squares his shoulders as if the burden of the mistress carrying their potential love-child is already confronting him. 'It'd be my fault, and my responsibility to sort it out.'

'*Sort it out*?' I repeat sarcastically. 'I'm talking about a baby – not a batch of ruined photographs. Not a prang in the car.'

'I know. But the theory is the same. My mistake . . . my responsibility.'

'Oh, bugger the theory, Andy. What would you actually *do*? Offer to marry her . . . divorce me and marry her?'

'Don't be ridiculous!' he says at once. 'Come on,

Gem, you're being stupid. It's not going to happen, so let's not argue . . .'

'But I want to know. Now that we've started this. I want to know what you'd do, exactly.'

'OK. I'd support her, obviously.'

'Financially?'

'Yes, of course. And I'd want to see the child, too. Regularly. I'd want to play a part in its life . . .'

'And what do you think *I'd* say to that?'

He laughs now. 'Well, as this isn't something we're ever going to have to worry about, I don't think I need to concern myself too much with that!' He tries to take hold of my hand and walk on, but I shake it off. I wish we hadn't started this. But we have, and I can't let it go. I know I should, but I can't. It's annoying me now.

'*If* it happened, Andy. Theoretically. Do you want to know what I'd say, if you came home and told me you'd got some bird pregnant, and not only that, you were going to spend *our* money supporting her kid – when you won't even agree to our having one ourselves?'

'Hang on, hang on!' he says. I know I've gone too far. But I can feel something dangerous just beneath the surface of my mind, bubbling away, beginning to boil over. It's like I'm powerless to stop it. 'What *are* we talking about here? This wasn't about us at all – it was about Mark and Jo. I *haven't* got anyone pregnant.'

'I know. But you're saying that, if you did . . .'

'And I *haven't* refused to have a baby with you! I thought we'd talked about this, the other day? I can't believe you're still sulking about it.'

'*Sulking*? Sulking, Andy? Is that what you call it? Because I'm saying I want a baby?'

'Yes, to be honest, that's what I do call it. It's not

112

about wanting a baby, Gemma – we both want that – it's about wanting *what you want, when you want it*. As usual.'

He turns away, like he's disgusted with me. And I just run. I'm so upset, so angry with him, I'm not even looking where I'm going. Back to the hotel, I suppose. Anywhere, I don't care, as long as it's away from Andy – away from this nasty, mean stranger who's suddenly taken the place of my lovely husband. What's happened to him? How has he gone, in less than a week, from smiling lovingly at me in church as he made his vows, to telling me, so harshly that it takes my breath away, that he'd like it if he was having a baby with some other woman, and that I'm *sulking* about it! I can't believe this. He's never spoken to me like this before. What can have changed him, in such a short time?

Caroline.

That's got to be it. Cow-face Caroline, turning up here, of all places, smiling that flirtatious smile at him, flashing her baby-blue eyes and her perfect figure, reminding him what he missed out on, all those years ago, making him wonder if he did the right thing, turning her down . . .

Always supposing he actually did.

That's the bottom line, isn't it? I've *said* I believe him, agreed to trust him. But do I? Do I really? Have I been fooling myself all this time – trusting him just because I *want* him to be perfect – when in fact there's no earthly reason to believe Andy's any different from all the other bastards out there who lie, and cheat, and break women's hearts. Like that Ben. Like my dad. Have I gone into this marriage, believing it to be different, better than my parents', better than everyone else's – when all the time it's *already showing cracks*? Why else would Andy have changed his mind about wanting to start a family? He's having second thoughts about me. About our marriage. About all of it! He's wishing he was with Caroline.

I've run blindly till I'm so out of breath I have to stop. Looking around me now, I realise I've got no idea where I am. I'm not on the coast road any more. I'm on a main road, with buildings on either side of me, and I don't know which way is the right direction back to the hotel. I'll just keep walking for a while. I'll probably recognise something in a minute. But the buildings gradually give way to woodland on one side and then the other. The road's climbing uphill, and I suspect leading away from civilisation, so I turn and head back the way I came. At least, I *think* this is the way I came. There's a turning on the left which could be the right way ... but after a while I pass a hospital, which I don't remember seeing before. A couple of people are coming out of the door, talking together in rapid Croatian.

'Excuse me,' I interrupt, jogging to catch them up. 'Can you tell me – which is the way back to the Hotel Angelo?'

The two girls look at each other, perplexed, and start to giggle. Probably bloody student nurses.

'No English,' announces one, sounding proud of herself nonetheless.

'No understand,' declares the other, before they both go off, giggling again.

There's no one else around. Where is everybody? Where do all the local people who speak English hide themselves? I suppose they work in the hotels and restaurants along the coast. If only I could *find* the coast. I carry on walking, telling myself there's no need

114

to panic. I'm not lost in a barren desert somewhere, for God's sake – I'm just on the outskirts of a strange town, and as soon as I find the sea, I'll be able to follow the coastline. Sure enough, in a couple more minutes I'm back at the spot where I ran away from Andy. I half expect to find him still there, waiting for me, waiting to apologise. In my mind, I'm rehearsing what I'm going to say. *Being sorry isn't enough this time, Andy.* I need to know he didn't mean it – any of it. I need to know why he said it; whether any of it's true. Otherwise . . .

Otherwise what? I'm too frightened to contemplate this. He's not there, anyway. I suppose he's gone back to the hotel. I start the walk back along the coast on my own, dragging my feet, my heart heavy. I can hardly believe this is happening on our honeymoon.

'Gemma!'

Someone's calling me, the voice breaking into my misery, making me look around in surprise. It's Ruby, sitting on her own on a bench overlooking the sea.

'Are you all right, dear?' she asks as I approach her. I guess I look a bit flustered or something.

'Yeah – I suppose so.'

'On your own?'

'Yes. Just . . . having a walk.'

She gives me a knowing look but doesn't say any more. Instead, she just moves up the bench a bit and pats the seat beside her. I hesitate, then shrug and sit down. Might as well. Nothing to rush back for.

'You're on your own too,' I say, stating the obvious.

'Yes. Harold's . . . still not really feeling up to doing much. I tried so hard yesterday to get him at least to come out for lunch down at the harbour or have dinner in the little restaurant next to the hotel. But it's no use.' She sighs, and then shrugs and laughs ruefully. 'I couldn't sit around any more – my bum was beginning to seize up! So I've come out, determined to walk all the way round the coast to the next bay, but already I've had to sit down again. Not fit, that's my trouble. Need to lose a bit of weight, I suppose, but with so many other miseries in the world, it always seems too much, somehow, to give up the things you enjoy as well. Red wine, chocolate cake, shortbread biscuits . . .' she counts them off on her fingers like a shopping list '. . . mint-choc chip ice cream, apple pie. . .' She glances at me and grins. 'Sticky toffee pudding!'

'You're making me feel hungry,' I tell her, trying to smile back but not quite managing it.

She fishes in her huge pink-striped bag and brings out a packet of biscuits.

'I won't tell the diet police if you don't,' she says, offering them to me. 'I never go out for a walk without sustenance. You don't know when you might get kidnapped by marauding pirates.'

'On land?'

'Don't rule it out. Better safe than sorry,' she says, still grinning as she takes a second biscuit. 'Eat up, girl. You need your strength.'

'Do I? What for?'

'To go back and sort it out. Whatever it is that's gone wrong.' She says this matter-of-factly, without looking at me. 'None of my business, of course,' she adds when I don't answer. 'But whatever it is, don't spoil your honeymoon over it. Wait till you get home, then give him hell.'

Despite myself, this makes me laugh. We sit in companionable silence for a few minutes, demolishing her packet of biscuits between us.

'But what if it's really serious?' I say, eventually, with a sigh. 'What if it's as bad as it could be?'

She looks at me now, a sad smile in her eyes. I suddenly feel a rush of affection for this nice lady who always seems to be ready with a smile and a reassuring chat – even though we hardly even know each other. She looks like someone I could confide in, someone who'd understand without judging.

'If it's that serious,' she says calmly, resting a hand on my arm in a gesture that's oddly comforting, 'then it deserves a lot of serious thought. A lot of serious talking. And I don't think honeymoons are the right time for all that seriousness.'

'I can't bear it, though, Ruby! I can't bear to think of Andy cheating on me! We've always been honest with each other, and now – this girl Caroline turns up, and he's lied to me, and he's changed his mind about having a baby, and he says he'd support her if she had one, and . . .' I stop, embarrassed. 'Sorry. I'm feeling a bit worked up.'

She looks at me carefully, then looks away again and tells me, apparently quite indifferently, as if it's of no relevance at all: 'My second husband was a womaniser – amongst other things. Even worse things. I call him Le Cochon. The Pig.'

No wonder. I hesitate and then admit, 'So was my dad. Still is, probably.'

'You say that as if you're ashamed of it. It's not your fault, dear.'

'I do feel ashamed of it. It coloured my whole childhood. It was shameful. I never told any of my friends, back then.'

'I know. It has that effect, doesn't it – makes the innocent parties feel embarrassed?'

'Yes. But Andy's never been like that.'

'No. He seems a really nice young man,' says Ruby, watching my face.

117

'I know. Everyone loves him. When we were younger he didn't have any friends, really. Sometimes I think he's making up for lost time. But up till now, I *never* thought he'd be interested in another woman.'

'Then I suspect you were right. It sounds like you know him well enough by now. This...business... could be a misunderstanding. Don't you think?'

'Maybe.' I sigh and rub my forehead, trying to collect my thoughts, running the conversation with Andy back over in my mind. Trying to convince myself I imagined half of it.

'Let's walk back to the hotel together, shall we?' suggests Ruby, getting to her feet with obvious effort. 'Let's go and see what those bloody silly men of ours are up to, eh?'

'Is Harold bloody silly, then?' I ask her as we stroll slowly back along the coast.

'Absolutely – aren't they all?' she laughs. She squeezes my arm and gives me a wink. 'They're very delicate creatures really, Gemma. Never forget that. We're much tougher than they are.'

'You think so?'

'Oh, yes.' She nods emphatically. 'We can cope with things, you see. We have to: we're built to withstand childbirth. If we fell apart at the slightest thing, we'd chuck our babies out with the rubbish and never have any more. You can laugh but it's true! Men don't *tell* you when they're going through a crisis. But we sure as hell know about it when they do.'

'You think Andy might be going through some sort of midlife crisis?'

'Oh, take no notice of me. I don't know anything.'

'I think you do, Ruby. I think you're very clever. Very wise.'

118

She laughs out loud at this. 'I wish my daughters could hear you! They think I'm an interfering old bat!'

'But at least you show them you care.'

'Yes. I do that, all right.'

We're approaching the back entrance of the hotel now. We walk through the foyer together and discover Harold, sitting on one of the sofas, checking his watch and looking anxious. His face breaks into a smile of relief when he sees Ruby.

'You see?' she whispers as we part company. 'Delicate creatures. Be gentle with them!'

'Thanks, Ruby. See you later.'

Andy's on our balcony, staring out at the sea. He looks round at me when I let myself into the room, but doesn't say anything.

'Sorry I ran off,' I start. 'But . . .'

He gets up and comes towards me, holding out his arms.

'My fault,' he says at once. 'I didn't mean to say that, Gem, about you sulking.'

'It's not that easy, though, Andy.' I'm not rushing straight into his arms. 'You can't just say you didn't mean it and expect everything to be OK again.'

'I know. I'm sorry. Please don't let's fight any more, Gemma. I don't know what's got into us both.'

'It's Caroline.'

'What?' He stares at me as if I've spoken in Hebrew. 'Caroline? It's nothing whatsoever to do with Caroline! Can't we forget about her? Why are you bringing her up again?'

'I don't want to go into it now, Andy. It's our honey-moon, and I want it to be special. I want us both to put all this out of our minds until we get home. Then we'll have to work it out.'

'Work what out?' He's dropped his arms to his sides now, looking perplexed.

'I think you might be going through some sort of crisis.'

'Crisis?'

'Yes.' I put up my hand to stop his protests. 'I understand. I know you're probably feeling stressed and anxious, and I know you don't want to talk to me about it, and that's why you're behaving strangely . . .'

'Me behaving strangely?'

'So I'm not going to take any notice. I'm just going to pretend everything's fine – OK? We'll have a lovely time here, and when we get home, we'll talk. We'll work things out somehow, Andy. If you need some counselling, or . . . I don't know . . . hypnotherapy . . .'

'What?'

'Or whatever it takes. We'll sort it out, OK?'

'Gemma,' he says faintly, sitting down on the bed and staring at me, 'I haven't got a clue in hell what you're talking about. I think you've had too much sun.'

Ruby

'Where did you go?' asks Harold, looking at me with a slightly hurt expression.

'Only for a little walk, I told you. I met that nice young Gemma along the road. We had a chat and she shared my biscuits.'

'You and your biscuits!' he laughs, hugging me. 'Always got some in your bag, haven't you, Ruby love?'

'I don't like to be without sustenance,' I retort. 'Never know when you might get ambushed by hordes of angry gorillas.'

'And you'd feed them biscuits to keep them quiet?' he teases, and we laugh easily together about my weakness, my sweet tooth. Neither of us mentions it but we both know it's better to have a fondness for biscuits than an inability to eat them. Or to eat anything at all.

'Gemma was telling me that poor Jo lost her wedding ring yesterday,' I tell Harold as we're sitting in our usual spot on the sun terrace later. 'Lost it in the sea. Apparently it was too loose, but she hadn't bothered to get it altered. Now she's upset because it was Mark's grandmother's ring.'

'These things happen,' he says with a philosophical shrug. 'They're not worth losing sleep over, Ruby, are they?'

'No. But we only know that because we've been through things that *are* worth losing sleep over,' I remind him. 'These young people probably haven't. They just think some things that happen are serious because the rest of their lives have been so easy.'

'That's a bit harsh.'

'Not really. Take young Jo. She's miserable and anxious because she's got pregnant before she wanted to ...'

'I think it's more serious than that, Rube. I think she's married Mark on the rebound. It's some other chap's baby.'

'Oh. God, that *is* more serious. I didn't know that.' I look at him suspiciously. How has *he* got hold of the gossip before me?

'Mark told me,' he says, smiling at my expression. 'We were chatting this morning while he was waiting for Jo outside. He seems surprisingly open about it. Poor chap's crazy about the girl, if you ask me – desperately wanted to marry her, couldn't believe his luck that she agreed. Now he's just worried that she'll regret it.'

'Yes, I can imagine. I wonder if that's why she's miserable, then – because of this other man.'

'Oh, it was a friend of Mark's. Sounds like a complete rat. Married man – didn't want to know her when she got pregnant. I doubt very much whether she's still wasting any time thinking about *him*.'

'If you think that, Harold Dimmock, then you know nothing whatsoever about women!'

'I don't, I admit it. They're a complete mystery to me!'

'We're not mysterious, not really. Just that we don't follow logic. Not when it comes to men.'

'You can say that again.' He sighs, smiles, and touches my hand. 'It was totally illogical that you spent half your life waiting for me.'

'No. The illogical part was getting married to those two other wastes of space. What on earth was I thinking of? Young and stupid, eh?'

He laughs. 'Now we're just old and stupid – both of us.'

'But at least we can be old and stupid together, Harold. That's the thing.'

I wasn't just young and stupid when I married Eddie at seventeen – I was little more than a baby, and I was having a baby myself.

I was still at school, of course. I'd never been one of the cleverest girls in my class, but I seemed to have a knack for languages, especially French. My teachers persuaded my parents that I should stay on and do A levels, maybe go to university. It caused arguments at home. Mum and Dad had been expecting me to go out to work as soon as I was sixteen – they needed the money. But Mum saw that I could possibly have a brighter future ahead of me.

'Let her have this opportunity, George,' she told my dad. 'Let her make something of herself.'

In the event, all I made of myself was a complete idiot. I had sex once with Eddie – just the once, out of curiosity – and I got pregnant. It'd been exciting, of course, doing it illicitly on his mum's sofa while she was at work. Unfortunately neither of us had thought any further than the excitement of the moment. I remember thinking that I'd better find out about getting the Pill, for the next time. It wasn't so easy in those days. It might have been the Swinging Sixties but there wasn't a whole lot of swinging going on in my neck of the woods. They were still looking at girls' fingers for wedding rings, or at least engagement rings, in the Family Planning Clinics, before prescribing it.

My French teacher, Mademoiselle Girard, was almost as disappointed in me as my parents were when I told her I was leaving school and getting married.

'You were destined for a degree in languages, Ruby,' she told me severely, 'and a wonderful career.'

She was young herself – a gifted teacher, who'd grown up in France with an English mother, and was completely bilingual. She loved the French language passionately, and brought it alive for us, reading us poetry and novels so that we listened, entranced by the fluidity and romance of the sound of it, and gradually, almost unwittingly, learning to speak it with the same degree of reverence and enjoyment.

'I can't help it. I've got to get married. I'm having

123

a baby,' I said, shrugging, pretending a nonchalance that I'm sure didn't fool anyone, least of all Mademoiselle.

'That's very sad.' She sighed and shook her head. 'But I hope that when you are older, Ruby, you'll have an opportunity to make up for what you're missing now. Meanwhile ... and this is very important, listen to me ...'

I did listen. I had a lot of respect for Mademoiselle, who was only in her mid-twenties and dressed in all the latest fashions.

'... you must not stop reading. No matter what you do, no matter how busy you are, promise me this. You must go to the library every week, and for every English book you read, you read a French book. And read them aloud.'

'Yeah, right!' I said, laughing, imagining the reaction of my future husband if I read out loud from Jean-Paul Satre in bed at night.

'I mean it,' insisted Mademoiselle. 'You will see, Ruby. It's important.'

'OK,' I said, only half seriously.

But I loved reading anyway, and after I'd had the baby, I couldn't make my weekly visit to the library without hearing Mademoiselle Girard's words echoing in my head. I resisted for the first couple of weeks; and then, feeling slightly silly, I made my way to the French literature shelves and borrowed *Bonjour Tristesse* by Françoise Sagan.

And that was it. I was hooked. Reading in two languages became a habit that I still have to this day. I'd read out loud while Eddie was at work and the baby was asleep. By the time Richard was born, I had two babies under a year old, and I was still only eighteen. I used to sit in my cold little kitchen with the nappies soaking in the sink and Trevor yelling his head off on my lap, and wonder what my life would have been like if I'd never gone to Eddie's house that day when his mum was out.

I carried on reading when I moved back home with Mum and while I was supposed to be helping her to run the household. I'd read rather than doing the dusting, or the ironing, and I'd forget to go shopping or cook the tea. Reading took me away from the disappointment of my life and the knowledge that I'd made a terrible, terrible mess of things. But it also meant that by the time my boys were both at school, I knew my French was still good enough. I knew I could go back to college, take my A levels and try for a degree course. Mademoiselle Girard had been right: and her advice had given me the means to change my life. She'd have been proud of me.

There's a barbecue being held tonight, out here on the sun terrace.

'That'll be nice,' I say to Harold. 'It'll make a change from cold fruit soup, and apple, pear, ice cream, cake.'

'Mm. Maybe.'

Oh, silly me. I suppose it'd be too much for him – the crowds of people all wanting to socialise, chat, and drink too much beer. He'd probably get a panic attack and want to scoot off back to our room.

'Don't worry.' I sigh. 'Tell you what, let's get away from it all instead. They won't be serving the normal meals here so it's a perfect opportunity to try out the little restaurant next-door that everyone's raving about. It's an Italian: Mario's.'

We both love Italian food, Harold and I, and these

coastal areas of Croatia have strong cultural links with Italy, which is after all only a short distance across the sea from here, so there's a noticeable Italian influence in the food. I thought this would tempt Harold, if nothing else.

'That sounds nice,' he says, less enthusiastically than I'd hoped.

'So we'll go tonight? Yes?' I persist.

'OK, love. If it makes you happy.'

It will, although that's hardly the point. I'd like to make *him* happy. But I think it's going to take more than a *Tagliatelle Carbonara*.

In the event, of course, it doesn't happen. Harold decides, as I'm getting ready to go out, that he's got an upset stomach and doesn't feel hungry.

I know I should be sympathetic. Correction – I *am* sympathetic. I know the upset stomach is probably – what do they call it? – psychosomatic. He's so churned up inside at the thought of going out and enjoying himself while Jeannie's possibly reproaching him from beyond the grave, it's no wonder his stomach's upset. It's nonsense, for a start, that Jeannie would ever reproach him, or me, for enjoying ourselves. She'd be glad. I don't know how long it's going to take Harold to accept that, but I know it can't be rushed. In the meantime, I'm sorry, but I need to eat tonight.

'Just come and sit with me at the barbecue, then,' I suggest lightly, pretending not to be disappointed about the restaurant. 'You don't have to eat. Just come and keep me company.'

'Ah, Rube – do you mind if I don't?' he says, pulling a face and rubbing his stomach. 'Why don't you just pop down, get a plateful from the barbecue and bring it back up here? We can sit out on the balcony together. It'll be nice.'

No, it won't. I don't want to spend the whole of my honeymoon sitting on a balcony. I want to protest, but I just smile and nod and head for the door. At the last minute, something in me rebels.

'Actually, I think I'll eat down there on the terrace with all the others,' I say cheerfully. 'You won't want the smell of my food wafting under your nose, will you, if you're feeling sick?'

I don't wait for him to answer. Downstairs, there's a happy sound of music, chatter and laughter coming from the terrace, and a smell of cooking that immediately makes my mouth water. I'll find someone to sit with and enjoy the company, the ambience, for a while. Harold will only be reading his book. It won't matter to him.

I hesitate, looking around the tables, searching for a friendly face, someone I recognise. There's Jo, looking fed up, picking miserably at a piece of meat, and Mark, watching her with concern, trying to cajole her into eating some more. My heart sinks slightly. I don't really feel like getting involved in that. I look around again and catch sight of Gemma and Andy. They're sitting together but slightly apart, eating in silence, an uncomfortable atmosphere emanating from them. I certainly don't want to get involved in whatever's wrong *there.* Maybe this was a bad idea. Maybe I *will* just get a plate of food and take it back with me. Sit on the balcony with Harold, reading his book.

Or maybe I won't.

Before I have time to ask myself what the hell I'm doing, I've walked out of the hotel, turned on to the coast path and headed straight for the Italian restaurant next-door. And I've actually walked in before I think: Don't be ridiculous, Ruby. You can't come and eat in here all on your own. But it's too late. A young waiter is already approaching me, slim and handsome in his tight trousers and tuxedo, smiling with delight as if I am the most special customer he's had the pleasure of greeting all evening. To be honest, I'm one of the few. Half the usual clientele are probably at the hotel barbecue.

'*Buona sera*, Signora,' he says, eyes twinkling, giving a little bow. 'You want a table for 'ow many, please?'

'Just one, thank you.' I could always make a dash for the door after he's got me seated.

'Just one?' His puppy-dog eyes become mock-serious. 'Signora is all alone? This cannot be!'

'Oh, don't start crying on my behalf!' I laugh. 'I'm only alone for tonight. My husband's not very well.'

'And you 'ave come *all alone* to 'ave your dinner?' He makes it sound like I've trekked over burning coals, at the very least, to get here. 'Please do not worry. I, Luciano, will look after you! Please, Signora, come this way, to our *best* table in the 'ouse. It will be an honour for me to serve you.'

'Thank you, Luciano,' I say, cheered up no end, as I follow him to the *best table in the 'ouse* without a moment's hesitation or any further thought of making a dash for it.

He's not kidding about the table, either. It's at the end of the veranda, sheltered from the evening breeze but overlooking the entire bay – from the twinkling lights of Korčula harbour on one side, to the remote dark shape of the mainland on the other.

'This is perfect,' I tell him gratefully as he holds out my chair for me, flicks a pristine white napkin expertly on to my lap, fills my glass with bottled water and hands me the wine list and the menu.

'Whatever I can do, Signora, to make your evening perfect, it will make me very 'appy to do it,' says Luciano solicitously. He can't be more than twenty-five, maybe thirty, but he's very smooth, very suave – almost to the point of being ridiculous.

Harold would love this, I think, sipping the water as I study the menu, choose a starter and a main course – no point doing it by halves – and ponder the wine list. If only I could get him here, just once. Maybe when I describe it to him, he'll overcome his reluctance . . .

'You are looking very un'appy, Signora,' says Luciano, returning soundlessly to my side. 'Is it the wine list? Too many to choose? Would you like me to 'elp you?'

'It's OK, thank you, Luciano. I'll have a small carafe of your house red, please. I'm not at all unhappy. It's just so beautiful here – the view over the bay.'

'I'm glad you like. But I think, still, you are un'appy. I think maybe you worry a little about the 'usband with the illness, yes?'

'Well. Maybe a little, yes,' I smile. It's difficult not to smile at this beautiful young Italian with his charming manners and eagerness to please.

'Signora, you must not be worried. The 'usband will be 'appy if you are 'appy. Then, because 'e is 'appy, 'e will feel better. *Pronto!*' He shrugs expressively as if this piece of wisdom is quite obvious.

'Thank you. I'm sure you're right.'

He takes my order and goes back to the kitchen, watching me, smiling at me, all the way. It makes me laugh to myself and, as I return to gazing at the view, I realise I'm humming a little song inside my head. It's 'Don't Worry, Be Happy'.

*

I'm full to bursting by the time I've finished the last mouthful of my risotto. But I still go on and order a *tiramisù*. I know I shouldn't. I shouldn't because I'm being greedy, and, more to the point, I shouldn't because I ought to go back to Harold, sitting alone on the balcony with his book and his sadness. I shouldn't, but still I do – for no other reason than that I'm enjoying myself. I'm having an evening out, a change of scene, and I'll have something to talk to Harold about when I get back. And, of course, it would be rude to leave without having coffee.

'Signora,' says Luciano, returning again with his polite little bow, 'I am so 'appy that you 'ave eaten this wonderful meal in our restaurant. Our chef, too, 'e is 'appy. Our second chef, 'e is 'appy too. Our kitchen staff, they are all 'appy. And I think, perhaps, you are a little bit more 'appy also?'

'I *am* more 'appy – I mean, happy, Luciano. Thank you very much for looking after me so well.'

'You must not thank me!' he protests, looking shocked. 'It 'as been my greatest pleasure, Signora . . .'

'Ruby.'

'Pardon?'

'My name's Ruby,' I tell him warmly. Warmed by the lovely meal, and the wine, and his cheerful, attentive service. 'Please call me Ruby.'

'Ruby.' He puts one hand to his heart, closing his eyes as if he's savouring the sound of it. 'This is indeed a fitting name for a beautiful lady such as yourself. The name of a beautiful jewel, precious and rare. I am honoured to call you by this name.'

'Good.' I feel a little embarrassed now, but I can't say it isn't fun to be buttered up with all this theatrical nonsense. It hasn't happened to me for a good many

130

years, I can tell you. 'And now, I think I'd better have my bill, please, when you're ready.'

When he brings the bill, he's accompanied by Carlo, the chef, who is introduced with much bowing and flourishing of arms, and a tall glass of Limoncello – *courtesy of the 'ouse, for the beautiful Signora Ruby.* By the time I've downed this, I'm feeling slightly pissed.

'Where are you staying, Signora Ruby?' asks Luciano anxiously. 'Shall I phone for a taxi to take you back to the town? You should not walk, a beautiful lady all alone, late at night.'

'It's fine, Luciano,' I say, laughing. 'I'm staying just next-door at the Hotel Angelo!'

'Ah! Then please permit me to accompany you to your 'otel.'

I know they're not busy, but this is ridiculous.

'No, honestly, that won't be necessary . . .'

'If I may insist? It is dark, and you are alone . . .'

'And there are brutes and beasties lurking in the shadows?' I laugh again – but it's no use protesting, he's walking beside me already, taking my elbow politely as if I were his eighty-year-old grandmother. That's how he probably sees me, I think to myself somewhat ruefully. A sad lonely old bat who can't even find her way home.

'Thank you very much.' I turn to face him as we arrive at the steps up to the hotel entrance. 'That was kind of you . . .'

'Ruby,' he says, looking at me with those entreating spaniel-puppy eyes, 'please forgive my impropriety.'

'Why?' I'm trying not to laugh at him. 'What have you done . . .?'

'It is not what I 'ave done,' he says softly, his eyes

boring into mine. 'It is what I am now going to do.' With which he leans forward and kisses me, just once, very firmly, on the cheek. 'You are a very lovely lady, Signora Ruby. I think your 'usband, 'e must be a very lucky, very 'appy man.'

I blink in surprise, raise my hand to the place where his lips touched my cheek, and murmur some sort of embarrassed response.

'I 'ope to see you again in the *ristorante*!' Luciano calls over his shoulder, giving me a wave as he jogs away from me.

'Yes. I 'ope so too, but I somehow doubt it,' I mutter to myself, climbing the steps slightly unsteadily. I need to tell Harold before the effects of the Limoncello and the surprise of the kiss wear off, probably leaving me feeling a little foolish and ridiculous, that he is considered, in some quarters, to be *a very lucky, very 'appy man.*

Because I'm beginning to think he might have forgotten it.

	S	M	T	W	T	F	**S**
					1	2	3
	4	5	6	7	8	9	10
June	11	12	13	14	15	16	17
	18	19	20	21	22	23	(24)
	25	26	27	28	29	30	

Gemma

I'm so glad I had that talk with Ruby. What she said to me about a male crisis makes perfect sense – in fact, the more I think about it, the more relieved I feel that this is obviously *all* that's wrong with Andy. If anything, I'm just annoyed with myself for not understanding that he was having a problem. When you think about it, a wedding is a peculiar time for a man. It's such a very girly thing, isn't it? All the fuss with the dresses, and the shoes, and the flowers, and the music. I suppose your average bridegroom feels a bit left out of it, really, although to be honest in Andy's case he seemed perfectly happy to leave it all to me – or, rather, to my mum. And then, after all the excitement, and all the eating and drinking, not to mention all the expense – wham! He's suddenly alone again with his wife. His *wife*. I think perhaps it's a scary moment of recognition for them all. Like, shit! I'm *married*. A reality check, you know?

So I guess me starting to talk about babies just at this precise time when he's probably feeling a bit nervous about everything – I don't know, maybe his responsibilities, the future, all that stuff – could have been a bit tactless, could have messed with his head slightly. And then, of course, he sees that Cow-faced Caroline bird, and really gets the jitters. Understandable. I'd feel the same if I suddenly ran into that Egyptian doctor who tried to touch me up in the sluice room, wouldn't I?

The point is, I'm aware *I'm* acting a bit out of character too. I'm being stroppy and demanding, and flying off the handle, just when I should be feeling calm and serene. Andy knows I'm not normally like this! So perhaps the stress of the wedding has got to us both.

I sat with him, calmly and serenely, last night at the barbecue, talking about nice neutral things like the food and the weather. We even touched on Croatian politics and the price of fruit here compared with at home.

'Why are we doing this, Gemma?' Andy asked me suddenly, just as I was getting into a debate on the varieties of apples and pears available.

'Doing what?'

'Talking like two strangers trying to pass a couple of hours at an airport. What's wrong? Are you still mad at me?'

'Mad at you? Of course not! I'm just trying to avoid any stressful subjects, Andy. Anything that might upset you. While you . . . settle down.'

'I am settled down. What are you talking about?'

'Having a nice relaxing time. Not worrying about anything. OK?'

'OK.' He gave me a strange look and shook his head. 'If you say so.'

Everything was fine until Jo and Mark joined us for a drink when we'd all finished eating. By then, I'd been concentrating so hard for so long on keeping to safe subjects of conversation that I hadn't noticed how much wine I'd been drinking, and I was beginning to get a bit giggly. Andy, of course, relaxed straight into his Buy Your Mate a Drink mode as soon as Mark sat down opposite him.

'Another beer, mate? Jo, another orange juice?'

'I'll have another glass of wine while you're up!' I called after him cheerfully when he got up to go to the bar – despite the fact that I already had a full glass.

'It must be a pain in the bum, going without alcohol,' I commented to Jo.

She shrugged. 'It's fine, really. I felt so ill at the beginning, I couldn't have touched a drop anyway. And now, all I care about is giving my baby the healthiest possible start.'

'Absolutely. Good for you,' I said, slurring slightly. 'I'll do exactly the same, when I'm pregnant. I can't understand those mums-to-be who keep on smoking or drinking . . .'

'Me neither. But you know what, Gemma? I think I've read somewhere that you can increase your fertility by cutting back on the alcohol when you start trying for a family, too.'

'Yes. That's true. As soon as we get home, I'm going to cut down, so I'll be ready for a baby when it comes along . . .' I giggle carelessly.

Andy, who'd just returned with the tray of drinks, stood stock still for a minute, looking from Jo to me and back again.

Jo, obviously clocking the look on his face and the

awkward silence, coughed discreetly as she took her drink from Andy.

'Well ... that is ...' I glanced at Andy and shrugged. 'Whenever we decide to have a baby. Not that we're in a hurry or anything.'

'Fair enough, girl!' said Jo lightly. 'Drink up while you've got the chance! I can hardly remember my boozy nights at uni any more ...'

I wish I hadn't told her, now, that I was looking forward to trying for a baby. After the arguments with Andy about it, I should just keep off the subject, really, at the moment – it's obvious he's still freaking out about it. Maybe when we get home, and discuss it again properly, I'll tell him I don't mind if he wants to wait for a year or so longer. I don't know *why* he's suddenly changed his mind, but I need to be under-standing about it. I *do* want a baby, but OK, I can wait. Christ, I didn't even *like* babies when I was younger. I totally hated it when my little sister was born!

I'm not sure what you're supposed to feel when you have a new baby sister. Let's put it this way – whatever you're supposed to feel, I didn't.

When Mum came home from the hospital with this red-faced, bawling bundle in a blanket, my first thought was: Take it away again. I didn't want to see her. I didn't want to listen to the endless talk about her, and I certainly didn't want to hold her, bath her, change her nappy or get involved in any of the yucky disgusting stuff that everyone seemed to think I'd enjoy. When I walked into Mum's bedroom and found her sitting up in bed breastfeeding the baby, I turned tail and bolted back into my own room.

'What's the matter?' she called after me.

'Nothing!' I shouted back, slamming the door behind me.

'It's *gross!*' I grumbled to my friend Cheryl on the phone. 'Totally *gross.*'

'It's only natural, though, isn't it, Gem? What did you think she was going to feed the baby on? Cornflakes?'

'It's not funny. She shouldn't even *have* a baby. . .'

'Oh, come on, not this again!' Poor Cheryl must have been fed up to the back teeth with listening to my whingeing over the past nine months. 'Now the baby's born you're going to have to get used to it.'

'No, I'm not!'

'What's she like? I can't wait to see her. Can I come round later on?'

'What do you want to see her for?'

I was so gutted at the thought of my friend – my best friend – wanting to come round to see the baby, rather than me, that I could hardly talk.

She laughed. ''Cos babies are *lovely*, silly! I wish *I* had a baby sister – you don't know how lucky you are.'

No, I didn't. But then again, Cheryl's parents were still happy together. *Her* dad wasn't carrying on with other women. *Her* mum wasn't crying on her own in front of the TV every night. If *they* had another baby, it wouldn't be so disgusting.

I scowled and sulked and banged around the house for the whole of Claire's first year. I don't think I ever held her, or played with her, or talked to her during that whole time. Mum gave up trying to get me to take an interest in her, and instead shut me out of their little magic Mother and Baby circle.

'I'm disappointed,' she told me once after I'd

childishly refused to look after Claire while she went to the doctor's. 'I thought you'd have grown up and got over this nonsense by now.'

She took the baby with her, slamming the door on me as she went out. I wanted to call her back and say I was sorry, I'd have the baby if it made her happy. If it made her love me again. But the tight knot of resentment I was carrying around inside me wouldn't let me do it.

Eventually the day came when I looked at my baby sister and saw not just an irritating reminder of the fact that my mum had let me down by having sex with my father, but a real little person, who toddled around the house on her fat baby legs, calling 'Mumma', laughing and smiling at Mum, who smiled back at her as if they were the only two people who mattered in the world.

'She never smiles at *me* like that,' I said moodily.

She also never tried to say my name, never came anywhere near me voluntarily or held her arms up to me the way she did to most people she saw.

Mum just stared at me in silence for a few seconds.

'What the hell,' she said eventually with something like real dislike in her voice, 'did you expect? It's quite clear you don't even like her.'

'I didn't expect,' I yelled back, smarting and hurt and knowing it was all my own fault, 'for you to *replace* me with *her*!'

We didn't talk to each other for about a week after that. But perversely, belatedly, I started trying to make friends with Claire. The impressions made in the first year of a child's life are obviously really important, though, because she never really took to me. Never trusted me or ran to me when she was hurt or wanted a cuddle. And it was all the more wounding because,

138

by the time she was a pretty and clever little two year old, I was actually besotted with her. I think it was because of her that I decided to be a children's nurse.

'Do you want to finish that walk?' says Andy this morning. 'The one we ... started... yesterday?'

I feel a twinge of panic. I don't want him talking about yesterday's argument. Now I've realised we might both be suffering from post-wedding stress, I'd rather avoid any tricky subjects completely.

'No,' I say quickly. 'I didn't really like that walk, Andy.'

'You were keen enough to do it, weren't you, before ...'

'Before I realised how high the hill is. I don't fancy the climb,' I joke, frantically trying to change the subject. 'I've developed a sudden fear of heights.'

He looks at me with amusement, shaking his head. 'OK, so shall we try a different walk? In the opposite direction? Without any hills?'

'That sounds good.' I smile with relief. 'Where have you got in mind?'

He unfolds the map and points to the road that follows the coast, out the other side of Korčula Town.

'This looks like an easy walk. See that village – God knows how you pronounce it, how can you say a Z, R and N together?' He laughs and points to it. Žrnovska Banja. I see what he means. 'In our guide-book it says there's a really good restaurant there, overlooking this little bay – here.' He points to the map again. 'How about we head there for lunch?'

This sounds more like it. A nice easy walk along the coast, followed by lunch in a restaurant overlooking a little bay – romantic or what? Now *that's* what I envisaged for this honeymoon.

*

We follow the road round the other side of the harbour. We haven't seen this area at all yet. I think we're coming out of the tourist part of town: there aren't any hotels or anything like that around here. Actually I remember reading in that feature in *Weddings Today* that there aren't all that many hotels on Korčula island at all. Apparently there are some campsites, and a few self-catering places to rent. We haven't seen any so far but now we suddenly come upon a row of sweet little cottages along the side of the road, looking out over the sea and back towards the harbour, and some of them have the traditional sign outside, picturing a bed and stating *Sobe* – rooms available.

'Maybe self-catering cottages – maybe B & Bs,' I suggest. 'Nice outlook.'

'Yes, although I still think our hotel would take a lot of beating, for location,' says Andy.

We walk on, swinging our hands together, enjoying the feel of the sun. It's hotter than ever today, and I'm quite glad we haven't chosen a long walk to do. And that there's a nice restaurant at the end of it to look forward to.

I'm so busy thinking about the nice restaurant that I don't even notice Caroline at first. A flash of yellow bikini, a stream of blonde hair, a rush of long, slim, brown legs and she's leapt off the swing-seat outside one of the cottages and skipped into the road beside us.

'Well, *hi*!' she purrs. 'This *is* a surprise!'

You can say that again.

'Hi,' says Andy, guardedly, glancing at me and back at Caroline again, hesitating, not sure whether to stop.

I don't stop. I turn away and keep walking.

'Where are you off to?' Caroline's asking Andy in her irritating sing-song voice. 'Not walking all the way to Račišće, are you? Apparently it's a lot further than it looks because of all the inlets along the coast, you know? Someone we were talking to the other night did it, but they were totally shattered and had to get the bus back, and it's very hot today, so you'll need to take water, and . . .'

I stop, turn round, and announce with a cold hostility I didn't know I could manage until now: 'No, we're not. We're only going as far as Zoronoska or whatever it's called. We're not quite that stupid.'

Andy looks at me wretchedly. He really doesn't know what to say. Why doesn't he just ignore her — walk on and pretend she doesn't exist? She doesn't deserve any more than that, the stupid spiteful cow. But he's just too nice for his own good. He can't even be nasty to someone who so obviously deserves it.

'*Wonderful* little restaurant there,' Caroline says, completely ignoring my cold hostility and addressing Andy instead. '*Wonderful views* as you walk along the coast here, too.'

'Good,' he manages to croak, quietly.

'Are you staying somewhere round here?' she asks sweetly.

'No,' I fire back. 'Nowhere near here.'

'Pity. We could have had a drink together tonight. We're staying right here.' She indicates the cottage behind her with a sweep of her thin bronzed arm. 'Little place belonging to a friend of mine. Basic but *wonderfully* cheap,' she giggles as if it's slightly risqué to admit this.

I turn away again and start to walk on, indicating to Andy that he should do likewise.

'Well, hopefully we'll bump into each other again!'

she calls after us. 'Come and join us at the cottage for a drink on your way back, if you like?'

I'd rather wrap myself in tinfoil and do a turn on the barbecue, thank you very much.

We walk on in silence for a while. The flavour of the day has soured. I'm trying to tell myself this is just as hard for Andy as it is for me. That he wouldn't have wanted to come face to face, on his honeymoon, with someone who was such a bitch to him, who insulted him and besmirched his reputation, who made him feel small and silly like the kids at school used to do. All over again. That I need to support him and help him, be tender and understanding. I'm struggling with myself – with my doubts and my suspicions and the new nasty side to my nature that I seem suddenly to have developed.

'How the fuck,' I demand eventually, giving up on the support and understanding, 'did you know that was where she was staying?'

'Don't be ridiculous, Gemma,' he says with a tired sigh. 'Of course I didn't *know*. If I had, I'd have avoided it like the plague.'

'Yeah, right,' I say.

We both look at each other, both sigh heavily, and walk on in silence. This is all Caroline's fault. It was a lovely day until *she* turned up again.

And if she interferes with my honeymoon one more time, you know what? She's not going to get away with it.

Jo

We're going for a nice long walk today. I've managed to convince Mark that it will do me good, it won't hurt the baby, and it's healthier than sitting around in the sun all day.

'There's a walk suggested in your guide book – all the way along the coast to Račišće We can take it steady and stop somewhere for lunch,' I suggested over breakfast.

So we set off from the hotel this morning before it got too hot. He's got bottles of water, fruit and sun cream in the rucksack on his back. He's not letting me carry anything. I'm wearing my hat, and my walking sandals, and I'm conscious, as we follow the road along the coast, that I've been looking forward to this all morning. There's a strange singing sensation in my chest that I can't quite recognise. I think it's the feeling of freedom that I'm enjoying – being out on the open road, in the fresh air, swinging my arms, looking up at the sky.

'Be careful, Jo. The road's a bit uneven just here. Mind you don't trip,' says Mark.

Not *quite* so free, perhaps.

The walk has brought us round the other side of Korčula Town, leaving the harbour behind and striking out along the coast road round the next bay. There's less traffic now; the road has become narrow and winding, and we've passed through outcrops of pastel-painted modern houses backed up against steep hillsides, looking down over millpond-still inlets of aquamarine water where little boats bob lazily and fish teem busily at the surface.

'This is beautiful,' says Mark. 'Look at the views some of these houses have. I wonder how much it costs to buy one like that!' He points out a large, white, tall-windowed property set back from the road, with steps down to its own jetty and a double garage built into its basement.

I daydream as we walk of living in a house like this: of preparing meals in a white-tiled kitchen with a window overlooking the sea; of children laughing as they play on the beach below; of eating fresh fish on the terrace in the warm evenings. Of living somewhere foreign, somewhere remote, somewhere where nothing of my previous life could reach me.

We pass through the village of Žrnovska Banja and the road begins to climb away from the coast. Now there's no traffic at all – nobody passing us on the road. Nothing but the sound of seabirds and our own footsteps on the dusty tarmac.

'Can we stop for a minute?' It's getting hotter now and I'm gasping for a drink.

'Are you all right?' Mark's immediately looking at me in concern. 'There's nowhere to sit down around here, Jo. Let's just get round the next corner.' The lane is edged now with tall hedges, so tall we can't see over them. I suddenly feel slightly panicky. Hemmed in, with no way out except the road ahead. 'Here – have some water,' adds Mark, passing me one of the bottles. 'Sure you're OK? We'll have a rest in a minute, when we can find somewhere off the road.'

'Yes. Thanks – I'm fine.'

We walk on: what seems to be a long way on. It's midday by now, and the heat of the sun is bouncing back at us off the tarmac, so intense it feels like I can almost touch it. Round the next bend is more narrow road, more tall hedge, still no verge to rest on, still no gaps in the hedgerow. I stop and hold on to a protruding branch, swaying slightly, hearing a sudden frightening buzzing in my head, like a swarm of angry bees attacking me from the inside.

'Are you *sure* you're OK, babe?' Mark takes my arm, supporting me, taking the water out of the rucksack again and holding it up to me. 'You're very hot.'

'I know. It *is* very hot,' I say, irritably, dipping my head and waiting for the humming to stop.

'Shall we turn back?' He unfolds the map and studies it for a minute, considering the distance we've come, the distance still to go to the next village. 'We're probably about halfway to Račišće, but there are a couple of smaller villages on the way where we could stop.'

Turn back? Round all those bends in the lane, down all that open road with no shade, nowhere to rest or get out of the sun?

'No. Let's keep going. I just need to sit down for a little while, that's all. In the shade. Then I'll be fine.'

He looks around, helplessly, consults the map again. I feel a wave of impatience. Maps don't show you where the hedge might give way to grass at the side of the road. There isn't a symbol on the map for shade, for degrees of heat, for the height of the vegetation bearing down oppressively, blocking out any chance of a breeze.

'Come on,' I say, pulling at his arm. 'There must be somewhere to sit, round the *next* bend.'

It takes fifteen minutes to get round the next bend – I keep checking my watch. And there's still nowhere to sit down apart from the middle of the road, which by now I'd be seriously considering if it didn't look hot enough to fry an egg on. And still no respite from the sun, so directly overhead that

145

even the height of the hedgerow offers only a two-inch strip of shade, like an inky black margin along the edge of the lane.

'We're nearly at this place now,' says Mark, showing me a huddle of grey squares on the map. 'Piske. We'll stop there, Jo. I don't think we should go on to Račišće. You're too tired.'

I'm actually too tired even to argue. I take the water bottle again and finish off the last drop. Mark stows the empty bottle and gets out the second one.

'Drink as much as you need. We can get some more at the village.'

Two more twists of the road, with nothing ahead, nothing behind, except the endless vista of road and hedgerow, and I'm beginning to wonder if this is how it feels to become delirious. Mark's looking too worried now even to discuss whether I'm OK.

'I'll carry you,' he says, readjusting the rucksack. 'On my back.'

'Don't be ridiculous. Keep going. It can't be far.'

One foot in front of the other. Heat rising from the road like mist. Not far, he said, to the next village. What did he say it was called again? Another swig of water. My throat's parched. It was stupid – stupid to walk in this heat, in the middle of the day, without being sure of the distance. I need to sit down. My head hurts.

'Round this corner!' calls Mark, who's gone on ahead to look. 'It must be round this corner. I thought we'd have come to it by now ...'

We're following the coast again now, although we can't even see it beyond the trees. But ten minutes later the road suddenly opens out and I finally catch a glimpse of the sea.

'A breeze!' I croak in relief. Thank God, a breeze. I hold up my face, feel the air moving.

'There's the village,' says Mark, the relief in his voice echoing mine. 'Let's find a restaurant. A bar. A café. Anything!'

Anything. That's a laugh. Two derelict cottages, a boat house, and we're walking out the other side of the so-called village.

'All right,' I say, and I'm practically on my knees. 'I want to go back.'

'This *can't* be Piske. It wouldn't be on the map just for this.' Mark's still walking, still holding the map out in front of him as if it's going to lead him to the promised land.

'I don't care if it's Piske, Račišće or sodding Manchester. I've had enough, Mark. I can't go any further.'

He turns and looks at me, his face creasing with anxiety.

'Come and sit down here,' he calls. 'There's some shade.'

At most it's about a metre of mottled shadow, from a dry knobbly tree at the edge of a tiny strip of shingle beside the sea. We perch together on a rock, passing the last of the water between us, sharing an apple, sucking hungrily on its juicy flesh. I pull off my sandals, slide off the rock and immerse myself up to my knees in the calmly rippling water, splashing cold salty handfuls over my face and neck. Heaven. I'll stay here. I'll wait till the sun goes down tonight and take my chances. Swim back, if necessary.

'We can't stay here, Jo,' Mark says quietly as if I've spoken aloud. 'We'll have to either go on or go back. We've got no more water.'

No more water. Oh, Jesus.

'We've got another apple. And a couple of bananas,' I say shakily. I peel one of the bananas and eat it, hungrily, but it just makes me thirsty again. 'Let's wait for a while and see if anyone comes past. There's supposed to be a bus, isn't there?'

We'd discussed getting the bus back from Račišće if the walk there took us too long. Already, the idea of walking all the way there, never mind considering the possibility of walking back, seems absurd, like a suggestion for a stupid dare.

'The bus only runs three times a day,' says Mark. 'The guide-book doesn't give the times. We might have missed them all, and anyway we don't know where to get it. *This* road obviously can't be the bus route.'

It's more of a bloody footpath; I feel angry with it for calling itself a road. Angry with the guide-book for suggesting this is a pleasant coastal walk. Angry with poxy Piske for being two tumble-down cottages and a boat house when it was supposed to be a village.

'We'll have to start walking back then,' I say. My voice comes out small and pathetic. I wonder what my mum and dad will say when they find out I died of thirst in a country lane in Korčula, with no water left and only a part share in an apple. All those years in the Girl Guides, for what?

'It might not be so bad on the way back,' says Mark. He doesn't sound very convincing. 'It'll be more downhill. Once we've gone uphill to start with.'

The uphill bit nearly kills me. My walking sandals, normally the most comfortable shoes I possess, are rubbing the tops of my toes and the skin is beginning to blister.

148

'My feet are swollen,' I pant, holding on to Mark's arm and letting him help me up the hill as if I was an arthritic octogenarian. 'I'm a wreck.'

What happened to my much-fêted personal fitness? The muscles in my legs seem to have turned to jelly. My ankles hurt, my back aches. Even the baby seems to be objecting, kicking me behind my navel with a steady thump that's making me feel sick.

'It's just the heat,' says Mark, stopping to shift the rucksack on his shoulders and wiping his brow with the back of his hand. 'I think it's even hotter today than it's been all week. We're not used to it. We should have done this in the early morning. Or the evening.'

'In the dark?' I retort sarcastically.

'No. Actually, babe, I don't think we should have done this at all. It was crazy. What the hell was I thinking?'

'My idea, wasn't it?'

'But I promised to look after you. I shouldn't have agreed to it ...'

'For God's sake! Does it matter whose fault it is?' I'm thirsty again, and the more I think about the fact that we haven't got any water, the more I want some. We walk slowly, trying to keep to the band of shade at the side of the road, which at least is a few inches wider now than before.

The long stretch of road is like a tunnel, trapping the heat and doubling its intensity. My feet are so sore now that I try walking without my sandals, but the surface of the road is too hot. A cyclist suddenly zooms past us, free-wheeling downhill.

'How far to Korčula Town?' Mark calls after him – but he's gone, whistling through his own happy breeze, not hearing us, barely seeing us plodding behind in his dust trail. Then, suddenly, there's a car. It's coming slowly towards us, an ancient blue Renault, the driver's thick brown arm hanging loosely out of the window. Mark waves at the driver, but he just waves back.

'How far to Korčula?' he calls again – but the driver shrugs, gesticulates, points in the direction we're headed and shouts something in Croatian.

'Well, at least it *is* a road, after all,' Mark comments, as if this is helpful, but I know what he means. I think we'd both begun to imagine that we'd somehow stumbled into another dimension – off the beaten track, or even off the planet. We'd hardly seen a soul since leaving civilisation this morning.

But now, gradually, the landscape begins to open out and I recognise something. A house, a particular bend in the road. Some more houses. There's another car, then two more. There's the sea again, and now we're coming into the village we walked through earlier.

'Žrnovska Banja,' announces Mark, still studying the map. 'Thank God. There was a sign for a restaurant here. I remember seeing it.'

My mouth feels even more parched at the thought of getting a cold drink; my feet even hotter at the thought of sitting down and resting them.

'Here!' Mark sounds excited now as he points to the sign, the crossed knife and fork symbol that represents everything I crave in life. We follow the direction of the sign, along a track that climbs cruelly uphill.

'I hope this is right,' I mutter. 'This is *definitely* not a road.'

150

But just as I'm beginning to think I can't go another step, we come out at a row of houses, perched high on the coast, overlooking the sea. *PANORAMA BISTRO* reads the sign outside the first of these. I feel like rushing in and screaming for a drink, but even now there's more torture. Another sign points up a flight of stairs to the side of the building. By the time I've climbed these, I'm ready to drop. It's a roof terrace, with wooden tables and chairs set mercifully in the shade and overlooking the bay, all the way back to Korčula Town. I couldn't possibly say the view is worth all the pain I've been through, but it's certainly superb. I collapse on to a chair and lean my head on my arms. The shade is heaven. Mark asks for a cold beer and an orange juice to be brought straight away, while he studies the menu.

'Actually, Mark, I don't think I want anything to eat,' I say as he passes the menu to me. 'I feel really sick.' Even the baby seems to have exhausted himself and stopped kicking me. In fact, he's not moving at all now.

'Would you prefer to get straight back to the hotel?'

'I'd love to, if only it didn't involve another half an hour's walk. I don't know if I can do it. Look at my ankles.' Now I've taken off my sandals, it's doubtful whether I'll ever get them back on.

'Hello, you two!' says a familiar voice suddenly. 'What's wrong, Jo? Hurt your feet?'

Andy's just got up from a table at the other end of the terrace, followed by Gemma who exclaims about the coincidence of us finding ourselves in the same tucked away little spot and adds: 'Did you walk here? You look absolutely worn out. God, look at your ankles!'

'I know,' I say, wearily. 'We tried to walk to Račišće, but it was so hot ... we were so thirsty ...'

'Račišće?' says Andy in surprise. 'Blimey, Mark, that was a bit ambitious, wasn't it? That must be a *hell* of a long walk, especially in this heat ...'

'Yes, we realise that now,' says Mark slightly stiffly. 'We didn't get much more than halfway, but Jo was feeling so awful ...'

'Poor you. You don't look too good, love. Have you eaten? Aren't you going to? The food's superb. I had seafood salad. Great big juicy prawns, dripping in garlic. Sardines; octopus ... have you tried the octopus over here yet?'

'Andy,' cuts in Gemma anxiously, 'I think you're making Jo feel worse.'

'I think I need to go ...' I begin, trying to stand on legs that feel like sponges. My head's swimming and I think I'm going to be sick. I don't know where I'm trying to go ... anywhere, away from this talk of fish, and garlic, and the smell of cooking, and the heat ...

'She's going to faint!' I hear Gemma say as the floor begins to tilt towards me. 'Quick, hold her, Mark – lay her down here. Let me check her pulse ...'

Everything's dark now. I'm whirling around like I'm on a fairground ride, but there's nothing to hold on to. Stop! Stop the ride, I want to get off! I don't like it – I feel sick, I feel ill. I want to go home. What am I doing here? I'm lonely and frightened. I can't see anything, or hear anything, apart from a ringing in my ears and somewhere, a long way off, someone crying.

'I want my mum,' the voice is crying. It's loud now, a terrible wailing inside my head. 'Take me home. Take me home. I don't want to be here! I want my mum!'

And then – nothing.

Nothing for what feels like forever.

June	**S**	M	T	W	T	F	S
					1	2	3
	4	5	6	7	8	9	10
	11	12	13	14	15	16	17
	18	19	20	21	22	23	24
	25	26	27	28	29	30	

Gemma

We're a bit subdued this morning. It shook us both up yesterday – seeing Jo being carted off from the restaurant in an ambulance – and when Mark came back to the hotel in a taxi during the evening to collect some things for her because she was being kept in hospital overnight, I was quite upset.

'I hope she's all right,' I keep saying to Andy. 'She looked so awful – I do hope the baby is OK . . .'

'She's in the best place, isn't she?' he reassures me. 'I expect they're just keeping an eye on her, being ultra-careful.'

'I just don't understand Mark at all. One minute he's a total health-and-safety freak, watching her every move, hardly letting her breathe unaided, and the next – he's taking her on a bloody *hike* in the middle of the hottest day . . .'

'To be fair, Gem, I don't suppose he knew it was

154

going to be the hottest day of the week. And perhaps it *doesn't* look that far to Račišće on the map.'

'Not if you're an idiot who can't read maps, no.'

'Aw, come on, give the guy a break. I'm sure he feels bad enough about Jo, without us adding to it.'

'Yeah, he must do,' I admit, thinking anxiously about all the things that can go wrong with a pregnancy, and about all the possible serious effects of heatstroke.

'The trouble is,' Andy says lightly, putting his arm round me, 'you hear all this stuff, being a nurse, and it just makes you worry more.'

'Well, of course it does! But then again, Mark's a bloody physiotherapist! Wouldn't you think he'd have more sense . . .'

'Not really. But if one of us sprains an ankle on these rocks, I guess he's our man! Come on, Gem, cheer up. I bet she'll be fine.'

In an attempt to stop me panicking about Jo, Andy's persuaded me to go on another bus trip today. This is going to be a longer trip – all the way to the other major town on Korčula island, Vela Luka, which is at the farthest end of the island, about thirty miles to the west. We've decided definitely not to bother with a hire car at all as it looks as though this bus journey will take us through nearly every other village on the island, and to be honest it's quite pleasant to have a complete rest from driving for a couple of weeks.

It's also quite pleasant to be spending a day getting as far away as possible from the prospect of running into Cow-face Caroline again. How she had the *bloody nerve* to come trotting over to us, bold as brass, yesterday and start chatting as if Andy was her best buddy, I really can't believe. I'm still, desperately, trying to convince myself he isn't lying to me about her. He was certainly as pissed off as I was yesterday. *Can't seem to get away from her*, he said moodily when we'd recovered enough from the shock of seeing her to talk about it sensibly. The trouble is, Korčula Town's such a small place, it's not easy to avoid someone here. All the more reason for going to Vela Luka. If she turns up *there*, I'll know she's actually stalking us. And I'm sorry, but I mean it: if she inflicts her stupid self on us one more time, I'm letting her have it. Andy might not be able to bear confrontation, but I sure as hell can.

It won't be the first time I've fought his battles for him. I guess we must have been in about Year Eleven at school when this boy Fatty Pete was giving Andy a hard time. He was an obnoxious kid – nobody liked him, but they pretended to because he was a nasty piece of work you didn't want to cross. Obese, smelly, ignorant and foul-mouthed, he nevertheless had this pathetic posse of dozy tossers who hung on his every word and sniggered with fake admiration whenever he threw his considerable weight around. He didn't like Andy because, basically, Andy chose to ignore him and tried to stay away from him. His way of dealing with Pete, and all the others like him, was to try to make himself invisible by sitting at the back of the class, keeping his head down, staying quiet – and most of all, never, ever telling anyone if he had his lunch money stolen or his ankles kicked. So Pete thought it would be really good fun to get a couple of his sidekicks to slash Andy's bike tyres. I was with him when he discovered the damage – in time to see Fatty Pete and his cronies giggling like the idiots they were as they ran away.

156

'I hope you're not going to let this go,' I said, furious that he was being picked on yet again.

'I've got no choice,' said Andy, wearily. 'I can't prove who did it, and anyway, you know how much worse Pete can make things for me. It's not worth it: it'll be easy enough to get the tyres repaired.'

Of course, it wasn't. One of the tyres was so badly slashed it was irreparable, and Andy had to get a new tyre. Three days later, they were slashed again. Andy reported it to the Head of Year, but apart from telling him that it was impossible to ensure security at all times and bikes were brought into school at the students' own risk, he didn't do much more than shrug his shoulders and shake his head.

Like most bullies, Fatty Pete was actually a coward, and fortunately I'd found out what his Achilles heel was. Marianne Parkes in our class, who lived next-door to him, had told me that his father was an even bigger bully than he was – a police sergeant with a raging temper, only surpassed by his slightly twisted method of putting the world to rights, starting with his own family. Walking home from school that evening with Andy, who was carrying his bike and wondering how he was going to find the money for more tyres, I told him I needed to make a detour to drop something off at Marianne's house. But I didn't. Instead, and ignoring Andy's protests, I knocked on Fatty Pete's door, taking a chance on his dad being home because I knew he did shiftwork. I was so angry about Andy's bike, I was trying not to think about my backup plan for the scary possibility of his dad being out and Fatty Pete answering the door himself – which was basically to leg it. Luckily Pete's dad – bigger than Pete and built like a brick shit-house – opened the door, and I immediately showed him his son's handiwork.

Andy was pulling me by the arm, horrified. 'Come on, Gemma – leave it!' he was begging.

'Is this right? You telling me the truth?' raged Fatty Pete's gigantic scary father. 'My boy did this?'

'Him and his mates,' I retorted, too angry to stop. Too frightened to back down and walk away now I'd started. 'And it's the second time, too.'

'Pete!' his father hollered up the stairs. 'Get down here! Tell me you *didn't* have anything to do with this lad's bike being vandalised?'

It was a sight for sore eyes – Pete cowering before his father's bellowing anger. He tried to lie his way out of it but his dad obviously knew him too well. We didn't hang around long enough to see what he was going to do to his son, but he did call after us: 'If my boy messes with you any more, lad – or any of his bloody stupid mates – you come straight round here and tell me, you hear?'

It was the first, and only, time in our lives Andy and I have been afforded police protection. We still laugh about it now. But you know what? Pete never did mess with Andy any more. I knew Andy was grateful that I'd sorted it out; but I also knew, even at that young age, that on another level he was mortified. Like he'd be mortified now, I know, if I got involved with this Caroline bird and told her what I thought of her. So let's just hope she stays away from us from now on so that I don't have to.

We're somewhat shocked by the bus timetable.

'This can't be right!' exclaims Andy, following the lines of figures on the list outside the bus station. 'There isn't another bus to Vela Luka until twelve-fifteen!'

'Because it's Sunday, I suppose. Look, some routes don't run at all on Sundays.'

'But there was a bus going there at five o'clock this morning, and another one at six-fifteen! What's that all about?'

'It's to tie in with the ferries, mate,' says someone with a Liverpool accent who's looking at the timetable over our shoulders. He's about eighteen, skinny and sun-tanned, with a rucksack the size of a small house on his back, bending him almost double under its weight. 'The ferry to Split, on the mainland, goes from Vela Luka, see. And to Hvar – one of the other islands. You been there? You should. It's cool.'

'Oh. Well – we were just going to Vela Luka for the day,' I say, feeling suddenly like a pensioner on a seaside coach outing beside this backpacker and his girlfriend, who's loitering behind him looking bored and carrying a much smaller rucksack.

'Ain't you been to any of the other islands?' she says now, displaying a mouthful of chewing-gum. 'What – you just got here, have you?'

'No. We've ... er .... been here a week,' admits Andy. 'But we've been to Lumbarda, and over to Orebic on the mainland ...'

'Boring,' pronounces the girl, sticking her hands in her pockets.

'You don't have to be rude, Pansy,' her boyfriend rebukes her.

Pansy? Anything less like a flower I've yet to see. She can't be more than sixteen, with cropped black hair and studs in her nose and lips. She's wearing combats and a tiny crop top, displaying a tattoo of a spider's web on her stomach. Apparently deciding not to listen to any more of our *boring* conversation, she adjusts the volume of her iPod and turns her back on us, watching the traffic.

'Sorry about her,' says the guy with a shrug, his

159

puny shoulders barely managing to move beneath the huge rucksack. 'She's got the arse-ache because we're going home today.'

'How long have you been here?' asks Andy, to be polite.

'Been bumming around Croatia for a couple of months. Just arrived on Korčula last night, though. Our last night. We only came here because of the bar in the tower.'

'The what?'

He looks at us as if we're completely stupid.

'The bar in the tower,' he repeats slowly, as if we're foreign or slightly deaf. 'Massimo Cocktail Bar. It's the best place on the island. Everyone goes there!'

'We don't,' I point out. 'We didn't know about it.'

'It's not in my guide-book,' complains Andy, taking it out of his pocket and thumbing through it to prove his point.

'Mate, you want to go there tonight. You'll be blown away. Trust me!' He readjusts his rucksack and has a last look at the bus timetable before turning away.

'Reuben,' whines Pansy, who's now leaning against a wall, hands in her pockets, kicking the pavement moodily, 'come on, we haven't got all day.'

'We have, actually, Pans. There's no buses yet, right? We might as well get a coffee and chill out. Long as we get the ferry tonight. See you later, guys,' he adds to us as they both slope off. 'Have a good day. Remember – Massimo Bar.'

'Where is it?' Andy shouts after him.

'In the tower!' he calls back, laughing at our stupidity. And they're gone, round the corner, dragging their heels in their worn-down trainers.

'We've never done that, have we?' comments Andy thoughtfully.

160

'What? Had our lips pierced and huge spider's webs tattooed on our stomachs?'

'No – gone travelling. Backpacking.'

'Well, we kind of did, didn't we? We had that island-hopping holiday in the Greek Islands one year . . .'

'No, Gem, that wasn't proper island-hopping. That was one week in Kos and one week in Rhodes. We stayed in four-star hotels. We've never just *taken off*, without any plans, and stayed in hostels, roughing it, travelling around on buses and ferries . . .'

'I've never wanted to!' I look at him carefully. 'Have *you*? You've never said.'

'I suppose I've never really thought about it. You've always booked the holidays . . .'

'Andy, that's not fair! If you'd ever said, even *once*, in all these years, that there was something – *anything* – you particularly wanted to do on holiday, there was nothing stopping you saying so. Nothing stopping you arranging it yourself, for once, come to that!'

'Maybe I will. Maybe next year we'll do something different, eh, Gem? Take some extra time off work and go backpacking in Australia? Or India?'

'But by next year I might be . . .' I stop myself just in time. I'm not planning on going to bloody Australia or India next year. I'm hoping by then that we'll have made some definite plans about starting our family. But we're not going to talk about that till we get home, are we?

'Might be what?' he asks casually.

'Too old,' I say, a bit snappily. 'Too old for bloody backpacking, and camping, and all that student stuff. Honestly, Andy, I'm sure you're having a mid-life crisis. Almost everything you've said this week has been weird.'

'What d'you mean – weird?'

'Oh, forget it. Come on, let's not stand around here – it's another hour and a half till this stupid bus. Let's at least get a coffee, if we're still going to wait for it.'

We decide, over coffee in the old town, that we'll still go to Vela Luka for the afternoon, just for the ride if nothing else.

'Anyway,' says Andy, sipping his coffee and staring at me over the cup, 'I'm not old enough for a mid-life crisis.'

'What is it, then? You're suddenly saying all these things.' I'm too nervous to bring up the baby thing. Or the Caroline thing. Or the thing about wanting to support her child if she had one. 'Like this, now, about wanting to go to Australia.'

'Not necessarily Australia. I just like the idea of the freedom of it: backpacking, going where you like, not having to book a hotel and stay in one place.'

'But it's what we've always liked doing!' I protest. 'You *loved* that hotel in Egypt last year! You wanted to go there again for our honeymoon.'

'I know I did. But I suppose I've never thought about the alternatives. Christ, Gemma, don't look so bloody upset! It was only a *thought*!'

Yes, but he's never had thoughts like this before. I don't know why he's started now. I'm beginning to feel like I don't know him any more.

We get the 12.15 bus, and it's just about to leave when Reuben and Pansy come haring round the corner, shouting to the driver to wait for them. They're falling about laughing as they jump aboard, unstrap each other's rucksacks and fling them in the luggage space at the front of the bus, finally collapsing on to a seat across the aisle from us.

'Oh, hi!' says Reuben when he sees us. 'Going for your day-trip, then?'

He makes it sound about as exciting as an appointment with the chiropodist.

'Yes. We'll get some lunch there, have a walk around the town ...' I'm not helping, am I? It sounds like an Arthritis Care charity beano. 'And then come back,' I finish quietly. 'Before it gets too late.'

'Got to be in bed early, have you?' says Pansy sarcastically through her chewing gum.

'Well,' says Andy with a grin, 'yes, as it's our honeymoon.'

'Oh, mate! You didn't say it was your *honeymoon*!' exclaims Reuben. He jumps to his feet, aims an exuberant high five at Andy, claps him on the shoulder, congratulates us both and announces to everyone on the bus: 'This guy's on his fucking *honeymoon*, for Christ's sake!'

'So am I!' I point out, laughing, but nobody's really listening. The English tourists are cheering and some are doing that strange whooping thing – they must be Americans – and the Croatians are looking at Reuben with undisguised distaste.

'Mate, if I'd known you were on your *honeymoon*,' he continues when the fuss has died down a bit, 'I'd have *understood*.'

'Understood what?' says Andy, looking pleased nonetheless at the attention, the excitement of having a new *mate*.

'Well, don't take this the wrong way, mate, but me and Pansy were saying, before we got on the bus, how you two seemed – you know – kind of *unadventurous*, right? Considering you're, like, still *almost* young, yeah?'

'Unadventurous?' repeats Andy, looking crestfallen.

163

I'm not crestfallen. Who wants to be adventurous anyway? Not sure about the *almost young*, though.

'Yeah, but you didn't say it was your *honeymoon!*' says Reuben again with a knowing grin. 'Mate, I'm surprised you're even out of the bedroom at all! When did you guys get married?'

'Last Saturday,' I tell him. 'But we've been together for eighteen years.'

'*Eighteen years!*' He whistles. 'Shit! That's longer than I've even been *alive!*'

'Longer than my *parents* have been alive,' says Pansy, exaggerating wildly.

I can't help laughing. Next thing you know, they'll be taking our photos to show everyone back home. 'Here, look: this is an old married couple we met on Korčula. Can you believe they've been together for eighteen years? And they're still alive! Amazing, yeah?'

We've stopped at a couple of villages along the road: little, out-of-the-way places that end almost as soon as they begin, where old women in black dresses and shawls climb aboard with baskets on their arms, shouting unsmiling greetings to other old people on the bus, waving at the neighbours who seem to be standing at their cottage doors to see them off on the bus. The whole journey takes almost an hour, but some of the villages look so similar that Andy, who's trying to follow it on the map, admits he's not sure where we are until we reach the town of Blato – recognisable from the wide, modern-looking square and tree-lined main street described in the guide-book.

'Not far now,' he says.

'You're right, mate,' says Reuben. 'We're in good time for the ferry.'

Pansy scowls and stares out of the window.

'The ferry takes us to the mainland – and we fly home from Split airport tomorrow morning,' he tells us with a shrug. 'Running out of money anyway, so what can you do?'

'Doesn't it worry you?' I ask him. 'Not knowing where you're going to be staying from one night to the next?'

'Nah!' He laughs cheerfully. 'Easy enough finding hostels. Anyway, we reckoned we deserved one last long trip, didn't we, Pans?'

'Yeah,' she mutters, without turning round.

'Why the last one, mate?' says Andy, looking surprised. 'What – you off to uni or something, are you?'

'Shit, no. Nothing like that. Pansy's pregnant, see? Three months gone,' he adds proudly. 'That's why she's getting away with only carrying the little back-pack.'

I look at her bare, flat stomach and imagine the spider's web tattoo being stretched to grotesque proportions with the growth of the baby.

'Congratulations,' I say faintly.

'Yeah! Er ... good for you, mate,' Andy looks almost too surprised to say any more.

'So we'll have to kind of settle down, I guess,' says the father-to-be, smiling at the sullen profile of his baby's juvenile mother. 'Rent a pad somewhere and get a job. All that stuff.'

'Well ...' We're arriving at Vela Luka now. The bus terminates here, at the port, and the last few passengers are grabbing their luggage and preparing to get off. 'All the best, then,' I tell them.

'Yeah – thanks, mate. You too. Enjoy the rest of your honeymoon,' he says cheerfully. 'Don't forget about the bar in the tower!'

Over lunch in one of the town's many seafront restaurants, I try, and fail, to think of a way to discuss with Andy the fact that we, at thirty-two, with an eighteen-year relationship, good jobs and our own three-bedroomed house with garden, apparently aren't yet ready to start a family and ought, moreover, to be considering backpacking round the world while supporting other people's children – whereas Jo and Mark, who aren't even a proper couple, are stumbling half-cocked into parenthood with a whole shed-load of problems stored up, and a couple of teenagers who look so wet behind the ears their mothers are probably still drying up their breast milk are nonchalantly going into it without a cent to their name or a care in the world.

I don't even know where to begin.

So instead I drink nearly a whole bottle of wine and fall asleep on the bus back.

Ruby

That poor young girl's in hospital, apparently. Harold said he was looking at the postcards on sale at the reception desk yesterday evening when he saw Mark running up to his room, looking scared out of his wits.

'Everything all right?' he asked, when a couple of minutes later Mark came tearing back down again with a bag.

'No – Jo's in hospital,' he said, running to the door. 'Sorry, mate, got to go. Taxi's waiting.'

Later, we saw Gemma and Andy and they told us Jo had collapsed with heat exhaustion. Gemma was really upset – they'd been with Jo when she collapsed, and Gemma was worrying about it developing into heatstroke which she said could be really serious, especially as Jo's pregnant.

'No good worrying now,' I told her firmly. 'They'll be giving her all the right treatment at the hospital, won't they?'

'I hope so,' she said, looking unconvinced – probably wondering if treatment at the hospital here would be as good as on the NHS. 'Poor Jo.'

Yes. And just as she was beginning to look better, too. Mark must be terrified.

We're halfway through our honeymoon now. It doesn't seem possible.

'Are you enjoying it, Rube?' says Harold when I point this out to him in the afternoon. 'Despite everything?'

'*Despite* everything?' I retort, laughing. 'What – despite being married to my dream lover?'

'Despite the dream lover being such a bloody disappointment.'

'Stop that,' I tell him, a bit more sharply than I intended.

'I just want you to be happy.'

'And I want the same for you, don't I, you daft old fool. *I'm* all right, but I want you to come out and see a bit of the island with me. Or at least the town. It's beautiful, Harold, and you've always loved driving around new places, exploring the countryside. It seems such a shame . . .'

'You go and explore, Ruby,' he says, looking wretched. 'You can tell me all about it.'

I'm torn between thinking, Yes, all right – sod it! I will go and look round – no point both of us missing out, and wanting to stay with Harold, keep him company, stop him from being miserable all on his own.

'Go on,' he says again, more insistently, picking up his book as if to show me he doesn't need me. 'Please, love. Take the camera. Take some pictures for me.'

Sighing, I get up, kissing the top of his head briefly.

'I'll just walk round the town for an hour, then. If you're absolutely sure you won't join me?'

'I'm sure. See you later.'

I'm staring out at the sea as I walk along, swinging my arms, humming to myself.

Don't worry, be happy.

Easier said than done. I *should* be happy, I know. But I can't help wanting Harold back the way he used to be – strong, cheerful, full of energy – before Jeannie was ill. He can't go on like this for ever.

Jeannie always managed to be happy, no matter what. Or perhaps it was more a case of her managing to *look* happy. For our sakes. She certainly never looked well. Even as a child, she was always slender and delicate – like a fragile plant, striving towards the sun. She was only twenty when she married Harold, and by the time they'd been married five years she'd had two miscarriages. She didn't seem to be able to conceive again, and Harold told me privately that although he'd have liked children, Jeannie's weakened state of health was of far more concern to him. Losing the babies seemed to have taken what little strength she had. It was as if she was fading away in front of our eyes. She saw various doctors, had batteries of tests, but they didn't find anything significantly wrong with her, concluding she was depressed and exhausted, and prescribing anti-depressants, rest and relaxation.

'I'm taking her away, Ruby,' Harold decided. 'She needs a change of scenery. Somewhere with a bit of sunshine and stimulation for her mind. I was thinking about a cruise.'

I'd been reading a novel set on a cruise boat on the Nile, and was captivated by the romance and mystery of it. I talked to a travel agent in London and showed Harold the itinerary.

'This looks just the thing!' he said enthusiastically. 'I'll talk to Jeannie about it. I'm sure it'll give her the boost she needs. Take her out of herself.' He stopped and looked at me. 'I don't suppose you'd come with us, would you, Rube?'

My heart lurched and swooped until I had to wrap my arms around my chest to stop the pain. I told myself he was only inviting me because he needed help in caring for my poor sister, but I knew from the look in his eyes that it was more than that. He wanted me around – as much as I wanted to be around him. I should have said no. It was an impossible situation: he was my sister's husband. I was already suffering; I'd been suffering ever since I met him, but at least I had my own life, my own work now, to keep me busy and occupy my mind. Being with them for two weeks was going to make it so much harder: for both of us. But I couldn't – I couldn't say no to him. I never have been able to.

We flew out to Luxor early the following March. From the moment we arrived, we were enchanted. The bustling streets where cars vied with donkeys, laden with bundles of straw and being led by men in djellabahs and turbans; the barefoot children running through the crowds, smiling and dusty in the baking hot sunshine; and then, confronting us like a mirage as our bus turned a corner – the majestic Nile, gleaming and mysterious like a silver-green ribbon stretched out across the land. Our cruise boat was a floating hotel, equipped with every luxury. I had a single cabin next to Harold and Jeannie's. We ate our first huge three-course meal in the sumptuous dining-room with all the other passengers, and Jeannie, who'd picked at her food with a great pretence at enjoying it, immediately retired to their cabin, tired out from the journey. Harold and I stood on deck, looking into the darkness at the lights of Luxor beyond. In the bar the other passengers were buying drinks and getting to know each other. There was music playing and the sounds of laughter and conversation floated out to us on the chilly night air.

'Are you getting cold?' said Harold eventually. 'We should go inside.'

'Yes. I think one of the tour guides is going to give us an introductory talk. It's a pity Jeannie's missing it.'

'I'll make notes and tell her in the morning,' he said with a smile of resignation that suddenly caught at my heart.

'Are you OK?' I blurted without thinking.

'Yes.' He looked back at me calmly, unsurprised. 'Jeannie and I have been married for five years, Ruby, and she still means the world to me. I love her,' he added in a whisper.

'Of course. I know you do. So do I.'

'But. . . but you and I. . .' He tailed off, staring back into the darkness beyond the river. 'There's something . . .'

'You and I,' I said, standing up straight and finding a strength and determination I didn't realise I possessed, 'will look after Jeannie, Harold. That's what we've come here to do.'

'And that's what I'll *always* do,' he added, turning back and shepherding me into the warmth of the bar. 'But I'm glad you're here too, Rube.'

The cruise was too much for Jeannie. It was my fault: I hadn't realised how much rushing around it was going to entail. She came on a couple of the trips with us: to the tombs of the Valley of the Kings, and to the Temple of Edfu. She held on to Harold's arm and walked listlessly, dragging her feet and blinking in the bright sunshine as our guide, Ibrahim, told us stories of Ancient Egypt that I was going to remember for ever afterwards. We kept her in the shade as much as possible, let her sit, rest and drink whenever we could, but still, by the third day, she'd decided she'd had enough. The option of lying under a parasol on the warm deck, reading a book and sipping lemonade, was more appealing for her.

'But *you* mustn't miss seeing the other temples!' she told Harold firmly. 'Ruby will stay and keep me company – won't you, Rube?'

'Of course I will,' I said at once. 'Harold will take photos for us, and come back and tell us all the stories.'

And so I sat with Jeannie, watching over her, worrying over her, while Harold went with the rest of our tour group to Kom Ombu temple, and visited the High Dam at Aswan. He wandered amongst the stalls of the Aswan bazaar and brought us back gifts – gold Key of Life earrings for Jeannie, a silver and blue Eye of Horus on a chain for me. The next trip was an evening visit to the island of Philae for the sound and light show at the Temple of Isis.

'You go too, Ruby,' said Jeannie suddenly as Harold was putting on his warm fleece ready for the short trip in the cool evening air. 'Please. You're missing everything because of me.'

'That's OK. I don't mind. I'm not leaving you on your own.'

'But I won't be on my own. Look – lots of people are missing this trip. It's an optional one, they can visit Philae during the day instead. I've been talking to Sandra: she's staying on the boat tonight. We'll keep each other company.'

Sandra was a formidable divorced lady of about forty who was travelling alone. She was very friendly and outgoing, but also very overweight and was finding the heat exhausting. She'd apparently decided to rest for the evening, hoping to be fit for the next day.

'Go on, you two, and enjoy yourselves,' she boomed at Harold and me. 'Jeannie and I have lots to talk about.'

I never knew what she found to talk about to our poor pale, sickly Jeannie, but she seemed to enjoy Sandra's company and the following morning they both opted to stay on board again, while we set off for a felucca ride on the river.

'I'd probably sink the bloody thing as soon as I set foot on it,' laughed Sandra, looking distrustfully at the dainty little sailing boats queuing up for passengers.

We were never alone together, Harold and I, even though Jeannie stayed on the boat with Sandra for most of the rest of the cruise. Our vindication was that she seemed happier and more rested that way. Everywhere we went there was Ibrahim, telling us about the history and the magic surrounding each beautiful place, and there were all the other tourists with their cameras and guide-books. To be honest, I was grateful for that, and I think Harold was, too. Being too close, for too long, would probably have tipped us over the edge of what we both knew was a dangerous, unmentionable precipice.

Jeannie relaxed and enjoyed the sunshine and the views of the fields of Egypt, the mud-hut villages and waving children, as we cruised down the river and back up again to Luxor. At meals she ate very little but always with the same pretence at enjoyment that had us fooled, and we all toasted each other in sparkling wine and promised we'd do the cruise again when her health had improved. I met Harold's eyes then, and saw the sadness and fear in them, and had to look away again quickly.

The last trip was to the mighty Temple of Karnak, built twenty centuries before Christ and dedicated to Amun, King of the Gods. Under a blazing sun we strolled to the entrance down an amazing avenue of sphinxes with the heads of rams and wandered through the giant pillars, cameras aiming always upwards at the pictures and hieroglyphics, so amazingly fresh and intact as if they'd been carved only a few years before. Outside the temple again, Ibrahim called the group together and pointed out to us a huge statue of a scarab beetle. He explained that the scarab was sacred to the Ancient Egyptians and that there was a superstition that if you walked the right way round the statue three times you would have good luck. Seven times round it, and you'd find love; nine times, you would have a child. He joked with us that he didn't know which was the right way round – but that it was probably safest to follow the crowd!

I glanced at Harold's face as we joined the throng and began to walk round the statue. I didn't want to ask him how many times he intended to make the circuit. He'd already found love, of course, but the thought of having a child was a cruel sadness to him.

'Let's stop after three,' he said quietly to me, taking my hand and giving it a squeeze. 'Whatever else happens, we need some good luck, don't we? Let's not give the gods too hard a time of it!'

He didn't let go of my hand straight away. And when he did, he squeezed it gently first and looked at me with some sort of apology in his eyes.

'I've enjoyed our time together,' was all he said.

'Me too.'

We both knew there was more to say – but that to say it would be dangerous. It would bring things to the surface that our loyalty and love for Jeannie couldn't allow.

I've still got the Eye of Horus necklace. I don't wear it all the time but I take it out and look at it occasionally, and I remember every day of that holiday, as clearly as if it were yesterday.

I'm not even aware that I'm daydreaming about it now until a sudden shout interrupts my thoughts.

'Signora Ruby!' It's the young waiter, Luciano, waving his arms at me as he runs to catch me up. 'You are all alone again!' he says as he falls into step beside me. 'The 'usband is still sick?'

'Yes. A little. He's getting better,' I add, more in hope than certainty. 'How are you, Luciano? Not working at the restaurant today?'

'I have a break. We finish the lunch, and I have a break before we begin the dinner.'

'I see. So you go home for a while?'

174

'Home? My home is too far, Signora Ruby – in Pescara, in *Italia*. Here in Korčula, I live in a room behind the restaurant. But is not my home. You understand?'

'Of course I do. You must miss your family.'

'I miss very much my mother, and my sisters and cousins. The restaurant, it is owned by my Uncle Mario and he is very good to me. I earn good money and send home to my mother. In my break I go to town to meet my friend who works at the big 'otel there.'

'Your girlfriend?' I say, smiling at him.

'Of course not! I do not have a girlfriend. One day, I hope . . . but I am afraid this will never happen.'

'I'm sure it will! There must be many young girls coming to your restaurant who would like to go out with you!'

He turns his solemn, beautiful eyes on me and smiles sadly.

'I do not like the young girls. I am not this sort of a man who is fooled by the giggling and the – how you say? – the eyelashes. These girls are empty in the head. They talk of nothing but the television and making the sex with strangers.' He shakes his head. 'My mother and my sisters would be ashamed to hear them talk.'

'That sort of talk is considered acceptable now, Luciano,' I say, thinking him oddly old-fashioned. 'But not all girls are like that.'

'If there are girls who are not like this, then they do not come on the 'oliday to Korčula,' he insists, 'or they do not come to my restaurant. This is why, when I meet a beautiful lady like Signora Ruby, I am – how you say? – I am overwhelmed by my feelings.'

'Now you're being absurd!' I say, laughing out

loud at his ridiculous flattery. 'I'm old enough to be your grandmother!'

'Age is not important. What is important, it is your *soul*.'

'My soul? Goodness.' I'm feeling slightly bothered by this conversation now. I'm not in the habit of discussing my soul with beautiful Italian boys who walk with me, uninvited, in the sunshine.

'Your soul is beautiful, I think, Signora Ruby. Like your beautiful name. I think your 'usband, he should not be feeling sick to be on 'oliday with such a beautiful wife. He should be 'appy and singing like the birds.'

'Well, Luciano, I don't think I need to discuss my husband's happiness or his illness with you, so if you don't mind, I'm going to leave you now ...'

'Oh! Signora, forgive me, I have offended you,' he says, stopping dead in his tracks and looking distraught.

'No, you haven't. I just don't feel in the mood for talking, so if you don't mind ...'

'I have! I have offended, with my stupid talk, my stupid words!' He claps his hand to his head dramatically. People are staring at us as they pass. 'My tongue – how you say? – it runs away with my words! I am a fool! I am an ass, a donkey, a sheep!'

'All right, no need for all that.' I'm trying not to laugh now.

'A dog! A goat!'

'OK, Luciano. Enough with the animals! Let's just leave it, please.'

'But I am unforgivable! I am a beast with no heart, to insult your poor 'usband, who is lying on his bed, sick, fevered, maybe even now close to his death!'

'Yes, well, let's hope not. You haven't insulted me

176

or offended me, but I really am going to leave you here or I won't get to the town and back before he starts to worry about me.'

I walk away, quickly, before he can come up with any more melodramatics. I daren't even look round, for fear of seeing him prostrate on the ground, weeping. Ridiculous boy! But I'm smiling despite myself as I climb the steps up to the old town to begin my sightseeing. Ridiculous, yes, but I can't deny it's brightened up my day. Maybe I'll tell Harold about it later and make him laugh. I need so badly to hear him laugh again.

	S	M	T	W	T	F	S
June					1	2	3
	4	5	6	7	8	9	10
	11	12	13	14	15	16	17
	18	19	20	21	22	23	24
	25	26	27	28	29	30	

Gemma

Jo's OK. Thank God.

Mark brought her back from hospital this morning – they arrived just as we were coming down for breakfast, very late because I had such a raging hangover. I was so relieved to see her looking better.

'Did they look after you well at the hospital? Did they rehydrate you straight away? Did they check the baby?'

'Gemma,' Andy warned me, 'I'm sure the doctors knew what they were doing.'

'Yes, they were marvellous,' Jo said. 'They only kept me in as a precaution. I was so worried because the baby didn't seem to be moving – but they explained that he would have been exhausted by the heat, too, because his temperature is always one degree Celsius higher than mine, and once I cooled down, he started to jump around again. I'm fine

178

now, honestly. Don't all look so worried!'

'She certainly had *me* worried,' says Mark, who looked like he was about to collapse with relief and fatigue.

'With good reason, for once,' Jo said. She was looking at him with something surprisingly close to gratitude and affection. 'The doctor said that if it had developed into full-blown heatstroke, I could have had convulsions and might have gone into premature labour.'

'I'm so glad you're all right, anyway.'

'Thanks, Gemma. Are *you* OK? You look really pale . . .'

It's my own fault, of course. I'd already had too much to drink yesterday afternoon, and then we decided to try out the bar in the tower in the evening. It was easy enough to find. It's in one of the towers on the town walls, but during the day, unless you knew about it being a cocktail bar, you'd just assume it was an old building, take its photo and walk on. At night, though, it's a different story, and we knew we were at the right place by the people gathering outside, looking up and chatting excitedly about going in.

We didn't really know what the big deal was until we got inside. It was pretty small and there didn't seem to be any seats downstairs – just the bar. A couple of English guys in front of us were climbing a ladder which looked like it was leading straight through a hole in the roof.

'Come on, Dave!' one of them called to his mate, who was waiting at the bottom. 'I think you'll be all right!'

I could see what he meant. Dave was a very large man, who looked extremely worried about squeezing through the hole at the top.

'Do we have to go through there, mate?' Andy asked him.

'Yeah, it's the only way if you want to sit up there and have a drink!' He heaved his considerable bulk up the ladder and, encouraged by the shouts of his friends, finally forced himself somehow through the gap at the top, leaving Andy and me below, staring up.

'Up you go, then!' said Andy cheerfully. 'Can't be any harder than it was for him!'

I can't say it was easy. The ladder was steep, and the gap at the top didn't seem to look any bigger as we got higher and closer. But once we'd scrambled through – what a sight! There were views all over the rooftops of the old town, and out across the bay. The top of the tower wasn't huge, but there was seating all round the edge, and some in the middle. We were lucky enough to get a couple of seats from some people who were just leaving – so we sat at the edge, leaning against the parapet.

'Please don't say we have to go back down to get our drinks,' I said to Andy. 'I'd never be able to climb up that ladder with a Piña Colada in one hand!'

'Would you like some drinks?' asked a very good-looking guy in a bright yellow T-shirt as soon as the words were out of my mouth.

'Oh – yes, please, mate.' Andy looked around in surprise. 'There isn't a bar up here too, is there?'

'No. I send the order down,' said the barman without further explanation. He wrote our drinks order on a piece of paper, and we watched in fascination as he pegged it to a wire basket which he then attached to the cable of a pulley on the side of the tower. He lowered this down, and a few minutes later it was winched back up again from below with our drinks inside the basket.

'Brilliant!' exclaimed Andy.

'It's certainly different,' I agreed, and as we sat back happily together, our arms round each other, to enjoy the sight of the sun setting over the sea, it felt suddenly like all our recent misunderstandings had been just an unpleasant dream.

I'd polished off several cocktails by the time she arrived with her mates. Wouldn't you just know it? Bloody Caroline, sliding through the hatch with her sleek blonde hair glittering like her serial silver chains, her perfect boobs barely contained in a little black strapless top, her skin-tight cropped jeans moulded like a second skin to her skinny thighs and pert bum. I had to take deep breaths to stop myself from running over and pushing her back down the ladder.

'I take it you've noticed who's just joined us,' I said caustically to Andy, who was gaping at her like a sexually repressed schoolboy. 'Better close your mouth — you'll get one of her false tits in your face as she walks past.'

'Don't be so hostile, Gemma,' he said, sighing. 'I'm just as gutted as you are that she keeps turning up everywhere we go.'

Too late for further discussion, she'd seen us.

'Well, *hello* again, Andrew darling!' she gushed, almost shoving one of her friends over the parapet in her haste to get to us. 'Hello, um, Jemima,' she added without even looking at me.

'Gemma. It's Gemma,' I snapped.

She gave me a pitying smile as if I was a five year old wanting her own way — and then, touching Andy's arm gently, purred at him flirtatiously, 'Darling, I'm so glad you're here!' as if the tower was her own private villa and we were there at her personal invitation.

'I've been *hoping* we'd bump into each other again!'

Andy, beginning to go pink, shrugged awkwardly, gave a feeble smile and looked like he didn't know where to put himself.

Right! I'd had enough.

'I can't think why,' I said coldly. 'From what Andy's told me, you hardly parted on the best of terms.'

'Oh!' She let out a silly, high-pitched girly giggle. 'Just a *little* misunderstanding, wasn't it, Andrew?'

'Telling lies about him? Ruining his reputation? I'd hardly call that a misunderstanding, Caroline.'

'Oh, really, Andrew!' she said coyly, waggling her boobs at him. 'Come on, you know it was all just a bit of fun.'

'Fun!' I tried to stand up so that, even if I couldn't exactly square up to her statuesque six-foot frame, I'd at least be within punching distance – but Andy held me back.

'Leave it, Gemma,' he said quietly. 'Let's just go.'

'No, Andy.' I rounded on him now. 'Why should we *just go* when we're here enjoying a nice romantic drink on our *honeymoon*, just because this *bitch* wants to make trouble and spoil everything!'

There was a shocked hush all around us. I'd raised my voice louder than I intended. Caroline looked back at me with big eyes, blinking fast, a picture of wounded innocence.

'Are you OK, Caro?' asked one of her cronies, leaning through the crowd to tap her on the shoulder. 'Is everything all right?'

'Yes, absolutely fine, Felicity,' she replied, smoothing her hair back from her face. 'Jemima, I don't know *why* you're being so aggressive towards me, but I can only assume it's some sort of a silly jealousy thing, which I suppose, in the circumstances, is quite understandable.' She looked straight at me for the first time and gave me a deceptively sickly-sweet smile. 'Don't worry, darling, it was only a little *fling*. I don't normally do it with freelance photographers. So frightfully *obvious* and *suburban*.'

'You didn't *do it* with him at all, you lying cow! He didn't want you! That's why you tried to wreck his career!'

'Gemma . . .' Andy tried again to stop me, but I was on my feet this time.

Caroline looked at me disdainfully, a cruel smirk on her face.

'Is that what he told you?' She laughed, shook her head and turned to Andy. 'Why don't you tell little Jemima the truth, Andrew darling – go on. Tell her how we made out at my flat after that long boozy lunch we had together. How you begged to see me again after I finished with you – kept on pestering me for more because, basically, it was better than what you were getting at home . . .'

My hand was raised to slap her but Andy gripped my wrist, forcing me away from her. His face was white, anger making his teeth clench in a snarl. I'd never seen him like that. It shocked me even more than Caroline's terrible allegations.

'I don't know what your problem is, Caroline,' he hissed, his face inches away from hers, 'but I think you need help.'

Still holding my wrist, he pulled me towards the hatch.

'Let's go,' he said, curtly, turning round and beginning the backward descent down the steep ladder.

'Why should *we* be forced to . . .?'

'Let's just *go*, Gemma!' he retorted, so sharply that I followed him down without another word.

We went straight to another bar on the edge of the town. I was already half pissed from the cocktails, on top of the wine I'd drunk at lunch, and we both proceeded to down enough beer to float home on.

'Please, just tell me it isn't true,' I said, before I became incapable of rational speech.

'She's a vicious lying cow,' said Andy, still sounding angry. He covered my hands with his on top of the table and added, much more gently, 'You know I love you, Gem. I've never loved anyone else. I swear it on my life.'

I wanted to believe him. I was trying desperately to blot out of my mind all the stuff Caroline said about having sex with him. And the quickest way to do it was to get totally slaughtered.

I don't feel too good at all today. I couldn't eat any breakfast, and even watching Andy eating made me feel nauseous.

'I thought we'd get the boat over to Badija today,' he said, munching cheerfully on his toast.

Badija is the nearest of the little islands off the coast of Korčula, and we've been promising ourselves all week that we'd have a trip. All that's there, apparently, is a monastery, so it would be a nice quiet day, away from everyone. But I can't face a boat trip today.

'Just looking at the sea is making me feel like throwing up. Sorry, but I think I need to lie down in the shade and drink water all day.'

'OK – no problem, we'll go tomorrow. Shall we just sit by the pool, then? Or will the swimming pool make you feel sick too?' he teased.

'Not unless there are waves in it. Oh, God, I just need to lie down, Andy . . .'

'Come on, then, you drunkard, you. Just can't handle it, can you!'

Now, I've been asleep under a sun umbrella for a couple of hours and I'm feeling a bit more human. I've actually eaten a sandwich and drunk some orange juice. I'm not touching any alcohol again — possibly not ever.

'Yeah, right!' laughs Andy when I tell him this. 'I've heard that before!'

'I wouldn't have drunk so much last night if it hadn't been for *her*.'

'I know.' Andy's face darkens. 'But let's not talk about her any more. She's not worth it.'

I look away and sigh. We've been over and over this, last night and this morning. It's not helping. I know he's right — we both need to put bloody Caroline out of our minds and try not to let her get to us. But it's easier said than done.

'OK if we join you?'

Jo and Mark are looking for chairs in the shade too.

'Of course! Come and sit with us. You look a lot better now, Jo,' says Andy warmly. 'In fact, I'd say Gemma looks a lot worse than you do!'

We chat for a while and end up telling them all about the bar in the tower, including the incident with Caroline.

'Blimey, what a mega-bitch,' says Jo. 'Sounds like she's still really got the hots for you, Andy!'

'What makes you say that?' I'm bristling, despite myself.

'She wouldn't bother keeping on with those lies and trying to make trouble between the two of you other-wise.' She raises an eyebrow at me. 'Are you jealous?' she asks softly.

'Not so much jealous as annoyed,' I admit. 'I know I shouldn't let her wind me up, but how dare she flirt with him like that in front of me!'

'Don't worry, Gemma,' Jo says kindly, putting her hand over mine. 'Any fool can see Andy's crazy about you. You haven't got anything to worry about there. *She's* probably jealous of *you*!'

'Fancy a walk into town?' says Andy a bit later, as Jo and I are still deep in conversation. We've progressed through her hospital treatment, to pregnancy, babies' names, and how important it is to breastfeed, so I suppose he's getting a bit bored listening to us. 'I want to have a look in that shop that had some English books for sale. I haven't got anything left to read.'

'No – if you don't mind, love,' I answer, 'I think I'll just stay here and keep cool today. I might have a swim in a minute.'

'I'll come with you, Andy,' offers Mark, 'if Gemma doesn't mind keeping Jo company for a little while?'

I'm expecting Jo to snap that she's not an invalid and doesn't need nursemaiding, but she just smiles back at Mark and says: 'OK. Don't be too long.'

'I won't. And you stay in the shade, OK? And keep drinking plenty of water. Will you make sure she does, Gemma?'

'Of course.' I look at Jo again, waiting for the retort about being perfectly capable of looking after herself – but she's still smiling at him as if being fussed over is exactly what she wants.

'It must have frightened you,' I say when the guys have gone, 'collapsing like that and being rushed into hospital.'

'Yes. It did. I was so scared I was going to lose my

186

baby, Gemma.' She pats her stomach lovingly. 'I think if that happened, I'd just give up altogether.'

'Don't say that. You're still so young – all your life ahead of you, as they say.'

'I know. I should feel grateful for what I have. And I do, now – more than ever. Since that scare, I've realised how lucky I am, with Mark.'

'He does seem like a really good guy.'

'Yes. And I do appreciate how much he cares about me. How much he wants to look after me and the baby. I'm going to try much harder now, not to be so irritable and grouchy with him. He doesn't deserve it.'

'Maybe not, but I think you're entitled to be a bit grouchy when you're pregnant!'

'Hopefully you'll find out for yourself one day soon.' She looks up at me, frowning slightly. 'Sorry – have I said the wrong thing, Gemma? Am I getting on your nerves, talking about babies all the time?'

'No, of course not!' I smile at her. 'I'm trying to keep off the subject at the moment with Andy, that's all. I don't want to sound like I'm obsessed with the whole issue of having a baby. He's right – I do tend to make all the decisions, and we need to discuss this one a bit more. It's just that he's been a bit strange, talking about going backpacking in Australia and all sorts of stuff we never wanted to do before.'

'I expect he's just got cold feet about having a family. Making excuses to put it off.'

'Probably!' I laugh again, a little uneasily. 'I wondered if the stress of the wedding has got to him.'

'Or perhaps he's just upset by all this stuff with that Caroline bird.'

'Yes. I wouldn't be surprised. God! *Why* did she

have to turn up here in Korčula at the same time as us!'

'Because life does that,' says Jo, with a philosophical shrug. 'Just when you think everything in the garden is lovely, it all turns brown and mouldy.'

'You don't know much about gardening, do you?' I say, giving her a grin.

'No, but I sure as hell know about life going brown and mouldy!'

We spend the rest of the afternoon chatting and we're laughing together like best old buddies when Mark comes back – without Andy.

'He couldn't find any decent English books in that shop, so he was going to go on and try somewhere else.'

'I don't think there *is* anywhere else.'

'Nor do I. But he wanted to look around, so I said I'd leave him to it. I didn't want to abandon Jo for too long.'

'Thanks, babe,' she says quietly, giving him another smile.

Thanks, babe! Christ. Things *are* looking up between them! A week ago, it wouldn't have surprised me if she'd decked him for being so over-protective. Now it looks like he can't do any wrong. Maybe some good has actually come out of the whole heat exhaustion scare.

I've had a swim, got a drink, and I'm beginning to think about going in for a shower when Andy finally turns up.

'Where have you *been*?' I ask him.

'Looking for a book.' He glances at Mark and adds, 'Didn't Mark tell you?'

'Yes, but where? Where was the shop? Vela Luka?'

He laughs. It's a strange, false laugh, and immediately I'm looking at him, wondering what's going on.

'Anyway, I couldn't find one,' he says with a shrug, sitting down next to me.

'A book, or a shop?'

'Either. Never mind. I'll read one of yours.' He picks up my girlie romance paperback and reads the blurb on the back, avidly, as if it's exactly what he's been looking for.

'Andy – are you trying to be funny? What's up? Where *did* you go to look for a book? There aren't any more shops around here selling them, are there?'

'No. Strange, that. I discovered the same thing!' He gives that silly false laugh again. 'Anyway – want a beer, anyone? I'm gasping!'

We all watch him as he heads for the bar.

'Seems a bit jumpy,' comments Mark.

'Maybe he's gone and bought you a surprise present, Gemma,' says Jo. 'He's got that look about him.'

'Hm.' He's got a look about him, that's for sure. And if I didn't know him better, do you know what I'd think it was? The look of a guilty conscience.

'I'm just going in to use one of the computers,' says Jo, getting up. 'Want to check my e-mails.'

'Still not heard back from your mum?' asks Mark.

'No.' She frowns. 'I've left messages on her phone, but she can't always check it while she's at work – she spends a lot of time in meetings. So I sent her an e-mail this morning. I just don't want her to keep worrying.'

'Jo made me phone her mum while she was in hospital,' Mark explains when she's gone. 'She was a bit delirious and kept on crying for her. I was frantic with worry. One of the nurses asked if she wanted to contact her mum, and she cried even more. "Yes, yes, I want my mum, I want my mum." In the end, the nurse said it would be better to call her and let Jo hear her voice on the phone – it might calm her down.'

'And did it?'

'Eventually, but her poor mum must have been scared out of her wits. I took the phone afterwards and told her to please not panic, I was sure everything was going to be OK, and I promised we'd let her know as soon as Jo was out of hospital. It's fine – I'm sure she will have picked up the e-mail by now.'

'Poor thing.' I look at him carefully. 'Her parents must have been really worried about her recently, one way and another.'

'Yes. But they're lovely people, her mum and dad. I can't tell you how grateful I am to them – they've welcomed me into the family as if Jo and I had been a regular couple for ever, like you and Andy.' He smiles at me. '*Your* folks must be like one big happy family, I should imagine, with the length of time you two have been together!'

I'd like to say this is true. OK, Andy's parents are great: I get on really well with them but, try as I might, I can't bring myself to get really *close* to them. Andy's an only child and I think Eleanor, his mum, would have liked a daughter. Sometimes she makes little hints to me about going shopping or to see a girlie film, and I know I ought to suggest we do those things together. She'd love it, and to be honest I'd probably love it too, but how can I do that? How can I build up some sort of pseudo-mother-and-daughter relationship with Eleanor, when I haven't even got that sort of bond with my own mum?

'Not really,' I tell Mark, trying to sound unconcerned. 'I don't see my dad. And my mum's kind of tied up with my younger sister most of the time.'

'That's a shame,' he says, looking genuinely sad.

'I know.' I swallow hard and look away, smiling my thanks at Andy as he comes back and puts a glass of orange-and-lemonade down in front of me.

I'd like nothing better than to have a nice happy family like Mark suggested. But that's not exactly going to happen now, not after all this time, so there's no point worrying about it.

Jo

While I'm waiting for this hotel computer to connect to the internet I'm leaning back in my chair, resting my hand over the baby's shape in my tummy, feeling him shifting around, stretching his little arms and legs, and imagining him, in four and a half months' time, kicking his legs like this when he's lying in his pram. Or in my lap. When I can look down at him and think: So here you are. The relief, when I felt him moving again after that terrible scare, was so overpowering I still feel shaky just thinking about it. My baby. I don't think I realised before just how much I want him. It's stronger than anything I've ever felt before. Yes, even stronger than my feelings for Ben.

That's a shock. I realise I've hardly even thought about Ben today. Maybe this is how it happens. First I might manage one whole day without thinking about him. Then perhaps I'll get through a night without dreaming about him. And eventually, surely to God, I'll suddenly realise I haven't given him a thought for a whole week. I suppose, like any addiction, you have to really want to get over it before you can begin to: and right now, that's what I want. I want to be free of it – this hopeless longing and misery. And then I can try to fall in love with Mark. It can't be that hard, surely, to fall for someone good, and kind, and decent, instead of hankering after a complete bastard who treated me like shit.

The internet connection finally fires up and I call up my e-mail. Thank goodness, there's a reply from Mum, from her work e-mail, her relief flooding out to me through cyberspace.

Dad and I were looking up flights last night. We were going to come straight over if we hadn't heard everything was all right today. Are you sure you'll be OK now? I'll call you later, darling, when I get home. xxxx

I send her another quick reply, reassuring her again that the baby and I are fine now and that Mark's looking after us brilliantly. I feel a strange little warm sensation as I type this, and realise I'm smiling to myself. And then I check the rest of my e-mails. And there's one from Ben.

There's so much spam in my Hotmail account, I didn't even notice it this morning, lurking between an offer of cheap Viagra and a fake banking message. It was sent three days ago. As I click to open it, I notice my hand's shaking. Bugger.

Joby. Even reading his special name for me makes my legs feel weak. *Joby, I've been a complete idiot. It was just such a shock – you know? – about the baby. I couldn't think straight. I didn't know how to cope with the situation. I was worried, if Leanne finds out about the baby, I might lose my kids. I didn't know what to do and I ended up doing the worst thing of all – turning my back on you, my Joby, my darling. What have I done? Now you're with Mark and, baby, I'm sorry but he's just not right for you! You know that, you must know that. He's not me. You can't tell me you've got anything with him – not anything like the love, the passion, you and I shared? We had something so good, baby. So special! Please don't tell me I've lost you now because of a few rash words, in the heat of the moment ... I didn't mean any of it – it was just the shock. I still love you, Joby. I miss you, I want you back. Please come back to me. We'll make a go of it somehow. You must know we were meant to be together. I'll be waiting, baby. Always, Your Ben xxxxxxx*

As I scroll down the screen, it's not just my hand that's shaking. I'm trembling like a leaf. And I know I can't resist replying.

I'm lying on the bed when Mark comes up to the room, looking for me.

'There you are!' he says, frowning anxiously. 'Are you OK? You don't feel ill again, do you?'

'No, I'm fine,' I say without moving, my eyes half-closed.

'Did you get an e-mail from your mum?'

'Yes.'

He looks at me uncertainly.

'Is everything all right?'

'Yes!' Sighing, I lift my head and look back at him. 'Sorry. Didn't mean to snap. I'm just tired, OK?'

'OK.' He still looks worried. 'Do you want me to close the curtains? Get you some water?'

'No. No – sorry, Mark, but please just leave me alone for a little while.'

'All right, then.' He turns and tiptoes out, closing the door very softly as if I was a baby myself and he'd taken an hour to rock me to sleep.

193

As soon as he's gone, I turn on to my side and cry.

I'm remembering a time, soon after Ben and I started seeing each other, when I came first in the 200-metre freestyle at the county championships and broke the previous record. I wasn't expected to win: I was competing against the current record holder, a big, muscular girl with a powerful crawl arm that looked deceptively steady until she streaked past you like greased lightning in the last twenty-five metres. I'd raced against her before so I knew her form, and this time I was ready for her, paced myself better and gave her a run for her money. We were head to head until I forced the last ounce of energy from my muscles and beat her by two seconds. Ben was ecstatic. He was practically screaming from the poolside, and in the changing area afterwards he lifted me bodily off the ground, hugged me and called me his 'shining star'. Later, we made love in my little narrow bed in the student house, and he told me for the first time that he loved me. It was probably the most wonderful moment of my life.

In the early hours of the morning, I woke up to find the bed empty beside me. Ben was getting dressed quietly, in the dark, trying not to wake me.

'Why do you have to go?' I asked him sleepily, reaching out for him from the bed. 'Why do you always have to go? Why not stay till the morning?'

'Your housemates ...' he began, looking awkward.

'They won't care. They all have their boyfriends staying over. It's normal. We can have breakfast together.'

'I have to get up early for work. Sorry, Joby. Another time, yeah?'

And he bent down and kissed me, hungrily, leaving me aching for more, leaving me wanting him back. Wanting him back the next night, and the night after, and every night I could possibly get my hands on him. I trusted him so much, I was sure he had a good reason every time he had to rush off home. When I eventually found out about his wife and kids, I couldn't believe how naive I'd been. Why hadn't I guessed? Why hadn't it been obvious? Had I *wanted* to stay blind to the truth? Or had I just been so stupidly, totally besotted with him that it never occurred to me that he was lying? And by then, of course, I was in so deep I had no idea how I was going to survive – with him or without him.

Mark's suggested we should have dinner at the hotel tonight. We normally eat at Mario's next-door, or one of the other restaurants on the way into town, having tried the dinner at the hotel once and found it a bit lacking. But I'm not arguing. By the time I've crawled out of bed, taken a shower and tried to make myself look even fractionally better than I feel, I haven't got the energy to walk anywhere.

Ruby and her husband are at the table next to ours. They've already finished their main course as we sit down.

'What's for dessert?' Harold's asking the waitress – a stocky, solemn-looking woman in her thirties with sensible shoes and a too-long skirt.

'Apple, pear, ice cream, cake,' she chants automatically, without any enthusiasm.

'I think, in that case,' says Harold, 'I'd like the trifle tonight, please.'

I study the list of main courses, trying not to listen.

'Trifle?' says the waitress. 'I don't understand *trifle*.'

'It's fruit, with sponge cake and creamy topping,' says Ruby, trying to be kind, trying to deflect Harold's teasing. The poor waitress has probably put up with this every night. Why do some men think it's so clever to take the rise out of people? I like Harold, and I'm sure he's just having a bit of fun, but I think Ruby's embarrassed by it.

'Leave her alone, Harold,' she says now, gently, 'and choose your dessert.'

He shrugs, does as he's told, and the waitress comes to our table to take our order.

'Oh, hello there,' says Ruby when she notices us. 'This is a change, for you, isn't it – eating here?'

'Yes. Jo's feeling a bit too tired to go out tonight,' says Mark, patting my hand.

'I'm sure you *must* be tired, love. But thank goodness you're all right,' she says kindly. 'No more long walks in the heat for you, eh!'

'No.' I shudder, rubbing my tummy, feeling a sudden need to soothe the baby inside me in case he can hear this suggestion. 'Definitely not.'

Ruby chats excitedly to me for a while about pregnancy and childbirth, how all four of hers were different – *the first is always the worst, but my second was breach, then the third had the cord round her neck so I needed an emergency Caesarian, and the fourth came so quickly I nearly had her in the taxi* – and what plans I've made for my own delivery. Just as I'm beginning to pray fervently for a change of subject, the

196

stocky waitress comes back with their desserts.

'Trifle,' she announces, loudly and solemnly, plonking a bowl down in front of Harold.

'What?' he asks, looking amazed, as well he might. It's a large clear bowl and inside are: an apple, a pear, a piece of cake and a portion of ice cream.

'Fruit, cake, and creamy topping,' she says, imitating Ruby's instructions. 'Trifle!'

'But ...' Harold's poking in the bowl with his spoon. 'This looks just like ...'

'Apple, pear, ice cream, cake.' She nods, the ghost of a smile flitting across her face. 'Enjoy!'

As she turns to walk away, her smile suddenly breaks out into laughter. She looks back at Harold, nods again as if to confirm that he's been beaten at his own game, and calls once more: 'Enjoy your trifle, sir!'

'And to think,' says Ruby, laughing now at Harold's expression as he surveys the contents of his bowl, 'we assumed she had no sense of humour!'

We join them outside for a drink when we've finished eating.

'Just one,' says Mark. 'We won't make it late. Jo needs her sleep.'

I'm not arguing. It's not actually sleep I need – just oblivion, really. Ruby smiles at me and begins to relate some more details about the horrendously scary arrival of her third baby. When she gets to the bit where she was being wheeled into theatre with the midwife running alongside, holding the baby back inside her to stop her being strangled by her own cord, Harold nudges her gently and says: 'I think you're making Jo nervous, love.'

'Oh – silly me. Sorry, dear. Don't worry, it

won't be like that for you. I'm sure it'll all go smoothly and you'll have a beautiful baby boy before you even have time to blink. Have you got all the classes booked that you're supposed to do nowadays? My Karen went to all sorts when she had her first one. Ante-natal classes, parentcraft, exercise-in-water ... and then after the baby was born, all sorts! Mother-and-baby groups, music therapy groups, baby massage classes – can you believe it? Massage for babies – supposed to be very good for them, but the teacher told her she had to ask her baby's permission to massage him. Whatever next? Whoever heard of asking a newborn baby for his permission? How would you know if he said no? What would you do?' She glances at Harold. 'What? Oh. Am I doing it again – asking too many questions?'

We all laugh.

'That's all right, Ruby,' I tell her. 'I can't answer the questions, but I do like to hear about all your experiences – and your daughter's. Apart from the gory bits!'

'Fair enough, dear,' says Ruby, laughing again.

We all take a sip of our drinks. The air is clear and warm, even though it's after ten o'clock. More pleasant sitting here now, really, than in the heat of the day, getting scorched by the sun.

'What about you, Harold?' I ask, to be polite. 'Did you have any children – from your first marriage?'

The words are out of my mouth before I remember. This is a disastrous topic of conversation, isn't it? His previous wife was Ruby's sister, who died from some awful wasting disease. Shit. I see him flinch slightly, shift his position in his chair, and I wish I hadn't spoken.

'Sorry, none of my business. I shouldn't have

asked ...' I begin frantically, but he shakes his head and gives me a sad little smile.

'It's OK, love.' He takes a deep breath. 'I owe you both an apology, anyway, for the way I snapped your heads off the other night. You were joking about anorexia. Maybe Ruby's told you: Jeannie, my first wife, was her younger sister. She was anorexic. It started after she miscarried our first baby, but ... the doctors didn't realise what was wrong ... and neither did I.'

He hangs his head. Ruby's got her hand on his arm, immediately, protectively.

'None of us did,' she asserts. 'It wasn't such a well-known thing in those days. Everyone just thought she was weak from the miscarriage. She was so tired all the time, so sad and thin ... we knew she was depressed, but we thought she'd pick up if she got pregnant again.'

'But she lost the second baby too,' says Harold, still hanging his head. 'And she got weaker and weaker ...'

'I'm so sorry,' I say, my eyes filling up with tears. I automatically put my hand over my stomach again, feeling my baby lazily shifting inside me. I conceived him so easily, with so little thought. How awful for that poor girl, married so young, having all her energy and enthusiasm for life sucked out of her by those two miscarriages.

'Were the doctors not able to do anything?' asks Mark quietly.

Ruby shrugs. 'At first, they told us she just needed to recover her strength after losing the babies. We needed to encourage her to rest, and persuade her to eat lots of nourishing food. She wasn't eating much, but we thought her lack of appetite was just because she was so weak.'

'It probably was, to begin with,' says Harold. 'But it became a habit. It got a hold of her. It became her consuming interest – to starve herself.'

'She hid it from us,' says Ruby. 'It was years before we understood what was going on.'

'And it was my fault,' says Harold. 'Because I was never there.'

'That's total nonsense.' Ruby dismisses this in the unemotional tones of someone who's said it over and over again, for months, for years. 'You were working. You couldn't watch her twenty-four hours a day, and even if you had, you know what the doctors told us eventually – anorexics become expert at pretending to eat.'

'They told us, years later,' Harold goes on as if she hasn't spoken, 'that the best chance of treating anorexia nervosa is to detect it early on. But I didn't do that. I missed my chance of saving her.'

'I'm sure that's not true,' I say, desperately, looking to Mark for confirmation.

'No. It might not have made any difference, mate,' he says. 'Even if you'd realised what was wrong, she still might ...' He tails off, awkwardly.

'She still might not have survived,' Ruby finishes for him. 'We know that, don't we, love?' Harold doesn't respond, just gives her a tiny sad smile. 'Harold finds that hard to accept,' she says simply.

'It must have been awful for you both,' I say, still blinking back tears. 'Your wife – and your sister, Ruby.'

'Yes. We did the best we possibly could for her, though.' She says this firmly, squeezing Harold's hand with every word, as if to reinforce it in his mind. 'Once she'd been diagnosed, she was treated

200

by the best psychiatrists, in a private hospital. She was admitted many times . . . so often we thought we had it beaten, but she always relapsed after a while. She couldn't help it. And it was nobody's fault.'

'Of course not. It's an illness, isn't it? An addiction,' says Mark.

'We know that,' says Ruby. 'But . . .' She stops dead in the middle of her sentence, and frowns, staring into the darkness. 'Sorry. I thought . . . I must be dreaming. I thought I heard someone calling my name.'

'So did I!' exclaims Mark, at the same moment that I hear it too.

'*Ruby! Signora Ruby! Are you there?*'

Harold gets to his feet and stares out over the path below.

'There's some young chap down there, looking up and calling "Ruby!"' he exclaims. 'Surely can't be you, love. Must be another . . .'

'No.' Ruby's looking slightly flushed. 'No, I think it's me he's calling, Harold. Take no notice. He'll go away in a minute.'

Mark and I raise our eyebrows at each other. This is a turn-up for the books. Ruby's got a secret admirer!

'*Ruby!*' comes the shout from below again. '*I am here, Luciano, your poor stupid donkey! I 'ave come 'ere with something for you. Please, Ruby! Please to come down and see me.*'

'What the hell . . .?' says Harold, staring at Ruby as if he's seeing her for the first time. 'Who *is* this person?'

'He's that waiter from the restaurant next-door. You know, I told you, he was very attentive when I had my dinner there.'

'Attentive? He looks like a bloody lovesick Labrador!'

201

'Oh, Harold, he's all right really. Just a boy.' Ruby looks quite uncomfortable. 'He doesn't mean any harm.'

'Ruby ... please, I 've come to say I am sorry for my offence!'

'What bloody offence?' asks Harold, frowning.

'Nothing. His English isn't very good. I'll ... look, I'll just pop down and tell him to clear off.'

'I'll tell him myself.' Harold leans over the balustrade at the edge of the terrace and raises his voice. 'The lady doesn't want to talk to you, young man. I think you'd better get lost.'

Mark looks at me and I have to look away. I'm going to get the giggles in a minute.

'Are you the 'usband of Signora Ruby?' asks the waiter. He's come closer now. We can just about make out his features in the darkness below. He's very young, and very good-looking. We've seen him at the restaurant ourselves, and Ruby's quite right – he's always very attentive. He's never followed *us* to the hotel, though!

'Is that any business of yours?' asks Harold stiffly.

'Please, forgive my impropriety.' He actually gives a little bow. Harold almost takes a step back in surprise. 'Sir, I do not wish to offend. I only say to you, sir, that you are a very lucky, very 'appy man, to be the 'usband of this beautiful lady whose name is like a jewel. And I am 'ere to bring Signora Ruby a token of my deep sorrow and sincerest regret, in case I 'ave offended.'

'My wife does not wish to accept any *token* from you, young man,' says Harold.

'You haven't *offended* me, Luciano,' Ruby shouts down. 'I've already told you that.'

'So just clear off, OK? Or I'll call the manager.

Please don't come around here any more pestering my wife.' Harold's obviously trying his best to sound stern, but I don't think he's a stern kind of man, not really. It sounds about as effective as a puppy dog's bark. 'Go and look for a girl of your own age, there's a good lad.'

There's a shocked silence at this before Luciano protests vigorously: 'You think I am trying to *molest* Signora Ruby? But I am not this kind of a man!' Even from here, I can see he has his hand on his heart. 'I do not make the hanky-panky with the ladies!'

'What does he do with them, then?' Mark whispers to me behind his hand. 'Embroidery?'

'I *talked* with Signora Ruby!' he says reverently as if he's describing a religious experience. 'She comes to my restaurant, a beautiful lady all alone, and I talk to her, to make her 'appy! And she walks to the town, again all alone, and again I talk to her. But I am a donkey, a mule, a goat ... my words they are stupid – so stupid I wished to cut out my tongue!'

'Don't be an idiot, Luciano,' says Ruby, still looking pink-cheeked and awkward. 'Everything's fine. Now go along home, please, like a good boy.'

'He's not one of your bloody pupils, Rube,' says Harold, looking at her in amazement. 'He's probably one of these rampant sexual predators who prey on lonely single women at seaside resorts ...'

'But I'm *not* a lonely single woman, Harold, am I?' she says flatly.

'I am *not* one of these *ramp sex pre-daters*!' argues Luciano indignantly.

'I'm not lonely at all, Harold. I'm just not with my husband when I should be. On our honeymoon.'

'I know. I'm sorry, Rube ...'

'I think we ought to go,' says Mark, looking at me meaningfully.

'Yes. We should. We'll ... er ... leave you to it ...'

'Signora Ruby!' calls Luciano again plaintively. 'Please to come down to receive from me this token!'

'Oh, bugger off, Luciano!' shouts Ruby, suddenly losing her patience. 'I don't want any token from you!'

'She is upset,' says Luciano, addressing us as we stand up to leave, dropping his voice confidentially, 'because of the sickness of the 'usband. I understand. I will wait, with my token, until Signora Ruby is more 'appy.'

'I think you might be wasting your time, mate,' Mark tells him cheerfully.

Luciano straightens up, this time with both palms pressed to his chest. 'I will wait! I cannot live until I have made the amends for the foolishness of my words. I will wait 'ere until she is 'appy to receive my token!'

'She's going home on Sunday,' I point out.

'Come on, Jo, it's none of our business,' whispers Mark. 'We shouldn't be getting involved.'

'No. You're right. Goodnight, Ruby. Goodnight, Harold. Will you be all right?' I add as an afterthought.

'Of course we will,' says Ruby brusquely. 'Luciano's just going.'

'If you wish me to go, Signora Ruby, then I must go, like a poor dog with no master. Like a poor 'orse with no cart. Like a ...'

'Like a bloody parrot that never shuts up!' mutters Ruby. 'Come on, Harold, I think we should go to bed too, and leave him to bugger off.'

*

204

'Well, that certainly brightened things up!' laughs Mark when we get back to our room.

'Yes. Can you believe it? A young lad like that, sniffing around someone of Ruby's age?'

'She's quite an attractive woman, really,' he says, thoughtfully. 'For her age, of course. If I was Harold, I'd be wanting to keep a closer eye on her, with random toy boys like that hanging around, wanting to give her tokens!'

'I wonder what it was? The *token*?'

'I dread to think,' he says with a grin. 'Something he keeps in his trousers, probably!'

'Mark! Surely not!'

'All young guys are the same,' he says with a shrug. 'It's all they think about.'

'Really? Including you?'

'Especially me,' he says, huskily, pulling me closer and planting a kiss on my cheek. 'You have no idea.'

I turn away and head for the bathroom to clean my teeth. My heart's hammering against my ribs, but it's with anxiety rather than passion. I know it's our honeymoon. But so far, I've been using the excuse of my pregnancy ... feeling too sick ... too tired ... too worried about the baby ...

How much longer can I keep up the excuses? Mark's been incredibly patient, agreeing to wait until after we were married ... until I was feeling less sick ... until I was ready. How much longer can I expect him to do that? Until the baby's born? Until I've stopped loving someone else?

The truth is, I don't want to make love to my husband. Because I'm so afraid that when I do, I'll be thinking of Ben. I might start calling out his name. I know Mark's put up with a lot already – but I think that might just kill him.

	S	M	T	W	T	F	S
					1	2	3
June	4	5	6	7	8	9	10
	11	12	13	14	15	16	17
	18	19	20	21	22	23	24
	25	26	(27)	28	29	30	

Gemma

We're going to make the trip to Badija today. We ask Tomislav, the manager, about booking a boat.

'I will arrange this for you,' he says importantly, smoothing his comb-over and straightening his bow-tie. It's green today. He seems to have a different coloured one for every day of the week. 'The boat will collect you from the jetty here, and come back for you later. You must tell the boatman the time you wish for him to come back.'

'OK. Sounds great!' says Andy cheerfully. We're both looking forward to this trip. We've got a packed lunch from the hotel, our towels, sun cream and books, and we're going to chill out on the island as there's nothing else to do over there. Peace and quiet!

We're sitting on the jetty waiting for our boat when Jo and Mark climb out of the water.

'You're early for swimming!' I comment.

'Yes. Best time – before all the children and teenagers get in there!' laughs Jo, who's not much more than a teenager herself. She seems better today – brighter and stronger-looking somehow since she's been out of hospital – but there's something else different about her too: a kind of determination, as if she's made up her mind to be cheerful whether she wants to or not. I guess the shock of her collapse has had some sort of effect on her.

'Where are you two off to today?' asks Mark, glancing at our bags.

'Badija. We've got a boat coming for us any minute.'

'Oh – have fun. Should be a relaxing day.' He looks at Jo thoughtfully. 'Perhaps we could try it another day?'

'As long as it's not too hot!' she says, wrapping herself in her towel as if to protect herself from the elements. 'There might not be much shade over there.'

'We'll let you know,' says Andy. 'Here's our boat coming now. What are you doing tonight?'

'Nothing special. Why?'

'We found a bar along the coast here, last night, where they have live music. They do food too – pretty basic, but good. D'you fancy it?'

'What do you think, Jo?' asks Mark. 'Would you be up for that?'

'Definitely.'

Again, I get the impression she's making a supreme effort: she's going to feel better, she's going to enjoy herself, if it kills her. It's good to see her looking more positive anyway. We arrange to meet them in the hotel bar at seven-thirty, and wave them goodbye as we climb into the little boat.

It's the same boatman who brought us over to Korcula when we arrived.

'You go to Badija, yes?' he says as we pull away from the jetty.

'Yes, please. Do you take many people over there?' asks Andy.

'Some – but not so many for the island to become crowded. It is quiet there, no shops.'

'That's what we're looking forward to,' I tell him. 'A quiet day on our own.'

'You will not be so very alone,' he amends. 'Already this morning I have taken some more people. But plenty of room on the beaches.'

'Good. We don't want to have to share our picnic!' I laugh.

'It is more busy at the weekends. Then, many local people from Korčula go to Badija. Many have their own boats and take their families, for picnics on the beaches, or to fish.'

'It sounds lovely.'

'If you like to relax, you will be happy. But for many years it was different. The monastery there, it was used as an army base in the war, and afterwards as a state sports centre and a hostel. Now is again a monastery, since 2003, when it was given back to the monks.'

I wonder whether he gives this same spiel to everyone he takes over to Badija. It's good to get some local knowledge from people like this who make their living on these islands. As we make the short journey across to Badija I find myself thinking how idyllic it would be to live in this simple way: ferrying passengers from shore to shore, living perhaps in a little cottage on the coast or one of the narrow red-roofed houses in Korčula Town. I don't suppose this guy can possibly earn very much but how much does he need? Enough to feed his family, to keep a roof over their heads – that's all. Why do we spend our whole lives rushing through traffic, stressed out of our minds, never having time to stop and smell the flowers or hear the birds singing – just so that we can afford the latest new technology, or new furniture before the old is even worn out, or new clothes to stay in fashion? What's it all about? Right now I think I could trade it all, to live somewhere peaceful and beautiful like this, and bring up my family in a cottage with a sea view.

'What you thinking about, Gem? You're miles away!' teases Andy.

'Sorry! Just thinking how lovely it is here. Wouldn't it be nice if we could live here, Andy? Never go back?'

'You'd miss your job.'

'Maybe,' I concede doubtfully.

'And I'd miss my family,' he adds.

I wish I could say the same.

We can see the monastery buildings as the boat approaches Badija. It's a very small island – only one kilometre square – and we've been warned that the far side is a naturist reserve.

'But on other beaches here also,' our boatman advises us as he ties up at the jetty, 'some people like to take off all their clothes.'

'I hope we're not expected to join in,' I comment.

'No one will expect this,' he replies, taking me seriously, so that Andy has to smother a fit of laughter.

We say our farewells to the boatman, confirming the time for our pick-up this evening, and as the boat chugs off back to Korčula, we start to follow a path from the monastery, along the coast, admiring the views over the sea. There are more people here than I expected, sunbathing or swimming from the rocks. After a while we come to a white pebble beach, surrounded by pine trees, and decide to settle down here.

'Plenty of shade – it'd be OK here for Jo,' I say. And it's a good thing, too, as it's very hot again today.

We spread out our towels and head straight for the sea. The water's clear and very warm, with lots of little fish swimming close to the surface. We're enjoying our swim so much, it's a while before I become aware of a small crowd gathering on the beach.

'What's going on?' I start – and then I see them: half a dozen or so small deer, venturing out of the shelter of the trees, tempted by people's picnics. The crowd has gathered to offer them titbits from their lunches. We join them quietly, not wanting to frighten the animals away.

'Give them apples!' someone suggests. 'That's supposed to be their favourite.'

A girl comes forward out of the crowd, offering an apple to the nearest deer who accepts it greedily. The others nuzzle up to her, looking for more, and she laughs excitedly, chatting with her friends in English about how cute they are.

There's something familiar about that girl. I look from her to her companions and suddenly it comes to me.

'They're that bloody Caroline's friends,' I exclaim.

'No – I don't think so,' says Andy. But he's looking uncomfortable. He knows perfectly well it's them. He's looking around him now, probably wondering the same thing as me.

'It *is* them, Andy. For God's sake! Don't say she's here, too.'

'Shall we move to another beach?' He's looking over his shoulder, probably expecting Caroline to sneak up behind us at any minute.

'No.' The little crowd is beginning to disperse now, as the deer move away back into the woodland. The girls have retreated to the other end of the beach without noticing us. 'No, let's say here, Andy. It doesn't look like she's with them. With a bit of luck, she's fallen overboard on the way out here.'

He doesn't laugh. Even the slightest mention of Caroline seems to have cast a cloud over our day. We get our picnic lunch out of our bag and eat it in silence, staring out at the sea. I wish to God Caroline had never come here on her stupid holiday. I wish to God Andy had never met her in the first place. I can't understand why he ever wanted even to be friendly with such a nasty, vicious, vindictive bitch – but then again, he always was too trusting. Too bloody nice for his own good.

I finish my lunch and lie back in the shade, trying to read my book but finding myself, instead, going over and over the stuff Caroline was coming out with at the bar in the tower the other night. I'm *sure* she was lying. She must have been! It's still hurtful, though, to think about her allegations, her outrageous claims about having sex with Andy at her flat, and about him pestering her for more *because it was better than he was getting at home*.

I've always thought our sex life was good – but then, how would I know any different? I've never been with anyone else; only ever snogged a few boys before Andy. What if Andy actually *did* want more – or better – than he was getting with me? What if, because he didn't want to hurt me, he'd never liked to tell me that he wasn't satisfied? You can love

211

someone despite having crap sex with them, and you can have fantastic sex with someone without loving them. Apparently. Like I say, how would I know? I've nothing to go on other than what my friends tell me, and what I read in novels. I'm suddenly aware of how limited my experience is. How can I actually be sure that I'm enough for Andy? I've always thought the fact that we were each other's first and only lover was something really special. But now I'm beginning to wonder if I'd have been better off sleeping around a bit when I was younger, to learn a few tricks, make sure I was good enough before expecting someone to commit himself to me for life.

After a while I put down my book and go for another swim. I'm aware of Andy watching me from the beach, but he doesn't come and join me. I turn on my back and float, staring up at the sky, wondering what he's thinking about. Is he comparing my grace-less flailing in the water with Jo's perfect streamlined action? Or comparing my large thighs, my big bum and rounded tummy with Caroline's stunning figure? I've never doubted Andy before – never, even for a minute, suspected him of thinking about other girls. I've never before been so consumed with self-doubt. And this is our honeymoon – the one time I should be feeling secure, cherished, totally loved up and sure of our relationship. It's just not fair.

By the time I come out of the water, Andy's turned over and fallen asleep. I pick up my book again but before long I've drifted off too. I dream that I'm living in an isolated cottage overlooking a rocky beach. I'm in a kitchen, stirring things on a stove, and then dishing up meat and vegetables on to plates on a long wooden table where half a dozen or more small dark children are banging their spoons, waiting for

212

their meal. A man comes in through the door, taking off his shoes, saying something about his day's fishing. I look up, expecting even in my dream that this, the apparent father of my brood of infants, must be Andy – but it's not. It's the Croatian boatman.

'Wake up! Gem, come on – wake up. It's time to go.' Andy's shaking me, laughing as I sit up, rubbing my eyes, wondering where I am. 'You've been asleep for hours!'

'Have I? Oh – sorry. I feel totally disoriented. I was having such a bizarre dream . . .'

'Who was it? Brad Pitt? George Clooney?' he teases.

'No. Nothing like that.' I shake my head, trying to clear the images from my mind. Normally I'd have described the dream to Andy and we'd have laughed about it; but right now, I don't feel it's a good idea to tell him I've been dreaming about having a big family, in case he thinks I'm picking a fight.

'Scary dream, then?' he asks sympathetically, stroking my arm.

'No. Just odd,' I say with a shrug, looking around for my clothes.

The dream's already fading as he starts to pack the bag, his back turned to me. And not feeling able to share it with him seems so wrong, and so sad.

At the jetty, there's a group of people waiting for the regular water-taxi back to Korcula Town.

'Can't we just get on this?' I suggest when it arrives. 'It's not quite full.'

'No – we've booked our man to come back for us specially. Anyway, I think these people all have return tickets. The water-taxi picked them up from the harbour in town.'

213

The boat chugs out, leaving us standing alone at the end of the jetty.

'He's late,' I remark after a while.

'Well, there's no hurry, is there?'

'I suppose not.' I sit down and drink some water. There's silence apart from the lapping of the water on the shore. Andy checks his watch, stares out to sea, checks his watch again. Suddenly, there's a stirring on the path behind us, a rustling of leaves, the sound of voices. Caroline's three friends appear from out of the undergrowth, staring from us to the sea beyond and back to each other again.

'Shit!' exclaims one. 'We haven't missed it, have we?'

'The water-taxi?' I look back at them with dislike, purely because of their association with the dreaded bitch queen. 'Yes. It went about twenty minutes ago.'

'Shit!' she repeats, looking at her watch. 'I *told* you it was six o'clock, Felicity.'

'Oh, bugger,' says Felicity, tottering up the jetty in her silly high-heeled sandals and peering out to the horizon as if she could conjure the boat back again. 'What're we going to do?'

'Wait for the next one?' I suggest sarcastically.

'That was the last one,' says the first girl. 'I *told* you it was six o'clock,' she repeats, glaring at Felicity.

'The last one?' says Andy, who's so far avoided even looking at these girls and has been standing on the edge of the jetty, contemplating the water below as if he wanted to jump in. 'That can't be right.'

'It is,' confirms the third girl. 'They told us six o'clock, on the way out, but we've been thinking it was half-past six.'

'I *knew* it was six o'clock, Nicky,' argues the first one, again, and the other two glare at her.

'What're you two waiting for anyway?' demands

214

Felicity rudely. 'You missed the boat too?'

'No, we've got a private boat booked,' says Andy. 'Going straight back to our hotel jetty.'

'If he turns up,' I point out. 'He's twenty minutes late now, Andy.'

We all gaze out to sea again in silence.

'Well, *fuck* knows what we're gonna do,' says one of the girls, squatting down on the jetty and lighting a cigarette. 'We'll have to get a boat off this bloody island somehow. There's nowhere to stay, and I've only got two fags left.'

'Never mind about your fags, Sara,' squawks Felicity. 'We've hardly got any water left, either.'

I think about the half-bottle of water we've still got in the bag. It's pretty warm, but at least it's drinkable. I'm not offering it to these three, though – at least, not unless it becomes a matter of life and death. It won't come to that, surely, will it?

'Do you think our boatman's coming?' I ask Andy quietly. 'Why's he so late?'

I have a sudden memory of my dream – of looking up and seeing the boatman walking in at the door of that cottage; of the realisation, in the dream, that he was the father of all my children. In actual fact the only interest I have in the guy is his boat and its ability to take us back to Korčula!

'I don't know, Gem,' Andy replies, equally quietly. I don't think either of us really wants to get into any further conversation with Caroline's friends. 'But he promised to come, so I suppose he's just been held up.'

'Any chance you guys can give us a lift?' asks Sara. 'If your boat does turn up? We'll pay. Otherwise, we're stuffed.'

'Yeah – we're here for the bloody night. Camping on the beach,' says Felicity.

215

I see Andy hesitating, struggling with himself. He's just not the sort to refuse to help anyone, especially in circumstances like this, but these girls represent Caroline, even if she's not with them, and I'm sure he feels the same as me – the less we have to do with them, the better.

'It'll be up to the boatman really,' he says at last, stiffly, not looking at them. 'But if it's OK with him, then yeah, sure.'

But another twenty minutes or so pass with still no sign of our boat.

'It's not looking good,' I admit at last. 'I don't know what we can do. There's not even anyone we can phone.'

'We could try Caro,' suggests Felicity.

I bristle, and I see Andy wince and swallow hard.

'How's that supposed to help?' retorts Sara, who's looking increasingly aggressive, probably at the thought of running out of fags. 'Always supposing she's come back anyway.'

Back from where? I can't help wondering. But I don't ask because, to be honest, as long as she's not around I'd rather not talk about her.

'She can get us a boat organised, can't she!' Sara's almost stamping her feet with impatience. 'She can go to the harbour, or whatever. Get us rescued.'

'OK, I'll call her.' Felicity opens her phone and finds the number while we all hang around, waiting. Andy's still facing the sea, staring at the horizon, distancing himself. 'No reply!' she calls out after a couple of minutes. 'Shit!'

'Where the hell *is* she?' demands Sara crossly.

'Who knows?' Nicky shrugs. 'Making out with some guy, I suppose. Bloody typical.'

Andy shuffles his feet, his back still turned.

'Caro, call me ASAP,' Felicity's saying crisply to Caroline's voicemail. 'We're stranded on this poxy Banjo island–'

'Badija,' interrupts Nicky. 'It's called Badija.'

'This poxy Badi-Yah or whatever it is,' goes on Felicity. 'We're stranded, and if we don't get a boat, Caro, we'll be here all bloody night. So do us a favour, get your arse out of wherever you are, whoever you're with this time, for Christ's sake, girl, and sort something out! Call me, OK?'

She hangs up and sighs.

'She's probably turned her phone off so she can shag non-stop without any interruptions. The bitch.'

Nice way to talk about your friend, I think despite myself.

We all sit down on the jetty. I'm beginning to gasp with thirst and it's no good, I just can't do it. I can't *not* share our half-bottle of water. I haul it out of the bag, take a glug and pass it round.

'Thanks,' says Felicity. 'Want a biscuit?'

She unearths a partly crushed packet of Digestives and offers them to us. I take one and nudge Andy. It's a few seconds before he shrugs, turns around and takes a biscuit, still not looking directly at the girls.

'Thanks,' he mutters.

I think it's a grudging kind of truce. But only because bloody Caroline isn't with them.

We don't talk a lot during the next hour or so. The peace between us is too fragile to allow for confidences or anything too personal. Felicity still has her phone out and seems to be texting constantly – whether to Caroline or someone else, nobody asks. We share the rest of the biscuits and ration the water, having another couple of sips each and putting the bottle away. Sara puffs moodily on one of her last cigarettes, inhaling deeply, watching the little smoke that escapes through her nostrils drift away on the breeze.

'I think we need to start looking for somewhere to camp out,' says the girl called Nicky eventually.

'Oh, surely it's not going to come to that?' I protest, looking at Andy anxiously. 'We must be able to contact *somebody*.'

'We haven't got any numbers, Gem. Not even the hotel.'

'Well,' says Felicity, suddenly snapping her phone shut and looking round at us all, 'why don't we go and talk to the monks?' And why didn't any of us think of that before? 'They're the only people living on the island,' she adds as if we didn't know. 'They'll help us, surely.'

'Yes. You're right – of course they will,' says Andy, looking annoyed that he didn't suggest it himself.

'Even if they can only give us a phone number, to get help from Korčula, that's all we need,' I agree with relief. God, I so don't want to spend the night on the beach here, with deer sniffing round us while we're asleep and God-knows-what strange creepy-crawlies all over us. 'Come on then, what're we waiting for?'

'We can't all go,' warns Andy. 'Just in case a boat turns up.'

'We'll go, won't we, Felicity?' says Sara, who seems to have perked up now she thinks help might be at hand – although I can't believe she thinks a bunch of Franciscan monks are going to help her out with half a dozen Marlboro Lights.

'Yes – come on, girls.' Felicity leads the way, tottering on her heels, calling back to us just as they go out of sight: 'Give us a shout if a boat comes!'

Their voices fade away and silence envelops us.

'Let's sit on the grass,' says Andy at length. 'We might as well be comfortable while we wait.'

'I wonder how long they'll be,' I sigh.

'I suppose it depends whether they can make themselves understood by the monks. Always supposing the silly cows can find the bloody monastery!'

'It's right there, Andy – you can see it from here!'

'I know. But they all seem to be particularly stupid.'

I laugh. 'Yes. But I guess it's not their fault.'

'What – that they're so stupid?'

'No: that they're Caroline's friends,' I say quietly. He doesn't answer. 'They didn't seem very complimentary about her,' I point out.

'So why come on holiday with her?'

'Search me.' I take a deep breath and add, 'Why would anyone want to be friendly with her? Have lots of cosy, friendly lunches with her . . .?'

'She seemed all right then,' Andy shoots back, defensively. 'I told you, she seemed nice. She was just . . . a laugh.'

'Yes. Laugh a minute.'

'Gem, let's not go over all this again.'

'OK.' I look at his face. 'OK, sorry. I'll shut up.'

We sit in silence again. It's so dead quiet, it's spooky. I thought I'd enjoy some peace, but this is beyond peaceful: it's getting a bit scary. Where are those bloody girls? What's taking them so long?

'I spy, with my little eye,' says Andy, giving me a grin, 'something beginning with B.'

'I wish it was a bloody boat. I don't know. Beach? Bag? Bikini?'

'I can't see your bikini,' he points out. 'You've got your clothes on over it.'

'Maybe you were looking down my top, I don't know.'

'Is that an invitation?'

'Maybe,' I laugh, loosening the neckline a bit.

'Take it off, then,' he says, pulling me into his arms and yanking my shorts down.

'Andy! No – not here!' I giggle.

'Why not? It's not exactly public, is it? There's nobody on the entire island except for a handful of monks and three stupid girls who've probably gone and got lost.'

'We might have to stay here for ever,' I speculate, not minding the idea quite so much now Andy and I are cuddled up together. Now I'm getting in the mood.

'Yeah. Sounds good to me!' He rolls me, laughing, into the shelter of the trees, unfastening my bikini top at the same time.

The ground's covered with pine needles, soft and dry like a springy carpet, scenting the warm evening air.

'You're sure nobody can see?' I ask breathlessly.

'Positive,' he mutters against my ear.

I'm past caring now, anyway. And, by the time we rouse ourselves from a post-coital doze, the boatman's calling from the jetty: 'Hello! Anyone there!' And there are three screeching girls and a bunch of monks searching for us.

Ruby

I've put a blue dress on tonight, one I haven't worn before. I'm looking at myself in the mirror, straightening the neckline, which is probably a bit too low, when Harold appears behind me, looking over my shoulder at my reflection.

'You look gorgeous,' he says, kissing the back of my neck.

'Do I?' I've never really become used to compliments. 'You don't think this is a bit too young for me?'

'Absolutely not. You only look about thirty-five anyway.'

'Oh, go on with you!' I laugh. I'm not daft. All right, people have said I've got a nice face. A nice smile. My skin's always been OK. My hair's not bad. But I've got the inevitable lines, age spots, varicose veins – oh, and, of course, I'm a bit overweight, but I never mention this, never ever suggest going on a diet. 'You're only saying that 'cos you want me to buy you a drink!'

'That'd be nice.' He smiles in response. 'But I'm actually saying it because it's true, Ruby. And I'm not the only one who thinks it. You've even got lads young enough to be your grandson running around after you.'

He's mentioned this several times since the episode with Luciano last night. I'm not sure whether he finds it funny, or whether it secretly bothers him, but I'm not having a conversation about it. I don't want to accord that much importance to it.

'I'm not interested in silly young lads,' I tell Harold lightly, turning away from the mirror to kiss him back. 'I know all about their daft nonsense – I had enough of it when I was a young divorcée in Paris all those years ago. Chasing after me with their flattery and their stupid compliments. All a lot of nothing.'

'Even so,' he points out, looking at me seriously for a moment, 'it would've been better by far to end up with one of them, than with Le Cochon.'

And I can't argue with that.

I was spending a few months in a private school in Paris when I met Jean-Léon Laroche. I'd finished my degree course and Mum had offered to look after my boys for the summer so that I could get some experience, teaching English to French children. I'd only been there a week when one of the teachers asked me if I was interested in doing some extra work as a private tutor.

'It's for one of our most influential parents,' he explained. 'A very wealthy businessman – you understand? He gives very much financial assistance to the school.'

Intrigued, wanting as much experience as I could get, and obviously tempted by the prospect of some extra earnings, I agreed to meet him. He was a widower with three very spoilt children – older than my own boys – who proved to be more of a trial than any of the kids in my classes at the school. But their father was charming – to the point of being flirtatious – and very good-looking in that smooth, tanned, sophisticated way that only the extremely rich can manage.

It was actually a relief to find myself attracted to him. Because the truth was, of course, that there was more than one reason for my stay in Paris. I'd needed to put some distance between myself and Harold. Not that anything had happened, or was going to happen, but every moment in his company, and every time I set foot in my sister's house ... seeing his jacket hanging in the hall, his slippers under the chair, the indentation of his head in the cushion where he'd been sitting ... all of these were a torture to me. And I know Harold found it equally difficult whenever I was around him.

'I can't bear it, Ruby,' he'd whispered to me once as we parted with our usual chaste kiss on the cheek.

That was all I'd needed to hear. It wasn't fair, on either of us: I had to get away, if only for a couple of months.

I worked hard, often for long hours, by the time I'd done the marking and the private tutoring too, and the other young teachers at the school made me welcome. I was only in my early-thirties and it was fun to be invited out to a succession of night-clubs, parties, and even on dates with those rampant young Frenchmen, but nothing helped to free my mind of the thoughts that plagued me at night: scary, shocking thoughts of my sister's husband that eventually drove me into the arms of the one person who helped me, briefly, to escape into a different world: Jean-Léon Laroche. Apparently he was besotted with my English accent and English Rose complexion. I wasn't bad-looking in those days: blonde and petite and a lot slimmer than I am now. Almost as soon as we started sleeping together, he told me he was in love with me. It was ridiculous, and I told him so. He said he'd never met anyone like me, which was probably true – unlike his circle of admiring, simpering Frenchwomen, I was feisty, independent and not easily impressed. We hardly knew each other, and I certainly didn't love *him*.

'But I want to be always with you,' he told me in the sexy Parisian accent that was half the attraction. 'I want to marry you, Ruby.'

'*Impossible*!' I retorted in French. 'I'm going back to England in a few weeks. My sons are staying with my mother ...'

'This is of no consequence,' he said, shrugging

and smiling at the same time. 'I have also a house in England. We shall live there, with your sons. My children will be back at their boarding school in September.'

I must have been half-crazy, lost and drowning in a sea of conflicting emotions. Perhaps I merely saw it as a chance to escape from my dangerous obsession with a man I could never have. Perhaps it was just the sex – he was a good lover, eclipsing terrible memories of Eddie and the few short-lived relationships I'd had since. Maybe I was purely, cynically, attracted to his wealthy lifestyle. Or perhaps, for a while, I really did imagine myself in love with him. Whatever it was, by the time I went home to England I was engaged.

After an enormous fancy society wedding we moved into his home in Dorset. Perhaps I should say *mansion*. I had my own suite of rooms, and more money than I knew what to do with. Trevor and Richard must have thought they'd died and gone to heaven – they learnt to ride, had their own ponies, their own dogs, their own swimming pool. Jean-Léon and I were together for long enough to produce the two girls, but by the time our second daughter, Jodie, was born I'd learnt a few lessons about the so-called good life. I'd learnt that everything has its price. That men who have accumulated great wealth have usually done it by upsetting a few people along the way, and that it can become a habit not to care very much about anyone else's feelings. Getting his own way was all that mattered to Jean-Léon, and if he was thwarted – for instance, by a wife who wanted to continue working as a teacher, an idea he found demeaning, and who caused scenes about the serial affairs that he treated so casually; or by children irritating him by crying too loudly, or too often, or not doing exactly as they were told – then it soon became apparent that lashing out was second nature to him. The more we fought, the more he turned to drink. And the more he drank, the more he lashed out.

I left him after the second time he physically abused me. I'd had the baby in my arms at the time and stumbled, almost dropping her. He expected to be forgiven; expected me to go back to him after I'd cooled off. When I divorced him I found out how really nasty he could be – especially when I came out of it with a decent chunk of his wealth, enough to buy a nice house for myself and my kids and not have to struggle for the rest of my life. Not that it made up for any of it – but it sure as hell made me feel better. I've never set eyes on him since and neither have our daughters. It's no loss to any of us.

Jo and Mark are at the bar tonight when we go down for a drink before dinner.

'Hello, love,' I greet her. I'm so pleased to see her looking better – and happier, too, I must say. 'How are you?'

'Good, thanks, Ruby. Look!' She holds out her left hand to me. She's got a beautiful new wedding ring – it's either white gold or platinum, I've never really known how to tell the difference. 'We chose it together this afternoon. Do you like it?'

'It's lovely,' I tell her warmly. 'And I can see you're both pleased with it!'

Mark's beaming from ear to ear. 'I'm just so happy that Jo's got the ring she really wants now.'

'I still feel bad about your gran's ring, though,' she says, her smile fading a little.

'Don't be. She wasn't the type to make a fuss about things like that. I bet she's looking down now, laughing about it, and thinking what a bloody fool I was to take so long to buy you a decent one!'

'I hope so!' Jo takes a sip of her orange juice and looks at her watch. 'What's happened to the others, do you think, Mark? Maybe they've forgotten!'

He checks the time himself.

'Yes, they're late! We were supposed to be meeting Gemma and Andy here at half past seven,' he explains to Harold and me.

'It's ten to eight,' says Jo. 'Perhaps they've muddled up the time.'

'I think I'll ask Reception to give their room a call and chase them up,' says Mark a few minutes later when they still haven't arrived.

He comes back from the desk looking puzzled.

'That's odd. There's no reply from their room, and Tomi says they haven't picked up their key. They're not back from Badija yet.'

'But Gemma said they were getting a boat back at six o'clock!' says Jo. 'And it's only supposed to be a twenty-minute crossing.'

'Well, maybe they've gone straight into town. Forgotten about us!' laughs Mark.

'Excuse me.' A German guy sitting opposite us leans across the table. 'I hope I am not being rude ... I think I heard you say that someone has gone to Badija, and they have not yet arrived back from there?'

'No ... we were expecting them to get a boat back at six o'clock, but perhaps they've changed their minds.'

'If you would like to take my advice,' he says in very formal English, 'I think you should tell this to the

226

manager. Last week, my wife and I went also to Badija. The boat did not come back for us. I had fortunately taken the precaution of having the telephone number of the hotel in my mobile phone and was able to telephone Tomislav. I was informed that this is unfortunately a common happening. Another boat was sent to bring us safely back.'

'Oh!' Jo looks at Mark in dismay. 'God, you don't think they're still over there, do you? Marooned?'

'Sounds possible, doesn't it? I'll go and have another word with Tomi. Thanks!' he adds to the German. 'Wouldn't you think Gemma and Andy should have been warned that this goes on, when they booked the boat?'

'Poor things,' I say. 'I hope they're all right. Badija doesn't have anywhere to stay, you know.'

Mark's back ten minutes later with the news that a phone call has been made to the boatman. Apparently he'd asked his son to make the pick-up and it had somehow been overlooked.

'Tomi was furious. He said this has happened before and the hotel won't recommend this chap any more. In future he's going to advise people to walk into town and get the regular water-taxis.'

'Great, saying it now!' says Jo crossly. 'Poor Gemma and Andy should have been told that this morning!'

'Well, at least they're being picked up now,' says Harold. 'It's a good thing you two were supposed to meet them tonight or I reckon they'd have ended up camping over there for the night!'

It's about a quarter to nine when the little boat finally pulls into the jetty. Harold and I have had dinner, but Jo and Mark said they weren't hungry and were going to wait for Gemma and Andy. We all go out on to the terrace to watch them coming ashore.

'Hello!' we chorus. 'At last!'

'Who were those others with you?' asks Jo as Gemma waves goodbye to three giggling girls who are now being ferried off towards the town.

'They missed the last water-taxi,' she explains. 'They were trying to get some help from the monks at the monastery when they saw our boat finally turn up. Thank God! Was it you who got hold of the boatman? Thank you so much! He was beside himself with apologies. Apparently he's been trying to get his son to help him with the business, but the son's not very reliable.'

'Well, I reckon that's lost him a lot of business now,' says Mark, 'from what Tomi said tonight.'

'Were you worried?' asks Jo. 'Did you think you'd be stranded over there all night?'

'It did cross our minds!' says Andy.

'What on earth did you do?' I ask them. 'Stuck there, waiting, for – well, about two and a half hours!'

They glance at each other, smiling. Andy's gone a bit pink.

'We played I Spy,' says Gemma quickly. She's trying not to laugh.

'Oh, well, – yes, that would have passed the time, at least,' I say. 'I play it with my students sometimes, you know? In French, of course. Who won?'

They grin at each other again.

'I think we both did,' says Andy.

	S	M	T	**W**	T	F	S
June					1	2	3
	4	5	6	7	8	9	10
	11	12	13	14	15	16	17
	18	19	20	21	22	23	24
	25	26	27	(28)	29	30	

Gemma

Despite yesterday's débâcle, we've been for another island trip today – to Mljet. We didn't do this one off our own backs, though – we booked it last week, with Jo and Mark, and we went by hydrofoil from Korčula harbour. Jo was a bit anxious about it and so was Mark, as you can imagine – he'd tried to persuade her to cancel – but Tomislav at the hotel reassured them that there's plenty of shade around the lakes on Mljet, and that the little town of Pomena, where the hydrofoil docks, has a selection of restaurants, bars and places to buy water.

We've all had a great day out. The trip included a guided tour through Mljet National Park, which covers the two lakes – imaginatively named Big Lake and Little Lake – and a small boat to take us out to the island in the middle of the big one, where there's a monastery and a restaurant. We took a slow stroll around the big lake, keeping to the shady forested area on the shore, and stopping frequently to rest and drink. Then we all had a refreshing swim in the lake which is saltwater, fed by a narrow channel from the sea and connected to the little lake by another channel. Our guide told us the lakes are very popular for swimming because they're about four degrees centigrade warmer than the open sea, calm and clear. After we'd dried off for a while in the sun we headed back to one of the restaurants in Pomena, where we found a table overlooking the harbour for a late lunch.

While we were eating, Jo was telling us about a conversation they'd had the other day with Ruby about her sister.

'She was anorexic. Apparently nobody realised that was the problem – she managed to hide it from them. Poor thing had had two miscarriages and everyone assumed she was weak and thin and depressed because of that, but she didn't get better, and she couldn't get pregnant again . . .'

'One of the first things anorexia buggers up is your fertility,' I told her.

'So she might even have been anorexic *before* the miscarriages?'

'Possibly. So was it the anorexia that killed her, in the end?'

'Apparently. Harold seems to feel guilty about the fact that he didn't realise what was wrong with her. He says he was too busy working, didn't spend enough time with her.'

'Poor guy shouldn't feel guilty. I don't think the people closest to anorexics ever realise what's going on at the beginning.'

'I know. And I think Ruby must spend almost her

whole time trying to tell him that, but he still blames himself. I suppose that's why he's ... well, kind of depressed, don't you think?'

'I should think anyone would be depressed if their wife died from anorexia,' put in Andy. 'But most people probably wouldn't try to get over it by having it off with her sister!'

'I don't think it was like that at all,' protested Jo. 'The sister died over a year ago. I get the impression Ruby's taken care of Harold – helped him get over the shock, perhaps.'

'You'd think he'd be a bit more cheerful now, wouldn't you? Now that they're married,' I said thoughtfully. 'Ruby says he's the love of her life.'

'Yes,' said Mark, looking at Jo. 'But if you marry the love of your life, and they're still grieving for someone else, there's only one option open to you.'

'What's that?' asked Jo, looking down, fiddling with her new wedding ring, turning it so that it caught the sunlight.

'Patience,' he said. 'You can't bully someone into loving you.'

'But I think Harold *does* love Ruby,' Jo protested, 'I think perhaps he loved both sisters.'

'That's crap,' I said. 'You can't love two people at the same time.'

'Can't you?' Jo looked up, some sort of pain so evident in her eyes that I had to look away. 'Why not? Who says you can't?'

'Jo's right,' Andy agreed. 'Logically, with so many millions of people in the world, why do we think we can only love one?'

'We *promised* to only love one!' I pointed out, slightly aggrieved but pretending to laugh about it. 'Only last week!'

'No. We promised to be faithful to only one,' he corrected me. 'If I met someone else I loved, Gem, I'd walk away from the situation. That's the whole point.'

There was an awkward moment, an uncomfortable kind of collective hiccup, where nobody wanted to speak. I opened my mouth, nearly said it, closed my mouth again. I imagined it blurting out of me like projectile vomit, unwanted, nasty: *That's what happened with Caroline, I suppose?* I swallowed it back quickly and shook my head to show I wasn't going to argue. I was determined to keep my niggling doubts about the Caroline thing under control – especially in front of the others.

Andy stood up and looked out at the sea. 'I'm going to find the Gents',' he said.

'This is probably a bad discussion to have while we're on our honeymoons,' I commented, when he'd gone, trying to make a joke of it. Jo and Mark shrugged it off, called for more coffee, and when Andy came back we talked about the live music bar in Korčula and everything was fine again.

We're all quiet and sleepy now, on the hydrofoil back to Korčula. I close my eyes and find myself thinking about Ruby and her poor anorexic sister. I wonder how close they were: I know Ruby said she was the oldest and Jeannie the youngest girl in the family, but had they played together, argued over clothes, lain in the dark at night and talked about boyfriends, or was the age gap too great for that? Did Ruby perhaps push her little sister in the pram, hold her hand and take her to the park, help her with her homework? That's the kind of big sister I should have been to Claire. The kind I wish I'd been. But, needless to say, it's a very far cry from the reality.

Of course, she was a bridesmaid at our wedding. It was what I wanted – what I'd always wanted: two bridesmaids – Claire and my best friend Cheryl. I'd been looking forward to asking Claire. I looked upon it as another chance for us to become proper sisters. I'd sit in her bedroom with her and discuss the wedding arrangements, treat her like an equal, like an adult. Take her out with me to the bridal shops to choose the style and colour of her dress. It'd be fun. We'd link arms in the street, laugh together and go somewhere nice for lunch.

In the event, Claire phoned me while I was still at the stage of enjoying my little fantasy.

'Mum says I've got to be a bridesmaid,' she said, sounding bored and hostile.

'No, you haven't got to.' I fought back annoyance at the way I'd been upstaged, yet again, by my mum, and cursed myself for not talking to Claire sooner. 'I'd like you to be. That's different.'

'Why? Why do you want me to do it? Haven't you got any friends of your own age?'

'Claire, you're my sister!' I gasped, unable to hide my disappointment, seeing the cosy chats and shopping trips of my daydreams fading into bitter oblivion. 'Of course I've got friends – but you're my first choice!'

'You wouldn't be mine,' she retorted.

'No, I wouldn't expect to be,' I sighed.

But then again, if she carried on as she was, she wasn't likely to be having a wedding. She'd be an unmarried mother before she was even out of her teens. I had a few concerns about Claire's lifestyle which I'd been planning to discuss seriously with her as part of our imagined new sisterly comradeship – but it looked like I'd lost that opportunity now.

The cold resentment I'd grown used to from my

233

sister continued throughout all the wedding preparations. We never did go shopping on our own together for her dress. Mum came with us and completely took over, telling Claire how pretty she looked in the pale green they chose together, only just remembering at the last minute to check with me that I liked it too, and that Cheryl would be happy with the same dress.

'Cheryl's expecting me to choose,' I said flatly. 'As it's my wedding.'

And Claire didn't just look pretty on my wedding day – she looked amazing. At the reception, in a fit of generosity and wanting everyone to be happy, I told her so and she responded with a smile of regal acceptance, far too knowing, far too aware of her charms, for her sixteen years. She was already eyeing up the best man, Andy's cousin Will, who's ten years older than her and married with a baby. Mum was smiling proudly in her direction, pointing her out to friends and relatives, taking the credit for her natural good looks and telling them about her potential for A levels and university as if this was some sort of coming-out party for Claire rather than my wedding.

Wanting to enjoy the day, wanting to look back and remember no ugly vibes, no subtle layers of unhappiness beneath the joy and perfection of it all, I stifled my nasty little fantasy of running up to those admiring middle-aged ladies and telling them some more about Claire. The things Mum didn't know about her golden girl – things I only knew because colleagues at work, student nurses who went to all the pubs and clubs in town, had told me about her using fake ID and her precocious self-confidence to gain admission to places she shouldn't be going, while Mum believed her to be staying overnight with friends. How they saw her hitting on men much too old for her, who'd buy her drinks and take her home with them in taxis.

'She's heading for trouble, if you don't mind my saying so,' commented one of the girls on my ward a few weeks before the wedding. 'If she was my little sister, I'd have to say something...'

I resented being told this, but it was probably true. Most people would discuss concerns like these with their sisters. Unfortunately, I haven't got that sort of relationship with Claire.

This evening, not having been held up by a forgetful boatman, we're back at the hotel in time to shower and change for the evening out we promised ourselves yesterday. The little restaurant-bar Andy and I particularly like is only a short walk away, and most nights they have two singer-guitarists there – a guy and a girl – who perform a lot of light English and American music, from Elvis through to the Beatles, Neil Diamond classics to Amy Winehouse hits. They're good, they create a great atmosphere, and the food's good too.

We've got here early enough tonight, with Jo and Mark, to grab an outside table as close to the singers as possible. We're too busy enjoying the music, singing along, clapping and cheering them and getting stuck into our meals, to have much conversation until they take a break halfway through the evening.

'I enjoyed today,' says Jo as she finishes her dinner. 'And I'm enjoying tonight, too. Thanks for asking us to come with you.'

'We've enjoyed your company,' says Andy at once – and I have to agree. It's turned out to be so nice having them and Harold and Ruby around, despite what I always believed about our honeymoon being a time for us to be alone.

'We're just so relieved that you're feeling OK now,' I tell Jo. 'You look one hundred per cent better than you did when we all arrived here – doesn't she, Mark?'

'Yes.' He smiles at Jo gently. 'I was worried about going ahead with this holiday, but now I'm glad we came. You do look heaps better, babe.'

'I'm almost daring to hope she's a little bit happier, too,' he adds quietly to us after Jo goes inside to use the loo. 'I realise these things can't be rushed . . .'

'But I'm sure she *is* happy with you,' I tell him. 'Oh, is that her phone?'

'Mm. Probably her mum – I'll get it.'

He picks up the phone and checks the ID, suddenly frowning to himself before turning away from the noise of the bar to answer it. Andy and I carry on talking quietly until we both become aware that Mark's voice is raised to a kind of strangled shout.

'What exactly do you want?' he's saying furiously. 'No, you *can't* talk to her. Piss off – I don't care, she doesn't want to talk to you, OK? You must be out of your mind – there's no way. . .' There's a silence. He frowns, looks around, catches sight of Jo, just coming back out from the Ladies', smiling at him, lifting her eyebrows in question as she sees him on the phone. '*What* e-mail?' says Mark in a deadly cold tone. '*When* did she send you an e-mail?'

Jo's smile falters. She holds out her hand for her phone but Mark turns away from her again, his face set with anger.

'You're lying, Ben,' he hisses into the phone. 'I don't believe you. Now, piss off and don't phone *my wife* ever again!'

He snaps the phone shut but doesn't turn round immediately. Jo's standing behind him, looking uncertain and uneasy.

'Ben seems to think you sent him an e-mail,' he says flatly, still not looking at her.

'Yes, I did.'

He closes his eyes and lets out a very low sound like a groan of pain. I feel my own heart sink to my boots. Poor Mark. Just as he believed she was getting over that bastard. Why? Why did she have to go and contact him?

'Well, I suppose that says it all, doesn't it?' Mark swings round suddenly and throws the phone down on the table. 'On our *honeymoon*, Jo! You couldn't even have the decency to wait till we got home – you couldn't even manage two bloody weeks with me, without getting in touch with the *love of your life*!'

He's spitting the words out at her. I'm aware that he's mimicking the phrase we used in our conversation this afternoon. Jo was so quick to say she believed it possible to love more than one person; Mark must have felt as threatened by that as I did when Andy agreed with her. But it's no good, is it? It's not enough for him to be just *one* of the people she loves, and I don't blame him. He's married her, he's taking on her child, he's done everything for her. He deserves more. She's not being fair.

'No, Mark!' she says, clutching his arm, trying to turn him to face her. 'Listen. He's not ... it isn't true! He's just trying to make trouble between us.'

'So you *didn't* send him an e-mail a couple of days ago?' he demands, piercing her with a look.

'Yes! But – I don't know what he told you, he's probably lying ...'

'Jo, I don't know who's lying and who isn't,' says

Mark, wearily. 'But, to be quite honest, I don't want to hang around and listen to your excuses. I've had enough of being second best. OK, I knew you still wanted him, but you promised you'd stay away from him. Maybe our getting married was just a huge mistake.'

'No! Mark, no – it wasn't a mistake. Don't walk away from me ... *Listen!* Let me explain ...'

But he's gone, shaking her off, disappearing into the darkness. And she's collapsed at the table, crying, telling me she loves him and it's all a misunderstanding.

'Don't tell *me*, Jo,' I say when she quietens down enough to hear me. 'It's Mark you need to tell. Whether he wants to hear you or not, you'll have to find a way of getting through to him.'

Always supposing she can find him. Because the way he looked when he walked off just now, I reckon he's angry and disillusioned enough to get the next flight back to London. And if Jo's really been e-mailing Ben while she's on her honeymoon then, to be quite honest, I couldn't really blame him.

Jo

Andy and Gemma walk back to the hotel with me. Our room key's still at reception; Mark's not in the bar or outside on the terrace. He's not in the hotel.

'I'll go up to the room and wait,' I say, shakily. 'Perhaps I'll try his phone, if he's got it on him.'

'Will you be all right?' says Andy, touching her arm briefly.

'Yes. Of course. I just wish he'd given me the chance to explain ...'

Gemma looks at me doubtfully. I suppose she's thinking I've got a lot of explaining to do. I feel a sudden wave of irritation and impatience. What does she know? In love with the same guy since she was fourteen – an easy, uncomplicated relationship that was always going to lead to marriage – how could she possibly understand what it's like to find yourself in my situation?

I always thought I'd be like her. There was nothing complicated, nothing needy or difficult, about my background. I grew up in a loving family. If you'd asked me before I started at uni how I saw my future, I'd probably have predicted being single, having a good time and a good career, until I was about thirty and then, hopefully, getting married and having a family. With someone nice, straightforward and kind. Yes, someone like Mark.

What happened to me? Why, when my life was perfect, my future looked good, I had everything going for me ... *why* did I have to be struck down with such devastating force by something I didn't want, didn't ask or go looking for? It wasn't fair. It took me by surprise, knocked the strength and the sense out of me, and changed my life forever. People can sneer and criticise all they like when I say I couldn't help it, but unless they've been there – unless they've experienced the sheer ferocity of feelings that completely take you over, mind and soul, the terrifying exhilaration of being swept away by something too big to control, the paralysing weakness of it, the breathtaking exhaustion of it – their opinions aren't even relevant. They haven't got a clue. They've never lived.

That's the horrifying enigma of having loved

somebody with such passion. Not a day goes by that I don't wish it'd never happened – and yet, at the same time, I wouldn't have missed it for the world. It's held me back – but it's made me grow up. It felt bad, and good, at the same time. It was awful, and wonderful. One of my brothers has a friend who's a recovered heroin addict, and this guy told me once that he hated and despised every moment of his addiction, but that on another level he'd always miss it. I know *exactly* how he feels.

'Where are you, Mark? Please call me.' It's the third message I've left on his voicemail, and I've sent three or four texts too. There's nothing else I can do other than sit on the bed, waiting. He'll come back. He's got to. I know he was upset, but he wouldn't walk out on me. Not Mark.

When I told Mum about Ben – about the baby being his, not Mark's – she sat, looking down at her hands in her lap, without saying a word until I'd finished. I was crying by then: crying because I was sorry. I love my mum and she didn't deserve to have this pain inflicted on her. The daughter she'd brought up to be good, caring and decent, had had an affair with a married man and was having his baby. And marrying someone else. I wasn't sorry about the affair, or about the baby, and I was too exhausted to be sorry that I was marrying someone I didn't love – that just felt like a lifeline in a stormy sea. No, I was sorry about hurting Mum and Dad.

'I know I've made a mess of things,' I mumbled through my tears.

'No, you haven't,' said Mum firmly, putting her arms round me. 'You've had a bad experience.

You've suffered. Life does that to us, Jo, but we come through and we survive.'

'I don't know if I can get through this,' I whispered.

'You have to. You have the baby to think about now.' She paused and stroked the hair out of my eyes, looking at me with the same gentle smile I remembered from when I fell and grazed my knees as a child. 'And Mark, too. You have him to think about.'

Mum and Dad had taken to Mark straight away. Even though they were surprised by the pregnancy, and even more surprised when I announced that we were getting married, they both seemed happy with what they presumed had been my choice – my partner, my lover. Now I'd told Mum the truth, she must be wondering if he was a fool or some kind of a saint, taking on his friend's pregnant reject, and whether our marriage was advisable or even sensible. But she didn't say any of this. If she had concerns, she didn't voice them. She merely said: *You have Mark to think about now.*

And I am thinking about him now. I'm thinking of how he looked on our wedding day: nervous and upright, smart and unfamiliar in his new suit and stiff collar. How he took my hand and smiled as he put his grandmother's ring on my finger – such a brilliantly happy smile, as if he'd been given the world and all its riches. I'm thinking about the times he's looked after me when I was horribly sick in the early weeks of my pregnancy. How patiently he cooked for me, trying to tempt me with different foods and drinks to see if there was anything I could keep down, when all I did was snap at him for his persistence. I'm remembering, too, the day of my twenty-week scan, just before our wedding day, when he sat beside me at the hospital, gasping with excitement at the image of the baby; laughing with delight at the news that I was having a boy. Squeezing my hand and immediately referring to the moving blob on the screen as little Jacob. I know Mark loves me – possibly in the way I loved Ben; possibly in a different way, a better way. And Mum's right. Because of that, I have to hold his heart carefully for ever. Even if the injury Ben inflicted on *mine* takes a lifetime to heal.

It's after midnight, and still no sign of Mark. No replies to my calls, no answering text messages. I can't sit here in the room any more, imagining all sorts of things – the very worst of things. I'm still dressed; I slip my shoes back on and head down-stairs, out of the hotel, and sit at the bottom of the steps leading to the coast path. As always, the night's still warm and the gentle breeze off the sea is a bless-ing. I sit for quite a while, just staring out at the lights on the water. Almost unconsciously I'm searching for the words to use in a prayer. *Please, God, let him come back to me. Help me make him under-stand. Please, just bring him back to me!*

Suddenly there's a cough and a shuffle of feet very close to me. I hold my breath, my heart racing. It seems so safe around here that I haven't even considered that I might be putting myself at risk by sitting outside on my own at this time of night. I tense, adrenaline flooding my limbs as I prepare to get up and run back up the steps.

'Hello?' calls a voice. 'Who is there?'

It's the waiter from the Italian restaurant next-door. Ruby's admirer.

'Hello.' I'm still a bit wary. 'I'm ... just going back into the hotel. Good night.'

'Wait!' He leans against the opposite wall, facing me. He doesn't look the least bit threatening, but one never knows. 'I'm sorry to disturb, Signora, but I 'ave only just finished the work, at the *ristorante*. I wished to deliver something for Signora Ruby but, of course, I am foolish, and did not realise it was already so very late ...'

'I should imagine she's fast asleep, with her husband.' I emphasise the word 'husband'. Really, this young man is being ridiculous. Does he honestly imagine Ruby's going to be remotely interested in him, especially at this hour?

'I do not come 'ere to be a bother to the Signora,' he says, indignantly, obviously interpreting my tone correctly. 'I came only to give her the token of my apology, for my bad manners, which I 'ave shown to her, by my mistake.'

'Well, the Signora – I mean, Ruby – told you there's no need, and she asked you to go away, so ...'

'I wish never again to bother Signora Ruby! I wish this with my heart! Please, Signora, please to give her this token from me, and I will not be a bother ever again.'

He tries to pass me something that's clutched in his hand but I shake my head, sighing. In the moonlight Luciano looks like a skinny little boy of about twelve and I feel about a hundred years older than him. I don't want to be sitting out here on the steps hearing about his token – whatever that means – just because he thinks he's offended an older lady he might, or might not, have a crush on. I want to be safe in my room with Mark. I want him to come back and tell me he still loves me.

'Why do you think you've offended Ruby?' I ask.

'Because I talk to her about the 'usband,' he tells me, apparently eager to share his burden. 'I tell her, the 'usband should be 'appy and singing like the birds, being married to such a beautiful lady. I tell her, she is not like the young girls who come to my restaurant with their bodies almost naked, and drink so much alcohol they are falling over and asking me to make the sex with them. I do not like these kind of girls,' he adds severely. 'I like the ladies like Signora Ruby – and like you too, Signora – who do not show their chests and their buttocks, who are beautiful in the soul ...'

'All right, OK, I get the picture,' I say quickly. 'I don't suppose Ruby was offended at all. She was probably flattered by what you said. But if you keep hanging around here, going on about it, she'll probably become really pissed off, and so will her husband. Yeah?'

'I would die!' he proclaims, clutching his chest dramatically. Bloody idiot. 'I would die before I would make Signora Ruby piss off because of me!'

'Look ...' I hesitate. I don't really want to get into all this, but the guy needs telling. 'I don't know whether you've got some kind of a ... *crush* on Ruby ...'

'A crush? What is this crush? I would not crush her! I kiss her cheek, this only, to say goodnight ...'

Oh, yes? I wonder if she mentioned *that* to Harold!

'No, no, a crush is – how can I put it? When you feel something for someone ...'

'Yes, yes! I feel something!'

I bet you do.

'I mean, you *think* you feel something, but it's

244

not real. It can't be real because you don't really know the person properly. Do you understand?'

'Ah, yes.' He mutters something in Italian that sounds far more romantic than *crush*. 'You think this is what I feel for the Signora?'

'I don't know, Luciano. Do *you* think so?'

He shakes his head vigorously.

'I do not crush her. I meet her in the restaurant – I think she is beautiful and alone. I meet her again when she walks to the town – I think again, she is beautiful and alone. This only. I respect a beautiful woman who is alone. But my stupid words are not good enough for her. This is all I wish to say. This is why I bring the token, so she will think of me, not as a clumsy goat, but as Luciano who respects her.'

'I see.' I'm not convinced. To be honest, I think he's slightly strange, but probably safe. 'What is this bloody token anyway?'

He holds out his hand.

I don't know what I was expecting. Some unusual pebble or shell, perhaps, that he's chosen 'specially for her. A lock of his hair ... something stupid like that.

But it's my ring.

It's *my bloody ring*!

I'm shouting at him before I even realise it.

'It's my ring – my fucking wedding ring! What the *hell* are you doing with my wedding ring? I lost it! I lost it in the *sea*, Luciano – it's mine!'

He's closed his hand around it again, holding it behind his back, stepping away from me, his eyes narrowed as if I'm a dangerous lunatic.

'This ring, it is mine. I buy it. I pay for it much money. I give to the Signora!'

'OK.' Breathe, breathe. Calm down. Don't panic him into running off with it. 'OK, yes – it's yours, and you're giving it to Ruby. So hand it over, and I'll make sure she gets it. Come on, give it to me, Luciano ...'

'I think I *not* now give you the token,' he says, looking at me suspiciously.

'It's not a sodding token, it's a ring! For God's sake!'

'I give only to Signora Ruby,' he says stubbornly. 'I am not a fool, to be tricked this way!'

'I'm not tricking you, you bloody stupid ...'

I stop, mid-shout. Luciano's looking past me up the steps. I turn, in the silence, to see Mark standing at the top. Thank God.

'Oh, thank God,' I murmur, running up to meet him halfway as he comes down towards me. I've forgotten Luciano already; forgotten his stupid stories, forgotten the ring. 'Thank God you're back. Where have you *been*?'

'What's going on?' he demands, ignoring this. 'What do you want?' he addresses Luciano.

'I come only to bring a token to Signora Ruby!' Luciano looks from Mark to me and back again, still holding his hands behind his back but looking worried now.

'It's my ring, Mark. He's got my ring – your gran's wedding ring! He says he paid for it!'

'I paid much money! Two nights' wages! I paid this to the cousin of the neighbour of the chef, who sells also the bad CDs and the videos that play with lines across the screen!'

Mark opens his wallet and offers Luciano a couple of notes. 'How much did you pay? This much?'

'No, Mark!' I protest. 'It's *ours* – we're not paying to get it back!'

'I'd have paid a reward,' he points out calmly, 'if someone had found it.'

Luciano's eyes are almost popping out of his head. He lifts one hand to take the money from Mark.

'The ring first,' says Mark sternly. 'And this is only because I happen to believe you, and because I don't want to get involved with your chef's cousin's mate or whoever the hell it is – but you should have more sense than to buy anything from someone who sells dodgy CDs and videos, should-n't you?'

'But he say to me, he buys the ring from a fisher-man ...'

'Yeah, whatever. Let's have it.'

'It's definitely the one,' I say as soon as it's in Mark's hand.

'How you know?' says Luciano sulkily, still holding out his hand for the money. 'Many rings the same, all over the world, like this one.'

'Not the same as this. The pattern's got a little chip in it, see?' Mark holds the ring up, but none of us can see, really – it's too dark. Luciano just pouts at us moodily. 'And, of course, there's the engrav-ing inside.'

'What is this – *engraving*?' asks Luciano.

'The initials of my grandmother and grandfather. GM – TW.' Mark shrugs. 'If you don't believe me, come inside in the light and I'll show you.'

'I believe you,' he says. 'I think, Signore, that you are not this kind of a man who speaks the lies, like the cousin of the neighbour of my chef. I am 'appy to take the money.' He gives a little bow.

'Of course you are,' I say, feeling slightly aggrieved

about it. 'Now clear off and leave us alone!'

'You will say, please, to Signora Ruby ...?'

'No! I'm not saying anything! Good *night*, Luciano!'

He disappears into the shadows and I turn to Mark, repeating softly as we stare at each other in the darkness: 'Where did you go? Where have you been?'

'Just walking. Just thinking. I'm sorry, babe.'

He takes me in his arms and I think for a minute that he's wet, that he's been swimming. But it's tears on his cheeks.

'Don't be sorry! It's my fault. I should have told you about the e-mail ...'

'No! I don't want to know. Please, whatever's going on with Ben, just don't tell me, OK? I can only bear it if I don't have to hear about it.'

'But nothing's going on ...'

'I shouldn't have reacted the way I did. I knew, didn't I, when I asked you to marry me: I knew you still had feelings for him. If I couldn't hack it, I should have walked away. I can't ask you to stop loving him. If that's how you still feel about him, I'll just have to ...'

'Mark!' I hold him at arm's length, shaking him gently. 'Shut up for a minute, will you, and listen.'

'What?'

'I've been trying to tell you, but you just assumed the worst. The e-mail ... It was in response to one Ben sent me a few days ago, saying a load of crap about still loving me, wanting me back ...'

'You didn't tell me.'

'No. I should have done, but I thought it'd just upset you. It upset *me* – but only because I hated him for doing it to me.'

'Doing what?' he asks softly, stroking my hair.

'Making things harder. Coming out with all that *crap* instead of staying away, giving me a chance, letting me get over him.' I pause, swallow back the pain that's still lodged somewhere between my throat and my stomach: even now, despite everything. 'Pretending still to love me, but not even bothering to ask how I am, how the baby is – just ignoring the whole situation of this pregnancy, the same way he ignores the fact of his wife and family! That's not love, Mark. I know that now – I can see it for what it is. Ben doesn't love me. He never did. *That's* what hurts.'

'I wish you'd told me,' he says again.

'So do I. I will, I promise – if he gets in touch again, I'll tell you every single lying word he says.'

'So what did you reply? Why did he phone tonight?'

'I can only guess why he phoned. Probably feeling slighted. Couldn't believe I'd actually given him a dose of his own medicine.' I smile to myself. I can quote my reply word for word. I'm rather proud of it, actually.

Dear Ben
Thank you for your e-mail. I read it with interest. You appear to be suffering from some sort of delusion. I'm not your 'Joby', or your 'baby', and you're not 'my Ben'. 'What we had' is over, and there's no way we could ever have 'made a go of it', as you belong to someone else – and so, now, do I. Please leave me alone. I'm on my honeymoon, and I love my husband.
Goodbye.
Jo

'Is it true?' whispers Mark huskily, his mouth close to my ear.

'Yes. It's over, and I want him to leave me alone.'

'And ... the other part? That you ...'

'... love my husband? Yes, I do, Mark. I know it's not exactly the way you want, not yet ...'

'That's OK. As long as you're not going to leave me for him!'

'Never,' I say, fiercely. 'I can't promise he's never going to sneak into my mind or my dreams, but it's not deliberate, Mark. I'm trying! I don't *want* him anywhere, not even in my subconscious mind. *You're* the one I want. When you walked away from me tonight, I was so frightened you weren't coming back. I don't know what I'd have done ...'

'Of course I was coming back. I was just being childish.'

'You're never that. You've put up with so much from me.'

'But you've *given* me so much! That's what you'll never understand,' he says softly. 'You gave me everything I could ever have wanted, when you agreed to marry me.'

	S	M	T	W	**T** 1	F 2	S 3
June	4	5	6	7	8	9	10
	11	12	13	14	15	16	17
	18	19	20	21	22	23	24
	25	26	27	28	(29)	30	

Gemma

It's quite a relief to see Jo and Mark together this morning – and looking happy, too. They're holding hands and smiling as they come in for breakfast.

'Everything OK?' asks Andy – and they smile and nod in response but we all keep off the subject of phone calls and e-mails.

'Look!' says Jo, holding out her hand. She's got her original wedding ring back – Mark's grandmother's ring – and she's wearing it on the ring finger of her other hand.

'Oh, that's fantastic!' I tell her. 'Did someone find it and hand it in?'

'Someone must have found it, all right,' says Mark. 'And it found its way into the hands of the cousin of the neighbour of the chef next-door – who seems to be the Del Boy of Korčula.'

'Luciano – that waiter who's got a crush on Ruby –

251

bought it from him to give her as a present,' explains Jo. 'I freaked out when he showed it to me.'

'We've got it back anyway,' says Mark, putting his arm round Jo's shoulders. 'That's all that matters.'

'I feel quite guilty now about having a new ring!' she laughs. 'But I'm going to wear them both, of course. It's funny, I really like the idea of wearing Mark's grandmother's ring now, but the ring Mark bought me himself feels more like my own. It's more special to me.'

'They seem happy,' comments Andy as we stroll into town a little later.

'Yes. They obviously sorted things out when Mark came back last night.'

I can't help sounding a bit wistful. I know, in my heart of hearts, that Andy and I have got things to sort out, too, but it's not going to happen until we get home, and I'm not looking forward to it. Right now we're on our way to look round the shops for souvenirs. I can't believe we've only got three days left here. It seems like only yesterday that we arrived on the island, when it was all new and exciting. So much has happened since – and a lot of it has been unsettling and upsetting.

We've never been the type of couple to have arguments, and I know that's mainly because of Andy: because he's always allowed things to drift on, without protest, without making his feelings known. But now, suddenly, I feel like there's a whole box full of unspoken disagreements sitting in the cupboard, with the lid half-off, just about to burst open. It's as if the wedding has been a catalyst: it's released something, and now an explosion is inevitable. It's got me feeling like I do before a storm – when the air around seems to press against my temples, hurting my brain. I know the thunderstorm, when it comes, is going to bring relief. But that doesn't mean to say I'm going to enjoy it.

We're looking at traditional Croatian embroidered tablecloths. Andy wants to buy his mum and dad a present, to thank them for helping out with the wedding costs. I think they'd have liked to get involved a bit more, to be honest, but they couldn't get a foot in the door, the way my mum orchestrated the whole show.

'What about your mum?' says Andy. 'Do you think she'd like one of these? Or would she prefer something else? Shall we look in that little shop with all the ceramics?'

'My mum?' I'm a bit flummoxed. 'I hadn't even thought about buying her anything.'

Andy looks at me in surprise.

'It'd be nice to thank her, wouldn't it, Gem? For everything?'

'I thanked her on the day. You thanked her in your speech.' I pout. 'I hope you're not going to suggest we buy something for my dad, too? Just because he put his hand in his pocket, having taken no interest in me whatsoever for the past sixteen years?'

'Maybe not. That's up to you, obviously. But, personally, I'd really like to buy your mum something.'

'OK.' I shrug. 'Let's buy her something. Not that she'll appreciate it, but . . .'

'Gemma!' Andy exclaims. 'Give her a chance!'

'What?' I'm so taken aback, I don't know what to say. Andy knows, better than anyone, what the situation is with my family. He's seen Claire grow up,

253

seen how she got all Mum's attention while I barely registered in her consciousness at all, even when I graduated with my nursing degree, even when Andy and I got engaged. 'The wedding's been the first thing she's ever been interested in about me!' I remind him.

'Don't you think that's a start, at least?'

'No. I think she just wanted a chance to dress up and show off in front of her friends.'

'Gemma,' he says gently, 'I haven't said this before, but . . .'

'There seem to be a lot of things you haven't said before, that you suddenly want to say now, to spoil our honeymoon!' I retort, before I can stop myself.

He doesn't respond. He hands over the embroidered tablecloth we've chosen for his mum and we wait in silence while a shop assistant wraps it and takes the money. When we're out in the street, he takes my hand and says: 'I don't want to spoil our honeymoon. I'm sorry if that's how it seems.'

'It doesn't, not really. Let's change the subject.' I smile, trying to show him it's OK, I'm not upset, I'm still the happy, smiling bride enjoying her romantic honeymoon, determined not to get drawn into arguments.

'But I do want to say this. I think it needs to be said.' He holds my hand tighter, as if he thinks I might snatch it away.

'Say it, then,' I tell him sharply, hating myself for the bossy tone of my voice and wondering what's happening to me. 'Get it over with.'

'I totally understand your feelings about your mum. I've always sympathised, always agreed that she put Claire first, neglected your needs.'

'Exactly.' I feel somewhat mollified. This is exactly my point, and has been for years. Andy knows that.

He's seen it with his own eyes. There's no reason to argue about it.

'And I agree with you about the wedding – up to a point. She did try to take it over, a bit. But loads of mums do that. And she only did it because she was desperate, Gemma – desperate to try to make things better between you.'

'It didn't seem that way to me.'

'I understand that, too. You're so used to the way things have been, you might not have noticed stuff that *I* noticed.'

'Like what?' I stare at him. We've walked through the steep cobbled streets of the old town and we're out on the walls now, looking out to sea. What the hell does he think he's noticed about my mum that *I* might have missed? I think he's just trying to make me feel better.

'Like the way she couldn't take her eyes off you all day.'

'You're joking! She never stopped looking at *Claire*.'

'Sometimes,' he says, smiling at me, 'I think we see what we expect to see – what we've always been used to seeing ...'

'Yes! And what I'm *sick* of seeing! I'm *sick* of always being second best, Andy. Always being ignored ... always being compared unfavourably with that spoilt brat!'

He puts his arms round me and pulls me close. Shit, I *really* did not want to get into all this stuff, not now, on our honeymoon. Not ever, to be quite honest, but certainly not now.

'You're entitled to your anger,' he says, kissing the top of my head. 'But I honestly think your mum's realising things now. I think she's probably beginning to

255

regret a lot of what's happened between you.'

'Well, maybe it's a bit too late,' I say, trying to sound like I don't care. But my heart's beating like a hammer. It's true. I *did* see the way Mum was looking at me during the reception. I did notice that she'd shed a few tears when we walked out of the church. I did catch something different in her tone of voice – less off-hand, more sincere – when she told me I looked beautiful. I noticed, but I couldn't really believe it. Was I perhaps not even prepared to believe it?

'Give her a chance, Gem,' Andy repeats softly. 'I'm not making excuses for her, but she's had a tough time. Be generous. There could be so much to gain.'

'Who for?' I retort sarcastically. He knows what I mean: we've talked about this often enough. How Mum's going to feel when Claire eventually leaves home. How she's suddenly going to find herself on her own, aware that she's been too cool, for too long, to her other daughter to rebuild any sort of relation-ship.

'For both of you.' He's silent for a moment, still holding me close to him. Then he adds, with sudden firmness: 'And for the sake of our own children, even-tually, too.'

I look up at him in surprise. Is he trying to be funny? 'I thought you'd decided you didn't want any . . .'

'I haven't said that, Gemma, you know I haven't. I've told you, I just don't want to rush straight home from the honeymoon and start making babies.'

'I know. OK. So let's drop the subject!' I wriggle out of his arms and turn away, pulling him by the hand. 'Come on. We came for souvenirs.'

We head back to the shops again and finish our shopping, including a painting of Korčula Town to take home and hang on the wall to remember our honeymoon by, and a brightly hand-painted ceramic jug and bowl set for Mum, that's been carefully packaged up for the journey home. Then we have lunch outside one of the restaurants that line the town walls, overlooking the harbour. The sun's shining like a thousand diamonds on the sea, the food is wonderful, the wine's smooth and fruity, and I'm feeling happier. At least on the surface.

'Thank you for talking me into buying Mum a present,' I tell Andy quietly. 'You're right: it's time I made some sort of an effort. It's worth a try, anyway. I'll go and see her when we get home.' I should leave it there. I shouldn't go on, and spoil it – but I do. 'I can't quite see what it's got to do with our *eventual* children, really, though . . .'

He shrugs. 'I want everything to be right before we have kids, don't you? Rather than have them born into a family with unresolved problems. That's what happened to Claire.'

'But surely, as long as *you and I* haven't got unresolved problems, that's all that matters,' I point out. 'And I didn't think we did. Not till the last few days, anyway.'

He sighs and shakes his head: like it's *me* being difficult! I can't help it – I just can't accept that the only reason he's suddenly wanting to put off having a family is that he wants me and Mum to make friends with each other first. It sounds like he's fumbling for excuses.

The diamonds on the sea have suddenly lost their sparkle. The wine seems to have soured in the glass. And we're barely talking to each other again now.

It's about four o'clock when we finally arrive back at the hotel.

'Mr Collins? There is somebody here who is waiting

to speak to you,' says Tomislav very formally, indicating the seating area of the lobby. Andy and I frown at each other in surprise. Who the hell would be waiting to speak to us? As we turn to look, there's a shout from one of the sofas.

'Here you are! We were just about to give up.'

Joy of joys, it's Felicity, Nicky and Sara – bloody Caroline's bloody stupid friends. The only thing to be thankful for is that she's not with them.

'I hope you don't mind us turning up here?' says Felicity. She's looking worried. They all are. 'We knew where you were staying because the boat dropped you off here the other night.'

'What can we do for you?' asks Andy, and looks from one to the other of them warily.

Somehow I just know this has to have something to do with . . .

'Caroline,' says Nicky. 'She's disappeared.'

'Disappeared?' I bite back the urge to cheer. It's about the best thing that could have happened to her.

'Yes. She was gone when we got back from shopping on Monday afternoon. Still not back when we woke up on Tuesday morning – you know, when we did the trip to Badija. She was supposed to be coming with us, but we all just presumed she'd gone off with some guy and stayed overnight.'

'She does that all the bloody time,' puts in Sara. 'It can be really annoying when she doesn't let anyone know.'

'So we weren't particularly bothered,' goes on Felicity. 'We went on the trip anyway, but she still wasn't back in the evening . . .'

'Or yesterday,' says Nicky. 'Or today.'

'And her phone's still turned off,' adds Sara.

They're all looking at Andy expectantly.

'So what are we supposed to do about it?' I ask

ungraciously. I mean – sorry, and all that, but we're hardly best buddies, are we?

'We've told the police,' says Felicity. 'We're actually really worried now. She's never done this before – not for days, you know, without even phoning. We're thinking maybe we should let her parents know, but we don't want to freak them out in case there's a harmless explanation and she turns up safe.'

'So what can *we* do?' I repeat. 'To help?' I add somewhat reluctantly.

'Did she say anything to you?' asks Nicky. She's looking straight at Andy. What the hell's she talking about? 'Did she give you any indication at all that she was . . . going off anywhere?'

He shakes his head, looking uncomfortable.

'She didn't seem upset or anything when you were talking?' persists Felicity.

'Hang on a minute,' I interrupt, as Andy seems to have been struck dumb. 'What's this got to do with us? We haven't spoken to her.'

We've gone out of our way to avoid her.

'Andrew has.' Sara looks at him and I bristle with indignation. What's she on about? 'He was the last one to see her before she vanished.'

'That's complete crap! The last time we saw her was in the bar at the top of the tower. Sunday night, wasn't it? You were all there. We left after Andy told her to stop telling lies . . .'

What? Why's everyone looking at each other like that? As if there's something I don't know, that no one's telling me?

Andy sits down with a huge sigh as if this has suddenly all become too much for him. 'Actually, Gemma,' he says quietly, 'I went to see her on Monday.'

259

'You *what*?' My voice sounds like an echo inside my own head. *You what, you what, you what?* I feel behind me for the edge of the sofa, sit down next to him with a thump. 'When?'

As if it matters when. As if, really, it even matters why. What matters is that he did it without telling me. And he wasn't *going* to tell me.

'You had a hangover, remember? I went into town with Mark. You stayed by the pool with Jo.'

'You said you'd been to look for a book shop,' I say, weakly. I can't look at him. I feel sick, thinking back to the way he lied to me. How easily he lied. How easily I believed him.

'I did. Because that's what I was doing.' The three girls are looking at each other impatiently, wanting to talk about Caroline. I couldn't give a monkey's about them, and even less about *her*. I want to know why Andy's been lying to me. Again. He shrugs now, as if it's not even important. 'When Mark decided to go back and check on Jo, I suddenly thought it'd be a good idea to go and see Caroline. We knew where she was staying, didn't we?' Andy's ignoring her friends now. He's turned away from them, taking hold of my hands, trying to get me to look at him, but I can't. 'I was thinking of you, Gemma!' he adds, sounding exasperated. 'I just wanted to make things all right. I wanted to tell her to leave us alone.'

'He turned up at our place just as we were going out shopping,' puts in Felicity. 'So Caroline stayed behind to talk to him. When we got back, they'd both gone.'

There's a silence. An interval fraught with suspicion.

'Did you have a fight?' asks Sara bluntly.

'Did you say something to her to make her storm off?' adds Nicky.

'Or ... do you know where she is?' says Felicity.

260

'Hang on a minute!' I'm looking up at them now. 'What are you implying? Andy doesn't know anything about this!' I get to my feet again and take hold of his arm, shaking it crossly. 'Tell them, Andy. For Christ's sake, it's bad enough that you went round there. Don't let them start *implying* stuff . . .' I look at his face and drop my voice to a whisper. 'Next thing you know, they'll be telling the police. . .'

'We have,' says Felicity calmly. 'That's why we came to see you. We've told the police you were the last person to see her. They'll be wanting to talk to you.'

'Thought we'd warn you, that's all,' says Sara. She gives Andy a look of dislike. 'In case you want to talk to us, instead. Tell us anything you know.'

He stares at the floor, not saying anything. I feel a chill like an Arctic wind blowing through my bones.

'*Do* you know anything, Andy?' I ask him in clipped, short tones.

He stares at me in surprise.

'Of course I don't! What do you think? That I murdered her or something?'

'That's not funny,' says Nicky, looking outraged.

'I don't know *what* to think, Andy,' I tell him, feeling close to tears. 'How can I decide what I think when you don't *tell* me anything? Did you go there to have sex with her? Stop *lying* to me!'

Andy looks from me, to the three girls, and back at me again. He shrugs his shoulders, shakes his head.

'That's what you all think, isn't it? We had sex, we had a row, I've somehow got rid of her. That's *really* what you think?'

'Yes,' says Sara quietly. 'If you want to know the truth, yes, we're thinking that. She says you never stopped pestering her for sex . . .'

261

'Then she's a fucking lying bitch,' he says bitterly, wiping his mouth as if he's just spat her out. 'And, to be honest, I don't give a shit where she is. I wish I'd never set eyes on her. If someone's done her in, they've done us all a favour.' Then he looks up and adds: 'Oh, Christ. Oh – great. Just fucking great.'

The police have arrived while we've been talking. And there's an officer standing right behind him, making notes. If his English is good enough, he's already got a transcript of Andy wishing Caroline dead.

RUBY

There's something going on here tonight. There's a strange atmosphere in the place – staff whispering and giving each other meaningful looks, and Tomislav striding around looking important and anxious, his bow-tie somehow quivering and his hair flopping forward over his face. The German couple we sometimes sit with in the bar have told us they saw two police officers here earlier.

'I believe,' says Herr Struckmann in a solemn undertone, 'that they have arrested an English person.'

'Yes, some people were saying,' adds Frau Struckmann, looking pleased with herself, 'that there are drugs involved.'

'And knives,' agrees her husband, nodding cheerfully. 'Possibly murder.'

'Oh, dear.' I look at Harold anxiously. 'This sounds worrying.'

'Well, if the police have arrested someone, we can all relax.' Herr Struckmann smiles knowingly. 'The police here, I do not think they will take chances.'

To be honest, I'm not taking much notice of this gossip. For all we know, given the language difficulties, things being translated badly from Croatian to German and then to English, it wouldn't surprise me to find out that it's all a storm in a teacup about a parking offence. I just hope our new friends are OK, that's all, I haven't seen any of them around this evening. I know we only met each other last week, but I've become quite fond of those two young girls and their husbands. I can't help smiling to myself when I hear them fretting about their various problems – mountains out of molehills, often as not, but of course it doesn't feel that way to them at the time, does it? They're both nice lads, too, Andy and young Mark. The girls have done all right. Even though Jo's married in haste, I reckon it'll work out OK if she gives it half a chance. And as for Gemma, well, if she doesn't know Andy by now, after living with him for all this time, she never will!

When Harold and I first lived together, we told ourselves it was for convenience. I'd been divorced from Le Cochon for several years by then, and had been living on my own with my younger two children. Within a couple of years of her diagnosis, the psychiatric unit was pretty well Jeannie's second home, and whenever she was discharged Harold stayed at home to keep an eye on her. He spent less and less time at work and the business was floundering. His father had died, leaving both the firm and his own family with huge, unsuspected debts, and his mother needed Harold's support to stay in her retirement bungalow. Before long the business went into liquidation and Harold was out of a job. Their lovely house had to be sold; he rented a small flat and got a job as a minibus driver for disabled children, so that he could pop home whenever possible to check on Jeannie. But before she even reached forty, she'd virtually withdrawn from the battle to stay alive. She needed constant supervision, a regime of feeding, weighing and counselling, that only specialist nurses and doctors could provide. We were warned that her heart and kidneys were showing signs of damage because of the years of self-starvation. She wouldn't be coming home again until her condition improved, she gained weight and could maintain it – and that would probably take many months.

Harold was struggling, trying to hold on to his driving job at the same time as visiting Jeannie every day and cooking and cleaning for himself. Our previous roles had been reversed. He'd been the wealthy young publishing executive with the world at his feet when I was an impoverished divorced mother and student teacher. Now, money wasn't an issue for me any more, whereas his world was crumbling – his business empire collapsed, his lovely young wife an invalid.

'Come and live with me,' I told him on one of my visits to his flat, where I'd found him sorting through bank statements at the kitchen table amongst unwashed plates and piles of laundry. 'You can't go on like this.'

Some men just don't do well on their own. They need a woman – not to keep house for them or anything un-PC like that. Just to be there. They need the company.

That's all we were: companions. My girls, now senior school age, were thrilled to have him around. Their Uncle Harold was a far better father-figure than their own wretched dad had ever been. We had our own bedrooms, and I knew Jeannie would share his as soon as she was well enough to come home. Oh, I can't deny I used to lie awake in mine, night after night, imagining him sleeping in the next room, hearing the movements of the springs, the little coughs and grunts and snores that accompanied his dreams.

At first we didn't even discuss it. Every night we'd give each other a chaste kiss on the cheek as we went our separate ways to our respective bedroom doors. Every night I'd touch the place where his lips had been, as if by holding on to it I could keep the kiss warm all night. Sometimes I'd catch him looking at me, while we were making dinner or washing up together, and see the look in his eyes that told me everything I needed to know – everything except for *why*?

Why was this fair? Why did we have to love each other but pretend we didn't? Why did this have to happen? And sometimes I'd ask myself the question that I tried not even to think about because doing so felt like a betrayal: why did he have to meet her first? Why Jeannie before me?

It all changed after a particularly gruelling visit to the hospital. The nurses told us that poor frail Jeannie had tried to commit suicide. They had no idea where she'd got hold of the razor. Maybe another patient ... they were so very sorry ... she hadn't been considered a particular suicide risk but from now on, of course, she'd be watched more carefully. She'd been found in time, stitched up, and sent back from Casualty heavily sedated for her own safety. We could see her if we liked, but we should-n't expect any response from her.

This time, Harold cried. He was exhausted from the strain of the daily visits, never knowing what to expect. Anger, abuse, tears, hysteria or total lack of interest in life – all were just as wearing. This time Jeannie stared back at him, her eyes glazed and fixed, a soft smile on her face as if she was already in a better place.

Back outside in the car park, we sat together in the car until he felt strong enough to drive home.

'There's something terrible I have to say, Ruby,' he muttered. 'And you're the only one I can say it to.' He took a deep breath and closed his eyes. 'When Sister told us what Jeannie tried to do today, I actually wished for one moment that she'd succeeded.'

I held his hand and squeezed it to show that I understood.

'Isn't that *terrible*?' His eyes shot open and gazed straight into mine. 'I wished her dead, Ruby. I actually wished her dead.'

'For her own sake, that's all. You just wanted the suffering to end. It's not terrible. It's understandable.'

'It can't be normal, Ruby – for a husband to wish his wife dead!'

'It's not a *normal* situation, Harold. You've done your best . . . God knows. Don't be so hard on yourself.'

For a minute we sat like that, holding hands, staring into each other's eyes. Rain beat against the car windows. A flock of gulls, blown in from the coast by the stormy weather, screamed overhead as they swooped and dived in the wind.

'But it isn't just for her,' he whispered finally. 'It isn't only for her sake that I wished it, Rube. *That's* what's so terrible.'

I remember wondering how it could be possible to

feel such pain and such elation at the same time. My heart hurt: I could feel each beat actually hurting me.

I touched his face with my fingertips, wiping away the traces of his tears, and finally, closing my eyes and leaning closer against him, I kissed him – gently at first, my lips following the route of my fingers across his cheek, around his chin, before settling with the touch of a butterfly against his mouth.

It was as if a dam had broken inside both our souls at the same instant. We kissed as if we were the last survivors of the human race: passion mixed with desperation, seasoned heavily with a grief that tore at our hearts so that we were gasping and sobbing as we kissed, and cried, and kissed until we were both weak.

'We'd best go home,' said Harold eventually, staring straight ahead as if he couldn't bear to look at me any more.

'Don't,' I pleaded, touching his hand. 'Don't feel guilty, Harold. Don't think it's wrong. It isn't! You know it isn't!'

But he started the engine without another word. When we got home, we spoke of other things: making the tea, helping the girls with their homework, watching the news. And, at bedtime, it was business as usual. A brotherly kiss on the cheek: separate rooms, separate beds.

When I thought about that kiss in the car afterwards, I began to wonder whether I'd dreamt it. But I knew I hadn't. It had changed everything – and that's why he couldn't bear it.

'There's one of them, at least,' says Harold now. We're sitting out on the terrace enjoying our evening

267

drink, and I've been worrying away at him about the fact that I haven't seen any of our friends since all the rumours and upset began.

It's Andy who's appeared – he's walking back towards the hotel along the seafront, staggering slightly as if he's had a lot to drink.

'He looks a bit the worse for wear,' I comment. 'I wonder where Gemma is?'

'None of our business, woman!' laughs Harold. 'Maybe they've had a row. Maybe it's her that's been arrested.'

'Oh, don't say that!' I gasp. 'Look, Harold, he's really none too steady on his feet. He's going to fall in a minute.'

He's heading out along the jetty, slipping and stumbling as he goes. He's still drinking, too – every now and then he stops, swaying, and drinks from a bottle he's got in his hand.

'Thank God for that,' I comment lightly when he finally reaches the end of the jetty and sits down abruptly, his legs hanging over the edge, staring out to sea. 'I thought he was going to jump in.'

'Honestly, Ruby,' says Harold affectionately, 'you see drama and excitement everywhere, don't you?'

I look at the pair of us, sitting side by side in exactly the same position that we've sat in almost every evening since we've been here, staring out at the sea, like two old codgers without a hope or a dream between us, and suddenly feel the hot threat of tears behind my eyes.

'A bit of drama and excitement wouldn't go amiss,' I retort before I can stop myself.

Harold sighs and looks away, and immediately I wish I could take it back.

'I didn't mean . . .' I try, but I know I'd be lying if I

carried on. I *did* mean it. Well, what can he expect? Yes, I understand; yes, I'm being patient, and loving, and encouraging. I haven't complained. I haven't made a fuss or made demands on him. How could I? 'I just meant,' I amend, blinking back the tears quickly before he notices, 'that it'd make a change to have something different going on.'

'Something other than sitting here with me, being bored half to death, wondering why we bothered to get married?' he says quietly.

I swallow, look straight ahead, without answering.

'Well?' he persists. 'Is that how you feel, Ruby? I wouldn't blame you. I'm not much of a catch, am I? Not much in the way of *excitement* . . .'

'Shut up!' I snap. 'What do you want me to say, Harold? Do you want me to agree with you? Will that make you feel better, if I say yes, you're boring, you're disappointing, I shouldn't have married you? Well, sorry, but I can't – I can't help you. If you want to wallow in your own damned self-pity, you'll have to inflict it all on yourself. I married a man I *know* can be exciting! Who can be fun, and spontaneous, and full of life! If I have to wait for months, or years, for that man to re-emerge, then *that's* a disappointment to me – yes, it is, I'll admit it! But what else can I do? I can't *force* you to get off your arse and bloody well pick up your life again, can I!'

The silence, when I stop, makes me suddenly aware of how loud I've been speaking. Almost shouting.

'Sorry,' I add quietly, automatically. Jesus, what am I turning into? A bloody fishwife. How's that going to help?

'Don't be.' He looks at me almost fiercely. 'Don't ever be sorry for telling me what I need to hear.

269

You're absolutely right. I'm a wimp, a pathetic disgrace of a man. You deserve so much more, Ruby, loving me all these years while I've been with Jeannie . . .'

'You loved *her*.' It doesn't hurt me to say this. It never did. She was my baby sister: she was beautiful, sweet, and fragile. How could anyone not love her?

'*And* you. I loved you too. Always.'

'I know. I know you did. Come on, Harold – let's not discuss this any more: we're both upset. Let's go in. It's getting late . . . What is it? Harold?'

He's jumped to his feet, staring down at the sea as if he's seen a ghost. Pushing back his chair with a scraping sound, he runs towards the steps, taking them two at a time as I follow behind, calling out, tripping as I try to hurry after him.

'Harold? What's happened? What's the matter? Harold!'

By the time I've jumped down the last two steps he's already at the jetty. He's running the length of it, slipping as he goes, stopping to pull off his shoes, and before I can even open my mouth to scream, he's jumped. With the speed and grace of a much younger man, he's jumped straight into the sea, disappearing for a heart-stopping moment beneath the surface and then coming up, gasping, turning his head from side to side, searching for something . . .

Not some*thing*. Some*one*. I cover my mouth with my hand to stop myself from yelling out in fright as I finally realise. Andy! Harold must have seen him slip off the end of the jetty, and even now he's diving beneath the surface for the second time, his shirt billowing out behind him as he disappears from view in the darkness of the water. There's nobody else around; no lifebelt, no means of attracting attention. I need to get help. I turn, desperately struggling to keep my footing on the slippery surface, and begin to pick my way back towards the hotel steps – but almost immediately there's a shout from below me. Unbelievably, Harold's bobbing to the surface again, pulling Andy alongside him, dragging him on to the rocks, coughing and wheezing and spitting out water.

'He's OK! But he's cut his head on the rocks and he's bleeding a lot. He needs some first aid.'

This time I don't even worry about the slippery planks. I run back to the hotel, waving my arms, shouting at the top of my voice.

'Help! I need some help! There's been an accident!'

By the time a posse of hotel staff, first-aiders and passers-by have rushed to the beach with blankets, bandages, towels and a flask of hot tea, the adrenaline's got me shaking so much I can hardly climb back over the rocks myself to reach Harold.

To my surprise, he's standing, strong and sure, wrapped in a blanket and sipping from the cup someone's already handed him, watching anxiously as they treat Andy's cut and help him sit up. He smiles at me.

'Sorry if I frightened you,' he says. 'There wasn't time to explain. I saw him stand up and he just ... fell straight in.'

I put my arms around him. For a minute I think he's shaking but then I remember – that's me.

'Are you sure he's going to be OK?'

'Yes, he's fine. The cut looks worse than it is, but he's a bit out-of-it. Pissed as a fart!' laughs Harold.

'You were amazing,' I tell him. 'You were like –

well, like a bloody Superhero. I've never seen anything like it!'

'Haven't you?' he says, teasingly. 'You've never seen me being amazing before, eh?'

'Not for a very long time!' I laugh. 'Come on, Superhero. Let's get you dried off and into some warm clothes, if these people are all right to look after Andy.'

'OK.' He takes my hand and helps me back over the rocks, stepping surprisingly confidently for someone with no shoes and heavy wet clothes. 'Who's going to be drying me off?' he asks, looking at me suggestively as we make our way up the stairs to our room, leaving a dripping trail of seawater behind us.

I look at him in surprise. Or, to be honest, astonishment would be nearer the truth.

'Well ...' I laugh and push him through the door into the shower room. 'I think perhaps you need a nice hot shower first. As you're so cold.'

'I'm not *that* cold,' he responds, winking at me as I help him out of his wet clothes.

Astonishment turns to downright disbelief. Has Harold had a knock on the head too?

'Come on, Rube,' he says, suddenly taking hold of me, kissing me hungrily, unzipping my dress at the same time. 'You're none too warm yourself. I reckon you'd better get in the shower with me, don't you? Help me soap myself down ... or whatever?'

I've got my clothes off before he's even finished speaking. Before he can change his mind.

'Enough drama and excitement for you now, Ruby Dimmock?' he mutters, pressing himself hard against me.

Bloody hell, I think to myself. This was certainly worth waiting for.

	S	M	T	W	T	**F**	S
					1	2	3
	4	5	6	7	8	9	10
June	11	12	13	14	15	16	17
	18	19	20	21	22	23	24
	25	26	27	28	29	(30)	

Gemma

I feel like I've climbed a mountain, done a jig on the top and climbed back down again, all in the space of twenty-four hours. OK, I guess I'll never know how it feels to climb a mountain, but if it involves aching from head to toe, experiencing breathing difficulties and light-headedness along with a sense of complete disbelief, then point me to Everest – it'll be a doddle after this.

Ruby says I'm probably in shock. I'm the nurse around here – I should know – but I don't even feel capable of making a diagnosis. My head's all over the place. How has this happened? How have we gone from enjoying a peaceful, quiet, romantic honeymoon, to having my husband questioned by police about a missing girl, and then being rescued from drowning, all on the same night? It's too much. I'm going to have to lie down again.

The ridiculous thing is that I didn't even know about it until this morning. I'd gone to bed early, in a bad mood. Well, look, what could you expect? I'd had to see Andy dragged – OK, maybe not dragged, but *led* – away by two police officers who took him into Tomislav's office, and didn't see him again for at least two hours. By that time I'd tortured myself with several terrifying possibilities, the least of which was that he was completely innocent but the police didn't believe him and were going to lock him up anyway. I won't even describe what the *worst* possibility was, but let's just say it took its lead from a thriller I'd watched on TV a few nights before the wedding, involving drugs and body parts. I don't ever want to think those thoughts again, or have the nightmares I had when I finally (after polishing off the entire alcoholic content of the mini-bar in our room) fell asleep. Alone. Andy, when he finally came out of the manager's office, looking pale, tired and angry, had stormed off on his own to get drunk.

Correction. I'm not being fair to him there. He did ask me to go and get drunk with him.

'I just want to *talk*, Andy,' I retorted. At least the police officers had gone without taking him with them, but what now? Were they coming back? Was he in the clear? Had he told them where he'd buried Caroline? I'm joking, now, but like I say – my imagination was playing horrible games with my common sense.

'We can talk in the bar. Come on, Gemma, please? I need to get out of here, and I need a drink so badly, I can't tell you . . .'

'There seems to be a hell of a lot, lately, that you *can't tell me*,' I snapped. I didn't mean to. It was just the anxiety. Two bloody hours, sitting in reception, biting my finger nails, wondering what was going on. Wondering what had happened.

'I'll tell you everything. Just as soon as I've downed the first pint,' he said, calmly, taking my hand.

'Well, if that's the order of your priorities ...'

'OK, forget it then. If we can't talk about this like civilised adults, don't bother. I'll go for a drink on my own. I'll see you later.'

At that point, any normal, nice, caring, loving wife (of less than two weeks) would have run after him, put her arms around him, told him she was sorry, that of course he needed a drink after his ordeal, that she'd wait till he was ready to talk, that she didn't want him going off on his own while he was still feeling so traumatised and shaken. I used to think I was normal, nice, caring and loving – but that all seems to have gone out of the window since the wedding. I seem to have become a nasty, suspicious, shrieking hyena.

'Sod off, then! Don't worry about *me*, thinking the worst, imagining you being locked up for rape, kidnap and bloody murder!' I called after him as he walked away. Very ladylike. A group of English holidaymakers who'd just arrived at the hotel and were checking in at the reception desk turned and stared, and one of the women actually took a couple of steps backwards. Probably wondering if it was too late to change hotels.

I slunk up to our room, feeling sorry for myself. The first beer out of the mini-bar went down so fast I opened a second, swiftly followed by a third. And then the red wine. Then the white. After that I wasn't too bothered by the taste of the cheap whisky – those little bottles only hold a couple of mouthfuls anyway, don't they? The brandy was better, but my lips had gone a bit numb so I spilt some of it. That only left some unidentifiable liqueurs. I kept looking at the time, expecting Andy to be back at any moment. I'd calmed down by then and wished I'd gone with him. Drinking separately was no way to sort out our problems – especially not on our honeymoon. But, then again, I hadn't exactly expected police interrogations when I booked our honeymoon, had I? I saved the last little bottle of liqueur for a while, in case Andy wanted it when he came back, but then I gave up and drank it. Eventually, I had to stop checking the time because I couldn't actually read the figures on my watch any more. And then I fell asleep.

Andy was asleep next to me when I woke up. I wasn't surprised; I'd got a headache and guessed I would have slept heavily apart from the terrible nightmares earlier on. I did wonder how he'd got into the room, but I supposed he must have asked at Reception for another key.

And then I saw the blood.

'Jesus!' I shouted, jumping out of bed and instantly falling over. I jumped out because he was bleeding and I was going to get a flannel. I fell over because I was hungover and the floor came up to meet me.

'Christ!' responded Andy, waking up and seeing me flat out on the floor. 'What's happened? What's the matter?'

'What's *happened*?' I pulled myself slowly to my feet and, holding my head gingerly, crept towards him. '*You* tell *me* what's happened! Did someone attack you? You've been hit over the head!'

'Oh – that,' he said, mildly, touching his forehead and looking at the smear of blood on his fingers. 'It's not as bad as it looks. I had a plaster on it. It must have come off.'

'Who did it? Was it the police? Did they come after you? Did they take you to the cells? Did they beat you?'

'What? Blimey, woman, you should write a thriller!' he said, laughing. 'Nobody beat me or hit me. It's not deep – just a graze, really. I don't know why it's started bleeding again. Maybe I scratched it in the night.'

'But how did it happen? One minute you're going off for a drink; next minute you wake up in bed, bleeding!'

'Not quite!' He was still laughing. 'It probably seems that way to you, Gem – judging by all the empty cans and bottles lying around the room. But one or two things did actually happen in between.'

'Like what?' I took a sneaky look around. He was right. It was a disgrace. Empties and booze spillages everywhere. I'd left the door of the mini-bar open, too – not that it mattered – there was only a packet of salted peanuts left in there.

Now Andy had stopped laughing and was looking a bit sheepish.

'Well, for a start, I got drunk too,' he admitted. 'Only beer, though. Not a complete mix of poisons, like yourself . . .'

'OK, OK, I'm suffering for it. Enough about me!'

'And then I fell off the jetty.'

'You *what*?' I screeched, before remembering that this would hurt my head. 'Bloody hell, Andy,' I went on in a whisper. 'Are you all right?'

'Well, as you can see, I'm fine apart from this little cut and probably a few bruises. But it could have been a whole different story if Harold hadn't come in after me.'

It took me a good minute to respond to this. Harold? *Harold* had jumped off the jetty to rescue Andy? Was I still drunk? Was it another nightmare?

'He saved my life, Gem,' added Andy quietly,

suddenly looking really choked up, like he'd only just woken up enough to realise it. 'I think I passed out when I hit my head on the rocks. I reckon I could have drowned.'

That did it. It knocked everything else completely out of the picture. Let's face it, did it really matter if some annoying bird from his past had turned up during our honeymoon? If he'd kept quiet about something that happened, or didn't happen, six years ago? Whatever else was going on – whatever had happened to Bitch Caroline – it was nothing, absolutely nothing compared with the fact that Andy could have drowned last night – out there in the dark, on his own, while I was getting stuck into miniature bottles of disgusting, unrecognisable bright red spirits. I threw myself into his arms, crying.

'Hey, it's not that bad,' he said, stroking my hair, smiling at me. 'I didn't lose my wallet. The bank notes need drying out, but the credit cards are still there.'

'You nearly *drowned*!' I sobbed, hanging on to him as if this was going to stop him going back and jumping in again.

'But I didn't. I do need to find Harold, Gem, and tell him how grateful I am.' He peeled me off him, gently, and got out of bed, looking for his clothes. 'He'd gone, last night, before I even recovered enough to thank him. They insisted on keeping me downstairs in Reception until a doctor came to check me over. Then someone came up here with me. I think they thought I was going to keel over again, but I was absolutely fine by then. The shock had sobered me up. They had to use the master key to let me in – you were totally dead to the world!'

'I'm so *sorry*! You should at least have woken me up. Told me . . .'

'I tried!' He chuckled. 'You turned over, shouted something about drugs and body parts, and started snoring again.'

We've found Harold and Ruby in their usual spot on the terrace. We both got ourselves so emotional, trying to find the words to thank Harold for his rescue operation, that all four of us ended up in tears. Well, Ruby and I were totally bawling; the guys just kind of swallowed and blinked and looked away.

'He was like a Superhero — absolutely bloody amazing,' Ruby keeps saying, now we've all had a coffee and calmed down a bit. She's looking at Harold like he's her very own film star. He's just smiling back at her, holding her hand. They're grinning like Cheshire cats, the pair of them. Well, perhaps the whole rescue thing has given them both a bit of excitement.

'I want to repay you in some way,' Andy says, looking a bit awkward. 'I just don't know what to suggest. Anything I offer would be an insult compared with you saving my bloody life, mate.'

'I just helped you out of the water,' says Harold modestly. 'You probably would have been OK . . .'

'I don't think so. But, whatever, what you did was . . . well, like Ruby says, bloody amazing. I owe you, big time.'

'Not at all. Glad I was there.'

'Well, look — let us, at the very least, take you both out for a slap-up meal, tonight,' I suggest brightly — before seeing the look on Ruby's face. Too late. Shit. I completely forgot about Harold's problem — his reluctance to do anything that resembles enjoying himself, in case his dead wife's watching from wherever she is. Sorry, that sounds nasty, and I don't mean

279

to be. But – why? I don't understand it. If he was OK about marrying Ruby, what's the problem with moving on from there and having some fun on his honeymoon? Still, it's not for me to say. 'We can eat here, in the hotel, if you prefer,' I add. 'But it'll be on us.'

'Actually,' says Harold slowly, giving Ruby another one of those grins, 'I think it'd be a very good idea to go out tonight.' Her mouth drops open, closely followed by mine. 'How about you take me to this Italian restaurant next door that I've heard so much about?' he adds cheerfully. 'Perhaps your young admirer might like to see that your 'usband is indeed 'appy to be out and about with you!'

'That'd be wonderful, Harold,' she says, wiping a tear from her eye again.

I think she's ecstatic about Harold agreeing to come out for the evening rather than the mere thought of an Italian meal – although I suppose if they've been eating the hotel food for two solid weeks then anything else probably does sound wonderful!

Amazingly, Harold and Ruby have now gone off for a stroll along the seafront.

'I'm so pleased for Ruby,' I say, watching them disappear down the coast path. 'At last he seems to have decided to get up and go.'

'Bit of a bummer that it's happened this late in the fortnight, though,' says Andy.

'I know. But Ruby said something to me earlier about them possibly coming back again next spring – having a second honeymoon, so to speak, pretty soon after the first! She said they'll treat this as a practice run, and do it properly next time. Bless her, she looks so happy now that he's coming out of himself.'

'Harold looks mighty pleased with himself, too.

Probably being a Superhero has perked him up a bit!'

We both fall silent for a moment. Neither of us seems to have the energy to go anywhere or do anything.

'Andy,' I say eventually. Tentatively. 'Are you going to tell me about it?'

He sighs. 'I suppose so.'

'I realise it must have been an ordeal, the police questioning you like that. I'm sorry I was stroppy about it . . .'

'No. It's my fault. Once again – I should have told you what happened. With Caroline. But I was worried you'd read something into it – me going round there to see her.'

I wait. He sighs again, not seeming to know where to start.

'I told the police everything I could,' he adds wearily. 'I think they believe me. But, at the end of the day, she's still missing.'

'No, she's not,' says a voice behind us.

Oh, just what we needed: flipping Felicity, without her two sidekicks this time.

'She's not?' repeats Andy, looking flummoxed. 'How come?'

'I thought I'd let you know straight away,' she says, sounding breathless, like she's run all the way here. 'Obviously we've told the police, but who knows when they'll let you know? If they do at all . . .'

'Just *tell* us, Felicity,' I say, irritably. 'Are you saying Caroline's turned up?'

'Well, yes. No. Not exactly . . .'

'What? She's come back and gone again?' I suggest.

'She hasn't come back at all. But she's finally phoned. She's OK, and we know where she is.'

Not too close, hopefully. The further, the better, as far as I'm concerned.

'In Dubrovnik,' she says, shrugging as if this is only to be expected. 'We went for a day-trip last week and met some guys there. Apparently she's been staying with them.'

'Without letting any of you know? I thought you were supposed to be her friends,' I comment. 'She's caused all this trouble . . .'

'I suspect that was the intention,' says Andy. 'Getting her own back on me again. She must have known how it would look, disappearing just after we'd had . . . a disagreement.'

I can't really comment on this, not yet knowing anything about the disagreement, but it wouldn't surprise me.

'All she said was that she'd gone away because she was upset,' says Felicity, giving Andy a look that implies this is obviously his fault. 'She needed space.'

'Pity she didn't get on a rocket, then, and get fired into it.'

'That isn't really going to help, is it, Jemima?' she rebukes me. I can't even be bothered to correct her. 'Caroline needs our support now. She's obviously been through some sort of major crisis of confidence.' Again, she shoots Andy a filthy look. 'She must have been distraught – she left without even packing a bag. Didn't even take her new designer bikini.'

'Well, I'm *sure* she'll survive somehow!' I've had enough of this. 'To be honest with you, Felicity, I couldn't give a flying fuck about Caroline: whether or not she's distraught, has or hasn't got a bikini, or whether she's stranded in the middle of nowhere with her knickers on fire! She's done her absolute best to ruin our honeymoon, but you can tell her from me –

282

no, you can tell her from *us* –' I grab hold of Andy's arm so violently he almost falls out of his chair '– that it hasn't worked. She can say, or do, what she bloody well likes, it makes no difference to us. She's the loser because Andy and I have got each other and always will have – and she's got nobody because she's such a total bloody bitch! Just tell her that, OK?'

I sit back, breathing hard, satisfied with myself. I nod a couple of times in the silence and repeat, just because I liked the sound of it: 'Just you tell her that!'

'I have,' says Andy quietly.

I look at him in surprise. He's flinching a bit from the way I've been squeezing his arm so tight.

'What?'

'I already have told her that. More or less word for word.'

'When you went round there?'

He nods. I loosen my grip on his arm, before he faints.

'Well,' says Felicity. Her hair has flopped forward over her face and she looks too stunned to push it back. 'Well! No wonder she was upset. No wonder she buggered off.'

'So at least it wasn't a waste of time, then,' says Andy, with a forced smile.

'It sounds like it had the desired effect,' I agree with him.

Felicity doesn't seem to be able to say anything else. We're obviously beneath her contempt. Her hair's still hanging over her face as she leaves. I think it's an improvement.

'So was that *it*?' I ask Andy when she's gone. 'The *disagreement*? You called her all those names . . .'

'And a few more besides.' He sighs. 'I don't know

why I thought it was a good idea, going round there. But after all that crap in the tower bar, I was so angry, I just wanted to make sure she wasn't going to bother us again. After her mates went out, she pretended to be all friendly and sweet. Asked me if I wanted a drink. "No, Caroline," I said. "I haven't come here for a friendly chat and a drink. I've come to tell you to stay right away from me and Gemma. We're on our honeymoon. I wish we weren't staying on the same island as you, but there it is. We don't want to talk to you."'

'How did she take that?'

'Oh, you can imagine. "Andrew darling, don't be like that!"' he mimics in her silly, pretentious voice. "I'm sorry if I've upset Jemima, but really, all I've been doing is talking about our shared memories . . ." I told her that *her* memories seemed to diverge wildly from mine. She pouted at me, called me a few names, and then she seemed suddenly to change tactics. "I'm sorry, Andrew. I'm so sorry if I've made trouble for you with Jemima." She was pretending to cry, trying to look all "hurt little girl" at me, and it was so getting on my nerves. When I got up to go, she became angry again, coming out with all those same old lies about me. That's when I told her she'd better give up because she was never going to come between me and you.'

'That girl has really got problems, Andy.'

'I know. She needs help. I told her that, too. Said she should see someone.' He stops and looks at me anxiously. 'I suppose Felicity's got a point, though, really, Gem – it might have been my fault that she buggered off like that. I probably made her feel pretty shit about herself.'

'Well, whose fault is that? Don't start feeling sorry

for her, Andy! Not after all the trouble she's caused you.'

'No, I don't. I don't feel sorry for her, but I did feel pretty worried when they said she'd disappeared. I really didn't want to think she might have ... done something silly ... because of me.'

I smile at him. 'You're just too nice for your own good, do you know that?'

'I've heard it said!'

He's smiling back, but the smile isn't reaching his eyes. This whole thing with Caroline has really got to him, maybe even more than it has to me. Well, thank God she's over in Dubrovnik now. All I can say is – let's hope she bloody stays there.

Jo

Mark and I are having some lunch at one of the cafés near the harbour when we catch sight of Ruby and Harold walking past.

'Am I dreaming?' says Mark. 'Or was that Harold, out and about?'

'You're not dreaming. It's him, all right. With Ruby. Holding hands and laughing, like they've just won the Lottery.'

'Well, that's good then, isn't it? I wonder how she finally persuaded him to leave the hotel.'

'I don't know. But what a shame it's taken him till nearly the end of the honeymoon. There's only two days left for them to get out and enjoy themselves.'

Only two days left. I feel a wave of sadness come over me – and, at the same time, a sharp jolt of shock at the sadness. I wasn't particularly looking forward to this honeymoon. To be honest, I felt so ill, and so miserable, it was as if I was somewhere outside my own body, letting everyone else take control, watching it all going on as if none of it – Mark, the wedding, his plans for the future – nothing apart from the baby had anything to do with me at all. But now I'm feeling better, I think I could have enjoyed it here. If the circumstances had been different. If I'd been with the man I really loved.

Even thinking that now feels like a betrayal – and not just of Mark, who's been so good to me he *deserves* for me to love him, but of myself, too. It doesn't make any sense, does it? I'm not stupid. I've got a brain in my head. I'm sensible and independent and even, according to my mum and dad, quite headstrong. So why? Why can't I get over loving someone who's hurt me, treated me like crap, never even really loved me? Am I a masochist or what? Don't get me wrong – I'll never go back to Ben. Never. That's the sensible part of me taking control, beating back the pathetic wimp who's still having those dreams every night. I'll say it again: *never*. Every time I say it to myself, I feel better, stronger, more positive. I'm going to beat this thing: not just for Mark's sake but for my own, too. I deserve better. Perhaps I even deserve Mark.

'Do you still think it's odd?' I ask him now, leaning back in my chair, sipping lemonade. 'Ruby and Harold – the whole thing of him loving both sisters?'

'I suppose I do, really,' he admits. 'If he loved the other sister so much, why was he having an affair with Ruby?'

'She says it was never like that. They didn't have an affair.'

'But what she was telling us the other day about that cruise on the Nile ... it all sounded pretty steamy to me!' he laughs.

'No. She said they were never alone together. They obviously knew there was something between them...'

'Yeah! He was married to an invalid, the sister was fit and available and fancied him rotten ...'

'I really don't think it was *like* that. It was just ... romantic,' I add wistfully. To be honest, it had sounded far more sensual than a quick fling in a cabin bunk. The river, the ancient temples, the sounds and scents of Egypt, the walking hand-in-hand around the scarab statue – all conducted under a blistering sun and with a smouldering, inner passion.

'Not very romantic for the poor sister, lying on the boat with her fat butch companion and her *declining health*. If you ask me, it still sounds a bit fishy. I wonder if any of the doctors she saw ever checked her for long-term poisoning!'

'I'm glad I know you're joking,' I tell him, giving his hand a playful smack across the table. He grasps mine and holds on to it.

'Yes, I am joking. I know perfectly well that it's possible to love someone passionately without there being anything physical going on.'

I pull my hand away and drop my eyes.

'I didn't mean ...' he adds quickly. 'That wasn't a complaint. Or a criticism.'

'I know. But it still makes me feel bad. I'm sorry, Mark.'

'Nothing to feel sorry about,' he says, stoutly. 'I told you from the start: I'm willing to wait.'

I don't know what to say. I can't make any promises, but this *is* supposed to be a honeymoon.

'I just hope it won't be for ever,' he whispers with a grin.

'It won't be,' I whisper back.

I *want* to love him. I'm looking at him now: his gentle smile, his kind brown eyes, his powerful physique and strong, clever hands. He's making a career out of healing people – knowing how to ease their pain and help them to move freely again. He's actually trying to do the same for me: I know that. I just need to let go and trust him. What am I waiting for? His patients don't wait for their pain, their disability, to go away on its own before they ask for his help. He's the therapist. He makes it happen.

When we stand up to leave the café, I put my arm through his and lean in closer to him. He gives a little blink of surprise and pulls me round to face him. The hope in his eyes almost kills me. When he lowers his face to kiss me, I don't resist.

'Let's go back to the hotel,' I suggest quietly. 'I think … a lie down might be a good idea.'

'Are you feeling tired?' he asks at once, looking concerned.

'No,' I reply, with a smile. 'Not in the slightest.'

In the event, I haven't thought about Ben at all. Mark's asleep now, one arm draped tenderly across my stomach as if to lay claim to it. To Ben's baby. And now I'm thinking: Is this going to work? Will he really accept this child, little Jacob, when he's born? Will we go on to have more children of our own? Will we be happy? Does anyone ever really know – even childhood sweethearts like Gemma and Andy, who've never wanted anyone else but each other? Can anyone really ever be sure it's all going to work out, for always?

In the midst of all this deliberation, I suddenly become aware that my phone's ringing its head off. It's in my bag, on the other side of the room. I shift Mark's arm, gently, and he turns over, grunting in his sleep as I pad across the room to retrieve it.

'Hello?'

For a few seconds there's silence and I wonder if it's a wrong number or one of those annoying sales calls. Then: 'Hello. Is this Jo?'

It's a woman's voice. She sounds slightly nervous, uncertain.

'Who wants to know?' I ask, cautiously.

Again the silence. I'm wondering whether to hang up. A crank caller who knows my name? I'm not happy about it.

'Who is this?' I ask again.

'This is Leanne,' she says eventually, in very clear, clipped tones now. 'You know who I am, Jo, don't you?'

Shit! I certainly do. She's Ben's wife.

It's the phone call I always used to dread. *One day*, I warned him, *one day she'll find out. Someone'll see us, or she'll find something – my phone number, my name somewhere. Or you'll slip up, call her by my name.* To be honest, I wanted him to. I wanted to know that he cared enough about me to slip up like that; to be thinking of me when he should have been thinking of her. But I wasn't sure if I'd be able to cope with the consequences. I think I always knew what those consequences would be: that he'd finish with me and stay with her.

'What do you want?' I ask quietly. My heart's knocking against my ribs. I take the phone into the bathroom, close the door, sit on the toilet lid with a towel wrapped round me.

'Just to tell you that I know all about it,' she says. Her voice is shaking. I feel a sudden overwhelming sympathy for her. It's so violent and unexpected, I actually think for a minute I'm going to vomit. I have to take deep breaths and lower my head. 'Are you still there?' she says.

'Yes. I'm ... so sorry.' It's totally inadequate. What else can I do? Hang up? That's the coward's way, I suppose.

'I found the e-mail,' she says, sounding suddenly stronger. Angry. I don't blame her. 'The e-mail he sent you – on your fucking *honeymoon*.'

'I'm sorry,' I whisper again.

'Oh, don't worry. I read your reply too. I can see you don't want any more to do with him. You've moved on. Lucky you.' Her bitterness is evident. She'd probably like to move on herself, right now. 'But what about the baby?'

Little Jacob rolls over inside me, and I put my free hand protectively over my stomach.

'He's mine,' I tell her fiercely. 'Nothing to do with Ben. He didn't want it. He told me to ...'

The words hang in my throat, unspoken. It's bad enough for his wife to find out about the affair, about the pregnancy, for God's sake, without also finding out her husband's a total heartless bastard.

'He says he's not convinced it's his,' she tells me.

There's a red mist in front of my eyes. I jump to my feet – not that I know how this is going to help. I almost throw the phone into the sink.

'He said that?' I yell. There's a snort of surprise from the bedroom and the thump of running feet. Mark's standing in the bathroom doorway, his hair on end, staring at me in shock. 'Who the hell?' he mouths. I realise I'm shaking. 'How dare he say that? Put him on! Put him on the fucking phone! He has *no right*! He *knows* . . .!' I take a deep, shuddering breath and go on, more quietly: 'He knows perfectly well it's his baby. If he said that, he's even more of a bastard than I thought.'

'Yes,' she says simply. 'You're right. He is.'

'I don't want anything from him. If that's what you're worried about, forget it. I don't want a penny – I don't want to see him again. Ever. I'm married now!' I glance at Mark, who's leaning against the door post, frowning, anxious. 'I'm married to someone who actually cares about me . . .'

'Yes. Mark.' I'd forgotten she must know him. 'You don't know how lucky you are, Jo.'

My eyes fill up with tears. I want to tell this woman I didn't mean it; I didn't mean to hurt her, to destroy her marriage, break her heart . . . but it won't make any difference. To her, I'll always be the other woman: the mistress, the slut who slept with her husband.

'I'm sorry,' I say again, wiping my eyes.

'Did you know?' she asks coldly. 'When you . . . started having sex with my husband, did you know he had a wife and children?'

'No,' I whisper.

'Well, I suppose that's one thing in your favour. Half the girls on the campus are always throwing themselves at him. I suppose it's inevitable he's going to be tempted now and then.'

He told me I was the first. I sit back down on the toilet lid with a defeated thump.

'But you're the first one to try the pregnancy trick,' she adds.

'It wasn't a trick! I ...' I stroke my stomach again; look at Mark, look away, shame making me flush. 'It was an accident,' I lie. 'My own fault. I'll live with the consequences.'

'Will you?' she says sarcastically. 'Well, so will I. I haven't any choice. I've got two little girls who love their daddy to think about. If it wasn't for them, believe me, I'd pack my bags right now. Just think about *that*, Jo, when you talk about the consequences. They aren't just for you. You've got a nice new husband to look after you. You'll be all right.' She's crying now. And I'm feeling like the scum of the earth.

'I can understand how you feel ...' I begin.

'No, you can't!' shrieks Leanne. I flinch. 'You have *no idea* how I feel. *You* ... you just saw something you wanted, and took it! You didn't bother to find out what his situation was ...'

'He didn't bother to tell me!'

'But when you realised, what did you do, Jo? Kick him out of your little student bed? Send him home to me? Oh, no. You carried on until you got what you bloody well wanted!'

'It wasn't like that! It wasn't! I loved ...' I blink back tears. Too late to stop. 'I loved him,' I whispered.

'Love!' she spits contemptuously. 'You call that love? How old are you, girl? Nineteen? Twenty?' I don't bother to answer. I can hear her breathing, heavily, harshly, and wonder whether she's had a drink before making this call. Probably, and who could blame her? 'You've got a lot to learn about love,' she finishes quietly, and hangs up the phone.

For a minute I sit still, tears running down my face, until Mark takes the phone out of my hand

and pulls me to my feet, wraps his arms around me, shushes me like a baby.

'She's right,' I sob. 'I deserve everything she said. I'm a horrible, cheating person. She's got two little girls, and her husband's a pig, and she can't leave him! I haven't given her a thought. I've been so obsessed with my own feelings ... I hate myself! I'm a bitch! Why did you marry me?'

'Because I love you,' Mark says without a moment's hesitation. 'And you're not any of those things.' He kisses the tears away from my eyes, rocks me in his arms. 'You're just a girl who's made a mistake, that's all. Leanne's hurt, yes – but so are you. You're both victims. There's only one nasty bastard in this story.'

'I know.' I sniff, wipe my face on a towel. 'I know that. He actually tried to pretend the baby might not be his!' My voice is rising again with indignation. 'How dare he! He's saying I slept around!'

'Like I said: a nasty bastard. I don't know how we were ever friends. I'm just glad ...' Mark lifts my face to his and smiles at me a little bit uncertainly. 'Glad you haven't still got any feelings for him?'

It's a question. A question that, in the circumstances – the circumstances of this phone call, to say nothing of the circumstances of our very satisfactory lovemaking a little while ago, definitely deserves an answer.

'No,' I say. 'No feelings left for him at all.'

It's almost the truth.

	S	M	T	W	T	F	**S**
							1
	2	3	4	5	6	7	8
July	9	10	11	12	13	14	15
	16	17	18	19	20	21	22
	23	24	25	26	27	28	29
	30	31					

Gemma

I'm having trouble getting Bitch Caroline out of my mind. I know, I know – I promised myself, when I found out Andy could have drowned the other night, that I'd stop all this: tormenting myself about Caroline. I actually don't mind too much that he went round there and confronted her. I'm glad he stood up to her. It's just the fact that he didn't tell me. He seems, suddenly, so full of secrets.

I keep going back, in my mind, over the things that have blown up during our time here: like when he said that if he fathered a child by another woman, he'd want to support it. I *know* I took that all the wrong way – got hysterical, made something out of nothing. It was quite a reasonable thing to say, after all, but I must admit, his reaction to meeting up with Caroline made me feel quite irrationally suspicious – and I was still upset about his sudden announcement that he wanted us to delay starting our own family. I've tried to take on board that, like Ruby suggested, Andy might be suffering some sort of stress himself, without even realising it. But all I can see is that he's behaving strangely, being secretive and wary.

'Are you sure everything's all right now?' I asked him last night when we were getting ready to go out. 'There isn't anything else you haven't told me, is there?'

'What do you mean?'

That's not an answer, is it? He looked awkward, evasive. Or am I still just being paranoid?

Well, like I say, I've promised myself nothing else matters since he came so close to drowning. If there's anything else to discuss, we'll just have to talk about it when we get home.

We went out with Ruby and Harold – our treat, to thank Harold for rescuing Andy. When I look at Harold – who strikes me as your typical middle-aged man who potters around in his slippers doing the crossword in the paper – it's hard to believe he actually leapt out of his chair, raced down that slippery jetty, threw himself into the water and dragged a younger, fitter, half-conscious guy out.

'Harold's quite a fitness fanatic himself, you know,' replied Ruby proudly when I said this to her.

'Really?' I didn't mean to sound quite so surprised. It's just that, until now, we'd hardly even seen him moving.

'Oh, yes. At home, he goes to the gym three times a week. Does about an hour on those strange machines.' Ruby grimaced. She obviously didn't share Harold's enthusiasm. 'And then he swims. I'm not saying he's as good as young Jo. He doesn't race, or anything like that. Just swims length after length of crawl. He says he's built for endurance rather than speed.'

'Well, good for him!' I was truly impressed. I glanced at Andy, who'd been listening. 'I doubt whether we'll be that fit when we're your age, Ruby.'

'Oh, you can count me out of it, love. I don't do anything like that – too much like hard work. I know I could do with losing a stone or two but I like my food too much. And my wine! My daughters are always nagging away at me: "Think about your heart, Mum."' She sighed. 'I reckon if my heart's managed to stand up to everything I've put it through, over the years, it'll be good for a while yet.'

I laughed. 'I'm sure you're right.'

'And anyway,' she lowered her voice, 'I actually think Harold overdoes it, at times. I think he works out so hard to put things out of his mind. You know what I mean?'

'Yes, I do.'

'Endurance. He's always talking about endurance, as if it's a goal he has to attain. Whereas, in fact, it's what he's been doing almost his entire life.'

From what we've seen, though, I reckon Harold's turned a corner. I don't know what happened the other night, when he rescued Andy from the sea. Perhaps something clicked in him – you know, like they show a bulb lighting up above someone's head, in cartoons – making him think about how easily Andy could have drowned if he hadn't been there, and how fragile life is (as if he didn't already know that, poor chap), and how we all need to live for the moment and try to be happy. Whatever, he certainly seems different now.

'I'm looking forward to this,' he said eagerly, a spring in his step as we walked the few yards from the hotel to Mario's restaurant. 'After everything you've all said about how good the food is.'

'It *is* good, Harold,' I told him.

I was suddenly aware that Ruby was the only one being quiet as we approached the restaurant. She actually didn't look quite herself and I found myself hoping she wasn't feeling ill or anything.

The door was opened for us by an oily-looking middle-aged waiter who showed us immediately to a table at one side of the restaurant. I noticed Ruby breathing sharply, looking around her – and suddenly I realised: she was worried about Luciano. Oh, bugger. We shouldn't have taken her here. Of all the places we could have brought her, why here? Why didn't we think? She was bound to be embarrassed if stupid Luciano started playing up to her, in front of us; in front of Harold.

Unfortunately, Harold didn't seem to have any such qualms.

'So where is he, then?' he joked as we all studied our menus. 'Where's Lover Boy, eh, Ruby? This is where he hangs out, isn't it?'

'Shush, Harold!' she whispered, miserably. She was trying to hide behind her menu.

And there he was. I wasn't even sure if Ruby had seen him yet – and he certainly hadn't seen her. He was attending to a couple of English ladies at the table behind us: they were both, probably, in their forties and looked like sisters. There was a lot of giggling and blushing going on, and Luciano was bending very close to them, bowing and smiling and fawning as he poured their wine.

'I cannot believe what I am 'earing!' he was saying.

297

'You beautiful ladies 'ave come *all alone* to 'ave your dinner? Please, ladies, do not worry! I, Luciano, will look after you! It will be an honour for me to serve you.'

'Ooh, isn't he cheeky, Maggie!' giggled one of the women.

'I'd like to take you home with me to Bolton!' sniggered the other.

'I am only 'appy to 'elp two lonely ladies enjoy their evening. Whatever I can do, Signore, to make your evening perfect, it will make me very 'appy to do it,' came the slick reply. I glanced at Ruby. She was looking straight back at me, but her expression told me she was listening. She wasn't going to turn round, but she was listening, all right.

'What is it, Ruby love?' asked Harold, suddenly noticing her expression.

'Nothing! Nothing at all, I'm fine,' she said, flustered, picking up her menu and fanning herself with it. 'What are we all having? Pasta? Pizza? There's loads of . . . um . . . pasta on the menu, and lots of . . . um . . . pizzas . . .'

'Are you all right, Ruby?' said Andy, frowning at her. I gave him a nudge and tried to indicate Luciano with my eyebrows, but it was no good. Men just don't do subtlety, do they? So I kicked him under the table instead.

'Ow!' He looked at me in surprise. 'What's that for, Gem? What's the matter with everyone? Why . . . oh. I get it. Hello, Luciano.'

He'd stopped at our table on his way to get more drinks from the bar for his *beautiful ladies*.

'This is a most wonderful surprise!' he exclaimed. 'My beautiful Ruby, *and* her 'usband, *and* my young friends from the 'otel! This is indeed a very wonderful evening for me! I am so honoured! I think it means we

298

must celebrate! I think we must 'ave the best wine in the 'ouse – I will bring this wine now, and it will be my pleasure, not only to serve this wine on the 'ouse, with the compliments of my uncle who is the owner of the *ristorante*, but also to join you, my friends, for a glass of this wine! If you will permit?' He bowed extravagantly, his eyes twinkling all the time at Ruby.

'That'd be very nice, mate,' said Andy at once, not about to pass up on a free bottle of wine.

Luciano swept off to the bar, returning in due course with a tray, balanced professionally on one hand, from which he dispensed two drinks to the table behind us, where we could hear the sisters giggling and protesting that he was *so sweet*, *so cute*, and (this one meant to be under the breath) had *such a great arse*.

He then returned to our table and took our orders, with much smacking of his lips and kissing of his fingertips to show how well we'd chosen. He then proceeded expertly to open and pour a bottle of Valpolicella, adding a small amount to a fifth glass for himself which he raised and declared: 'I wish to make the toast to my very special friends who 'ave done me the great honour – despite my most shameful mistake and impropriety with the matter of the ring, which was on account of the dishonesty of the cousin of the neighbour of the chef who sells the bad CDs – of coming to my *ristorante* tonight, to enjoy the wonderful delicacies of my chef, who is the friend of my uncle, who has taken me in and taught me my trade, and provided for me and cared for me as a mother loves her child. *Salute*, my friends!'

He was close to tears at this point, and personally I was so staggered by the length and formality of this toast that all I could do was raise my glass and echo: '*Salute*'. As we gulped our wine I noticed Ruby looking down at the table in front of her, still looking quite uncomfortable. Not that Harold seemed to be aware of her discomfort – not a bit of it.

'So, young man!' he began, plonking his glass down on the table. 'I believe you had something to say to me – something about me being happy?'

Ruby groaned softly and looked like she wanted to leave, if not fall down and die, but Luciano, standing almost to attention in front of us, nodded calmly and agreed.

'Yes, Signore, this is true. I, Luciano, 'ave wished only to see the beautiful Signora Ruby smiling and 'appy as she deserves to be. And – if you will excuse my impropriety, Signore – I 'ave seen that only if the 'usband is 'appy will this beautiful lady also be 'appy. Is this not so?'

'It's very much so, Luciano,' said Harold, getting to his feet with great dignity and shaking his hand. 'I'd like to thank you for that very intelligent observation. And for looking after my wife when she was, unhappily, alone, because her husband was too foolish to look after her himself.'

'Not foolish, Harold!' exclaimed Ruby, looking up at last.

'Not foolish, Signore, to be sick and un'appy,' agreed Luciano with another little bow. 'And now, I think, I bring your starters and also, perhaps, because this is a special celebration, I bring more wine. Yes?'

'Yes, please,' said Andy. 'You're right – it's a *very* special celebration tonight, Luciano. This guy here –' he indicated Harold, '– dived into the sea last night to rescue me when I fell in and hit my head on the rocks. If it hadn't been for him . . .' He shook his head and looked down at the table. 'This is why we're celebrating,' he added after a suitable pause.

300

Luciano stood rooted to the spot, staring at Harold, his mouth open in amazement.

'You are this hero?' he asked in hushed tones. 'You are this Superman who has been spoken of by my friends who work at the 'otel? You are he? He are you?' His emotions had apparently run away with his grammar temporarily. 'This I cannot believe! I am thinking, this hero, he must be a young, strong man of many muscles, who runs, who jumps, who flies into the water and carries out the poor drunken fool who has fallen! Forgive me, my friend, but this is the story they are telling me,' he adds to drunken fool Andy without shifting his gaze from Harold the Hero. 'My friend, I am honoured to be in the presence of such a man as you! I kiss your hand!' He grabbed Harold's hand, almost knocking over the rest of his wine, and held it to his lips, his eyes wide with admiration. 'I am 'umble! I prostrate myself . . .'

'No, no – for Christ's sake, don't do that,' said Harold quickly, looking very uneasy. 'Just get the starters, there's a good chap, and we'll forget about the other stuff, eh?'

'You will forgive my impropriety, Signore Hero, with the token of the ring, which was on account of the dishonesty of the cousin of the . . .'

'. . . neighbour of the chef. Yes, no problem – we all get taken in by that kind of thing from time to time, lad. Just don't go around giving rings to ladies any more, eh? Not always a very sensible idea, unless you've got ideas of marrying them.'

'I am grateful for your advice, Signore, grateful for your wisdom, and your patience, and your great understanding, and . . .' He saw the look on Harold's face and added quickly, 'And now I go right away for your starters.'

301

We were all thoroughly pissed by the time we left. The food was as wonderful as Luciano had promised; Harold was great company, telling us stories about his work with the special needs children whose bus he drove, and about his old days in the publishing industry when he personally signed deals with some of the great contemporary authors. He also talked about things Ruby had already told us: about their life together, about their famous holiday in Egypt – which, of course, I found really exciting and romantic because of my own long-held fascination with Ancient Egypt – and about her children of whom he seems tremendously fond, the two boys from her first marriage and two girls from the second, all grown up now. When he mentioned Jeannie, his first wife, he looked down at the table and we all flinched slightly, thinking he shouldn't have done that – but then he just cleared his throat, looked up and carried on. Ruby was the one who had to dab her eyes.

We stayed until the restaurant was empty and the staff, including Luciano, were leaning against the walls, looking like they were ready for their beds.

'We're very sorry,' said Ruby as we got up to leave. 'We've talked so much, and eaten so much . . . and drunk so much! . . . we didn't realise how late it was.'

'Signora Ruby,' replied Luciano solemnly, taking her hand, 'if I had to stay awake all night, it would have been my privilege and my greatest honour to have served yourself and the Hero 'usband, and my young friend here who was brought back from the dead!' He put his hands together as if thanking God for the walking miracle that was Andy. 'Please give me and my uncle, and the chef, and the second chef, and all our staff in the kitchen, the honour of coming again to

302

our *ristorante* before you go 'ome to the England.'

'Sadly, we have only one more night,' said Ruby, who seemed to have recovered her composure around Luciano as the wine began to flow. 'But perhaps . . .'

'Tomorrow is your last evening at Korčula' he gasped, putting his hand over his mouth in horror. 'Please, tell me this cannot be true? You leave us already?'

'We'll have been here for two weeks,' I said. 'But we don't want to go home, either.'

'In this case, then tomorrow must be another party!' he declared. 'Tomorrow evening our *ristorante* will be at your disposal – the best table in the 'ouse, the best wine, the best dishes of the chef's creation! You will come, yes? To 'ave the last evening of your 'oliday with poor Luciano, who will be lonely and bereft when you 'ave gone?'

I think we said yes. We were all so slaughtered, we might have agreed to anything. I do remember what Ruby said, though, as we staggered, arm-in-arm, back to the hotel.

'Bloody lonely and bereft, my arse! The cheeky little bugger! Did you hear him carrying on with those two women from Lancashire on the table behind us? *You beautiful ladies, all alone*!' she snorted, and then said, a little sadly, half under her breath: 'I almost thought he meant it when he said that to me. Silly old bat!'

'I think he did mean it, actually, Rube,' said Harold, giving her a hug. 'And who could blame him, eh? Who could blame him?'

This morning we lie in bed late, neither of us wanting to think about the fact that we oly have one more morning like this. We leave tomorrow.

'Come on,' says Andy eventually, getting up and heading for the shower. 'Let's enjoy our last day in the sunshine. It's probably pissing it down with rain at home.'

'Oh, *don't* say that!' I groan, hiding my head under the pillow. 'I don't think I can get up, Andy. I still feel full of wine and food from last night.'

'A nice stodgy breakfast will sort you out,' he says, coming back to pull me out of bed. I stagger to my feet and we stand for a moment, holding on to each other, swaying together as if we're dancing. 'What do you want to do on our last day, then?'

'Hm. Let's think. Well, I *don't* want to go back to Badija and get stranded there again ...'

'Spoilsport,' he laughs gently. 'How about getting the ferry over to Orebić again? It looks like being really hot today. There were sandy beaches there, and we can do some swimming ...'

'Yes, that sounds great.'

'And there was that really nice restaurant where we had lunch last time ...'

'Andy!' I protest, pushing him away. 'How *can* you even think about eating!'

But I do manage breakfast, amazingly, and it does make me feel more human. Jo and Mark come in and join us at our table, and we tell them about last night's dinner at Mario's.

'We said we'd go back there tonight,' says Andy. 'At least – I think we did! Do you want to come with us?'

'That'd be really nice, wouldn't it, babe?' says Mark.

She agrees, but I notice she seems a bit subdued.

'Is everything all right?' I ask her quietly when Mark gets up to get another cup of coffee.

'Yes. Sorry, I still feel a bit ... shell-shocked. I had a call from Ben's wife yesterday.'

'Christ! She's found out about you?'

Jo nods. 'And about the baby. She read our e-mails.'

I wait, not knowing what to say.

'I feel like shit,' she whispers, looking down at her breakfast plate. 'I feel ... so ashamed.'

'It wasn't your fault!' I protest, stoutly. Andy's eating his breakfast next to me, noisily, looking the other way, pretending not to listen.

'Yes, it was. I've kept telling myself that, Gemma – that it wasn't my fault, I was the innocent victim in all of it – but after talking to her – Leanne – I can't feel sorry for myself any more. Of course I didn't know he was married at the beginning, but when I did find out, I should have finished with him straight away. I told myself I couldn't because I loved him so much.' She looks up at me and smiles. 'But, as my dad used to tell me when I was little – *there's no such thing as can't.*'

'But at the time,' I tell her, putting my hand over hers on the table, 'at that time, it obviously *felt* like you couldn't.'

'Yes. And now I realise that she, his wife, *really* can't walk away. She's got two little girls: she needs to stay with him. I feel sorry for her. I wish I'd tried harder to think about her at the time. I just blocked her out, like she didn't exist.'

'So did he. That was worse, much worse! She was his *wife!*'

'I know.' Jo sighs, gives me another weak little smile. 'And now it's all come out, he's telling more lies to try to save his marriage. Do you know what he's told her? That he's not convinced my baby is his.'

305

'The bastard!'

'Exactly. I hate him for that – and for telling me it was the first time he'd had an affair. His wife said he was always at it.'

'Then more fool her, for putting up with it. Kids or no kids, she'd be better off without him.' I'm thinking bitterly now of my dad – of course. And, with a sudden pang, of my poor mum. Of all those lonely years on her own, with a baby to bring up and an elder daughter she couldn't get along with.

'Easier said than done, I suppose.'

'Yes. But there's something to be happy about in all this, Jo.'

'Is there?' She looks at me doubtfully.

'You've just told me you hate him – Ben. I think that's a step in the right direction.'

She actually laughs at this. Another step forward. I thought she might have hit me.

'You're right! And it's true – the anger I feel now, when I think about him, is such a relief it's almost exhilarating!'

'Good for you. Focus on that, girl!' I watch Mark walking back, carrying his coffee cup and a glass of fruit juice for Jo. He smiles at her across the hotel dining-room. 'And on him,' I add quietly. 'He's lovely, Jo.'

'I know.' Her eyes grow soft as she watches him approaching. 'He is. And I *am*, Gemma – he's all I'm focusing on now, believe me. Him and my baby.'

'You'll be OK then,' I tell her firmly. 'You'll survive.'

We walk the length of the promenade in Orebić until we reach one of the furthest beaches where it's peaceful and uncrowded. The sand's soft here, the sea's warm and shallow. We have to wade out quite

306

a way to be able to swim. Afterwards, we lie on the sand, holding hands, drying off. This is perfect. A perfect last day of a perfect honeymoon. Well – almost perfect.

I close my eyes, trying to blot out thoughts of that bitch who almost ruined everything for us. Caroline.

'I wonder why she's like it?' I muse, before I realise I've spoken aloud.

'What? Who?' Andy's half asleep beside me.

'Caroline. I wonder if there's a *reason* for her being such a bitch?'

'Oh, Gem, let's not start on that again. Not today,' he says, opening his eyes, raising himself on one elbow to look at me.

'I'm not. I'm not *starting* anything. I just can't help wondering.'

He sits up straight suddenly, giving himself a little shake and looking out at the sea.

'I know,' he admits eventually. 'I've been wondering, too.'

'You have?' I'm too surprised to be annoyed.

'Yes. She's obviously such a mess. So mixed up. I just wish I'd realised it, when I first met her. Sorry, Gem . . .'

'Wel, no point being upset about it now, is there?' I shrug. 'I guess I can't blame her for trying to get her hooks into you. You *are* a bit special, I suppose.'

He laughs and pushes me back down on the sand, leaning over me, planting little kisses on my face and neck until I can't stand it any more and reach round the back of his head to pull him closer and kiss him properly.

Poor bloody Caroline. She knew something special when she saw it – and, for once in her life, she didn't get what she wanted.

At least – I don't *think* she did, says the little voice

in the back of my head that I'm trying my hardest to ignore.

Ruby

'That was such a good night, last night!' says Harold, for probably the tenth or twelfth time this morning. 'Wasn't it a great meal, Ruby? And such good company – that young Luciano is certainly a character.'

'Yes,' I agree somewhat doubtfully. We're having a walk this morning, along the coast the other side of the hotel, having explored Korčula Town together yesterday. We're trying to make up for lost time, but there just aren't enough hours left now to go dashing around the island seeing all the places I wanted to see. They'll have to wait for next time.

'You don't seem too sure about him,' comments Harold.

The quantities of wine I drank last night must have somewhat blunted my inhibitions. I didn't feel awkward around Luciano, even after I heard him using the same old chat-up lines on those two women sitting behind us. But, if I'm honest, character or not, I still think he's full of shit. Far too much to say for himself, for someone so young.

'Well, I suppose it brings in the punters,' I say grudgingly.

'That's a bit cynical!' Harold looks at me with amusement.

'Remember, I'm talking from experience now. Middle-aged ladies, on their own, get subjected to that torrent of flattery, delivered in that wonderful accent, and inevitably go away thinking they've got an admirer.'

I feel a fool, obviously. Not that I was completely taken in, you understand.

'You *have* got an admirer, Rube. But he's a tired old Englishman rather than a virile young Italian!'

I laugh. There's been quite enough virility around here for me, the last couple of nights, thank you very much. And that's still something of a surprise, I can tell you. We might have been together a long time and I've always realised what some people must think, but I've tried not to let it bother me. If they don't understand – don't know the truth – why should I care? I'm open about it because I've got nothing to hide. Yes, I fell in love with my brother-in-law. Yes, he did with me. But we didn't fall into bed together as some people obviously imagine – we *wanted* to, but we didn't. We made that sacrifice for all those years. Most young people think everything begins and ends with sex. They don't understand that, nice though it is, it doesn't actually matter as much as the media would have you believe. There's so much more to loving someone. Some of them might be surprised to know that the truth is – until this week, we'd only actually had sex once. And that was a disaster.

It was the night Jeannie died.

A couple of months after her suicide attempt, we were warned that the doctors were almost certainly fighting a losing battle. Jeannie's kidneys were failing, her heart wasn't beating properly, and the chemical balance of her body had been so disturbed over the many years she'd been starving herself that it was now impossible to turn back the clock. They were doing their best – but she was slipping out of their grasp.

'I just want her to go quickly,' said Harold when we came home from the hospital on what turned out to be the last day of her life. He closed his eyes as he said it, as if he couldn't bear to see my reaction. 'As quickly as possible – it's what she would want.'

'Yes. It is.'

We hugged each other, and cried, and talked about Jeannie and how her life had become a burden to her. We fell asleep for a while, holding each other, and when we woke, we lay for a long time in each other's arms, looking at each other in silence.

'I love you, Ruby,' he whispered suddenly. It was the first time he'd ever actually voiced it.

'I love you, too.' The words hurt my throat and scalded my lips. 'I've always loved you!'

'It's not right...' he began to say as I leant over him and started to kiss him. 'She's lying there ... in the hospital ...'

But I kissed him harder, so that he couldn't speak, couldn't protest. Within minutes, we were tearing off each other's clothes. Years and years of holding back and waiting had made us both greedy and desperate. Now we'd finally stepped over the mark, nothing was going to stop us. No thoughts of Jeannie, no fears of breaking marriage vows, no reminders of the hospital, the sickness, the approaching end. He was actually inside me when the phone rang. We nearly didn't answer it, but it wouldn't stop. The ringing was a constant, throbbing accompaniment to the throbbing of my body.

'It was the hospital,' said Harold, pushing away from me after he'd finally reached out and grabbed the phone. 'She's gone, Ruby. She passed away while you and I were ...' He hung his head and groaned. 'She slipped away in her sleep and *died*. What the *hell* were we thinking of?'

*

310

It's been over a year now since that night. Harold and I have slept together since then: oh, yes, we both needed the comfort, the warmth of another body next to our own during the long cold nights, when it felt tempting to give in to the same misery and despair that Jeannie herself must have known so well. We came through it, of course, as everybody always does – and eventually started to allow ourselves to enjoy being together, guilt-free at last. But whenever Harold tried to make love to me it brought back the memory of that terrible first time, and ended up with him being so distressed I had to tell him it didn't matter, it wasn't important – we'd been all these years without it, we didn't really need it, did we?

So – what can I say? It's come as a surprise. A bonus, if you like. The icing on the cake. I thought I had everything I'd ever wanted already ... But now – well, I'm the luckiest old woman in the world.

There's a little restaurant just round the next bay. We decide to stop here and have some lunch.

'Ah, this is so romantic!' I sigh contentedly as we sip our wine at a table on the terrace, overlooking the sea.

'You sound like Gemma,' he teases. 'That's all that girl seems to talk about – *romance*. I bet she reads scores of paperbacks where girl meets boy and they all live happily ever after.'

'Don't be so patronising and dismissive, Harold Dimmock. There's nothing wrong with a bit of romance. We need it more than ever in this world today, to escape from all the awful things that go on.'

'Fair enough.' He grins. 'I apologise. Yes, it's very romantic here.' He suddenly sighs and adds quietly,

'Actually, Ruby, it *is* lovely. I wish I hadn't been such a bloody fool and missed so much of it.'

'No point crying over spilt milk,' I tell him briskly. 'We're coming back again, that's the main thing.'

'Yes.'

'And ... you're all right,' I add more softly. 'That's *really* the main thing. You're ... a lot better. Aren't you, Harold?'

'I seem to be, don't I, Rube?' He grimaces. 'Stupid old fool, skulking away like that, feeling sorry for myself.'

'You weren't feeling sorry for yourself. You know what the doctor said. It's all part of the grieving process. It affects everyone differently, you can't rush it, you just have to work through it and ...'

'He was wrong, Ruby.'

I look at him in surprise. 'What do you mean, he was wrong? I don't think so, Harold. I mean, I think he knows what he's talking about. He was very good, very kind ...'

'Yes, yes, of course he was. Because he thought this was all about Jeannie. All about my grief at losing her. But he was wrong. It wasn't about her at all. It was all about me.'

'You've lost me now, love.' And I'm slightly worried, to be honest. I thought we were heading *out* of the Slough of Despond. You know? Leaving behind all the misery and self-recrimination. 'It wasn't about *you*. It was about Jeannie. We *both* felt it. We both loved her.'

'Not at the end.' He puts down his wine glass and drops his head, rubbing his hand over his mouth as if he's not sure whether to go on. 'This is what I've never told you, Ruby ...'

'Then don't, Harold!' I feel suddenly very alarmed.

I don't want him to say anything that's going to hurt him. It doesn't matter. Whatever it is, it doesn't matter! 'Don't tell me now, if you don't want to. I don't care what . . .'

But he lifts his head again, meets my eyes, and tells me very directly.

'I didn't love her, Ruby. Not at the end. I don't know when I stopped – some time during those last few years, or those last few terrible months maybe, when she was destroying herself. We were doing everything we could to save her – and I used to look in her eyes and think: You just don't care. You don't care what you're doing to me – to Ruby – to everyone who loves you. You're not even trying to get better.'

'She couldn't help it, Harold.'

'I knew that! Of course I did! Why do you think I felt such terrible, terrible guilt? It was bad enough, knowing how I felt about *you*. But when I realised I'd stopped loving Jeannie, I . . . just couldn't forgive myself. I couldn't let myself admit it. I had to pretend . . . and keep on pretending. I couldn't even tell the doctor.'

'Or me,' I say, holding his hand.

'Especially not you, Rube. What would you have thought of me? She was your baby sister. You entrusted her to me, back then when we first met. I promised when I married her that I'd love her for ever. *In sickness and in health.* I broke that promise, Ruby. It's taken me till now to admit it. Some husband, eh?'

'Harold,' I tell him, gripping his hand more firmly, 'what *are* you talking about? You were a fantastic husband to my sister. You never let her down; never betrayed her, never left her. Most men would have done! She tried our patience. Yes, she was sweet, and beautiful, and everyone loved her ... but let's be honest! She was also self-obsessed, and weak, and given to those terrible depressions. I adored her, but she wasn't easy! You *loved* her to the end, Harold Dimmock, whether you *felt* like you did or not. You loved her in the way you cared for her, and put her first. Don't you dare be telling yourself anything different! Hold your head up, Harold, and be as proud of yourself as I am!'

'Are you, Ruby?' he asks quietly with tears in his eyes. 'Even now?'

'Especially now!' I retort. I realise I'm sounding almost cross, I'm so vehement, and I lower my voice and touch his face gently, smoothing away the lines of worry. 'I'm more proud of you than ever. You've admitted something to yourself now that must have been horrifying the life out of you, every time you thought about it.'

'It has been. You're right.'

'And now – look! Have you been struck down for saying it? Has the world stopped turning?'

'No.' He smiles. 'Actually, the world feels absolutely great. I feel like I've set myself free.'

'Thank God for that,' I say, giving him a quick kiss. 'Here's the waiter with our lunch now. I couldn't bear the world to stop turning before I've eaten it.'

We're laughing together before we've even taken a mouthful of our food – laughing like two silly children on a school outing. Or like two lovers on their honeymoon, if you like.

I'm sorry, Jeannie. So sorry, my darling sister. You know we both did our best. But the legacy you left us with is just this: the determination to eat, drink, and be merry. For tomorrow ...

Bugger tomorrow. Today's wonderful.

July	**S**	M	T	W	T	F	S
							1
	②	3	4	5	6	7	8
	9	10	11	12	13	14	15
	16	17	18	19	20	21	22
	23	24	25	26	27	28	29
	30	31					

Gemma

Ruby and Harold are leaving first. We're all on different flights. They have an afternoon one to Gatwick, ours isn't till this evening. Jo and Mark are flying to Luton. We've all gathered on the sun terrace to say our goodbyes.

'I'm going to miss you!' I tell Ruby, giving her a hug. 'I feel like I've known you for ever!'

'Yes. I'll miss you all, too. You take care of your-selves now!' She turns to hug Jo. 'And you look after little Jacob, won't you?'

'Of course I will.' Jo's actually got tears in her eyes. I know how she feels: it's quite odd how close we've all become during the last two weeks. I suppose there's been a lot of emotional turmoil between the six of us, what with Jo being rushed to hospital with heat exhaustion, Andy falling off the jetty and nearly drowning, and Harold rescuing him. We girls have all

315

done a lot of talking, too – we didn't feel like strangers to each other somehow. It seemed natural to confess things to each other that we might not even have told our friends back home. Maybe that was actually because we thought, after today, we wouldn't see each other again.

Now, though, the thought of our parting for ever is making my eyes start to fill up. I want to know whether there's a happy ending for them all. I want to know about Jo's baby, and whether she completely gets over Ben and is happy with Mark. I want to be sure that Harold's not going to slide back into his depression, and that he and Ruby are going to be as happy together as they deserve. OK, I know life's not like the paperbacks I read. But I want Happy Ever After for my new friends!

'I need to know!' I burst out, rummaging in my bag for a pen. 'It's no good – I've got to have your phone numbers. Or your e-mails, whatever. I know we said we wouldn't, but I can't bear it. I want to hear from you all again!'

'Me too!' says Jo, wiping her eyes. 'Ruby, Harold – your boat's here. Quick, write down your phone number.'

'I thought you'd never ask!' says Ruby. Her hand's shaking as she takes the pen.

It was what we all agreed last night, in the restaurant. Most of us had had a few drinks and we were getting sentimental.

'Shall we all keep in touch?' I suggested, linking hands with Jo and Ruby around the table. 'Maybe we can actually meet up again? You know, for our tenth anniversary or something. A reunion here on Korčula!'

'Harold and I will be nearly seventy by then,' Ruby

laughed. 'We might both be using walking frames or going into a retirement home.'

'You speak for yourself, woman,' protested Harold. 'You're only as old as you feel – and personally, I feel about twenty-five right now!'

He looked it, too. He'd gone from being stooped and weary-looking to bright-eyed, upright and cheerful – a transformation.

'And *we*'ll have a ten-year-old son!' added Jo. I noticed the emphasis on *we*. Mark noticed it too, and squeezed her hand, smiling into her eyes with a kind of gratitude. She smiled back, took a deep breath as if this was going to be a huge gamble, and added, very deliberately: 'And who knows? Maybe another child or two as well!'

Mark looked like he was about to burst. He couldn't talk. He just kept hold of Jo's hand and stared down at his plate.

'Well, God only knows where Gem and I will be in ten years' time!' said Andy brightly, to change the subject. He looked at me and laughed, and I made myself smile because I knew he was only trying to lighten the atmosphere. But if we'd been on our own, and if we hadn't had the upsets we've had during the past couple of weeks, I'd have asked him what the hell he was talking about! Ten years' time? God, if he hasn't got over his reluctance to have a baby by *then*, I'll be getting past it!

The conversation moved on to other holiday destinations: places everybody would like to visit in the future. Mark said he'd always dreamed of seeing India; and Jo explained that she had an aunt and uncle in Canada she'd always wanted to visit.

'Egypt was wonderful,' said Ruby, looking at Harold wistfully. 'I'd like to go back one day.'

'We loved it, too, didn't we, Gem?' said Andy. 'But we haven't seen all the ancient sites – we went to the Red Sea. Maybe we'll do a Nile cruise another year.'

'That'd be wonderful,' I agreed. 'I've always been interested in all that Ancient Egyptian history.' Not exactly the sort of holiday you'd take a child on, of course, but I purposely held back from mentioning that.

'And I quite fancy backpacking in Australia,' he reminded me cheerfully.

I decided at that point that I might as well accept we weren't going to have children until our forties!

'Of course, we're all just discussing our *dream* holidays here,' Jo said thoughtfully. 'There's no way Mark or I will really be jetting off to India or Canada. Not for a long time!'

'And the truth is,' added Harold, 'that I've promised Ruby, before we even think about going anywhere else in the world, we're coming back to Korčula to see it properly. Next spring. That's a definite.'

'That'll be lovely for you both.' I smiled at them. 'You deserve that.'

Yes, we'll all be thinking of you!' said Jo.

'So *are* we going to keep in touch?' I asked again. I looked around the table. Jo was nodding eagerly, Ruby and Harold smiling easily, Mark looking at Jo as if he'd do whatever she wanted in the world.

'I'm not sure it's a good idea,' said Andy.

I stared at him. 'Why not?'

'Oh, not that it hasn't been great, with you guys!' he added quickly. 'But, you know – every year, when we go on holiday, we make friends with people, don't we, Gem? I must admit, I like meeting new people, having a meal or a few drinks with them, like this. And, over the years, we've always exchanged

318

addresses, or phone numbers, or whatever, and they've promised to keep in touch. Sometimes we talk about meeting up again, like Gemma said earlier, for an anniversary or something. Then we go home and never hear from them again. I send e-mails. Sometimes I ring them and they say "Oh, great to hear from you – we must get together some time!" And then it all goes quiet. Gemma sends them Christmas cards, and occasionally we get one back. And that's it.'

It's true, of course, but I've never thought much about it. I'm pretty sure it happens to everyone. People mean it at the time, don't they? They've enjoyed each other's company for two weeks and think it'd be fun to stay in touch, but when they get back to the reality of their lives at home, they don't find the time. And then they can't be bothered. I've never taken it personally. But perhaps Andy has. Each time it's another rejection. Another echo of the past.

'It doesn't mean anything,' I told him gently. 'It's just the way people are.'

'I know. So maybe it's best to accept that from the start: we're not going to keep in touch really, so let's not pretend we are. Let's just say, it's been fun, it's been great, but it's not going to go on for ever.'

The others all shrugged and nodded as if they could see the sense of this. I didn't say anything, but looking from one of our new friends to the other, I just couldn't imagine never hearing from them again. This hasn't been like any ordinary holiday friendship. There was something deeper, more meaningful, going on here. Surely I wasn't the only one to feel it?

*

319

I've got the piece of paper with Ruby's e-mail address and phone number on it safely in my purse now. Andy's looking at me with a mixture of exasperation and affection. I know what he's thinking: Don't come crying to me if they don't keep in touch! I've written down our details for Ruby and Harold, and Jo and I are just exchanging ours when Harold picks up his suitcase with a grunt and a nod to Ruby.

'We're off, then. The boatman's waiting, Rube.'

She hugs us all again and says a cheery goodbye.

'Have a safe journey!' I tell her.

'I'll let you know about the baby!' calls Jo.

We wave until the little boat becomes a dot in the distance.

'It's going to be weird,' I remark to Jo as we sit for a while with them, lingering over a last cup of coffee. The two guys are deep into a conversation about football teams, and Jo and I are leaning back in our chairs, lazily watching the morning getting hotter and busier, as those lucky people whose holidays aren't coming to an end lay their towels on the rocks and enjoy their swimming.

'What is?'

'Going back home; going back to work. After all the months of planning and stressing about the wedding – here we are, married. Mr and Mrs Collins. But when we go home everything's still going to be exactly the same as it was before. Weird.'

'Not for me,' she says, quietly. 'My life's going to be changed completely.'

'Oh, yes, of course.' I smile at her. 'You've got the baby to look forward to.'

'Not just that. Mark and I have only just started living together. I've never lived with a guy before – it

320

felt so strange when we moved into our flat. We were more like friends than an engaged couple, about to get married. But now . . .'

'You've had two whole weeks together, in each other's company the whole time. You seem a lot happier than when you arrived here.'

'God, yes. Do you know, it feels like a lifetime ago since we stepped off that boat. I was feeling tired, and sick, and emotional – and wondering if I'd made the biggest mistake of my life.'

'And now?' I ask her pointedly.

She smiles in response. 'I know what the biggest mistake of my life was now. It was Ben. I've been pining after something that would have been disastrous for me, and all the while, something so much better was sitting here waiting. I'm so lucky.'

'You've been through a lot. You're entitled to be happy now, Jo. I really hope it all works out for you.'

'Thanks, Gemma. And how about you? Have *you* got your happy ending?'

'Of course,' I say automatically. 'Andy and I have always been happy together. We were the *really* lucky ones – we were always going to get married. We promised each other that when we were about sixteen! Our lives have been one long fairytale romance!'

Jo smiles at me again and says, 'I'm glad.'

She doesn't need to know about the doubts lurking in the back of my mind. I don't even want to acknowledge them to myself.

'OK – we're off,' says Mark a bit later. 'Ready, babe? Got everything?'

'Yes.' Jo passes him her bag to carry, and I find myself smiling as I remember how stroppy she was, two weeks ago, about things like that. How she insisted she was capable, she wasn't an invalid, didn't need looking after. Now I think she realises she could be grateful for a bit of pampering after all.

We walk down to the jetty with them, to see them off.

'I'll e-mail you,' Jo promises as she gives me a farewell hug.

'Yes. You must let us know when the baby arrives!'

She looks at me in surprise. 'You don't really think I'm going to leave it till then, do you? I'll be e-mailing you every week, Gemma. I haven't got a job yet, remember. I'll be on the computer all the time!'

'Oh, yes – you must let us know about your degree, too. When you get your results!'

'I will, I promise. 'Bye, then, Gemma. I'm going to miss our chats.'

'Me too. Take care!'

It's only me and Andy this time, standing on the jetty, waving goodbye. He puts his arm round me.

'Cheer up, Gem,' he says. 'It's not over yet.'

'Not quite!'

'Let's go and have a slap up lunch on our own. And a farewell drink. Yes?'

'You say the nicest things!' I laugh, as he takes hold of my hand and pulls me back down the jetty towards the hotel. 'Hold on!'

'What's the matter?'

'Nothing. I just want to stand here for a minute and get a good long look at this view. So it's imprinted in my memory for ever.'

'My superb photographs will do that for you! Come on, that's long enough. I'm starving.'

No romance in his soul – that's his trouble!

Jo

I keep looking back until Korčula disappears from view over the horizon.

'I want to go back one day, too,' I tell Mark as the boat chugs towards the mainland. 'When I'm not pregnant, and can enjoy a long walk without getting carted off to hospital!'

'And enjoy a boozy evening with everyone else!'

I laugh. 'We'll have the baby with us. We won't be able to have evenings out at all – boozy or otherwise.' I look at him thoughtfully. 'Will you mind? I suppose we can get babysitters occasionally ...'

'Mind?' He kisses me briefly by way of an answer. 'I'm looking forward to it! I know he's not actually going to be mine, but ... I want to be a good pseudo-dad to him.'

'You will be. I know that already. We've got a lot to look forward to, haven't we? I was talking to Gemma, earlier, and she was feeling a bit strange about going back to exactly the same life they had before they got married. I suppose that's how most people feel, but ...'

'Nowadays, yes. But for our parents and grandparents it wasn't like that, was it? Most of them didn't live together before they were married, and in lots of cases they lived with their parents right up till their wedding day. So it was a much more significant point, really, in their lives.'

'I don't think I could possibly feel anything was any more significant than our wedding.'

'Really?' He looks at me with surprise. 'I thought you probably felt pushed into it. Like you had very little choice. I actually thought you were regretting

323

it almost as soon as we'd exchanged our vows.'

'To be honest, I didn't know what the hell I was feeling, I was so mixed up. But it's only taken me two weeks to realise how glad I am that I agreed to it.' I shrug and grin at him. 'Some people spend half their lifetime wondering if they married the right person. At least it only took me two weeks!'

I don't want to tell Mark that I'm actually a bit concerned about Gemma. On the face of it, she and Andy have got the perfect relationship – childhood sweethearts, growing up together, knowing all there is to know about each other and all that. She likes to talk about the romance of it, as if she's describing some fictional characters in a chick-flick film rather than herself and her husband. I wanted to say to her: *Gemma, you're real people, with real worries and insecurities, not two mythical personifications of Perfect Love.* But how could I even attempt to talk to her like that? I wouldn't have the cheek. I'm only twenty-one; compared with her, I haven't even begun to live. She's a nurse, dealing with sick children every day, seeing their frightened parents, helping them to cope. How can she not see that she and Andy are just as vulnerable, just as unlikely to be whole and perfect, as any of her patients?

I don't believe in Perfect Love. But then, I wouldn't, would I, after my recent experiences. What I do believe in, though, is the sort of love that can grow and flourish despite people's differences, despite their flaws and their mistakes and even their disagreements. I might be young but I think I've learnt that much, at least. It's no good Gemma pasting on that smile and telling me everything in the garden's wonderful, when in actual fact anybody can see it isn't. There's a bloody great quagmire where the lawn should be, and she and Andy are just tiptoeing around it, pretending it doesn't exist. I don't know what it is, or what's caused it, but I'm worried they're going to go home from here, open the door and fall straight into it.

I fall asleep on the bus journey from Orebić back to Dubrovnik, and when I wake up we're nearly at the airport.

'Are you OK, babe?' Mark asks me anxiously.

'Yes, fine.' I stretch and try unsuccessfully to get comfortable in my seat. The baby's squirming about madly and I'm glad I haven't got long to wait for the toilets and a cup of tea.

We have plenty of time before we have to board our flight. I stretch my legs for a while and then we find somewhere quiet to sit and wait.

'Is anyone sitting here?' a girl asks a few moments later, indicating the seat next to me.

'No, go ahead,' I tell her, and return to my book. I'm aware that she's looking at me.

'When's the baby due?' she asks when I look up.

'October.' I smile at her. I'm getting used to this, now the pregnancy's beginning to show – complete strangers asking about the baby: how far on I am, whether we know what sex it is and what we're going to call it!

'Oh! Lucky you.' She sighs and adds quietly, almost to herself, 'I'd love to have a baby.'

I feel a flicker of unease. She's probably harmless but obviously not quite right – to start talking about this to a stranger at an airport.

'Well,' I say, to be polite, 'I hope you do, one day.'

I turn away, not wanting to get into any further conversation with this girl. But she carries on, despite me lifting my book again to show that I'm keen to get back to my reading.

'Are you on your honeymoon?'

'Yes!' I look at her in surprise. 'How can you tell?'

'Your ring.' She nods at my left hand. 'It looks brand new.'

'Oh, yes, it is.' I smile, despite myself. I can't be bothered to tell her it wasn't even the ring I was married with.

'Lucky you,' she says again, sighing heavily and looking up at the ceiling. 'I'm on my own, unfortunately.'

What am I supposed to say to this? 'I'm sorry to hear that.'

Mark nudges me, giving me a look of concern.

'Do you want to move?' he whispers.

I shake my head. 'It's OK,' I whisper back.

'I thought I was pregnant once,' she ploughs on regardless. 'But it was a false alarm. And it's never happened since. No matter how many guys I sleep with.'

She's sleeping around, just to try and get pregnant? This is one very weird lady. I'm certainly not getting into this. Perhaps Mark's right. It might be better to move away. 'I think ... we're just going to get a cup of tea now,' I begin, closing my book and giving Mark a nudge.

'I wouldn't have cared!' this girl's saying at the same time. Her voice is getting louder. I definitely think there's something not quite right about her. 'Even if it was *his* baby, I wouldn't have cared! I told him I'd have got rid of it – but I was only saying that to spite him. I'd still have wanted it, even if it was bloody Andrew Collins' baby!'

'Oh, Christ,' says Mark softly.

And, right on cue, the girl starts to cry, noisily and without any inhibition.

'I wanted it! I wanted to have Andrew's baby! I did!'

I can't think of anything to say, other than to echo Mark. Oh, Christ. What the hell do we make of *this*?

Gemma

We're on the boat across to the mainland when my phone bleeps. That's surprising in itself. Nobody's called me, or sent me text messages, the whole two weeks we've been away. My family wouldn't anyway – and my friends promised not to disturb me on my honeymoon.

'It's from Jo!' I exclaim to Andy, looking at the screen. Her number's only been in my phone since this morning.

'Probably just testing, making sure she's got the right number,' he says with a shrug as I open the message.

'They're at the airport,' I announce as I start to read it.

And then I don't say any more.

HI GEMMA. WE'RE AT THE AIRPORT AND I JUST WANTED TO WARN YOU. WE MET THAT GIRL CAROLINE. SHE'S HANGING AROUND THE AIRPORT AND ACTING VERY STRANGELY. MAYBE SHE'LL BE GONE WHEN YOU GET HERE. BUT IF NOT – IGNORE HER. SHE'S NOT QUITE RIGHT. I'LL E-MAIL YOU LATER. JO XXX

327

'What's up?' says Andy, leaning across me to look at the message.

'Nothing.' I close the phone with a snap. 'She was just letting us know they'd arrived at the airport OK.'

'Oh. Bit strange, isn't it!'

I shrug and look away. 'Well, as you say, probably just checking the number.'

I feel uneasy all the rest of the journey. Andy falls asleep on the coach, and I'm trying to read my book but I can't concentrate. I can't stop thinking about bloody Caroline. Just when I thought I'd heard the last of her! Why did Jo bother to send that text? So what if the silly cow was at the airport when they got there? She's probably gone home by now, on an earlier flight. And so what if she was acting strangely? From what I can make out, that's par for the course. What did Jo feel the need to warn me about? It's no good being forewarned if you don't know why!

We finally arrive at the airport and join the queue to check in for our flight.

'Are you OK?' Andy asks me, suddenly becoming aware that I've been quiet for the past three hours. And then, before I even have time to answer, he adds in a whisper: 'Oh, God. Look who's here.'

I wheel around, expecting the worst, but it's actually only the three stupid friends – Felicity, Nicky and Sara. No Caroline, thank God.

'Hello there!' calls Felicity cheerfully. They're behind us in the queue. Obviously on the same flight – although not with our tour operator as they weren't on our coach. It looks like we're lumbered with them now. 'Going home?'

'No, we're on our way to the North Pole,' I mutter sarcastically. Andy giggles nervously.

'You haven't seen Caro by any chance, have you?'

she continues. Next to me, I feel Andy's spine go rigid. 'She's supposed to be meeting us here, for the flight back. She's been staying in Dubrovnik, as you know . . .'

'We haven't seen her,' I say, coldly. 'And if we do, we'll be keeping well away from her. She's caused us enough trouble.'

'Leave it, Gem,' Andy says, quietly.

'You know it's true!' I tell him. I turn back to her friends. 'I don't know how *you* put up with it, to be honest! She's a pain in the neck. And as for disappearing off like that, without telling you where she'd gone — what sort of a friend is she? Getting you worried, getting the police out . . .'

'She can't help it, Jemima,' says Nicky stoutly.

'*Gemma*! My name's Gemma!' I tell her crossly. 'And sorry, but that's crap! Of course she can help it!'

'I know she's a pain at times. But basically, she's depressed.'

'Aren't we all! Christ, Nicky — if Caroline was my friend, I think I'd be bloody suicidal!'

The three of them look at each other, shaking their heads like I'm being particularly thick.

'I mean,' says Nicky with particular emphasis, 'she's *clinically* depressed.'

'It makes her seek affection all the time,' explains Sara. 'That's why she tends to . . . um . . . sleep around.'

'And accuse people of sleeping with her, even when they haven't?' I add crossly.

'Please — just leave it, Gem,' says Andy again.

'I'm sorry, but depression's no excuse for the way she carries on. She should be on medication.'

'She won't take anything. Because she wants to get pregnant.'

329

'She does?' I retort, shocked. Even Andy's eyebrows have shot up. Caroline doesn't exactly give the impression of being broody. 'Well, it might help if she finds herself a man of her own, first!'

The three girls are all talking at once now, trying to tell me that, yes, they know she can be difficult, yes, she drives them up the wall too, but she's got problems, she can't help it.

'You'll have to stop it,' I say with heavy sarcasm. 'You'll have me feeling sorry for her in a minute.'

'I know she's upset you a bit,' says Felicity, qualifying for the understatement of the year. 'And, yes, she's been a bit of a handful to us, too. But she's our friend.'

Fortunately we've reached the front of the queue now and we need to go to the desk to get checked in.

'What the hell are they talking about?' I demand indignantly as we move away from them. 'Trying to get pregnant, my arse! She's just a bloody trouble-maker!'

'Just ignore them, Gemma. Don't worry about it. Here – you need your passport. Put the cases on the luggage belt.'

When we've finished at the desk, I direct Andy to a place where we can sit down and get a drink. I know I need to calm down. I feel such extreme dislike for that girl, I've almost wanted to murder her during these past two weeks. Knowing that she's clinically depressed doesn't make me feel any more charitable towards her for the way she's treated Andy, but perhaps her friends are right, up to a point. Perhaps she can't always help her behaviour. Not that it means she has to be a complete bitch!

'Let's just forget about her, for God's sake,' says Andy impatiently. He still looks totally pissed off.

Maybe he's thinking back to when he first knew her, wondering whether her heavy flirtation was an attempt to get him to father a child with her, rather than a genuine interest in his manly charms! If, of course, it really *was* only heavy flirtation. I glance at him again and swallow back the urge to voice these niggling doubts. I'm *not* going to doubt Andy. It's *obviously* Caroline that's the problem!

'I wish I could forget about her,' I retort, 'but we can't seem to get away from her. Even now. What next – is she going to follow us all the way home?'

'We still haven't found her,' sings out a now-familiar voice a few minutes later. Felicity plonks herself down at our table without being asked. 'She'd better hurry up or she'll miss the flight.'

'Oh, dear,' I say without much conviction.

'She *has* texted me to say she's at the airport, though,' Felicity goes on. 'That's what I can't understand. Where the hell is she?'

Andy's sighing and looking down at his feet. 'Come on, Gemma,' he says, finishing his drink quickly. 'Let's go and . . . er . . . look at the shops.'

Too late. As I swallow the rest of my coffee, the other two girls appear from the cafeteria counter, carrying cups of tea.

'Caro's here!' calls Sara gaily to Felicity. 'We've found her!'

'We're off, then,' I say sharply.

But she's already seen us.

'Ah, Andrew!' She stops in front of us, staring. 'I've been looking for you.'

'Well, sorry. But we're just going.' Andy pulls at my arm.

'I've been looking for you all day,' she goes on.

She raises her voice. 'I wanted to tell you something. About the baby.'

There's a horrible silence. It kind of rings, vibrating in the air like electricity. I can almost see the sparks.

'What baby?' I hear myself asking, my own voice echoing inside my head.

'The one I thought I was having.' She's looking directly at Andy. He keeps tugging at my arm as if he still wants us to go, but he doesn't seem to be able to move. 'You know, Andrew. Back then.'

'What's she talking about, Andy?' I ask him quietly.

'I've no idea.'

'I just wanted to tell you,' she goes on, her voice now sickly-sweet, dangerously sweet, like honey-coated arsenic, 'that I didn't mean it. I wouldn't have got rid of it really. I'd have loved it.' Her voice is wobbling now. Her eyes fill up with tears. 'I wanted it, all right? It was what I wanted, Andrew. To have ... your baby!'

'She's nuts,' says Andy crossly as we finally walk away. 'Totally fucking loopy! Someone's going to punch her lights out one day if she's not careful, going around saying stuff like that ...'

'It's all right, Andy,' I tell him wearily, rushing to keep up with his fast angry strides.

'I mean, she could get herself into trouble, never mind about being depressed or whatever. Her friends ought to keep her fucking locked up, if you ask me ...'

'Andy! Slow down! I said ... it's all right. Don't worry.'

He stops, looking around him anxiously as if he's expecting her to be following him. He's trembling slightly. I take hold of his hand and say, carefully,

332

without looking him in the eyes: 'Let's not get ourselves upset about it. She's not worth it.'

'But . . .'

'She can't hurt us, Andy.' I don't know why, but I actually feel almost deadly calm now. I almost feel like smiling. It's like we've reached some sort of a climax, and now it's over, things can only get better. 'She's just a stupid, mixed-up girl. She's got nobody, and she wants to hurt us but she can't. We've got each other.'

I can feel him relaxing slightly; feel his breathing returning to normal.

'So let's just go and board the plane, and make sure we're not sitting anywhere near her,' I add. 'And we'll say no more about it, OK?'

'OK,' he agrees, giving me a grateful smile.

'Until we get home,' I add under my breath.

And then, I think, we're going to need a very long talk.

	S	M	T	W	T	**F**	S
			1	2	3	4	5
August	6	7	8	9	10	(11)	12
	13	14	15	16	17	18	19
	20	21	22	23	24	25	26
	27	28	29	30	31		

Six Years Before: Kensington, London

It was a hot afternoon. As they walked back to her apartment the heat was bouncing off the pavements of the dusty city streets, scorching the tops of their heads, the backs of their necks. He was drunk; not drunk to the point of collapse or incapability, but drunk enough to have forgotten what he was doing and why. Why was he going back with her? Why had it seemed like a good idea, at the end of the long, boozy lunch that had rounded off the morning's work under the hot lights of the studio, to accept her offer of a coffee back at her place, instead of heading straight for the train, and home?

Now, in her pristine top-floor apartment, with its polished floors and white rugs, its leather sofas and soft music, he watched her kicking off her shoes, curling her long, slim legs beneath her as she settled herself next to him on the sofa, and noticed the glass of brandy she'd put on the table next to him.

'I thought you said coffee,' he muttered, suddenly feeling sleepy, feeling the need of the caffeine, 'not brandy.'

'I've put the percolator on,' she replied, sinking back against the cushions, brushing against his shoulder so that her perfume wafted across his face and the hem of her silky blue dress rode a little higher up her thighs. 'Have your brandy while we wait.'

He felt uncomfortable, and drank the brandy for something to do. She'd refilled his glass before he remembered that she still hadn't brought the coffee, but by then he didn't really want it any more. She'd been good company in the restaurant. She'd always been good company, come to that – prepared to listen to him, laugh at his jokes, make him feel as though he was somebody interesting and amusing; somebody who was used to having lunches with top models. It was just a working friendship, nothing more than that. But he'd enjoyed the illusion of being, for once in his life, one of the popular ones. A guy who was invited out to lunch with a beautiful woman instead of creeping off home on his own after work.

Now, she didn't seem such a lot of fun. She looked serious, and sultry, and was trying to force more brandy on him when he was sure he'd already said he couldn't possibly drink any more. Everything was going out of focus.

'Take your shoes off,' she was telling him. 'Here – let me undo your collar. You look so hot. Is that better?'

It was. It was very nice, actually, having had his legs lifted up on to the sofa, resting his head in her silky lap, having her cool hand stroking his forehead. He'd fall asleep in a minute, if he wasn't careful. Or at least . . . he might have done, if she hadn't started kissing him.

There wasn't any thought of being unfaithful in his head. There wasn't any thought in his head at all – the drink had numbed his mind to thought until all that was left was sensation. The feel of soft lips, silk and sweet flesh, the scent of perfume, the sounds of music and muffled whispers. The sudden overwhelming pressure of need. At the exact moment of climax, a sudden and terrifying shard of pure clarity pierced the fog of his drunkenness, so that he struggled to sit up, opened his eyes wide and shouted: '*Gemma!*'

'What have I done?' he moaned, holding his head, scrambling for his clothes. 'What have you made me do?'

'You seemed eager enough,' she retorted, looking angry now, the soft smile replaced by harshness. 'I didn't exactly have to force you.' She wrapped the blue silk dress around her. 'Is that *it*?'

He didn't bother to reply. Staggering, but sober enough now from the shock of realisation to get into his clothes and shoes and find his way to the door, he remembered his inbred good manners sufficiently to turn and apologise.

'I was drunk. I'm sorry, but I didn't mean for this to happen. I didn't *want* it to happen.'

'Well, thank you very much!' she screeched. 'Fuck off then! Go on, back to your boring little life and your boring little girlfriend!'

'She's not . . .' He leaned against the door, close to tears. How had he allowed it to get this far? All because of his stupid, stupid conceit at being liked and admired by a beautiful model. He should have known she was after more than just his pleasant company and

336

his silly jokes. Now he'd broken all his promises to Gemma and behaved like the ignorant, lecherous prats he'd always despised. Worse, he'd done the most awful thing possible in Gemma's eyes. He'd acted like her father.

By the time he'd made his way home, he was stone cold sober, and he'd made some decisions. He was going to learn from this experience. He was going to grow up and stop looking for approval from people he didn't even care about. He was never again going to drink a drink he hadn't asked for and didn't need. He was never, ever going to let himself down again like that. And he was never going to tell Gemma about it. It would hurt her more than he could even imagine. Instead, he'd have to live with his own shame and self-disgust. It served him right.

There were rumours circulating about him during the next few weeks. He squared his shoulders and ignored the nudges and the sniggers. He'd moved beyond caring what Caroline or any of her cronies thought about him. He shrugged off the implied criticisms of his sexual performance. It didn't matter. If it helped Caroline to save face, so be it. The next round of rumours were more fanciful and outrageous: that she'd dumped him because he was rubbish in bed; that he'd pestered her to continue the 'relationship'; that she'd had to threaten to tell his girlfriend about it, to get rid of him. And then, a few weeks later, the most frightening rumour of all: that she was pregnant.

He didn't sleep for a week. He sat in the darkness of his bedroom, night after night, watching Gemma sleep, wondering if he was about to lose her for ever because of five minutes of drunken madness. If there was a baby, and if it was his – what could he do other than agree to support it? If he was nothing else, and despite recent appearances to the contrary, he was a decent guy – a gentleman. He'd have to take responsibility for what he'd done. And Gemma would leave him, and hate him like she hated her dad. And he couldn't blame her.

Eventually he confronted Caroline.

'There's talk,' he said abruptly. 'You've been saying you're pregnant. Is it true?'

'Might be,' she said, smugly, infuriatingly.

'Is it mine? Is that what you're saying? I need to know!'

'It could be.' She smiled nastily. 'Although it'd be a miracle, to be honest. I wouldn't have thought there was enough time for it to happen.'

He ignored the sneer.

'So it could be someone else? The father?'

She looked at him pityingly. 'Did you really think you were the only one? They're queuing up for it, Andrew. You were lucky I even gave you a chance – and you blew it.'

'You call that lucky?' he threw back at her as he walked away.

Weeks went by. Gradually, people lost interest, as they do, and found someone else to gossip about. He didn't see Caroline for a long time – he was working on different jobs, she was in another part of the country. He tried to put it out of his mind, but it was impossible. He'd wake up in the night, sweating and shaking from a nightmare about child support. When he eventually saw her again, her stomach looked as flat as ever, and as ever she was surrounded by slavering, adoring sycophants. It sickened him to think that he'd been like that himself. She was drinking Champagne cocktails and smoking. She couldn't be pregnant. But he was shocked to find himself

338

thinking: If she is, and it's my baby, I'll have something to say about it.

When he got the opportunity, he approached her and asked her directly.

'Oh, that!' she said airily. 'False alarm.' She looked at him with disdainful amusement. 'Why? Were you hoping to hear the patter of tiny feet?' She laughed wildly, in his face, and when she'd stopped leant closer, spitting out the words venomously: 'Listen, Andrew *darling*. If I'd been having a *brat*, I'd have got rid of it by now. Especially if I thought it was *yours*. Got it?'

Sometimes, over the following months and years, he thought about her; about that last exchange; about how nasty and dirty it had made him feel. Not that he didn't deserve it. He heard eventually that she'd moved away, gone to New York for a couple of years, and gradually he allowed the memory to sink to the basest corner of his consciousness, where it lurked, unpleasant but untended, to prick at his conscience from time to time when something happened to remind him. By the time he and Gemma were getting married, Caroline and her spiteful taunts could not have been further from his mind, so that, seeing her again in Korčula, during his honeymoon of all times, was the stuff of his nightmares all over again. His mind went into a whirl of panic. He dreaded any confrontation with Caroline – any conversation, any opportunity for her to hint, in front of Gemma, at what had gone before. Eventually, he knew, he'd have to tell Gemma about it. He hated himself for the half-truths and half-lies he was feeding her: knew she was suspicious, knew she deserved to hear the truth.

But how could he? How could he do that to her on

their honeymoon? Especially when she was talking about having babies – the very thing he didn't want to think about right then!

And especially when she was so insistent on everything being *perfect*. He knew it wasn't. *He* wasn't perfect at all, and when she found that out perhaps it would all be over. Almost before it had begun.

	S	M	T	W	T	F	**S**
							1
	2	3	4	5	6	7	8
July	9	10	11	12	13	14	(15)
	16	17	18	19	20	21	22
	23	24	25	26	27	28	29
	30	31					

Six Years Later

Gemma

I've only been back at work for two weeks, but it feels like an eternity. It's been really busy on the ward, so that by the time I've come home I'm so exhausted from work, and from my own thoughts going round in circles in my head, I haven't got the energy to cook anything, never mind eat it. I'm existing on the odd slice of toast between the glasses of wine that help me sleep. I can't stop thinking about the way my whole life has changed. Why did I ever think everything was perfect? It's just made it harder, almost unbearable, to come to terms with the truth, the reality: that our relationship was a sham, that Andy was another lying, unfaithful bastard like my dad.

Even before he admitted what really happened with Caroline, I'd kind of guessed but was refusing to acknowledge it, even to myself. I couldn't bring myself to discuss it with him on the journey home from Croatia. I kept quiet on the flight, pretending to be asleep: kept telling myself it was going to be OK – that we'd have a long talk about it all when we got home. I'd tell him, frankly, that I'd run out of ways to believe him. Then he'd come up with some perfectly logical explanation for everything, one that I hadn't thought of. He had to! I closed my eyes and prayed, hard, that he would, and I waited, my heart in my mouth, for the talk that was going to save our relationship.

Instead, it was the talk that ended everything. We sat up all night, without a wink of sleep between us, crying, talking, and crying some more. And here I am, alone. Married and separated, all within the space of a month.

Cheryl comes round almost every night. She brings me takeaways, or heats up soup and tries to get me to eat, but the sight of the food makes me feel sick. She looks so distressed on my behalf, I'd feel guilty if I were capable of feeling anything. I try to talk to her about other things – her job, my job, the weather. She listens, looking at me with sad, sympathetic eyes, until I run out of mundane topics to discuss and realise I'm crying yet again.

'You need to tell your mum,' she said one day last week, holding my hand tight as I dripped exhausted tears on to her shoulder. 'You need your mum right now, Gemma.'

I shook my head. 'No point. You know how it is, we're not that close.'

'She's your *mum*, Gem! No matter what's happened, over the years . . .' She stopped talking, and tilted my chin so that she could look into my eyes.

'In fact, she'll probably understand better than anyone what you're going through.'

It was hard to explain to Cheryl that this was exactly why I didn't relish the thought of talking to Mum about the break-up. I hated the idea, more than anything else, of Andy being compared with my dad. It hurt so much I could hardly bear it. But in the end Cheryl must have phoned Mum herself because last night I had a call from her, and I could tell straight away from the wobble in her voice that she knew.

'Come and stay with me,' she said without any preamble. 'Please. Cheryl's worried that you're not looking after yourself.'

'It's OK,' I said dully, staring out of the window. 'I have to get up, and get dressed, and go to work, and look after sick children . . .'

'I know. But are you eating properly?'

'Yes,' I lied, looking down at the way my clothes are already hanging loosely on me. 'I'm all right.'

I held on to the phone for half an hour after I'd hung up; lying on the sofa, cradling it as if it was a lover – a child – a parent. I wished I'd been able to tell her that I wasn't all right, not at all, I was falling apart, I needed someone's arms around me, needed looking after. Needed my mum. But that's as much of a fantasy as my marriage seems to have been.

I was on an early shift this morning and I'm half-asleep on the sofa at four o'clock in the afternoon when the doorbell rings. I open the door and am greeted by a huge bouquet on four legs. The bouquet shifts slightly and the legs acquire two bodies.

'Hello, Gemma,' says Claire.

'My poor baby,' says Mum.

We're in a group hug before I can even think about it. And all three of us are crying.

They haven't just brought flowers. Claire's got cakes and chocolates in a carrier bag; Mum's brought a home-made pie and a frozen casserole. The kettle's on and they're arranging the flowers, and tidying up for me, and suddenly the house begins to feel like a home again.

'I'm going to cook you eggs and chips,' says Mum firmly, looking me up and down critically. 'You can have the pie tomorrow and the casserole on Monday.'

'OK,' I say meekly, surprising myself. 'I'll try . . .'

'You need your strength,' she says calmly. 'Now then, Claire, the kettle's boiling – go and make the tea, there's a good girl, while I talk to Gemma.'

I wait for Claire to pout and protest, but to my surprise she smiles agreeably and goes out to the kitchen, where I hear her beginning to wash up my sinkful of dirty mugs.

'Do you want to tell me about it?' Mum asks quietly, sitting down beside me.

I shrug. 'Not much to tell. I trusted him, he let me down. Cheated on me, lied to me. You know how it goes.'

'But you still love him,' she says.

It's a statement, not a question, but I retort immediately: 'Do I? Is that what you think? That I'll do what you did – spend my life crying for him, taking him back, waiting for him to do it again?'

'That's not what I said. This is nothing like what happened with your father, Gemma.'

'How can you say that?' I stare at her crossly. It feels good to be cross. Better than lying around feeling sorry for myself. I want to shout now – scream and shout and stamp my feet. Maybe I'd feel a whole lot better if I did. 'OK, so it was only once – so he *says*. But if he can do it once, he can do it again ... and again ... there's no difference – it's *just* what I always despised about Dad.' More quietly now, looking away, I add: 'And I'm sorry, Mum, but I despised the way you still loved him, still wanted him, when he treated you like *shit*.'

'I didn't,' she says.

'What? You didn't what?'

'I didn't love him. Not for a long time. Not after the first couple of affairs. Possibly not even before then.'

'Oh, come on, Mum! All those nights, crying over Claire's head when she was a baby ... and for Christ's sake! The fact that you even *had* her!'

'I wasn't crying for your father.' She lowers her head. I can hardly hear her. Hardly believe what I'm hearing anyway. 'I was crying for *Claire's* father, Gemma.'

Time seems to be suspended. I'm staring out of the window at the garden. There's a blackbird on the lawn, with a snail in its beak, and a butterfly dancing around the flowerbed, its wings pure white in the late-afternoon sunshine. I'm watching them as if they're all that matters. I can't take this in.

'She wasn't ... Dad's baby?' I say eventually. My throat's so tight, I can hardly force the words out. 'You had an affair?'

'I fell in love,' Mum corrects me softly.

'Who with?' I croak, staring at this stranger who looks like my mum.

'His name was Michael ...'

'Michael? Michael? I don't remember any *Michael*!'

'You wouldn't. He never came to the house. I met him at work — you remember, when I had the part-time job at the school . . .'

'You were a teaching assistant. What was he — a teacher?'

She nods, looks down. 'He was married, Gemma. That's why I've never told you. I had an affair with a married man. I was too ashamed to tell you.'

I find myself suddenly thinking of Jo — of how she described the affair with Ben. How passionately she'd loved him, how impossible she'd found it to give him up when she found out he was married.

'No wonder you were always so unhappy,' I say, my voice shaking with shock.

'I didn't realise you noticed,' she says.

'We weren't exactly looking out for each other, were we?'

'No. And that's something I've had to live with, and regret, ever since. I clung to Claire because she was all I had left of Michael. He went to live in New Zealand with his family. It was probably for the best. We . . . weren't together very long. All I had was memories . . . and his daughter.'

'But, Mum, doesn't he know about her? Surely he knows he's got a daughter over here!'

'Yes, he knows. But we agreed he wouldn't contact her. I didn't want that sort of emotional turmoil for Claire — a father who sent her birthday cards every year but never came to see her. I told your dad I didn't know who her father was. We were separated by then, of course, but he still called me all sorts of names, which was priceless, really, considering his behaviour all the way through our marriage!'

'I wish I'd known all this,' I say weakly. 'Why didn't you tell me? I could never understand why you were still crying for Dad, still loving him. I hated him so much, I almost hated you for still loving him! I . . .' I look down, realising something I've never admitted to, even to myself. 'I almost hated Claire for being his baby.'

'I think I knew that. But I couldn't tell you. I tried, so many times . . . but everything was so difficult back then. I had a new baby . . . you were being awkward . . . and I'd lost the man I loved.'

'I'd have understood,' I say in a whisper. But I know it isn't true. I wouldn't have done. I'd have been furious, and indignant, and disgusted. I'd have taken the moral high ground, and probably never spoken to Mum again. I correct myself: 'At least, I understand now.'

'Do you?' Mum gives me a false, bright smile. 'I always hoped I could confide in you when you were grown up, but somehow it just never happened. The longer I left it, the harder it got. But I had to tell Claire.'

'She didn't know either?' I exclaim.

'Not for a long time, no. I know that sounds terrible. But she found out last year. Your father kindly told her she wasn't his. That's why she's been so jealous of you.'

'What?' I nearly fall off my chair. 'Claire – jealous of me? That's a joke!'

'She has a funny way of showing it. But she resented the fact that you knew who your father was.'

'Some father!'

'I can't disagree with you there.' Mum smiles thinly. 'But, in Claire's eyes, any father was better than none. And, of course, she was angry with me for letting her grow up believing he was her dad. She was right to be angry. Especially as she'd been told by him that I didn't even know who her real father was. It's been . . . difficult for her.'

'Is that why she's started behaving the way she has?' I ask, without thinking.

Mum looks at me guardedly.

'What do you mean? Has she said anything to you?'

'I've heard it from other people,' I admit. 'You know she barely speaks to me. But she's been seen getting drunk with men old enough to be . . .' I trail off quickly before saying it: *her father*. 'She's been lying to you, Mum. She's been going out to pubs and nightclubs when she's pretended she's staying over at her friend's. I should have told you before.'

'It's all right. I found out what's been going on. What else could I expect? She'd had her world turned upside down. When I talked to her about her behaviour, she gave me some backchat about following in my footsteps. So I sat her down and told her everything. About Michael. About how much I'd loved him, how much I'd longed to have his baby. How special she was to me. Every bit as special to me as you are, Gemma,' Mum goes on. 'You were both wanted, both loved. But I wasn't a very good mum to either of you. I did everything wrong.'

We're hugging each other before she even finishes speaking. I'm crying again now. Will I ever stop?

'You didn't do anything wrong! You did what you thought was best. I wish I'd known all this, Mum.'

'That was my fault too. I should have talked to you, years ago, but – I was so afraid you'd hate me for it. Right from when you were a kid you'd had your perfect relationship with Andy . . .'

She stops, looks at me apologetically and strokes my hair.

'Sorry, darling.'

'Well, you're right. I was totally smug and self-righteous,' I admit, sniffing miserably. 'I thought I knew all the answers. Now look at me.'

Claire comes in quietly with a tray of tea and some biscuits.

'Shall I go and tidy upstairs for you, Gemma?' she asks gently. She gives Mum a questioning look, and I realise she's actually being discreet – leaving Mum and me alone to talk. My God, this is a new side of Claire I'm suddenly seeing. The world's gone mad.

'You'd better not risk going up there,' I tell her, trying to sound flippant. 'I haven't made the bed or cleaned the bathroom since . . .' I tail off. Since my wedding. The memory of it makes my eyes overflow with tears again. I actually want to throw myself on the floor and howl.

'I don't mind doing it,' says Claire. She hovers in the doorway for a moment, watching me hesitantly, and then suddenly she flies across the room and throws herself at me, almost knocking me sideways. 'Oh, Gemma, I'm so sorry! About Andy, and . . . about everything! Please don't cry! I'll stay here with you till you feel better. I'll cook for you, and clean for you, and do whatever you want! I've been such a bitch, and I just want you to be happy again. I can't bear it!'

'Stop it!' I'm laughing and sobbing at the same time. The noise is horrible. 'Don't be silly, it's not your fault.'

Mum mutters something about cooking chips, and goes out to the kitchen, sniffing into her hanky.

'It's not Mum's fault either,' I add quietly to Claire when I've stopped crying.

'Has she told you? About Dad? *Your* dad, I mean.'

'Only just now. I haven't really begun to take it in yet, to be honest.'

'Me neither.'

349

'You're not upset with her?' I ask frankly. 'For not telling you sooner?'

Claire thinks about this. 'I was, yes, at first. But she didn't actually lie to me, I suppose — she just let me *assume*. And I guess it was for my own good.'

'How do you mean?'

'That Michael — my real father — he couldn't have cared much about me, could he? Just buggering off to New Zealand like that, and never even bothering to keep in touch? How could he do that?'

'He and Mum thought it was for the best. Perhaps that was a mistake.'

'I guess everyone makes them.' Claire grimaces. 'I've made a few myself, recently. Older guys,' she adds, giving me a conspiratorial look.

'Probably not a good idea. But maybe you had to find that out for yourself.' I pause, looking at her thoughtfully. Suddenly seeing not so much a spoilt, difficult teenager as just a girl who's been unhappy. Has it really taken such deep misery of my own for me to recognise this? I put my arm around her. 'I can imagine what a shock this has all been for you. But from what Mum said to me . . . well, it seems like your dad was the love of her life. And she told me she wanted you very much. I was sixteen when you were born, and I always knew one thing for sure: she loved you desperately. Still does.'

'I know,' my sister whispers, biting her lip. 'I know that.'

'And you might find it hard to believe,' I add, trying to lighten my tone, 'but so do I.'

'I think I knew that too,' she responds without looking at me. 'But I could never work out why. I haven't exactly been lovable.'

'You should have seen *me* at your age!' I snort. 'The bitch from hell!'

350

We're cuddled up together when Mum comes back in the room. And the look of relief on her face when she sees us almost makes me start crying yet again.

We eat eggs and chips together, and I manage almost to clear my plate. I keep wanting to talk to Mum about the wedding, the honeymoon, but every time I start, I remember all over again that the end of my honeymoon was also the end of my marriage, and I break off, floundering and gasping with the pain.

'I just don't know how to carry on,' I say at length, resting my head on my hand. 'I don't know where to go from here.'

For a moment Mum doesn't say anything. Then she takes a deep breath, looks me in the eye and says: 'He still loves you, Gemma.'

'How can you say that?' I retort. 'You don't know . . .'

'I've heard the whole story. Cheryl came round. Don't look at me like that – she did the right thing. She's a brilliant friend, Gemma, but we're your family, and although we haven't managed to make a very good job of it in the past, perhaps it takes something like this to change that.'

'I know. You're right.' I give her a weak smile. 'But it *doesn't* change what Andy did.'

'It happened six years ago. From what I've heard, he got drunk, got taken advantage of by a megabitch . . .'

'You can say that again!'

'. . . and he's gone through hell himself because of it. Cheryl's seen him.'

'Has she? She didn't tell me.'

'Probably thought you wouldn't want to hear it. But she says he's almost in a worse state than you. Can't

351

work, can't even go out; he's staying at his parents' place, and they're distraught too.'

'I'm sorry, Mum, but I can't really care about that!'

'No.' She hesitates, sighs, and then goes on firmly: 'I know you need time, love, to get over this. I understand that. But don't throw everything away because of one stupid mistake in the past.'

'I don't even know if it *was* only one stupid mistake, though, do I? How can I believe anything he tells me now? Did you forgive Dad after *one stupid mistake*?'

'That was different. He didn't care. He didn't love me any more. It hurt, Gem – it hurt terribly. But you *know* this is different. You do know that, don't you? You *know* Andy is nothing like your father. He's a good man, a lovely, kind, loving man.'

'I thought he was,' I whimper miserably.

'No. You thought he was *perfect*. You thought your relationship was perfect.'

'I know! Yes, I did! What's wrong with that? What's so wrong with wanting everything to be perfect?'

I know the answer, though, before she even says it:

'This isn't a fairytale – it's real life. Nobody's relationship is perfect. Andy's human, and he's made a mistake.'

'Then he should have told me at the time.'

'To get it off his chest? Make himself feel better? No, he chose to go on suffering the guilt and regret on his own rather than hurt you!' Mum shakes her head and hands her plate to Claire, who's taking them out to the kitchen. 'I'm sorry, Gemma, I should probably mind my own business. But I don't want to see you unhappy for the rest of your life. Please don't be too unforgiving. You and Andy love each other. Give him another chance. We *all* make mistakes.'

She's looking at me meaningfully. Mistakes like

falling in love with a married teacher and having his baby. Keeping the truth about that child's father a secret for all these years.

Mistakes like not bothering to repair my relationships with my mum and my sister. Being so intolerant – demanding perfection from everyone else when I'm obviously not perfect myself. For God's sake! Am I never going to grow up?

'I'm sorry,' whispers Mum, getting up to give me a hug. 'I've made you cry again.'

'No.' I try to smile at her through the tears. 'No, you haven't. You've possibly just made me start to understand things.'

'Well, it's never too late!' she teases gently. 'We should have talked more like this years ago, shouldn't we?'

'I wouldn't have listened,' I admit.

'Will you phone Andy?' she asks gently. 'Just talk to him?'

'Yes.' I nod slowly. 'I expect I will.'

Maybe not tonight. Maybe in a day or two, when I can do it without crying. When I can hold a sensible conversation with him and perhaps start to move on. Perhaps start to back down, be generous, be forgiving. It won't be easy, but in my heart of hearts, I know it's what I want to do. Caroline was never supposed to come between us. If I let her, it's as much my fault as Andy's. We're worth more than that.

September	S	M	T	W	T	F	S
						1	2
	3	4	5	6	7	8	9
	10	11	12	13	14	15	16
	(17)	18	19	20	21	22	23
	24	25	26	27	28	29	30

Gemma

Saturday morning. We're lying in bed late, discussing whose turn it is to make a cup of tea. Sunlight's flickering through the gap in the curtains, highlighting specks of dust floating like fairies' dream powder near the ceiling.

'What shall we do today?' Andy asks me sleepily, turning on to his side, encircling me with his arm. 'Shopping? Tidying up the garden?'

'Nah. Boring.' I grin at him. 'Let's just stay in bed all day. We haven't done that since . . . for ages.'

I feel a quick stab of regret at nearly slipping up. Nearly straying on to unsafe ground – opening up the dialogue we've both agreed is now closed.

'That sounds like a very interesting proposition, Mrs C.' He pulls me closer to him and begins kissing me. 'The cup of tea can wait, I think.'

We've been back together for nearly a month now.

We talked a lot on the phone at first. It wasn't too polite. I needed to be angry, and he needed to convince me he wasn't telling any more lies. It took time. We met, eventually, on neutral territory – at a restaurant – and finally managed to hold a civilised, if stilted, conversation. By about the fourth or fifth meeting, I'd asked him to move back.

'I want to get over this and move on,' I told him, still finding it difficult to meet his eyes. 'It's not going to be the end of us. I won't let it.'

'I want that too – more than anything,' he said quietly. 'But will you really be able to forgive me, Gem? Or is it always going to be the skeleton in the cupboard, jumping out at us, causing rows and bitterness?'

'I hope not. That's something I'm going to have to work at.'

He'd made his commitment to me then: no more lies, no more secrets. I'd got to make one myself, possibly a harder one: no recriminations. No constant reminders. Moving on had to mean just that. You can't move on if you're always looking behind you.

'I think we should plan another holiday,' Andy says when he's finally brought me the promised cup of tea.

'Already?'

'For next year. In the spring, perhaps.'

I smile at him. I don't have to ask him to explain his thinking. We both know that, sadly, the honeymoon in Korčula is always going to be associated in our minds with Caroline and the problems she caused us. We're going to need some completely different memories to take their place.

'I'd like to go back to Korčula I say thoughtfully. 'But not just yet. I'm not sure I'm ready for that.'

'No. Of course not. Maybe Greece? Or Italy?'

I look at him in surprise. 'I thought you wanted to go backpacking in Australia?'

He shrugs, looking a bit sheepish.

'Bit of a holiday fantasy, I suppose. Guess I was trying to escape, in my mind . . . from everything.'

'Well, I'm glad you're not up for it any more. It's not really *us*, is it, the whole backpacking thing? We never went camping, or even caravanning.'

'No, you're right. We both like proper beds and a meal put in front of us, don't we?' He pauses for a moment and then adds quietly, 'The thing is, Gem – I think maybe we should have one more really nice holiday, fairly soon. Before we have to think about going downmarket a bit, and maybe having bucket-and-spade type holidays in Devon or Cornwall.'

He looks at me meaningfully but I'm just staring at him, wondering if I'm understanding him right.

'We'll be on a tighter budget, you know, when there's three of us, and you're on maternity pay . . .' he adds, smiling at the expression on my face.

I'm now sitting straight up in bed, wide awake. This is one subject we haven't broached at all since the separation. To be honest, I haven't even thought about it. When your whole marriage is in jeopardy, the question of having children suddenly becomes a total irrelevance.

'I know you might think it's too soon for me to say this,' Andy goes on when I still don't respond, 'but I want to say it anyway.' He hangs his head and looks even more sheepish. 'I never meant any of it, Gem . . . I hadn't changed my mind about having a family. I just couldn't face talking about it right then. With the other stuff going on . . . driving me crazy, frightening the shit out of me.' He takes a huge breath that's almost a sob. 'I was terrified out of my life that I was going to lose you. Who cared if we never had children, compared with *that*?'

I hold on to him, closing my eyes.

'I know. You're right. While we were ... apart ... I realised none of that mattered. Not at all.'

'But now?' He leaves the question hanging in the air between us.

'Do you think we're ready?' I ask him carefully.

'It was what we both wanted, before. And perhaps to go ahead with those plans and dreams we used to share would be the best way forward, Gem. Maybe, for me, it's the best way of proving to you that I'm still the guy you used to love.'

'I never stopped loving you,' I tell him hoarsely. 'Even when I stopped trusting you.'

'Do you still want to have a baby with me as its father?'

'Don't be ridiculous!' I manage to laugh. 'Who the hell else would I want as the father?'

'Someone ... perfect?' He raises his eyebrows at me.

'Well, yes, that would be nice, I suppose,' I tease him. 'But as there doesn't seem to be a queue of Mr Perfects waiting to batter down my door ...'

'You'll make do with me?'

'Oh, yes.' I snuggle up to him happily. 'Yes, please.'

'Shall we have a ceremonial Binning of the Pill Packet?'

'And a last bottle of wine? Before I have to cut it out?'

'Sounds good!' he laughs. 'When can we start practising?'

'Oh –' I pretend to think about it '– I'd say in

about five minutes' time. If you can manage it?'

'You're very demanding these days, Mrs C. I suppose you're expecting me to become a mere stud animal now?'

'With a bit of luck!' I growl.

'Thank God for that!'

It'll be Charlie for a boy; Emmie for a girl. My mum and sister are going to be over the moon. I hope it happens soon. But if not, we can wait. We've got each other, and our families. The future, finally, is looking good.

June	S	M	T	W	T	F	S
	1	2	3	4	5	6	7
	8	9	10	11	12	13	14
	(15)	16	17	18	19	20	21
	22	23	24	25	26	27	28
	29	30					

Two Years Later
Korčula, Croatia

Gemma

It's evening when our little boat approaches the island from the mainland, the sun sinking behind the dark huddle of land that gradually takes shape, as we chug nearer, into folded mountains, gently rippling into slopes of vivid green, and, finally, rising out of the twilight as if they'd been hiding from the night, clusters of houses perched precariously on cliff-tops and hillsides and down on the shore. We hold our breath, watching the dusky landscape gradually drawing nearer. Korčula. It's welcoming us back again.

'Nearly there, Emmie,' Andy whispers to our sleeping daughter, kissing the top of her head, stroking back the soft dark curls from her hot little face.

359

'Nearly there!' he adds to me, smiling as if we're sharing a secret. We are, of course. We're returning to the one special island that holds both our dreams and our demons – the place where, I think, looking back, we both finally had to grow up.

It was a bit of a challenge, coming on this journey with an eleven month old. But when Jo suggested it, we couldn't say no – and Ruby and Harold agreed to come out again, too, and make it a reunion for all our second anniversaries.

'If Jo and Mark can manage it with Jacob, so can we,' declared Andy confidently.

'He's nine months or so older than Emmie,' I pointed out.

'Yes, but in some ways that probably makes it harder – he'll be running around. And Jo's pregnant again,' he reminded me.

'Yes, but thank God, she says she's feeling absolutely fine this time. I'd have hated for her to feel as sick and ill as she did before.'

We've all been keeping in touch, of course. Andy's had to admit he was wrong about holiday friendships always fizzling out. It's been two years now, and the six of us seem to have become even closer, if anything. We've only actually met up on a handful of occasions, but we e-mail each other all the time, and phone, and send each other pictures of the babies. Grandchildren, in Ruby's case: her elder daughter Karen has re-married, and produced twin boys, much to Grandma's delight. We've all been to stay for a weekend at Ruby and Harold's lovely new bungalow in Sussex where they moved to start a new life together, away from the sad memories, now that they've both retired. And we've had long summer days together at Jo and Mark's house, and they at ours. But this was the ultimate reunion: coming back to Korčula. It just had to be done, and by now Andy and I feel strong enough to replace all those difficult honeymoon memories with better ones.

We're pulling into the little jetty and the boatman jumps out to tie up the boat.

'Please be careful,' he says, holding out a hand to Andy as he lifts Emmie out of the boat. 'It is slippery.'

'We know,' says Andy ruefully. 'I fell off this jetty two years ago, hit my head on a rock. Lucky I didn't drown – my mate jumped in and saved me.'

The boatman looks at him in surprise, leans closer to scrutinise his face, and then claps him heartily on the back.

'I remember! You are the one who was brought back from drowning by the Superhero!'

'That's right!' Andy laughs in surprise at being recognised. 'Harold is the other guy's name. He's back here again, too.'

'I think I remember him also. I brought him across on the boat this morning. Welcome back to Korčula, my friends.'

'Thank you.' I smile at him. 'We're happy to be back.'

'Here they are!' Ruby's running across the sun terrace, flying down the steps at a rate that defies her sixty years. 'Come on, Harold, they're here! Come and help them with their cases. They've got the baby to carry. Oh!' She stops at the bottom of the steps, staring in surprise. 'She's walking!'

'Not really – just tottering like a drunk, if she's got something to hold on to!' Andy's stood Emmie, still half-asleep, down on the ground while he picks up the cases from where the boatman left them. I'm holding her hand as she sways on her feet, rubbing her eyes with tiredness, taking a few stumbling baby steps around my legs. I pick her up again as Ruby envelops us both in a hug, followed swiftly by Harold who gives Emmie a big smacker of a kiss on her little pink cheek, making her pull a face and start to cry.

'Wise girl,' pronounces Ruby as we all start to laugh. 'Don't let any strange old man kiss you, eh! Wait for the handsome prince!'

'I thought I was the handsome prince!' says Harold, looking at her in mock disappointment.

'Only to me,' she says cheerfully. 'That's all you need to worry about.'

We've unpacked and laid Emmie in her cot when there's a tap at the door.

'Can we come in?' whispers Jo. 'Is Emmie asleep? Will we wake her up?'

'Don't worry!' I'm hugging Jo, laughing with excitement at seeing her again. 'She's completely out of her routine, with that long journey. God only knows whether she'll sleep tonight.'

'Same with Jacob. Say hello to Auntie Gemma and Uncle Andy, Jacob!'

He twines himself around her legs, his thumb in his mouth, smiling shyly.

'Hello, Jacob,' I say, squatting down to his level. At twenty months he's a proper little boy now, although I suspect Jo's still going to have her hands full when his new baby sister arrives in time for his second birthday. I turn to look at her. 'How are you? You look positively blooming!'

'I am! I feel great! I can't believe how different I feel from last time.'

'The difference is in yourself,' I tell her gently. 'You were so unhappy when we met you here two years ago. And look at you now!'

'I know. And I've got some wonderful news, Gemma – I've got to tell you straight away!' She smiles at me. 'Mark's adopting Jacob! We're going through the formalities now. He's going to be his real daddy!'

'Oh!' I give her a hug. 'I'm so pleased. But what about –' I pull a face '– Ben?'

She shrugs as if the name means nothing to her. 'He agreed straight away. Never wanted anything to do with Jacob anyway, and quite honestly, it suits him to be able to wash his hands of any responsibility.' She looks at me and shakes her head. 'Just about sums him up, doesn't it?'

I don't know what to say to this, so I just hug her again to show her how pleased I am.

'Mark's always been Jacob's daddy really, of course,' she says with a bright smile. 'But it's so good to be making it official. Do you know what, Gemma? Sometimes I'm scared this is all a dream – Mark, Jacob, the new baby, everything so wonderful – I'm afraid I'm going to wake up and I'm on my own again, abandoned by Ben, terrified at the mess I've made of things . . .'

'It's not a dream,' I tell her, laughing. 'Shall I shake you? Pinch you?'

'No, that's OK, I believe you! But look at *you*, too! So happy, with your own little daughter. Who'd have believed *that*, last time we were here?'

'I know.' I meet her eyes and allow myself the relief of honesty. 'I wasn't happy either when we were here

363

before. I was pretending to be, but I knew there was something badly wrong.'

'Poor you,' she says. She knows everything, of course. 'What a horrible time you went through.'

'But *you* know how it is, don't you? At the time, you think you're never going to feel better. But when you do ... it's like ... *doubly* good. I think I appreciate everything so much more now.'

'And look at how much good has come out of it all,' she says softly, smiling down at our sleeping baby. 'You were brave to come back here, Gemma. I hope it doesn't upset you.'

'Well, we went to Venice last spring, when I was pregnant, and pretended *that* was our honeymoon. It was wonderful – everything was good again between Andy and me, and we had such a lovely time. But ... something perverse in me still felt like I ought to be here in Korčula!'

'It's so great, being back here together,' says Mark when we're all gathered in the bar later, having a celebratory drink.

'It is,' agrees Jo, smiling across at me. 'I know we all had our various problems when we met here two years ago. But this place still holds some sort of magic, doesn't it?'

'You're right. It does,' says Harold very seriously, putting his arm round Ruby's shoulders. 'It seems to have worked a spell on all of us. Look at us! We picked up our bus passes this year, and we're still like a pair of young lovebirds – aren't we, sweetheart?'

'Silly old birds, more likely,' scoffs Ruby – but there's a telltale pinkness to her cheeks and a sparkle in her eyes. 'Come on, drink up, everyone. The table's booked for nine o'clock. Let's get going while the babies are asleep.'

They're both out for the count, in their buggies. We carry them, between us, down the steps and wheel them round to Mario's next-door. Ruby and Harold booked the table as soon as they got here this morning. It seems completely natural to have our Reunion Dinner here.

'I wonder if Luciano's still here?' I muse when we arrive.

'He wasn't when we came back last spring,' says Ruby. 'We asked after him, and they said he'd gone home to Italy.'

'What a shame. I'd have liked to see him again.'

The door's opened for us by one of the other waiters I remember from last time.

'Dobar dan,' says Ruby.

That's the first surprise. She might have been speaking Double Dutch for all I know, but it's pretty obvious from the waiter's pleased response that it was Croatian.

'I've been learning,' she says as we're settled at our table. 'I started when we came back last year, and I've carried on at home. I got a book with a CD so you can play it out loud and repeat it. It's difficult, though. A lot harder than French!' she adds, laughing. 'Although maybe that's because I'm so much older now!'

'Well, good for you.' I'm very impressed. I bet they don't get many tourists here who have a shot at speaking the language. 'I'm sure that's going to be useful, when you go off on your travels.'

Ruby and Harold are only with us for a couple of days on Korčula. Because they've already been back once – last spring, for their 'second honeymoon', as they promised they would – they're making this year's holiday more adventurous, touring the mainland and some of the other islands as well.

'Backpacking!' laughs Andy.

'Not quite,' admits Harold. 'We're being a bit more civilised than that. We're booked into various hotels, and we've got holdalls on wheels, rather than rucksacks!'

'I don't blame you. We met a young couple last time who were doing the whole rucksack and hostel thing, didn't we, Gem? At the time I thought I envied them – but actually I know I'd hate it!'

'But it *is* going to be fun, seeing other islands and other parts of Croatia,' says Ruby. 'Bit of an adventure for us.'

'And it's a practice run for next year,' adds Harold.

'Next year?' We all look at them. 'So what are you up to next year?'

'We're off to Australia.' Ruby grins with excitement. 'In February. It'll be nice and warm there then. We're staying with my Trevor in Melbourne, of course, for part of the time – it'll be lovely to see him and his family. I've three grandchildren out there, and I've only ever met them twice!'

'And then we're going off travelling around Oz!' says Harold, looking even more excited than Ruby. 'We're going to hire a car, drive from Melbourne to Sydney, spend a few weeks there, then fly on to Brisbane and up to Cairns, see the Great Barrier Reef . . .'

'Wow, that all sounds fantastic!' I say.

Harold grins and squeezes Ruby's hand. 'So we're off on our Gap Year in February. Although what it's a gap between, I'm not quite sure!'

'Middle age and old age?' she suggests, teasing.

'First childhood and second childhood, more like!' I joke.

'No. Between responsibility and freedom,' says Mark. He raises his glass of water solemnly. 'Here's to freedom!'

'To freedom!' we all repeat cheerfully – and then Jo and I look at each other and burst out laughing. We're hardly living up to the toast ourselves, are we – with two babies between us and another one on the way!

'And,' adds Andy, seeing the look pass between us, and raising his glass again, 'to families. Even more precious than freedom.' He leans down and tenderly straightens the blanket over our sleeping daughter's legs. 'More precious than anything.'

'But why are we making all these very important toasts . . . with *water*?' demands Harold. 'Let's order the wine, for God's sake!'

And it's at this point that the door from the kitchen opens – and there stands Luciano.

'Oh, my friends!' he cries, coming to shake all our hands and looking like he's about to cry with emotion. 'I could not believe my eyes. I could hardly believe it was you! All of you together again, like before, and with the beautiful *bambini*!' He kisses the air, staring from Emmie to Jacob and shaking his head as if he can't quite comprehend their beauty. 'This is too wonderful to speak of! My English, it is not enough words to say the wonderment! Please, let me bring you the best wine in the 'ouse, with my compliments, and please to allow me to join you for a glass of this very best wine? You will allow?'

'Of course, Luciano!' I watch him run back to the bar, before saying to the others in a whisper, 'Did you notice – he didn't say it was with the compliments of *his uncle who is the owner of the* ristorante?'

'No. We heard when we came last year that the

367

owner had passed away,' says Harold. 'We presumed it was under new management and thought that was why Luciano wasn't here.'

He's back with the wine before we have time to wonder any further. He pours, takes our food order to the kitchen, and then comes back to join us.

'I wish to make the toast,' he says gravely, holding his glass aloft. At this rate, the toasts are going to go on all night! 'To friendships made in Korčula May they last a lifetime.'

'We'll all drink to that,' agrees Andy as we clink glasses.

'And also,' goes on Luciano, 'I 'ave some sadness to share with you, my friends, and then some 'appiness.' He pauses, takes a gulp of wine and a deep breath, and then goes on: 'The sadness, it is because my Uncle Mario, who was the owner of the *ristorante*, last year 'e passed away, very sudden, very quick, from the 'eart attack. I miss 'im every day. He was like the father to me, teaching me all I know about the *ristorante*. I love the *ristorante* with all my 'eart, like I loved my uncle. I cry for him every day, I pray for his soul, I look up to 'eaven and pray him to look over me as I run his *ristorante* as best I can.'

'You're running the *risto* ... restaurant now, Luciano?' I exclaim.

'But of course!' He looks surprised. 'Of course my uncle left to me the *ristorante*, as he would to his son, because he had no son, only poor Luciano who weeps for his soul ...'

'But that's wonderful news!' says Ruby, before amending quickly, 'I mean, I'm so sorry to hear about your poor uncle, of course, but you now own the restaurant! We're very happy for you.'

'But this is not the 'appiness of which I spoke,' he

says, a wide smile now spreading across his face. 'My 'appiness is even more great than this. It is greater than the sky, the stars, the sun! Greater even than the 'eavens! It is so great, I cannot even speak of it!'

'Will we ever find out?' mutters Andy behind his hand.

'What is it, Luciano?' I beg him. 'Please tell us. We're dying to know what it is that's greater than the sun and the heavens!'

'It is love,' he says, reverently, placing his hand over his heart. 'In my sadness of losing my uncle, in my necessity of returning to Italia last year for the burial of my dear uncle – in the middle of my sadness and grief, I found also at his funeral my one true love! The cousin of the neighbour of my uncle's oldest friend, who was at the funeral along with everybody in the town who knew my uncle, fell in love with poor unworthy Luciano that very day, over my uncle's grave – and I with her!'

'Oh, how romantic!' I respond, although in fact it does conjure up a very strange picture of furtive glances across the coffin. 'What's her name?'

'She is Gabriella.' He rolls the name off his tongue as if it were a love song. 'And my greatest 'appiness is that she 'as done me the very great honour of becoming my wife and coming to live with me 'ere, in Korčula, to 'elp me with the running of the *ristorante*. And –' he gives us a shy smile '– we 'ope one day to 'ave many, many *bambini*!'

'That's wonderful news, Luciano!' says Jo. 'We're all delighted for you. Are we going to meet Gabriella?'

'Of course. I wish you to look upon this wonderful woman, who 'as been sent to me by the angels from 'eaven to dry my tears of sadness at the loss of my poor dear uncle. Gabriella!' he calls, marching to the door of the kitchen. 'Come, I wish you to meet my dear friends.' The door swings shut behind him as he continues in a torrent of rapid-fire Italian before re-emerging, pink with pleasure, holding the arm of a plump, round-faced and friendly-looking woman, dressed in a voluminous apron that does nothing to conceal the size of her enormous bust.

'Good evening,' she says in faltering English. 'I am pleased to meet you.' She takes each of our hands in turn, giving a little nod of the head as we announce our names, and smiling continuously throughout.

'You see, my friends,' says Luciano on completion of this introduction, 'what a fortunate and 'appy man your poor Luciano has become, to 'ave the love of this beautiful woman, and although I am undeserving, I thank God every day for this great and wonderful gift.' He bows with a flourish as if ending a show, and adds: 'And now I will bring to you your starters, and I wish you *Buon Appetito*.'

'Thank you, Luciano,' we chant together, in slightly dazed tones.

Nobody speaks for a few moments after they leave us. And then Harold starts to chuckle. Ruby nudges him and bursts out laughing. And immediately we're all so completely convulsed that we have difficulty composing ourselves before he returns with our starters.

His wonderful Gabriella certainly seems to have plenty of pretty obvious charms. But I'm not quite sure how they intend to go about having their *many, many* bambini, unless adoption's a possibility. She's fifty if she's a day.

Ruby missed out there, all right – or perhaps I should say she had a lucky escape. He did say he liked older women!

We've all enjoyed a few drinks by the time we finish our delicious meal – except for poor Jo who complains jokingly that she's the only one on orange juice again, just like last time! Promising Luciano that of course we'll come back again, we head back to the hotel and take our little ones up to bed.

'How does it feel to be back here?' asks Andy softly as we're getting undressed. 'Is it bringing back any terrible memories?'

'No.' I smile at him. 'Only good ones.'

'It wasn't *all* bad, then? Last time?'

'Of course not. We'd just got married, and we were here on our honeymoon in this beautiful place.' I hesitate and then go on, looking at him only slightly wistfully, 'It was just a pity we were both so totally immature and unrealistic. We thought we were perfect, Andy. We'd been together so long, neither of us had really grown up.'

'Perhaps nobody really grows up completely until they have their own children.'

'That's very philosophical, Mr Collins! And probably very true.' I pause in the middle of brushing my hair, look at him in the mirror and sigh, before going on gently: 'Do you ever wonder how she is? Whether she actually ended up having a baby of her own?'

He doesn't have to ask me who I mean. And he doesn't have to lie to me, either. Not any more.

'I prefer not to think about Caroline. But yes, I do wonder, occasionally,' he admits. 'I hope, really, that she's not still a miserable, nasty, vindictive bitch. I'd rather think that she'd got herself sorted out and was

371

happy. At one time I couldn't have cared less, I just hated her so much for trying to wreck our lives. But now . . . I suppose because we're so lucky, because we've got each other, and Emmie, and we're so happy . . .'

'It's hard to wish anyone else unhappiness, isn't it?'

'Yes. Even if they deserve it.'

'So do we deserve this happiness? Or should we be saying, like Luciano, that we are undeserving of this wonderful gift from the heavens?' I add teasingly.

'I think we should accept it as our right and proper due,' he laughs, pulling me down beside him on the bed. 'And as part of the magic that you seem to believe Korčula worked on us all!'

'Let's see if it still works that magic, then, shall we?' I suggest, cuddling up close to him. 'Let's see . . .'

There's a picture in my head as I fall asleep a little later. It still happens occasionally. It's a picture of a girl with shining blonde hair, glossy red lips, a perfect figure and long slim legs. She's smiling, beckoning to Andy, pursing her lips at him suggestively, wiggling her hips and batting her eyelashes. I watch the image with resignation, accepting the cruelty of its recurrence, like a nightmare that terrifies you even though you know it's not real. But this time it's different. This time, instead of leering at me triumphantly before walking off into the distance, the girl suddenly begins to dissolve. Like a sugar statue, she slowly melts – from the head down – dripping grotesquely into a puddle on the floor. Her silky hair washes over her eyes; her make-up runs down her cheeks as they collapse. Her perfect mouth goes into an unattractive downward scowl before folding into her chin, running down her chest. Her boobs droop like an old lady's and melt along with her stomach and then her legs. I watch, fascinated, as her feet finally disintegrate into the puddle, and with a pop, like a cartoon character being zapped, she's disappeared.

I think I'm actually dreaming now, but it's hard to know. Because I'm sure I just heard Andy laugh out loud and say, with a surprising new firmness to his voice: 'She's gone now, Gemma. Gone for good. She can't touch us now. Nothing can any more.'

And *that's* the magic of Korčula.

Watch out for the other titles available in Olivia Ryan's delightful trilogy about three subjects close to every woman's heart

TALES FROM A HEN WEEKEND

It should the happiest time of Katie Halliday's life: after four years together she's about to get married to Matt Davenport. They're the perfect couple and her family are determined to give them the perfect wedding.

While Matt is off to Prague with the lads, Katie has arranged to spend her last days of freedom in Dublin with her mum, sister and closest friends. But – fuelled by party games and too much Guinness – some strange secrets start to emerge. Soon Katie's seeing a whole different side to her friends and family. But Katie is keeping some secrets of her own – and perhaps this weekend is not the best time for her to develop a serious case of pre-marital jitters. Especially when a hen night treasure hunt introduces her to Harry who easily wins item number three on the list: *find a gorgeous man*.

It *should* be the happiest time of Katie Halliday's life . . . If she survives the next 48 hours.

978-0-7499-3806-2

TALES FROM A WEDDING DAY

Today is the big day – Abbie Vincent's best friend,
Samantha Patterson, is getting married! As chief
bridesmaid, Abbie's taking her duties very seriously
and she's utterly determined that the wedding will
go off without any hitches. However, with Sam's
good-intentioned (if overbearing) parents, her
obnoxious teenage sister and her brother's tantrum-
prone little boy to keep in check, disaster is only a
heartbeat away. And to top it off, though Abbie's
never forgiven their old best friend's betrayal of
their friendship, Sam has some misguided notion of
burying the hatchet by inviting her to the wedding.

It's supposed to be the bride who gets nervous
before the wedding but unlucky-in-love Abbie's on
tenterhooks in case anything goes wrong and ruins
Sam's special day – she's even willing to put her
lack of faith in romance to the side.

In fact, she's so busy ensuring that everything runs
smoothly that she doesn't even notice that all eyes
are *not* actually on the blushing bride.

978-0-7499-3929-8